SUBTROPICAL SPECULATIONS

PROJECTILE TRAINS FOR THE MOON.

Anthology of
FLORIDA SCIENCE FICTION
SUBTROPICAL SPECULATIONS

Rick Wilber and Richard Mathews, Editors

Pineapple Press, Inc.
Sarasota, Florida

Inquiries should be addressed to: Pineapple Press, Inc.
P.O. Drawer 16008
Southside Station
Sarasota, Florida 34239

LIBRARY OF CONGRESS CATALOGING-IN-PUBLICATION DATA

Subtropical speculations : an anthology of Florida science fiction / edited
by Richard Mathews and Rick Wilber. — 1st ed.
    p. cm.
   ISBN 0-910923-82-5 : $12.95
   1. Science fiction, American—Florida. 2. Florida—Fiction.
  I. Mathews, Richard, 1944-   . II. Wilber, Rick, 1948-
  PS648.S3S84   1990
813'.08762089759—dc20   90-37793
                                                              CIP

First Edition
  10 9 8 7 6 5 4 3 2 1

Design by Joan Lange Kresek
Composition by Creative Typography, Palmetto, Florida
Printed and bound by BookCrafters, Fredericksburg, Virginia

Dedications

*For the bright and beautiful Robin
and for R.A., my front-yard basketball buddy.*
—R.W.

*For Julie
and for our most exciting subtropical speculations,
Emily and Joseph*
—R.M.

Acknowledgments

The editors gratefully acknowledge research assistance in preparation of this volume from the trustees and staff of the British Library, London; Marlyn R. Pethe-Cook and Mickey Wells of the Merl Kelce Library, University of Tampa; and Jim Shelton of the Tampa/Hillsborough County Public Library. We would also like to express our appreciation to Ellen Datlow for her help and advice, and a special thanks to Joe Haldeman for his encouragement and for his judging of the entries in our contest for new Florida writers. Special thanks also to photographer Daniel Alarcon for his photographs of several of the authors and of the editors, and heartfelt thanks to Julie and Robin for their continual support and encouragement.

Contents

TAMPA TOWN, PREVIOUS TO THE UNDERTAKING.

INTRODUCTION

Richard Mathews and Rick Wilber

Modern science fiction has its roots in nineteenth-century romantic literature — and some of those roots are anchored fast in Florida's sandy soil. Jules Verne, arguably the founding father of what we now call science fiction, enjoyed immense popularity toward the end of the last century writing "scientific" tales that used the science of his time as a starting point for flights of imagination that took his characters to the center of the Earth, deep under the oceans, or on voyages to the moon. Verne's adventurers in *From the Earth to the Moon* lifted off near Tampa in 1865. Florida, with its pioneering people carving out a life from an exotic and primitive jungle, was a perfect setting for such an adventurous launch. (See the illustration across from the title page and the one opposite this page for reproductions of the original art from *From the Earth to the Moon*. The first shows the rocket on the way to the moon and the second shows the Florida launch setting.)

Science fiction has branched out considerably since then, and truly blossomed in the post–World War II years as the field moved from its dependence on Verne and H.G. Wells and its pulp magazine beginnings to a much wider popular, and critical, acceptance. Florida, if anything, has gained in importance as the field matured. Several of the Florida authors included in this volume — Damon Knight, Kate Wilhelm, Walter M. Miller, Andre Norton, Martin Caidin and Piers Anthony, among others — were important to the growing interest in science fiction short stories and novels in the 1950s and 1960s.

The field began as a fiction of prediction and ideas. It is startling to reread Verne's prescient work as he describes a spaceship nearly identical in height and weight to the Apollo moon rocket of a century later. His ship traveled at a nearly identical speed (25,545 miles per hour to Apollo's 24,226) and carried an identical crew of three. Verne even had his vehicle splash down in the Pacific

Ocean not far from where the actual event occurred. Verne delivers it all combined with a shrewd satire; American technological advances in weaponry during our Civil War so disturbed his pacifist nature that he wrote the novel partly as a satiric explanation of where the military might next turn its attention when the war was over. Even in this regard, he was prophetic. The American space program is often criticized for being driven by an ironically similar purpose.

The relatively narrow scientific extrapolation that marked the field's early years began to widen in the post-war era, and underwent rapid expansion in the 1960s and 70s. Contemporary science fiction encompasses a variety of sub-genres ranging from the "hard" science fiction of futuristic spaceships and laser blasts to "soft" science fiction (and its own sub-genres, like the 1960s' New Wave and the 1980s' cyberpunk) not so heavily dependent on scientific accuracy and prediction. Indeed, many critics, readers, and writers include within the field's broad definition some highly imaginative flights of fantasy and horror that rely far more on magic and mythology than on the scientific method.

In fact, that wide definition of contemporary science fiction and fantasy has resulted in a blurring of the lines between science fiction and the literary mainstream. Margaret Atwood's *The Handmaid's Tale* is clearly a work of predictive science fiction, though it was marketed — and became a bestseller — as a mainstream novel. Paul Theroux's *O-Zone* and W.P. Kinsella's *Shoeless Joe* are among other novels to be treated in similar fashion, and the short stories of Kinsella, James W. Hall, T. Coraghessan Boyle, David Foster Wallace, and many more all contain elements of science fiction and fantasy that certainly qualify them for inclusion in the genre — though none of the authors are thought of as science fiction writers.

Meanwhile, many of the field's practitioners are, in turn, writing stories that fit easily within the mainstream, as several of the stories in this collection display.

Subtropical Speculations first came to mind in an Italian restaurant in downtown Tampa, where the two of us were sharing a meal, some wine and some conversation. It dawned on us, as we chatted, that many of science fiction's important writers were Floridians, and that the state was the setting for several classic tales as well as many contemporary stories.

One of us had just returned from Gainesville and an interview with Hugo-winner Joe Haldeman for a profile in *The Tampa Tribune*'s short-story supplement, Fiction Quarterly. The other was just back from Inverness and a conversation with Piers Anthony as background for a book-length study of his work. These were not just minor figures in the field, but major, ground-breaking writers whose influence has been felt throughout the world. And they weren't, by any means, the only famous current science fiction authors for whom the state has had extraordinary importance. Damon Knight and Kate Wilhelm had written in a Gulf Coast beach house. Andre Norton still lives and writes in central Florida. Martin Caidin lives in Gainesville. . . . The list went on.

And that's how it began, one name leading to another until we quickly had a dozen or so science fiction writers with a Florida connection, and a growing catalog of stories in which the state was a key element. Something clearly had to be done about this, and we shook hands on the job right there. Certainly some publisher would realize, as we had, that Florida was a very singular locale for science fiction. Jules Verne, after all, had picked up on that a century ago, and we were certain that others would recognize the natural connections. You are reading the product of our certainty.

What is it about Florida that prompted these tales?

Certainly, in the widest sense, the answer has something to do with Florida's very special sense of place, and science fiction writers are far from the only group to recognize that and find it useful.

Florida is a land of fundamental, often ironic contrasts. Primordial swamps flow past pavement and condominiums; a teeming, natural aboriginal fecundity vies with a nature too often in retreat as we struggle to save our state's few remaining panthers, its gentle manatee, its colorful roseate spoonbill and stately wood stork. And yet, in the midst of that encroaching pavement, our climate helps make certain that nature is always ready for a sudden return. With ample rain and year-round warm weather and sunshine, things take hold here quickly, plants and animals and people, many of them imported from elsewhere: the fire ant, the Asian cockroach, the cattle egret, the drug smuggler, the drifter, the happy retiree, the ambitious entrepreneur, and many more. Florida welcomes them all with the same open arms that beckon the tourist, with offers of sunshine, warm weather, golden sand, and gentle waves against a palm-lined shore.

The brochures from the travel agents and housing developers don't always tell the whole story, of course, and many a writer has enjoyed pointing that out. From mystery writers like John D. MacDonald and the currently popular James W. Hall, to mainstream writers like Stephen Crane and Ernest Hemingway, Marjorie Kinnan Rawlings and Janet Burroway, Wallace Stevens and Donald Justice, and many, many more — Florida has been worth writing about and living in.

Science fiction writers, we think, have found the state interesting in their own uncommon fashion. Whether they are writing hard, extrapolative science fiction (and thus see the Kennedy Space Center as especially important to their story), or wide-open fantasy (perhaps only California can come close to Florida in laying claim to such an array of the fantastic — ranging from the make-believe of our theme parks to our sunshine-and-beach reputation), the state provides science fiction writers with memorable settings and any number of interesting characters, as well as a wonderful place to live.

We have included both classic and new stories, and this collection brings together some of the field's best-known as well as its up-and-coming writers.

We began the process by asking several writers to contribute stories in which Florida was an important part of the tale. We then opened *Subtropical Speculations* to general submissions, and received several gems from both well-established writers and those with just a few stories published. We also made it a point to reach out to new writers by announcing a contest for unpublished authors where the best story (chosen by Joe Haldeman, who graciously took on the duties of judge) would be included.

The result is a collection of sixteen stories that vary widely, ranging in their setting from the state's well-known cities and beaches to its almost unknown and still quite rural interior; in their characters from the logical and precise thinking of scientists to the sometimes vicious and sometimes charming entanglements of backwoods Florida crackers; and in their vision from dismaying predictions of economic, social and environmental collapse to more upbeat images of hope and promise for our state's future.

Several of the stories focus on interior, rural Florida, that part of the state rarely seen by tourists. Hugo- and Nebula-winning Joe Haldeman, for instance, offers a delightful Florida cracker tale that mixes aliens and moonshine in a classically-styled piece, "All the Universe in a Mason Jar." Haldeman was Guest of Honor at the World Science Fiction Convention in The Hague, Netherlands, in August of 1990.

Walter M. Miller, Jr., whose 1961 Hugo-winning novel *A Canticle for Leibowitz* is one of the field's seminal works of merit, also tells a story from rural Florida in "A Triflin' Man," which describes the power of the simple, straightforward approach to problem solving. And Tilden Counts, a mystery writer, detours the reader a long way away from the Florida that the tourists see, to a place where a humble reporter, some alien visitors, some native Americans and a potent cultural mix lead to murder. "The Weather After This" seamlessly blends the mystery genre with science fiction.

Florida's abundant wildlife, both on land and in the sea, is important to several stories. Piers Anthony, most famous for his fantasy novels but a writer of hard science fiction as well — and one of the state's best-selling authors in any genre — contributes "Beak by Beak," which connects parakeets (which can be found in the wild in Florida) with aliens and Earth's salvation. Joseph Green, who works for NASA while also finding time to write novels and short stories, contributes "Raccoon Reaction," which shows perfectly how a humble element of natural Florida can teach things of global importance to those who work with the latest in high technology. And James B. Johnson gives us a picture of how man's intricate and sometimes tragic interaction with animals can be destructive. In his memorable "Flankspeed," we see a dolphin who suffers terribly from his relationship with humans, even while he helps a human to new insight.

There are several bleak visions of Florida's future here. Award-winning author Kate Wilhelm tells a dystopian tale of a scientific team from a future United States that is near collapse. The team members investigate an abandoned Miami, and learn as much about each other, and themselves, as they do about the city. Novelist Charles Fontenay, who has returned to science fiction after a long stint in the newspaper world, also sees a dismal future in his greenhouse-affected "The Savior," where only the strong survive. And Rick Wilber's story, "Finals," takes a dark look at what life would be like for the Floridians of the next century if Europe and Japan continue to prosper economically while the U.S. economy slowly crumbles.

A more hopeful view of Florida's future comes from celebrated fantasy author Andre Norton, who has delighted millions of readers during fifty years of writing. Norton shows her concern with Florida's serious pollution problems in "Desirable Lakeside Residence." Norton was Guest of Honor at the 1989 World Science Fiction Convention in Boston.

Two of the field's most famous names give us off-beat stories that highlight the authors' frequent themes. Damon Knight, a trailblazer in modern science fiction (and one of its first great critics), contributes "Down There," a story which predicts a quirky future that may not be too far from us. Knight sees a world where beautiful facades drive a man to search for reality, no matter how ugly it may be. The point is particularly well taken in Florida, where the fantasy of our facades all too often masks our very real social problems. Martin Caidin, author of a slew of bestsellers, several films (*Marooned,* for one) and the television series *The Six Million*

Dollar Man and *The Bionic Woman,* gives us an excerpt from a recent novel, *Prison Ship,* which shows us that a good pilot, no matter where he's from, can fly just about anything. Caidin is himself an accomplished pilot.

Two of the stories in this collection are traditionally literary in tone and only tangentially touch upon science fiction motifs, a stylistic tack increasingly found in contemporary science fiction as the field often blurs with mainstream writing. Joe Taylor's intriguing "Welcome to the Pleistocene and Land," makes a wonderful satiric statement about life in modern Florida. And novelist Jack C. Haldeman honors us with the collection's most avant-garde story, "Quartet for Strings and an Occasional Clarinet," a piece, like Taylor's, that would fit every bit as well in a literary magazine as it does in a science fiction anthology.

Florida is the retirement or winter home for many people in show business, and Don F. Briggs uses his background knowledge of show people to good effect in "Miss Molly and the Alien," which has an alien visitor, a once-beautiful woman, a would-be musician, and a carnival act that all combine to tell us something about greed.

And we welcome a newcomer, Clark Perry, whose story "Killing Time" gives us a distinctly subtropical perspective on time travel. Perry's story was the winner of our contest for new writers of Florida science fiction.

These stories range from the worrisomely predictive (just how far into the future will we be able to go before St. Petersburg does indeed slip beneath the rising waters of the Gulf of Mexico?) to the wildly speculative, from the compellingly serious to the delightfully good-humored. That is the sort of varied, literate mix that helps explain science fiction's huge, and growing, audience. Readers by the millions continue to enjoy the field as much as the writers, who obviously relish the creation of these marvelous excursions into the imagination.

Florida has always been a land of bright opportunity and dark poverty, of fresh starts and frequent failures, of speculative land booms and the inevitable busts that go with them. The state leads the nation in new business starts — and in bankruptcies. It is a state of both great promise and great peril, with a future that could be as wondrous and inviting as our sunshine and golden beaches, or as dismal and disturbing as our crime rate and disappearing wildlife.

These authors embrace the climate, the geography, and the contradictions of Florida with their art to make the familiar strange and wondrous, to challenge our assumptions, and bring us to reconsider our own values in the light of their brave new visions. They display a good portion of the field's entertaining variety, and challenge your imagination, we think, every bit as much as Verne's work challenged and entertained the readers of more than a century ago. We hope the stories nourish your imagination as they have ours, and that they enhance your pleasure in this bright and boundless place we call our home.

— Rick Wilber and Richard Mathews, Editors

SUBTROPICAL SPECULATIONS

Piers Anthony

Piers Anthony has lived in Florida since 1959, and has written full-time since 1969. Author of more than fifty books, including *Chthon, Macroscope,* and *Race Against Time,* Anthony is especially acknowledged as a master of the fantasy novel, with the famous Xanth series and others bringing him world-wide recognition. Having lived at first in St. Petersburg, Anthony later moved to a more rural setting. As he explains, "We moved out of the city to the forest of Central Florida and bought horses for our daughters. The Florida landscape became that of the fantasy land of Xanth, and horses in various forms galloped through my fiction."

"Beak By Beak" is based on our experience with parakeets in Florida. We inherited one from a relative who was moving out of Florida, so got another to keep it company, and then another, until we had six. I believe that birds should be allowed to fly, but ours were not house-trained, so we made a cage big enough so they could fly within it. Those birds were a lot of fun, each with its separate personality. Then they started dying of natural causes: heart attack, cancer, and so on. The loss of each one was so painful to us that we decided not to keep birds after that. It was from this joy and sadness that I wrote the story. Parakeets can live wild in Florida, and many do, but we only really get to know the caged ones. Who knows what secret lives the ones we don't know may have?

BEAK BY BEAK

by Piers Anthony

The red bird was perched fetchingly on the mailbox as Humbert ambled out in slippers and tousled iron hair to pick up the morning newspaper. A gust of wind blew the front door open behind him, and a squawk came from inside.

The red visitor perked up. It fluttered across the lawn to cling precariously to the front hedge.

Humbert stopped, the banded paper in one hand. "Lost, little fellow?" he inquired. "Why . . . you're no cardinal. You're a parakeet!"

He peered at it more closely. "A beautiful, blood-red, male parakeet. I never saw your like before."

There was another angry chirp inside. "My pets don't like the draft," Humbert explained. "I'll have to shut this door."

The red bird hopped to the doorstep and up to the closed screen, fluttering against it and falling back.

"You *are* a tame bird!" he said. He squatted down and held out his hand, but the bird skittered nervously away. He laughed. "Not *that* tame, I see!"

As he opened the screen the bird hopped forward again. "You want to come in? Where's your home?" But he held the door open and allowed it to fly into the living room.

His wife bustled in from the kitchen holding a jar of instant coffee. "Humbert, did you forget the door again? You know Blue doesn't . . . " She froze. "Humbert — there's a bird in here!"

"Several, Meta," he said, gently closing the door.

"I mean a wild bird. Look at that color!"

The red parakeet flew up to the tall decorative lamp and perched on the shade, looking at her.

"He seemed to want to come in," Humbert said. "He's a remarkable specimen, and half tame."

Her attitude changed immediately. "What a beautiful bird! I've never seen a parakeet that color."

The bird spied the large cage and flew over to it. The three parakeets inside spooked, plastering themselves against the sides in mad retreat.

Humbert approached and put his hand to the stranger again. "Let me have a look at you, Red. I can't put you in with our family without good references. You might have the mites." But it jumped away from him.

"Check the newspaper," Meta said. "Maybe there's an ad for a lost pet. Such a distinctive bird must be valuable." She disappeared into the bedroom with her coffee.

Humbert eased himself into the easy chair. He had made it a point, since his heart attack, to move slowly and remain unexcited. He spread the paper.

The black headline leaped at him, ALIEN SPACESHIP ORBITS EARTH.

"Meta!" he called.

"Dear, I have to hurry down to the office," her muffled protestation came back. She was active in numerous volunteer capacities as well as holding a part-time clerical position. She preferred to keep herself occupied, now that their children were married and on their own, even though money was no problem.

Humbert shrugged and did not push the matter. Probably the headline would only upset her. He read through the article, finding the information too scant. The newspaper really knew little more than the fact: a strange ship appeared a thousand miles above Earth, and now hung in an oblique orbit. There were statistics: how many minutes it took to circle the Earth, at what times it would pass over which cities, and so on, but nothing essential. There had been no communications, no threats. Just — observation?

Meta bustled through. She always bustled, never walked. "Is there any notice?"

He'd forgotten the bird! "I haven't seen it," he said.

She was already through the door, and soon he heard the car start up. She would be gone for several hours. He glanced at the red parakeet, who was on top of the cage again, searching for some way to enter.

"Oh, all right, Red," he said, smiling. "I'll introduce you." He opened the cage door and reached in to catch a bird. There was the usual panicked flutter, for the birds, tame as they were, did not really like to be handled.

He snared one and brought it out. "Take it easy, Yellow," he said. Yellow was the youngest and most energetic of their family: a spectacular yellow harlequin with a green underside. He set the bird on top of the cage. "Yellow, this is our visitor from Outside. Red, this is Yellow."

Yellow shook out his feathers, stretched one wing, and sneezed. Having suitably expressed his indignation at being handled, he eyed the other bird warily. It was always this way; parakeets took time to become acquainted.

Humbert reached in for Blue. She was a timid, retiring bird given to nervous starts and loose droppings, but of very pretty hue. In the right light, a green overcast could be seen above the deep blue breast, as though the yellow of her head had diluted the blue. She bit his finger, not hard, and did not struggle as his hand closed over her wings. Sometimes the birds would perch on his fingers, but he hadn't really tried to train them. He set Blue down beside Yellow, but she took flight immediately, afraid of the stranger, and came to rest on top of the front curtains. She settled down to preen her wingfeathers.

"Well, that was Blue," he said apologetically.

He did not try to catch Green, but shooed her out with a wave of his hand. Green was the eldest of the brood and had had more than one owner before. She was a conventional green-bodied, dark-winged female with a neat yellow bib sporting four to six black dots — they kept changing — and she bit viciously when handled. She would come quickly to eat some treat from the hand, however.

"And that's Green," Humbert said as she flew to displace Blue from the curtain. "You'll get to know them all in due course." Green was contentedly chewing the edge of the curtain.

Yellow, seldom cowed very long by anything, was already making the first overture. He strode over to Red and pecked at him. Red sidled away.

"That's the way it is, Red," Humbert said as he reached into the cage to remove the fouled newspaper on its floor. "Very important to establish the pecking order — not that much attention is paid to it here." Yellow was chasing the disgruntled visitor more boldly now. "Just give him a sharp rap on the beak," he advised Red. "You have to assert yourself sometime."

He put in new paper and filled the treat-cups with oats, installing a fourth cup for the newcomer. He stepped back. "Soup's on!"

Green, always alert, arrowed across the room, the beat of her wing washing a breeze past his face. She hopped into the cage and mounted to the row of cuts. Seed scattered noisily upon the fresh newspaper as she scraped energetically.

Yellow heard the sound and scrambled across the top and down the side of the cage, using both feet and his beak to hold on. Blue, realizing what she was missing, flew in at the same time. They collided at the door, fluttering for balance, and fell inside. In a moment both were upon the feeding perch, while Green chattered angrily in an effort to protect her claim.

"This is what we call 'King of the Perch,' or maybe 'Musical Treat-Cups,'" Humbert explained to Red, who peered through the wire in some alarm. "The object is to get a cropful of seed without letting anybody else eat in peace. You'll get the hang of it soon enough."

He returned to his chair and watched while Green and Yellow, owners of the two end cups, converged on Blue in the middle. None of the three went near the new cup. While Blue's attention was taken up by Yellow, Green pecked her neck from the other side. Blue squawked and flew across the cage.

"They don't mean anything," he said reassuringly, "it's just a mealtime game, and there's plenty of ordinary seed available in the main dish in case anyone does go hungry. Watch."

Sure enough, Blue flew back immediately to the row of cups,

the whir of her wings startling Green into flight. Now Yellow and Blue forgot their differences long enough to do some serious seed-scattering, picking up the hard grains and hulling them adeptly in their beaks. Green scrambled up the side of the cage, using both feet and bill as Yellow had done, and recovered her place before her end cup. All three ate contentedly.

"You'll catch on, Red," he said. "I'll let you be, now." The bird didn't seem to hear him.

Humbert went into his study, turned on the radio, and settled down to work on his toothpick models. The artistic constructions he had fashioned from the simplest materials were all around the house: boats and statues and geometric shapes made from slender wooden splinters and drops of cement.

The whir of wings made him look up. "That you, Yellow?" But it was the newcomer. "Not ready to mix yet, huh, Red?"

The bird perched upon his toothpick sculpture of Meta. "Oh . . . you want to know what I'm doing? Well, I make things like that bust of my wife you're sitting on. Don't worry — it's strong enough to hold a hundred of your kind. Well, fifty, maybe. But don't mess on it, if you don't mind. Personal dignity, you know."

He studied the bird more carefully. Its breast and tail feathers were lighter than the back and wings, but still red. Four dark-red dots showed up against the pink throat plumage; otherwise its coloration was nearly uniform. The cere, above the vertical parakeet bill, was blue, the signal for the male of the species, and this was the only deviation.

"You're a strange one," he said. "Not just your color, but your manner. You aren't tame enough to be handled, yet you're more interested in what I'm doing than in others of your kind. It's almost as if you — "

He stopped as he became aware of the radio news broadcast. " . . . in orbit ten hours without acknowledgment of signals or any apparent effort to communicate with us. Experts are divided on whether it should be considered friendly, indifferent, or hostile.

The present assumption is that its purpose is merely observational. However — "

Humbert tuned the words out of his mind. "It's so hard to trust each other, let alone an unknown quantity. We don't know what that ship is doing in our skies, and probably it doesn't know what to make of us. But I'll bet it isn't much different from any meeting between strangers. You and me, for instance: I've never seen a bird quite like you, and you could be a dangerous alien from some other system for all I know. And you can't afford to trust me, either, because my hand could crush you in a moment. But you see, we get along. In a little while we'll really get to know each other, and then mutual trust will come. Some things just can't be pushed."

He spread a group of picks on the table and heated his cement. "You know, Red, I think I'll make a ship — a spaceship like the one in the sky. There's a picture of it in the . . . no! Stay clear of that glue. It's hot, and it gets awfully hard when it *isn't* hot, and they say the fumes can make hallucinations. You dip your bill in that and I'd have to scrape it off with a file. Believe me, Red, you wouldn't like that."

He rose to fetch the newspaper, and the bird, startled, flew ahead of him into the living room. The three local residents were still inside the cage, though its door was open. Green was braced on one of the ladders, pecking industriously at its plastic rungs, while Yellow was reaching forward surreptitiously to tweak Blue's unguarded tail.

"That's another thing you'll have to learn, Red," he said, smiling. "Feather-tweaking. Keep your wings and tail out of range, or you'll wind up with a bent feather. It just isn't parakeet nature to pass up a good tweak." He thought about that a moment. "I hope they don't try to tweak that spaceship before they get to know it well."

Red did not accompany him to the study this time. The radio had lapsed into popular music. The melody of "Sipping Cider" was on.

"Hey . . . I remember that one!" Humbert said, pleased. He matched the words with his own off-key accompaniment:

"So cheek by cheek and jaw by jaw,
We both sipped cider through a straw."

For a little while the years rolled back.

Later he emerged to discover Red inside the cage with the others. Yellow was friendly, but Blue still kept her distance, and Green was sleeping on an upper swing, one foot tucked up and head behind a wing. According to the handbook, a sleeping bird never raised a foot and folded back the head simultaneously, but Green evidently didn't read much.

Red cocked an eye at him. "Right," Humbert said. " 'Stone walls do not a prison make, nor iron bars a cage.' That's the way Mr. Lovelace put it. Our birds have the run of the house — but a familiar cage is more comfortable than a strange world. I only lock things up at night so nobody can get hurt in the dark."

Red had been largely accepted by the time Meta came home. Less hurried now, she admired him again. "He's just what we needed to fill out the set. Four birds, four distinctive colors. But are you sure he doesn't belong to anybody?"

Humbert admitted he'd forgotten to check the paper. It made no difference, as it turned out; there was no notice about any missing red parakeet, that day or in the ones following. Red was theirs, as long as he chose to stay.

Weeks passed. While Humbert's elaborate spaceship model grew, Red learned every facet of parakeet existence as locally practiced. He splashed seed industriously from both the main feeder and the treat-cups, then descended to the floor of the cage to search out the fallen morsels and swallow bits of gravel. He banged at the plastic toys and threw them about as though they were enemies. He raced up and down the ladders and took flying leaps at the dangling length of clothesline. He tweaked tail feathers, and played tug-of-war with stems of millet. When ushered from the cage during cleaning time, he flew merrily over to Meta's curtains to peck at stray threads.

There were three unusual things about him. The first was his color; the second his almost-intelligent interest in human affairs; and he was mute. Humbert never heard him chirp or warble. But since Red seemed to be perfectly healthy otherwise, it was not a matter for concern. He was one of the family.

The spaceship remained in orbit, uncommunicative. Humbert remembered that it had appeared the same day Red came, so it was easy to keep track. After a while the matter ceased to make headlines. Humbert wasn't certain why no Earth ship was sent to link with the interstellar visitor and attempt direct contact; something about a deadlocked UN session. It was easier to do nothing, in a democracy, than to agree on any positive course of action. Yet this did not explain why the spaceship made no effort to communicate, either. Surely it had not come all this way just to orbit silently?

Red became friendly with shy Blue. They groomed each other's neck feathers and shared a treat-cup. "Do you think they would mate, if we set up a nesting box for them?" Meta inquired. "If that mutation bred true — "

Humbert agreed it was worth a try. He read up on parakeet nesting procedures, for they had never bred their birds before, and bought a suitable enclosed box. "Beak by beak, and claw by claw," he sang to the melody of "Sipping Cider."

But tragedy struck before the arrangements were complete.

The birds scrambled in normal fashion for their preferred roosts on the highest swinging perches as Humbert turned out the light. They went everywhere in the day time, but always sought the heights at night.

There was a bump. Alarmed, Humbert turned on the light — and found Blue beating her wings on the floor. Something was wrong: she was unable to fly!

Red came down solicitously, but Blue was not aware of him. She got to her feet and climbed to the lowest perch and clung there, her little body quivering.

Meta came to watch. "What's the matter with Blue?"

"I'm afraid it's a . . . a heart attack," he said. He knew the symptoms too well, and knew that parakeets, along with men, were subject to such things.

Blue tried to fly back up to the swinging perch, but fell to the floor again. Humbert opened the cage and reached in to pick her up. She struggled, afraid of him, but had no strength to fight. He held her and stroked her neck with a finger, knowing he could not help her.

After a while she became quiet, and he returned her to the cage. He set her on a lower perch, afraid she might fall again, but her feet grasped it securely. He turned out the living-room light, but as an afterthought left the hall light on so that she could see enough to find the top perch, just in case. It would be better if she remained put, but —

There was a flutter. He and Meta could not resist checking — but Blue remained where she was. Red had come down to join her. "Isn't that sweet," Meta said.

In the morning Blue was dead. She lay on her back on the bottom of the cage, and her eyes were open and already shrunken. The two others seemed not to notice, but Red hopped about nervously.

"You don't know what to make of it, do you?" Humbert said. He felt unaccustomed tears sting his eyes as he picked up the fragile body.

He inspected Blue carefully, but there was no way to bring her back. He wrapped her tenderly in his handkerchief and took the body into the back yard for burial.

Red came with him. "We all have to go sometime," Humbert said as he dug a shallow grave beside a rose bush.

He laid the body in the ground and covered it over. "I know how you must feel," he said to Red on the bush. "But you did what you could to give her comfort. I'm sure you made her life brighter, right up to the end. I think she died knowing she was loved."

Red flew to the fence and looked at him. Humbert knew even before the bird took flight again that this was the end of their acquaintance.

Meta was too upset to go to work that day. She looked at the cage, suddenly too large for the two birds within, and turned away, only to look again, perversely hopeful, a moment later. Humbert turned on the radio and sat before his toothpick spaceship, the model almost complete, but could not work.

"We interrupt this program for a special news bulletin," the radio said urgently. "The alien spaceship is gone. Just a few minutes ago — "

Humbert listened, surprised. Just like that? It had left without ever making contact with Man. All that effort to come, then a departure as mysterious as the arrival.

He smiled. Perhaps they had been wise to avoid contact with Earth's officialdom, for that was representative in name only. Still, in their place he would at least have sent down a representative, perhaps incognito, in an attempt to come to know the temper of the common man of the planet. That was where the truth inevitably lay — in the attitudes of the common individual. Once that was known, little else was required for decision.

Yes — he would have gone down quietly, and not for any overnight stand. He would have observed for a reasonable length of time, and if the standards of the world differed somewhat from his own — well, there were still ways to judge, given sufficient time.

His hand halted before the model. A representative — perhaps a creature very like a native animal, neither wild nor tame. Something like a parakeet, free to enter certain homes without being challenged or held; free to observe intimately. . . .

Free also to love a native girl, who might not be as intelligent, but still was beautiful and affectionate. Free to love her — and lose her?

Free to run from grief — but never to escape it entirely, though a world be forgotten, and its other inhabitants never contacted at all.

Andre Norton

In the midst of a successful career as a writer of books for children and adolescents, Andre Norton published her first science fiction story, "The People of the Crater," in *Fantasy Book* magazine in 1947. Author of more than one hundred titles, she is well-known for her Dane Thorson books, including the classic *Sargasso of Space*. A Floridian since 1967, in recent years she has turned to editing anthologies in addition to writing. Her popular Witch World novels have sold over ten million copies worldwide, and the Witch World anthology series, which she edits, has enjoyed success through several volumes. Along with publishers Betty and Ian Ballantine, she was a Professional Guest of Honor at Noreascon Three, the 47th World Science Fiction Convention, held in Boston in 1989.

When I wrote that story I lived out in the country, out on Lake Howell, and there was much talk there about it becoming polluted — they wouldn't let anyone swim in it. I got to thinking what would happen if the whole outside became polluted. This story led me to a book, called Outside, *in which people have been imprisoned in great domes that cover the cities for so long they don't think that outside exists.*

DESIRABLE LAKESIDE RESIDENCE

by Andre Norton

I went to the river
to drown all my sorrow
But the river was more
to be pitied than I . . .
            — *Scots ballad*

Her face felt queer and light without her respirator on — almost like being out here without any clothes. Jill thumbed the worn cords of her breather, crinkling them, smoothing them out again, without paying attention to what her hands were doing, her eyes were so busy surveying this new, strange and sometimes terrifying outer world.

Back home had been the apartment, sealed, of course, and the school, with the sealed bus in between. Sometimes there had been a visit to the shopping center. But she could hardly really remember now. Even the trip to this place was rather like a dream.

Movement in the long ragged grass beyond the end of the concrete block on which Jill sat. She tensed —

A black head, a small furred head with two startling blue eyes —

Jill hardly dared to breathe even though there was no smog at all. Those eyes were watching her measuringly. Then a sinuous black body flowed into full view. One minute it had not been there, the next — it just was!

This was — she remembered the old books — a cat!

Dogs and cats, people had had them once, living in their houses. Before the air quotient got so low no one was allowed to keep a pet in housing centers. But there was no air quotient here yet — a cat could live —

Jill studied the cat, sitting up on its haunches, its tail laid straight out on the ground behind it, just the very tip of that twitching a little now and then. Except for that one small movement it might have been a pretend cat, like the old pretend bear she had when she was little. Very suddenly it yawned wide, showing sharp white teeth, a curling pink tongue, bright in color, against the black which was all the rest of it.

"Hello, cat — " Jill said in that quiet voice which the bigness of Outside caused her to use.

Black ears twitched as if her words had tickled them a little. The cat blinked.

"Do you live here — Outside?" she asked. Because here things did dare to live Outside. She had seen a bird that very morning, and in the grass were all kinds of hoppers and crawlers. "It's nice" — Jill was gaining confidence — "to live Outside — but sometimes," she ended truthfully, "scary, too. Like at night."

"Ulysses, where are you, cat?"

Jill jumped. The cat blinked again, turned its head to look back over one shoulder. Then it uttered a small sound.

"I heard you, Ulysses. Now where are you?"

There was a swishing in grass and bush. Jill gathered her feet under her for a quick takeoff. Yet she had no intention of retreat until that was entirely necessary.

The bushes parted and Jill saw another girl no bigger than she was. She settled back on her chosen seat. The cat arose and went to rub back and forth against the newcomer's scratched and sandy legs.

"Hello," Jill ventured.

"You're Colonel Baylor's niece." The other made that sound almost like an accusation. She stood with her hands bunched into fists resting on her hips. As Jill, she wore a one-piece shorts-tunic, but hers was a rusty green which seemed to melt into the coloring of the bushes. Jill had an odd feeling that if the other chose she could be unseen while still standing right there. Her skin was brown and her hair fluffed out around her face in an upstanding black puff.

"He's my Uncle Shaw," Jill offered. "Do — do you live Outside, too?"

"Outside," the other repeated as if the word were strange. "Sure,

I live here. Me — I'm Marcy Scholar. I live over there." She pivoted to point to her left. "The other way's the lake — or what used to be the lake. My dad — when I was just a little old baby — he used to go fishing there. You believe me?"

She eyed Jill challengingly as if expecting a denial.

Jill nodded. She could believe anything of Outside. It had already shown her so many wonders which before had existed only in books, or on the screen of the school TV they used when Double Smog was so bad you couldn't even use the sealed buses.

"You come from up North, the bad country — " Marcy took a step forward. "The colonel, he has a big pull with the government or you couldn't get here at all. We don't allow people coming into a Clear. It might make it bad, too, if too many came. Bad enough with the lakes all dead, and the rest of it."

Jill's eyes suddenly smarted as badly as they did once when she was caught in a room where the breather failed. She did not want to remember why she was here.

"Uncle Shaw walked on the moon! The President of the whole United States gave him a medal for it. He's in the history books — " she countered. "I guess what Uncle Shaw wants, he gets."

Marcy did not protest as Jill half expected. Instead she nodded. "That's right. My father — he worked on the Project, too, that's how come we live here. When they closed down the big base and said no more space flights, well, we moved here with the colonel, and Dr. Wilson, and the Pierces. Look here — "

She pushed past Jill and swept away some of the foliage. Behind those trailing, yellowish leaves, was a board planted on a firm stake in the ground; on it, very faint lettering.

"You read that?" Marcy stabbed a finger at the words.

"Sure I can read!" Jill studied the almost lost lines. "It says, 'Desirable Lakeside Residence.' "

"And that's what all this was!" Marcy answered. "Once — years and years ago — people paid lots of money for this land — land beside a lake. Of course, that was before all the fish, and turtles and alligators and things died off, and the water was all full of weeds. You can hardly tell where the lake was any more — come on — I'll show you!"

Jill eyed the mass of rusty green doubtfully. But Marcy hooked back an armful to show an opening beyond. And, at that moment, Ulysses came to life in flowing movement and disappeared through it. Fastening her respirator to her belt, Jill followed.

It was like going through a tunnel, but the walls of this tunnel were alive, not concrete. She put out a hand timidly now and then to touch fingertips to leaves, springy branches, all the parts of Outside. Then they were out of the tunnel, before them what seemed to be a smooth green surface some distance below where they now stood. However, as she studied it, Jill could see there were brown patches which the green did not cover and which looked liquid.

This was very different from any lake in a picture, but then everything was different now from pictures. Old people kept talking about how it was when they were young, saying, yes, the pictures were right. But sometimes Jill wondered if they were not just trying to remember it and getting the pictures mixed up with what they wanted to believe. Perhaps the pictures were stories which were never true, even long ago.

Marcy shaded her eyes with her hand, stared out across the green-brown surface.

"That's funny — "

"What's funny?"

"Seems like there is more water showing today — like the weeds are gone. Maybe it's so poisoned now even the old weeds can't live in it." She picked up a stick from the ground by her feet, and then lay full length to reach over and plunge the end of it into the thick mass below, dragging it back and forth.

Ulysses appeared again. Not up with them, but below. Jill could see him crouched on a slime-edged stone. His head was forward as he stared into the weeds, as if he could see something the girls could not.

"Hey!" Marcy braced herself up on her elbows. "Did you see that?"

"What?"

"When I poked this old stick in right here" — she leaned forward to demonstrate — "something moved away — along there!" She used the stick as a pointer. "Watch Ulysses, he must have seen it too!"

The cat's tail swept back and forth; he was clearly gazing in the direction Marcy indicated.

"You said all the fish, the turtles and things are dead." Jill edged back. Once there had been snakes, too. Were the snakes dead?

"Sure are. My dad says nothing could live in this old lake! But something did move away. Let's see — " She wormed her way along, striking at the leaves below, cutting swaths through them, leaving the growth tattered. But, though they both watched intently, there were no more signs of anything which might or might not be fleeing the lashing branch.

"Bug — a big bug?" suggested Jill as Marcy rolled back, dropping the stick.

"Sure would be a *big* one." Marcy sounded unconvinced. "You going to live here — all the time?"

Jill began to twist at her respirator again. "I guess so."

"What's it like up North, in the bad country?"

Jill looked about her a little desperately. Outside was so different, how could she tell Marcy about Inside? She did not even want to remember those last black days.

"They — they cut down on our block quota," she said in a rush. "Two of the big breathers burned out. People were all jammed together in the part where the conditioners still worked. But there were too many. They — they took old Mr. Evans away and Mrs. Evans, too. Daddy — somehow he got a message to Uncle Shaw, and he sent for me. But Daddy couldn't come. He is one of the maintainers, and they aren't allowed even to leave their own sections for fear something will happen and the breathers break down."

Marcy was watching her narrowly.

"I bet you're glad to be here."

"I don't know — it's all so different, it's Outside." Now Jill looked around her wildly. That stone where she had sat, from it she could turn around and see the house. From here — now all she could see were bushes. Where was the house — ?

She got to her feet, shaking with the cold inside her.

"Please" — somehow she got out that plea — "where's the house? Which way did we come to get here?" Inside was safe —

"You frightened? Nothing to be frightened of. Just trees and things. And Ulysses, but he's a friend. He's a smart cat, understands a lot you say. If he could only talk now — " Marcy leaned over and called:

"Ulysses, you come on up. Nothing to catch down there, no use your pretending there is."

Jill was still shaking a little. But Marcy's relaxation was soothing. And she wanted to see the cat close again. Perhaps he would let her pet him.

Again that black head pushed through the brush and Ulysses, stopping once to lick at his shoulder, came to join them.

"He's half Siamese," Marcy announced as if that made him even more special. "His mother is Min-Hoy. My mother had her since a little kitten. She's old now and doesn't go out much. Listen, you got a cat?"

Jill shook her head. "They don't allow them — nothing that uses up air, people have to have it all. I never saw one before, except in pictures."

"Well, suppose I let you have half of Ulysses — "

"Half?"

"Sure, like you take him some days, and me some. Ulysses" — she looked to the cat. "This is Jill Baylor, she never had a cat. You can be with her sometimes, can't you?"

Ulysses had been inspecting one paw intently. Now he looked first at Marcy as if he understood every word, and then turned his head to apply the same searching stare to Jill. She knelt and held out her hand.

"Ulysses — "

He came to her with the grave dignity of his species, sniffed at her fingers, then rubbed his head back and forth against her flesh, his silky soft fur like a caress.

"He likes you." Marcy nodded briskly. "He'll give you half his time, just wait and see!"

"*Jill!*" a voice called from nearby.

Marcy stood up. "That's your aunt, you'd better go. Miss Abby's a great one for people being prompt."

"I know. How — how do I go?"

Marcy guided her back through the green tunnel. Ulysses disappeared again. But Marcy stayed to where Aunt Abby stood under the roof overhang. Jill was already sure that her aunt liked that house a great deal better before Jill came to stay in it.

"Where have you been — ? Oh, hello, Marcy. You can tell your mother the colonel got the jeep fixed and I'm going in to town later this afternoon, if she wants a shopping lift."

"Yes, Mrs. Baylor." Marcy was polite but she did not linger. There was no sign of Ulysses.

Nobody asked Jill concerning her adventures of the morning and she did not volunteer. She was uneasy with Aunt Abby; as for Uncle Shaw, she thought most of the time he did not even know she was there. Sometimes he seemed to come back from some far distance and talk to her as if she were a baby. But most of the time he was shut up at the other end of the house in a room Aunt Abby had warned her not to enter. What it contained she had no idea.

There were only four families now living by the lake, she was to discover. Marcy's, the Haddams, who were older and seemed to spend most of their time working in a garden trying to raise things. Though Marcy reported most of the stuff died off before it ever got big or ripe enough to eat, but they kept on trying. Then there were the Williamses and they — Marcy warned her to stay away from them, even though Jill had no desire to explore Outside alone. The Williamses, Marcy reported, were dirt-mean, dirt-dirty, and wrong in the head. Which was enough to frighten Jill away from any contact.

But it was the Williamses who caused all the rumpus the night of the full moon.

Jill awakened out of sleep and sat up in her bed, her heart thumping, her body beginning to shake as she heard that awful screaming. It came from Outside, awakening all the suspicions her days with Marcy had lulled. Then she heard sounds in the house, Uncle Shaw's heavy tread, Aunt Abby's voice.

The generator was off again and they had had only lamps for a week. But she saw through the window the broad beam of a flashlight cut the night. Then she heard Marcy's father call from the road and saw a second flashlight.

There was another shriek and Jill cried out, too, in echo. The door opened on Aunt Abby, who went swiftly to the window, pulling it closed in spite of the heat.

"It's all right." She sat down on the bed and took Jill's hands in hers. "Just some animal — "

But Jill knew better. There weren't many animals — Ulysses, Min-Hoy, the old mule the Haddams kept. Marcy had told her all the wild animals were gone.

There was no more screaming and Aunt Abby took her into bed with her so after a while Jill did sleep. When she went for breakfast, Uncle Shaw was in his usual place. Nobody said anything about what had happened in the night and she felt she must not ask. It was not until she met Marcy that she heard the story.

"Beeny Williams," Marcy reported, "clean out of his head and running down the road yelling demons were going to get him. My father had to knock him out. They're taking him in town to a doctor." She stopped and looked sidewise at Jill in an odd kind of way as if she were in two minds whether to say something or not. Then she asked abruptly:

"Jill, do you ever dream about — well, some queer things?"

"What kind of things?" Everyone had scary dreams.

"Well, like being in a green place and moving around — not like walking, but sort of flying. Or being away from that green place and wanting a lot to get back."

Jill shook her head. "You dream like that?"

"Sometimes — only usually you never remember the dreams plain when you wake up, but these you do. It seems to be important. Oh, stuff!" She threw up her hands. "Dad says to stay away from the lake. Seems Beeny went wading in a piece of it last night, might be he got some sort of poison. But all those Williamses are crazy. I don't see how wading in the lake could do anything to him. Dad didn't say we couldn't walk around it, let's go see — "

They took the familiar way through the tunnel. Jill blinked in the very bright sun. Then she blinked again.

"Marcy, there's a lot more water showing! See — there and there! Perhaps your dad is right, could be something killing off the weeds."

"Sure true. Ulysses," she called to the cat crouched on the stone below, "you come away from there, could be you might catch something bad."

However Ulysses did not so much as twitch an ear this time in response — nor did he come. Marcy threatened to climb down and get him, but Jill pointed out that the bank was crumbling and she might land in the forbidden lake.

They left the cat and worked their way along the shore, coming close to a derelict house well embowered in the skeletons of dead creepers and feebler shoots of new ones.

"Spooky," Marcy commented. "Looks like a place where things could hide and jump out — "

"Who used to live there, I wonder?"

"Dr. Wilson. He was at the Cape, too. And he walked on the moon — "

"Dr. Morgan Wilson." Jill nodded. "I remember."

"He was the worst upset when they closed down the Project 'cause he was right in the middle of an experiment. Tried to bring his stuff along here and work on it, but he didn't have any more money from the government and nobody would listen to him. He never got over feeling bad about it. One night he just up and walked out into the lake — just like that!" Marcy waved a hand.

"They never found him until the next morning. And you know what — he took a treasure with him — and it was never found."

"A treasure — what?"

"Well, he had these moon rocks he was using in his experiment. He'd picked them up himself. My dad said they used to keep them in cases where people could go and see them. But after New York and Chicago and Los Angeles all went dead in the Breakdown and there was no going to the moon any more — nor money to spend except for breathers and fighting the poison and all — nobody cared what became of a lot of old rocks. So these were lost in the lake."

"What did they look like?"

"Oh, I guess like any old rock. They were just treasures because they came from another world."

They turned back then for they were faced with a palmetto thicket which they could not penetrate. It was a lot hotter and Jill began to think of indoors and the slight cool one could find by just getting out of the sun.

"Come on home with me," she urged. "We can have some lemonade and Aunt Abby gave me a big old catalogue — we can pick out what we'd like to buy if they still had the store and we had any money."

Wish buying was usually a way to spend a rainy day, but it might also fill up a hot one.

"Okay."

So they were installed on Jill's bed shortly, turning the limp pages of the catalogue and rather listlessly making choices, when there was a scratching at the outside door just beyond the entrance to Jill's bedroom.

"Hey" — Marcy sat up — "it's Ulysses — and he's carrying something — I'll let him in."

She was away before Jill could move and the black cat flashed into the room and under Jill's bed as if he feared his find would be taken from him. They could hear him growling softly and both girls hung over the side trying to look, finally rolling off on the floor.

"What you got, cat?" demanded Marcy. "Let's see now — "

But though Ulysses was crouched growling, and he had certainly had something in his mouth when Marcy let him in, there was nothing at all except his own black form now to be seen.

"What did he do with it?"

"I don't know." Marcy was as surprised as Jill. "What was it anyhow?"

But when they compared notes they discovered that neither of them had seen it clearly enough to guess. Jill went for the big flashlight always kept on the table in the hall. She flashed the beam back and forth under, where it shone on Ulysses' sleek person, but showed nothing else at all.

"Got away," Marcy said.

"But if it's in the room somewhere, whatever it is — " Jill did not like the thought of a released something here — especially a something which she could not identify.

"We'll keep Ulysses here. If it comes out, he'll get it. He's just waiting. You shut the door so it can't get out in the hall, and he'll catch it again."

But it was not long before Ulysses apparently gave up all thoughts of hunting and jumped up to sprawl at sleepy ease on the bed. When it came time for Marcy to leave Jill had a plea.

"Marcy, you said Ulysses is half mine, let him stay here tonight. If that — that thing is loose in here, I don't want it on me. Maybe he can catch it again."

"Okay, if he'll stay. Will you, Ulysses?"

He raised his head, yawned and settled back.

"Looks like he chooses so. But if he makes a fuss in the night, you'll have to let him out quick. He yells if you don't — real loud."

Ulysses showed no desire to go out in the early evening. Jill brought in some of his food, which Marcy had delivered, and a tin pie plate full of water. He opened his eyes sleepily, looked at her offering and yawned again. Flashlight in hand, she once more made the rounds of the room, forcing herself to lie on her stomach and look under the bed. But she could see nothing at all. What *had* Ulysses brought in? Or had they been mistaken and only thought he had something?

A little reluctantly Jill crawled into bed, dropping the edge of the sheet over Ulysses. She did not know how Aunt Abby would accept this addition to the household, even if it were temporary, and she did not want to explain. Aunt Abby certainly would not accept with anything but alarm the fact that Ulysses had brought in something and loosed it in Jill's room.

Aunt Abby came and took away the lamp and Ulysses cooperated nicely by not announcing his presence by either voice or movement under the end of the sheet. But Jill fought sleep. She had a fear which slowly became real horror, of waking to find *something* perhaps right on her pillow.

Ulysses was stretched beside her. Now he laid one paw across her leg as if he knew exactly how she felt and wanted to reassure her, both of his presence and the fact he was on guard. She began to relax.

She — she was not in bed at all! She was back in a sealed apartment but the breather had failed, she could not breathe — her respirator — the door — she must get out — away where she could breathe! She must! Jill threw herself at the wall. There were no doors — no vents! If she pounded would some one hear?

Then it was dark and she was back in the room, sitting up in bed. A small throaty sound — that was Ulysses. He had moved to the edge of the bed, was crouched there — looking down at the floor. Jill was sweating, shaking with the fear of that dream, it must have been a dream —

But she was awake and still she felt it — that she could hardly breathe, that she must get out — back — back to —

It was as if she could see it right before her like a picture on the wall — the lake — the almost dead lake!

But she did not want — she did — she must —

Thoroughly frightened, Jill rocked back and forth. She did not want to go to the lake, not now. Of course, she didn't! What was the matter with her?

But all she could see was the lake. And, fast conquering her resistance, was the knowledge that she must get up — yes, right now — and go to the lake.

She was crying, so afraid of this thing which had taken over her will, was making her do what she shrank from, that she was shivering uncontrollably as she slid from the bed.

It was then that she saw the eyes!

At first they seemed only pricks of yellow down at floor level, where she had put the pan of water for Ulysses. But when they moved —

Jill grabbed for the flashlight. Her hands were so slippery with sweat that she almost dropped it. Somehow she got it focused on the pan, pushed the button.

There was something squatting in the pan, slopping the water out on the floor as it flopped back and forth, its movements growing wilder. But save for general outlines — she could hardly see it.

"Breathe — I can't breathe!" Jill's hoarse whisper brought another small growl from Ulysses. But she could breathe, there was no smog here. This was a Clear Outside. What was the matter — ?

It was not her — some door in her own mind seemed to open — it was the thing over there flopping in the pan — it couldn't breathe — had to have water —

Jill scuttled for the door, giving the pan and the flopper a wide berth. She laid the flashlight on the floor, slipped around the door and padded towards the kitchen. The cupboard was on the right, that was where she had seen the big kettle when Aunt Abby had talked about canning.

There was moonlight in the kitchen, enough to let her find the cupboard, bring out the kettle. Then — fill it — she worked as noiselessly as she could. Not too full or it would be too heavy for her to carry —

As it was, she slopped water over the edge all the way back to the bedroom. Now —

The floppings in the pan had almost stopped. Jill caught her breath at the feeling inside her — the thing was dying. Fighting her fear and repulsion, Jill somehow got across the room, snatched up the pan before she could let her horror of what it held affect her and tipped all its contents into the kettle. There was an alien touch against her fingers as it splashed in. But — she could hardly see it now!

She knelt by the kettle, took the torch and shone it into the depths.

It — it was like something made of glass! She could see the bulbous eyes, they were solid, and some other parts, but the rest seemed to melt right into the water.

Jill gave a small sound of relief. That compulsion which had held her to the creature's need was lifted. She was free.

She sat back on her heels by the kettle, still shining the torch at the thing. It had flopped about some at first, but now it was settled quietly at the bottom.

A sound out of the dark, Ulysses poked his head over the other side of the kettle to survey its inhabitant. He did not growl, and he stood so for only a moment or two before going to jump back on the bed with the air of one willing to return to sleep now that all the excitement was over.

For a time the thing was all right, Jill decided. She was more puzzled than alarmed now. Her acquaintance with things living Outside was so small, only through reading and what she had learned from Marcy and observation these past days. But how had the thing made her wake up, know what it had to have to live? She could not remember ever having known that things which were not people could think you into doing what they wanted.

When she was very little — the old fairy tale book which had been her mother's — a story about a frog who was really a prince. But that was only a story. Certainly this almost transparent thing would never have been a person!

It came from the lake, she was sure of that from the first picture in her mind after she woke up. And it wanted to go back there.

Tonight?

Almost as if she had somehow involuntarily asked a question! A kind of urgency swept into her mind in answer. Yes — now — now! It was answering her as truly as if it had come to the surface of the water and shouted back at her.

To go out in the night? Jill cringed. She did not dare, she simply could not. Yet now the thing — it was doing as it had before — pushing her into taking it back.

Jill fought with all the strength of will she had. She could *not* go down to the lake now —

But she was gasping — the thing — it was making her feel again something of what it felt — its earlier agony had been only a little relieved by the bringing of the kettle. It had to be returned to the lake and soon.

Slowly Jill got up and began to dress. She was not even sure she could find the way by night. But the thing would give her no peace. At last, lugging the kettle with one hand, holding the flash in the other, she edged out into the night.

There were so many small sounds — different kinds of bugs maybe, and some birds. Before the bad times there had been animals — before the Cleanup when 'most everything requiring air men could use had been killed. Maybe — here in the Outside there were animals left.

Better not think of that! Water sloshing over the rim of the kettle at every step, Jill started on the straightest line possible for the lake. When she got behind the first screen of bushes she turned on the flash and found the now familiar way. But she could not run as she wished, she had to go slowly to avoid a fall on this rough ground.

So she reached the bank of the lake. The moon shone so brightly she snapped off the flash. Then she was aware of movement — the edges of the thick banks of vegetation which had grown from the lake bottom to close over the water were in constant motion, a rippling. Portions of leaf and stem were torn away, floating out into the clear patches, where they went into violent agitation and were pulled completely under. But there was no sign of what was doing this.

In — in! The thought was like a shout in her mind. Jill set down the torch, took the kettle in both hands, dumped its contents down the bank.

Then, fully released from the task the thing had laid upon her, she grabbed for the flash and ran for the house, the empty kettle banging against her legs. Nor did her heart stop its pounding until she was back in bed, Ulysses once more warm and heavy along her leg, purring a little when she reached down to smooth his fur.

Marcy had news in the morning.

"Those Williamses are going to try to blow up the lake, they're afraid something poisonous is out there. Beeny is clear out of his head and all the Williamses went into town to get a dynamite permit."

"They — they can't do that!" Though Jill did not understand at first her reason for that swift denial.

Marcy was eyeing her. "What do you know about it?"

Jill told her of the night's adventure.

"Let's go see — right now!" was Marcy's answer.

Then Jill discovered curiosity overran the traces of last night's fear.

"Look at that, just look at that!." Marcy stared at the lake. The stretches of open water were well marked this morning. All that activity last night must have brought this about.

"If those invisible things are cutting out all the weeds," Marcy observed, "then they sure are doing good. It was those old weeds which started a lot of the trouble. Dad says they got in so thick they took out the oxygen and then the fish and things died but the weeds kept right on. Towards the last, some of the men who had big houses on the other side of the lake tried all sorts of things. They even got new kinds of fish they thought would eat the weeds and dumped those in — brought them from Africa and South America and places like that. But it didn't do any good. Most of the fish couldn't live here and just died — and others — I guess there weren't enough of them."

"Invisible fish?" If there was a rational explanation for last night,

Jill was only too eager to have it.

Marcy shook her head. "Never heard of any like those. But they'd better make the most of their time. When the Williamses bomb the lake — "

"Bomb it?"

"Use the dynamite — like bombing."

"But they can't!" Jill wanted to scream that loud enough so that the Williamses 'way off in their mucky old house could hear every word. "I'm going to tell Uncle Shaw — right now!"

Marcy trailed behind her to the house. It was going to take almost as much courage to go into Uncle Shaw's forbidden quarters as it did to transport the kettle to the lake. But just as that had to be done, so did this.

She paused outside the kitchen. Aunt Abby was busy there, and if they went in, she would prevent Jill's reaching Uncle Shaw. They had better go around the house to the big window.

To think that was easier than to do so, the bushes were so thick. But Jill persisted with strength she did not know she had until she came to use it. Then she was looking into the long room. There were books, some crowded on shelves, but others in untidy piles on the floor, and a long table with all kinds of things on it.

But in a big chair Uncle Shaw was sitting, just sitting — staring straight at the window. There was no change in his expression, it was as if he did not see Jill.

She leaned forward and rapped on the pane, and his head jerked as if she had awakened him. Then he frowned and motioned her to go away. But Jill did as she would not have dared to do a day earlier, stood her ground, and pointed to the window, made motions to open it.

After a long moment Uncle Shaw got up, moving very slowly as if it were an effort. He came and opened the long window, which had once been a door onto the overgrown patio.

"Go away," he said flatly.

Jill heard a rustle behind her as if Marcy were obeying. But she stood her ground, though her heart was beating fast again.

"You've got to stop them," she said in a rush.

"Stop them — stop who — from doing what?" He talked slowly as he had moved.

"Stop them from bombing the lake. They'll kill all the invisibles — "

Now his eyes really saw her, not just looked at something which was annoying him.

"Jill — Marcy — " he said their names. "What are you talking about?"

"The Williamses, they're going to bomb the lake on account of what happened to Beeny," Jill said as quickly as she could, determined to make him hear this while he seemed to be listening to her. "That'll kill all the invisibles. And they're eating off the weeds — or at least they break them off and pull them out and sink them or something. There's a lot more clear water this morning."

"Clear water?" He came out, breaking a way through the bush before the window. "Show me — and then tell me just what you are talking about."

It was when Uncle Shaw stood on the lake bank and they pointed out the clear water that Jill told of Ulysses' hunting and its results in detail. He stopped her from time to time to make her repeat parts, but she finally came to the end.

"You see — if they bomb the lake — then the invisibles — they'll all be dead!" she ended.

"You say it talked to you — in your mind — " For the third time he returned to that part of her story. She was beginning to be impatient. The important thing was to stop the Williamses, not worry over what happened last night.

"Not talked exactly, it made me feel bad just like it was feeling, just as if I were caught where a breather broke down. It was horrible!"

"Needed water — Yet by your account it had been quite a long time out of it."

She nodded. "Yes, it needed water awfully bad. It was flopping around in the pan I put down for Ulysses. Then I got the kettle for it, but that wasn't enough either — it needed the lake. When I brought it down — there was all that tearing at the weeds — big patches pulled loose and sunk. But if the Williamses — "

He had been looking over her head at the water. Then he turned abruptly. "Come on!" was the curt order he threw at them and they had to trot fast to keep at his heels.

It was Marcy's house they went to, Marcy's Dad she was told to retell her story to. When she had done, Uncle Shaw looked at Major Scholar.

"What do you think, Price?"

"There were those imports Jacques Brazan bought — "

"Something invisible in water, but something which can live out of it for fairly long stretches of time. Something that can 'think' a distress call. That sound like any of Brazan's pets?"

"Come to think of it, no. But what do you have then, Shaw? Nothing of the old native wildlife fits that description either."

"A wild, very wild guess." Uncle Shaw rubbed his hands together. "So wild you might well drag me in with Beeny, so I won't even say it yet. What did Brazan put in?"

"Ought to be in the records." Major Scholar got a notebook out of his desk. "Here it is — " He ran his finger down a list. "Nothing with any remote resemblance. But remember Arthur Pierce? He went berserk that day and dumped his collection in the lake."

"He had some strange things in that! No listing though — "

"Dad," Marcy spoke up. "I remember Dr. Pierce's big aquarium. There was a fish that walked on its fins out of water, it could jump, too. He showed me once when I was little, just after we came here."

"Mudskipper!" Her father nodded. "Wait — " He went to a big bookcase and started running his finger along under the titles of the books. "Here — now — " He pulled out a book and slapped it open on the desk.

"Mudskipper — but — wait a minute! Listen here, Shaw!" He began to read, skipping a lot. " 'Pigmy goby — colorless except for eyes — practically transparent in water' — No, this is only three-eighths of an inch long — "

"It was a lot bigger," protested Jill. "Too big for the pie pan I had for Ulysses. It flopped all over in that trying to get under the water."

"Mutant — just maybe," Uncle Shaw said. "Which would fit in with that idea of mine." But he did not continue to explain, saying instead:

"Tonight, Price, we're going fishing!"

He was almost a different person, Jill decided. Just as if the Uncle Shaw she had known since she arrived had been asleep and was now fully awake.

"But the Williamses are going to bomb — " she reminded him.

"Not now — at least not yet. This is important enough to pull a few strings, Price. Do you think we can still pull them?"

Major Scholar laughed. "One can always try, Shaw. I'm laying the smart money all on you."

After dark they gathered at the lake edge. Uncle Shaw and Major Scholar had not said Jill and Marcy could not go too, so they were very much there, and also Aunt Abby and Mrs. Scholar.

But along the beds of vegetation there was no whirling tonight. Had — had she dreamed it, Jill began to wonder apprehensively. And what would Uncle Shaw, Major Scholar, say when no invisibles came?

Then — just as it had shot into her mind last night from the despairing captive in the pan — she knew!

"They won't come," she said with conviction. "Because they know that you have that — that you want to *catch* them!" She pointed to the net, the big kettle of water they had waiting. "They are afraid to come!"

"How do they know?" Uncle Shaw asked quietly. He did not say he didn't believe her, as she expected him to.

"They — somehow they know when there's danger."

"All right." He had been kneeling on the bank, now he stood up. But he stooped again and threw the net behind him, kicked out and sent the water cascading out of the kettle. "We're not going to try to take them."

"But — " Major Scholar began to protest and then said in another tone, "I see — see what you mean — we reacted in the old way — making the same old mistake."

They were all standing now and the moon was beginning to silver the lake. Suddenly there was movement along the edge of the beds, the water rippled, churned. The invisibles were back.

Uncle Shaw held out his hands. One of them caught Jill's in a warm grip, with the other he held Aunt Abby's.

"I think, Price, perhaps — just perhaps we have been given another chance. If we can step out of the old ways enough to take it — no more mistakes — "

"Perhaps so, Shaw."

"You won't let the Williamses — " began Jill.

"No!" That word was as sharp and clear as a shout. It even seemed to echo over the moon-drenched water, where there was that abundant rippling life. "Not now, not ever — I promise you that!" But Jill thought he was not answering her but what was in the water.

"The moon is very bright tonight — " Aunt Abby spoke a little hesitatingly.

"Perhaps it calls to its own. Pierce's creatures may have provided the seed, but remember," Uncle Shaw said slowly, "there was something else down there — "

"Those moon rocks!" Marcy cried.

"Shaw, surely you don't think — !" Major Scholar sounded incredulous.

"Price, I'm not going to think right now, the time has come to accept. If Wilson's suspicions were the truth and those bits of rock from the last pickup had some germ of life locked into them — a germ which reacted on this — then think, man, what the rest of the lunar harvest might mean to this world now!"

"And we know just where — "

Uncle Shaw laughed. "Yes, Price. Since they are now dusty and largely forgotten why shouldn't we make a little intelligent use of them right here. Then watch what happens in a world befouled!

It could be our answer is right up there and we were too blind to see it!"

On the lake the moonlight was shivered into a thousand fragments where the invisibles were at work.

Walter M. Miller, Jr.

Walter M. Miller published his first science fiction short story in *Amazing* in 1951, and subsequently has written and published dozens of stories, including "The Darfsteller," which won the Hugo Award for best novellette in 1955. His influential novel *A Canticle For Leibowitz* won the Hugo in 1961 and is generally recognized as one of the great classics of the field. A new novel, *Leibowitz and The Wild Horse Woman,* is in progress for Bantam Books.

I was born in Florida and have lived here all my life, except for twelve years in the 1940s and 50s. This story came to me in those years, when I was living in Texas and feeling nostalgic for the backwoods and the good old scrub palmetto and pine tree environment I'd grown up in.

A TRIFLIN' MAN

by Walter M. Miller, Jr.

The rain sang light in the sodden palmettos and the wind moaned through the pines about the unpainted shack, whipping the sea grass that billowed about the islands of scrub. The land lay bathed in rain-haze beneath the pines. Rain trickled from the roof of the shack and made a rattling spray in the rivulets under the eaves. Rain blew from the roof in foggy cloudlets. Rain played marimba-sounds on the wooden steps. A droopy chicken huddled in the drenched grass, too sick to stir or seek a shelter.

No road led across the scrublands to the distant highway, but only a sandy footpath that was now a gushing torrent that ran down to an overflowing creek of brackish water. A 'possum hurried across the inundated footpath at the edge of the clearing, drenched and miserable, seeking higher ground.

The cabin was without a chimney, but a length of stovepipe projected from a side window, and bent skyward at a clumsy angle. A thin trail of brown smoke leaked from beneath the rain-hood, and wound away on the gusty breeze. In the cabin, there was life, and an aura of song lingered about the rain-washed walls, song as mournful as the sodden land, low as the wail of a distant train.

Whose hands was drivin' the nails O Lord?
Whose hands was drivin' the nails?
Lord O Lord!
My hands was drivin' the nails O Lord!
My hands was drivin' the nails
And I did crucify my God!

The song was low and vibrant in the cabin, and Lucey rocked to it, rolling her head as she sang over the stove, where a smoked 'possum simmered in pot-likker with sweet-taters, while corn bread toasted in the oven. The cabin was full of food-smells and sweat-smells, and smoky light through dusty panes.

From a rickety iron bed near the window came a sudden choking sob, an animal sound of almost unendurable torment and despair. Lucey stopped singing and turned to blink toward the cry, sudden concern melting her pudgy face into a mountain woman cherub's face, full of compassion.

"Awwwwwww . . ." The sound welled unbidden from her throat, a rich low outpouring of love and sympathy for the sallow twitching youth who lay on the yellowish sheets, his eyes wild, his hands tensing into claws.

"Awwwww, Doodie — you ain't gonna have another spell?" she said.

Only a small hurt this time, my son. It can't be helped. It's like tuning a guitar. You can't do it without sounding the strings, or pulsing the neural fibers. But only a small hurt this time . . .

The youth writhed and shuddered, stiffening into a puppet strained by steel springs. His back arched, and his muscles quivered. He flung himself suddenly into reflexive gymnastics, sobbing in small shrieks.

Lucey murmured softly. An immense mass of love, she waddled toward the bed in bounces of rubbery flesh. She bent over him to purr low in her throat.

"Poor Doodie . . . poor li'l Doodie. Mama's lamb."

The boy sobbed and thrashed. The paroxysm brought froth to his lips and jerked his limbs into cramped spasms. He jerked and writhed and tumbled on the bed.

"You jus' try to lay calm, Doodie. You jus' try. You gonna be all right. It ain't gonna last long, Doodie. It's gonna go away."

"No!" he whimpered. "No! Don't touch me, Mama! *Don't!*"

"Now, Doodie . . ."

She sat on the edge of the bed to gather him up in her massive arms. The spasms grew more frantic, less reflexive. He fought her, shrieking terror. She lay beside him, moaning low with pity. She enveloped him with her arms, enfolding him so that he could no longer kick. She pulled his face into the hollow of her huge bosom and squeezed him. With his tense body pressed tightly against the bulky mass of her, she melted again with love, and began chanting a rhythmic lullaby while he twitched and slavered against her, fighting away, pretending to suffocate.

Gradually, as exhaustion overcame him, the spasm passed. He lay wheezing quietly in her arms.

The strings are tuned, my son, and it was only a small hurt. Has the hurt stopped, my son?

Yes, father, if only this monstress would let me be.

Accept my knowledge, and be content. The time will come.

"Who you whisperin' to, Doodie? Why are you mumblin' so?" She looked down at his tousled head, pressed tightly between her breasts.

His muttering ceased, and he lay quietly as if in a trance. It was always so. The boy had fits, and when the paroxysm had passed, he went into a rigid sleep. But it was more like a frozen moment of awareness, and old Ma Kutter said the boy was "witched." Lucey had never believed in "witchin'."

When he was tensely quiet, she tenderly disengaged herself and slid off the bed. He lay on his side, face toward the window, eyes slitted and mouth agape. Humming softly, Lucey returned to the stove and took a stick of oak out of the bucket. She paused to glance back at him — and he seemed to be rigidly listening to something. The rain?

"Doodie . . . ?"

"When are you coming for us, father?" came in a ghost whisper from the bed. "When, *when?*"

"What are you talking about, Doodie?" The cast-iron stove-lid clattered on the hot metal as she lifted it nervously aside. She glanced down briefly at the red coals in the stove, then back at Doodie.

"Very soon . . . very soon!" he whispered.

Lucey chucked the stick of wood in atop the coals, then stood staring at the bed until the flames licked up about the lid-hole to glisten orange on her sweat-glazed face.

"Who are you talkin' to, Doodie?"

She expected no answer, but after several seconds, his breathing grew deeper. Then it came: "My *father.*"

Lucey's plump mouth went slowly shut and her hand quivered as she fumbled for the stove lid.

"Your pa is dead, Doodie. You know that."

The emaciated youth stirred on the bed, picked himself up slowly on one arm, and turned to look at her, his eyes blazing. "You lie!" he cried. "Mama, you lie!"

"Doodie!"

"I hate you, Mama. I hate all of you, and I'll make you pay. I'll be like *him.*"

The stove lid clattered back in place. She wiped her hands nervously on her dress. "You're sick, Doodie! You're not right in the mind. You never even *seed* your pa."

"I talk to him," the boy said. "He tells me things. He told me why you're my mother. He told me how. And he told me who *I* am."

"You're my son!" Lucey's voice had gone up an octave, and she edged defensively away.

"Only half of me, Mama." the boy said, then laughed defiantly. "Only half of me is even human. You knew that when he came here, and paid you to have his baby."

"*Doodie!*"

"You can't lie to me, Mama. *He* tells me. *He* knows."

"He was just a man, Doodie. Now he's gone. He never came back, do you hear?"

The boy stared out the window at the rain-shroud. When he spoke again, it was in a small slow voice of contempt.

"It doesn't matter. He doesn't want you to believe — any of you." He paused to snicker. "He doesn't want to warn you what we're going to do."

Lucey shook her head slowly. "Lord, have mercy on me," she breathed. "I know I done wrong. But please, punish old Lucey and not my boy."

"I ain't crazy, Mama."

"If you ain't crazy, you're 'witched,' and talkin' to the dead."

"He ain't dead. He's Outside."

Lucey's eyes flickered quickly to the door.

"And he's comin' back — soon." The boy chuckled. "Then he'll make me like him, and it won't hurt to listen."

"You talk like he wasn't a man. I seed him, and you didn't. Your pa was just a man, Doodie."

"No, Mama. He showed you a man because he wanted you to see a man. Next time, he'll come the way he *really* is."

"Why would your pa come back," she snorted, summoning courage to stir the pot. "What would he want here? If you was right in the head, you wouldn't get fits, and you'd know you never seed him. What's his name? You don't even know his name."

"His name is a purple bitter with black velvet, Mama. Only there isn't any word."

"Fits," she moaned. "A child with fits."

"The crawlers, you mean? That's when he talks to me. It hurts at first."

She advanced on him with a big tin spoon, and shook it at him. "You're sick, Doodie. And don't you carry on so. A doctor's what you need . . . if only Mama had some money."

"I won't fuss with you, Mama."

"Huh!" She stood there for a moment, shaking her head. Then she went back to stir the pot. Odorous steam arose to perfume the shack.

The boy turned his head to watch her with luminous eyes. "The fits are when he talks, Mama. Honest they are. It's like electricity inside me. I wish I could tell you how."

"Sick!" She shook her head vigorously. "Sick, that's all."

"If I was all like him, it wouldn't hurt. It only hurts because I'm half like you."

"Doodie, you're gonna drive your old mother to her grave. Why do you torment me so?"

He turned back to the window and fell silent . . . determinedly, hostilely silent. The silence grew like an angry thing in the cabin, and Lucey's noises at the stove only served to punctuate it.

"Where does your father stay, Doodie?" she asked at last, in cautious desperation.

"Outside . . ."

"Gitalong! Wheah outside, in a palmetto scrub? In the cypress swamp?"

"*Way* Outside. Outside the world."

"Who taught you such silliness? Spirits an' such! I ought to tan you good, Doodie!"

"From another world," the boy went on.

"An' he talks to you from the other world?"

Doodie nodded solemnly.

Lucey stirred vigorously at the pot, her face creased in a dark frown. Lots of folks believed in spirits, and lots of folks believed in mediums. But Lucey had got herself straight with the Lord.

"I'm gonna call the parson," she grunted flatly.

"Why?"

"Christian folks don't truck with spirits."

"He's no spirit, Mama. He's like a man, only he's not. He comes from a star."

She set her jaw and fell grimly silent. She didn't like to remember Doodie's father. He'd come seeking shelter from a storm, and he was big and taciturn, and he made love like a machine. Lucey had been younger then — younger and wilder, and not afraid of shame. He'd vanished as quickly as he'd come.

When he had gone, it almost felt like he'd been there to accomplish an errand, some piece of business that had to be handled hastily and efficiently.

"Why'd he want a son?" she scoffed. "If what you say is true — which it ain't."

The boy stirred restlessly. "Maybe I shouldn't tell."

"You tell Mama."

"You won't believe it anyway," he said listlessly. "He fixed it so I'd *look* human. He fixed it so he could talk to me. I tell him things. Things he could find out himself if he wanted to."

"What does he want to know?"

"How humans work inside."

"Livers and lungs and such? Sssssss! Silliest I ever — "

"And brains. Now they know."

"They?"

"Pa's people. *You'll see.* Now they know, and they're coming to run things. Things will be different, lots different."

"When?"

"Soon. Only pa's coming sooner. He's their . . . their . . ." The boy groped for a word. "He's like a detective."

Lucey took the corn bread out of the oven and sank despairingly into a chair. "Doodie, Doodie . . ."

"What, Mama?"

"Oh, Sweet Jesus! What did I do, what did I do? He's a child of the devil. Fits an' lies and puny ways. Lord, have mercy on me."

With an effort, the boy sat up to stare at her weakly. "He's no devil, Mama. He's no man, but he's better than a man. You'll see."

"You're not right in the mind, Doodie."

"It's all right. He wouldn't want you to believe. Then you'd be warned. They'd be warned too."

"They?"

"Humans — white and black and yellow. He picked poor people to have his sons, so nobody would believe."

"Sons? You mean you ain't the only one?"

Doodie shook his head. "I got brothers, Mama — half-brothers. I talk to them sometimes too."

She was silent a long time. "Doodie, you better go to sleep," she said wearily at last.

"Nobody'll believe . . . until he comes, and the rest of them come after him."

"He ain't comin', Doodie. You ain't seed him — never."

"Not with my eyes," he said.

She shook her head slowly, peering at him with brimming eyes. "Poor little boy. Cain't I do somethin' to make you see?"

Doodie sighed. He was tired, and didn't answer. He fell back on the pillow and lay motionless. The water that crawled down the pane rippled the rain-light over his sallow face. He might have been a pretty child, if it had not been for the tightness in his face, and the tumor-shape on his forehead.

He said it was the tumor-shape that let him talk to his father. After a few moments, Lucey arose, and took their supper off the stove. Doodie sat propped up on pillows, but he only nibbled at his food.

"Take it away," he told her suddenly. "I can feel it starting again."

There was nothing she could do. While he shrieked and tossed again on the bed, she went out on the rain-swept porch to pray. She prayed softly that her sin be upon herself, not upon her boy. She prayed for understanding, and when she was done she cried until Doodie was silent again inside.

When she went back into the house, he was watching her with cold, hard eyes.

"It's tonight," he said. "He's coming *tonight,* Mama."

The rain ceased at twilight, but the wind stiffened, hurling drops of water from the pines and scattering them like shot across the sagging roof. Running water gurgled in the ditch, and a rabbit ran toward higher ground. In the west, the clouds lifted a dark bandage from a bloody slash of sky, and somewhere a dog howled in the dusk. Rain-pelted, the sick hen lay dying in the yard.

Lucey stood in the doorway, nervously peering out into the pines and the scrub, while she listened to the croak of the tree frogs at sunset, and the conch-shell sounds of wind in the pines.

"Ain't no night for strangers to be out wanderin'," she said. "There won't be no moon till nearly midnight."

"He'll come," promised the small voice behind her. "He's coming from the Outside."

"Shush, child. He's nothing of the sort."

"He'll come, all right."

"What if I won't let him in the door?"

Doodie laughed. "You can't stop him, Mama. I'm only *half* like you, and it hurts when he talks-inside."

"Yes, child?"

"If he talks-inside to a human, the human dies. He told me."

"Sounds like witch-woman talk," Lucey said scornfully and stared back at him from the doorway. "I don't want no more of it. There's nobody can kill somebody by just a-talkin'."

"*He* can. And it ain't just talking. It's talking *inside.*"

"Ain't nobody can talk inside your mother but your mother."

"That's what I been saying." Doodie laughed. "If he did, you'd die. That's why he needed *me.*"

Lucey's eyes kept flickering toward the rain-soaked scrub, and she hugged her huge arms, and shivered. "Silliest I ever!" she snorted. "He was just a man, and you never even seed him."

She went inside and got the shotgun, and sat down at the table to clean it, after lighting a smoky oil lamp on the wall.

"Why are you cleaning that gun, Mama?"

"Wildcat around the chicken yard last night!" she muttered. "Tonight I'm gonna watch."

Doodie stared at her with narrowed eyes, and the look on his face started her shivering again. Sometimes he did seem not-quite-human, a shape witched or haunted wherein a silent cat prowled by itself and watched, through human eyes.

How could she believe the wild words of a child subject to fits, a child whose story was like those told by witching women and herb healers? A thing that came from the stars, a thing that could come in the guise of a man and talk, make love, eat, and laugh, a thing that wanted a half-human son to which it could speak from afar.

How could she believe in a thing that was like a spy sent into the city before the army came, a thing that could make her conceive when it wasn't even human? It was wilder than any of the stories they told in the deep swamps, and Lucey was a good Christian now.

Still, when Doodie fell asleep, she took the gun and went out to wait for the wildcat that had been disturbing the chickens. It wasn't unchristian to believe in wildcats, not even tonight.

Doodie's father had been just a man, a triflin' man. True, she couldn't remember him very clearly, because she had been drinking corn squeezin's with Jacob Fleeter before the stranger came. She had been all giggly, and he had been all shimmery, and she couldn't remember a word he'd said.

"Lord forgive me," she breathed as she left the house.

The wet grass dragged about her legs as she crossed the yard and traversed a clearing toward an island of palmetto scrub from which she could cover both the house and the chicken yard.

The clouds had broken, and stars shone brightly, but there was no moon. Lucey moved by instinct, knowing each inch of land for half a mile around the shack.

She sat on a wet and rotting log in the edge of the palmetto thicket, laid the shotgun across her lap, stuffed a corncob pipe with tobacco from Deevey's field, and sat smoking in the blackness while whippoorwills mourned over the land, and an occasional owl hooted from the swamp. The air was cool and clean after the rain, and only a few nightbirds flitted in the brush while crickets chirped in the distance and tree frogs spoke mysteriously.

"*AAAaaaAAaaarrrwww . . . Na!*"

The cry was low and piercing. Was it Doodie, having another spasm — or only a dream? She half-arose, then paused, listening. There were a few more whimpers, then silence. A dream, she decided, and settled back to wait. There was nothing she could do for Doodie, not until the State Healthmobile came through again, and examined him for "catchin'" ailments. If they found he wasn't right in the mind, they might take him away.

The glowing ember in the pipe was hypnotic — the only thing to be clearly seen except the stars. She stared at the stars, wondering about their names, until they began to crawl before her eyes. Then she looked at the ember in the pipe again, brightening and dimming with each breath, acquiring a lacy crust of ashes, growing sleepy in the bowl and sinking deeper, deeper, while the whippoorwills pierced the night with melancholy.

"*. . . Na na naaaAAAAhhhaaa . . . !*"

When the cries woke her, she knew she had slept for some time. Faint moonlight seeped through the pine branches from the east, and there was a light mist over the land. The air had chilled, and she shivered as she arose to stretch, propping the gun across the rotten log. She waited for Doodie's cries to cease.

The cries continued, unabated.

Stiffening with sudden apprehension, she started back toward the shack. Then she saw it — a faint violet glow through the trees to the north, just past the corner of the hen house! She stopped again, tense with fright. Doodie's cries were becoming meaningful.

"Pa! I can't stand it any closer! Naa, naaa! I can't think, I can't think at all. No, *please* . . ."

Reflexively, Lucey started to bolt for the house, but checked herself in time. No lamp burned in the window. She picked up the shotgun and a pebble. After a nervous pause, she tossed the pebble at the porch.

It bounced from the wall with a loud crack, and she slunk low into shadows. Doodie's cries continued without pause. A minute passed, and no one emerged from the house.

A sudden metallic sound, like the opening of a metal door, came from the direction of the violet light. Quickly she stepped over the log and pressed back into the scrub thicket. Shaking with fear, she waited in the palmettos, crouching in the moonlight among the spiny fronds, and lifting her head occasionally to peer toward the violet light.

She saw nothing for a time, and then, gradually the moonlight seemed to dim. She glanced upward. A tenuous shadow, like smoke, had begun to obscure the face of the moon, a translucent blur like the thinnest cloud.

At first, she dismissed it as a cloud. But it writhed within itself, curled and crawled, not dispersing, but seeming to swim. Smoke from the violet light? She watched it with wide, upturned eyes.

Despite its volatile shape, it clung together as a single entity as smoke would never have done. She could still see it faintly after it had cleared the lunar disk, scintillating in the moon-glow.

It swam like an airborne jellyfish. A cluster of silver threads it seemed, tangled in a cloud of filaments — or a giant mass of dandelion fluff. It leaked out misty pseudopods, then drew them back as it pulled itself through the air. Weightless as chick-down, huge as a barn, it flew — and drifted from the direction of the sphere in a semicircle, as if inspecting the land, at times moving against the wind.

It was coming closer to the house.

It moved with purpose, and therefore was alive. This Lucey knew. It moved with its millions of spun threads, finer than a spider's web, the patterns as ordered as a neural array.

It contracted suddenly and began to settle toward the house. Glittering opaquely, blotting out half the cabin, it kept contracting and drawing itself in, becoming denser until it fell in the yard with a blinding flash of incandescent light.

Lucey's flesh crawled. Her hands trembled on the gun, her breath came in shallow gasps.

Before her eyes it was changing into a manlike thing.

Frozen, she waited, thinking swiftly. Could it be that Doodie was right?

Could it be —

Doodie was still whimpering in the house, weary now, as he always was when the spasm had spent itself. But the words still came, words addressed to his father.

The thing in the yard was assuming the shape of a man — and Lucey knew who the man would be.

She reared up quickly in the palmettos, like an enraged, hulking river animal breaking to the surface. She came up shotgun-in-hand and bellowed across the clearing. "Hey theah! You triflin' skunk! *Look at me!*"

Still groping for human shape, the creature froze.

"Run off an' leave me with child!" Lucey shouted. "And no way to pay his keep!"

The creature kept coming toward her, and the pulsing grew stronger.

"Don't come any nearer, you hear?"

When it kept coming, Lucey grunted in a gathering rage and charged out of the palmettos to meet it, shotgun raised, screaming insults. The thing wobbled to a stop, its face a shapeless blob with black shadows for eyes.

She brought the gun to her shoulder and fired both barrels at once.

The thing tumbled to the ground. Crackling arcs danced about it, and a smell of ozone came on the breeze. For one hideous moment it was lighted by a glow from within. Then the glow died, and it began to expand. It grew erratically, and the moonlight danced in silvery filaments about it. A blob of its substance broke loose from the rest, and wind-borne, sailed across the clearing and dashed itself to dust in the palmettos.

A sudden gust took the rest of it, rolling it away in the grass, gauzy shreds tearing loose from the mass. The gust blew it against the trunk of a pine. It lodged there briefly, quivering in the breeze and shimmering palely under the moon. Then it broke into dust that scattered eastward across the land.

"Praised be the Lord," repeated Lucey, beginning to cry.

A high whining sound pierced the night, from the direction of the violet light. She whirled to stare. The light grew brighter. Then the whine abruptly ceased. A luminescent sphere, glowing with violet haze, moved upward from the pines. It paused, then in stately majesty continued the ascent, gathering speed until it became a ghostly chariot that dwindled. Up, up, up toward the gleaming stars. She watched it until it vanished from sight.

Then she straightened her shoulders, and glowered toward the dust traces that blew eastward over the scrub.

"Ain't nothing worse than a triflin' man," she philosophized. "If he's human, or if he's not."

Wearily she returned to the cabin. Doodie was sleeping peacefully. Smiling, she tucked him in, and went to bed. There was corn to hoe, come dawn.

Report: Servopilot recon six, to fleet. Missionman caught in transition phase by native organism, and devastated, thus destroying liaison with native analog. Suggest delay of invasion plans. Unpredictability factors associated with mothers of genetic analogs. Withdraw contacts. Servo Six.

Joe Haldeman

Joe Haldeman achieved international acclaim with his novel *The Forever War,* which received the Hugo, Nebula, and Ditmar awards as the best science fiction novel of 1975. His story "Tricentennial" won the Hugo for best short story the following year, and another novel, *Mindbridge,* won the Galaxy Award in 1978. His other books include *All My Sins Remembered, Worlds, Worlds Apart, Tool of the Trade, Buying Time,* and *The Hemingway Hoax.* His short stories have appeared frequently in all the major science fiction magazines as well as other literary and mainstream publications, and he is also a well-published poet and songwriter. He was Professional Guest of Honor at ConFiction, the 48th Annual World Science Fiction Convention in The Hague, Holland, in August of 1990.

"All the Universe in a Mason Jar" is pure old Brooksville. When I lived there I got along with the people just fine, but was very uncomfortable with the town.

I wanted to put a person into the story who is totally inappropriate in that milieu and have him get along. Then I put in a basic 'National Enquirer' flying saucer, but made it real. I wrote it as a goof, after a hard novel. It was my first Florida story. I realized I'd lived here all these years and had never written one. I don't know when I've had such fun writing a story.

ALL THE UNIVERSE IN A MASON JAR

by Joe Haldeman

New Homestead, Florida: 1990.

John Taylor Taylor, retired professor of mathematics, lived just over two kilometers out of town, in a three-room efficiency module tucked in an isolated corner of a citrus grove. Books and old furniture and no neighbors, which was the way John liked it. He only had a few years left on this Earth, and he preferred to spend them with his oldest and most valued friend: himself.

But this story isn't about John Taylor Taylor. It's about his moonshiner, Lester Gilbert. And some five billion others.

This day the weather was fine, so the professor took his stick and walked into town to pick up the week's mail. A thick cylinder of journals and letters was wedged into his box; he had to ask the clerk to remove them from the other side. He tucked the mail under his arm without looking at it, and wandered next door to the bar.

"Howdy, Professor."

"Good afternoon, Leroy." He and the bartender were the only ones in the place, not unusual this late in the month. "I'll take a boilermaker today, please." He threaded his way through a maze of flypaper strips and eased himself into a booth of chipped, weathered plastic.

He sorted his mail into four piles: junk, bills, letters, and journals. Quite a bit of junk, two bills, a letter that turned out to be another bill, and three journals — *Nature, Communications* of the American Society of Mathematics, and a collection of papers delivered at an ASM symposium on topology. He scanned the contributors lists and, as usual, saw none of his old colleagues represented.

"Here y' go." Leroy set a cold beer and a shot glass of whiskey between *Communications* and the phone bill. John paid him with a five and lit his pipe carefully before taking a sip. He folded *Nature* back at the letters column and began reading.

The screen door slapped shut loudly behind a burly man in

wrinkled clean work clothes. John recognized him with a nod; he returned a left-handed V-sign and mounted a bar stool.

"How 'bout a red-eye, Leroy?" Mixture of beer and tomato juice with a dash of Louisiana, hangover cure.

Leroy mixed it. "Rough night, Isaac?"

"Shoo. You don' know." He downed half the concoction in a gulp, and shuddered. He turned to John. "Hey, Professor. What you know about them flyin' saucers?"

"Lot of them around a few years ago," he said tactfully. "Never saw one myself."

"Me neither. Wouldn't give you a nickel for one. Not until last night." He slurped the red-eye and wiped his mouth.

"What?" the bartender said. "You saw one?"

"*Saw* one? Shoo." He slid the two-thirds empty glass across the bar. "You wanta put some beer on top that? Thanks.

"We was down the country road seven, eight klicks. You know Eric Olsen's new place?"

"Don't think so."

"New boy, took over Jarmin's plat."

"Oh yeah. Never comes in here; know of him, though."

"You wouldn't hang around no bar neither if you had a pretty little . . . well. Point is, he was puttin' up one of them new stasis barns, you know?"

"Yeah, no bugs. Keeps stuff forever. My daddy-in-law has one."

"Well, he picked up one big enough for his whole avocado crop. Hold on to it till the price is right, up north, like January? No profit till next year, help his 'mortization."

"Yeah, but what's that got to do with the flying — "

"I'm gettin' to it." John settled back to listen. Some tall tale was on the way.

"Anyhow, we was gonna have an old-fashion barn raisin' . . . Miz Olsen got a boar and set up a pit barbecue, the other ladies they brought the trimmin's. Eric, he made two big washtubs of spiced wine, set 'em on ice till we get the barn up. Five, six hours, it turned out (the directions wasn't right), *hot* afternoon, and we just headed for that wine like you never saw.

"I guess we was all pretty loaded, finished off that wine before the pig was ready. Eric, he called in to Samson's and had 'em send out two kegs of Bud."

"Got to get to know that boy," Leroy said.

"Tell me about it. Well, we tore into that pig and had him down to bones an' gristle in twenty minutes. Best god-dern pig *I* ever had, anyhow.

"So's not to let the fire permit go to waste, we went out an' rounded up a bunch of scrap, couple of good-size logs. Finish off that beer around a bonfire. Jommy Parker went off to pick up his fiddle and he took along Midnight Jackson, pick up his banjo. Miz Olsen had this Swedish guitar, one too many strings but by God could she play it.

"We cracked that second keg 'bout sundown and Lester Gilbert — you know Lester?"

Leroy laughed. "Don't I just. He was 'fraid the beer wouldn't hold out, went to get some corn?"

John made a mental note to be home by four o'clock. It was Wednesday; Lester would be by with his weekly quart.

"We get along all right," the bartender was saying. "Figure our clientele don't overlap that much."

"Shoo," Isaac said. "Some of Lester's clientele overlaps on a regular basis.

"Anyhow, it got dark quick, you know how clear it was last night. Say, let me have another, just beer."

Leroy filled the glass and cut the foam off. "Clear enough to see a flyin' saucer, eh?"

"I'm gettin' to it. Thanks." He sipped it and concentrated for a few seconds on tapping tobacco into a cigarette paper. "Like I say, it got dark fast. We was sittin' around the fire, singin' if we knew the words, drinkin' if we didn't — "

" 'Spect you didn't know many of the songs, yourself."

"Never could keep the words in my head. Anyhow, the fire was gettin' a mite hot on me, so I turned this deck chair around and settled down lookin' east, fire to my back, watchin' the moon rise over the government forest there — "

"Hold on now. Moon ain't comin' up until after midnight."

"You-god-damn-*right* it ain't!" John felt a chill even though he'd seen it coming. Isaac had a certain fame as a storyteller. "That wa'nt *nobody's* moon."

"Did anybody else see it?" John asked.

"Ev'rybody. Ev'rbody who was there — and one that wasn't. I'll get to that.

"I saw that thing and spilled my beer gettin' up, damn near trip and fall in the pit. Hollered, 'Lookit that goddamn thing!' and pointed, jumpin' up an' down, and like I say, they all did see it.

"It was a little bigger than the moon and not quite so round, egg-shaped. Whiter than the moon, an' if you looked close you could see little green and blue flashes around the edge. It didn't make no noise we could hear, and was movin' real slow. We saw it for at least a minute. Then it went down behind the trees."

"What could it of been?" the bartender said. "Sure you wa'nt all drunk and seein' things?"

"No way in hell. You know me, Leroy, I can tie one on ev'y now and again, but I just plain don't get that drunk. Sure thing I don't get that drunk on beer an' *wine!*"

"And Lester wasn't back with the 'shine yet?"

"No . . . an' that's the other part of the story." Isaac took his time lighting the cigarette and drank off some beer.

"I'm here to tell you, we was all feelin' sorta spooky over that. Hunkered up around the fire, lookin' over our shoulders. Eric went in to call the sheriff, but he didn't get no answer.

"Sat there for a long time, speculatin'. Forgot all about Lester, suppose to be back with the corn.

"Suddenly we hear this somethin' crashin' through the woods. Jommy sprints to his pickup and gets out his over-and-under. But it's just Lester. Runnin' like the hounds of hell is right behind him.

"He's got a plywood box with a half-dozen Mason jars in her, and from ten feet away he smells like Saturday night. He don't say a word, sets that box down, not too gentle, jumps over to Jommy and grabs that gun away from him and aims it at the government woods, and pulls both triggers, just *boom-crack* twenty-gauge buckshot and a thirty-caliber rifle slug right behind.

"Now Jommy is understandable pissed off. He takes the gun back from Lester and shoves him on the shoulder, follows him and shoves him again; all the time askin' him, just not too politely, don't he know he's too drunk to handle a firearm? and don't he know we could all get busted, him shootin' into federal land? and just in general, what the Sam Hill's goin' on, Lester?"

He paused to relight the cigarette and take a drink. "Now Lester's just takin' it and not sayin' a thing. How 'bout *that?*"

"Peculiar," Leroy admitted.

Isaac nodded. "Lester, he's a good boy but he does have one hell of a temper. Anyhow, Lester finally sets down by his box and unscrews the top off a full jar — they's one with no top but it looks to be empty — and just gulps down one whole hell of a lot. He coughs once and starts talkin'."

"Surprised he could talk at all." John agreed. He always mixed Lester's corn with a lot of something else.

"And listen — that boy is sober like a parson. And he says, talkin' real low and steady, that he seen the same thing we did. He describes it, just exactly like I tole you. But he sees it on the ground. Not in the air."

Isaac passed the glass over and Leroy filled it without a word. "He was takin' a long-cut through the government land so's to stay away from the road. Also he had a call of nature and it always felt more satisfyin' on government land.

"He stopped to take care of that and have a little drink and then suddenly saw this light. Which was the saucer droppin' down into a clearing, but he don't know that. He figures it's the sheriff's 'copter with its night lights on, which don't bother him much, 'cause the sheriff's one of his best customers."

"That a fact?"

"Don't let on I tole you. Anyways, he thought the sheriff might want a little some, so he walks on toward the light. It's on the other side of a little rise; no underbresh but it takes him a few minutes to get there.

"He tops the rise and there's this saucer — bigger'n a private 'copter, he says. He's stupified. Takes a drink and studies it for a while. Thinks it's probably some secret government thing. He's leanin' against a tree, studying . . . and then it dawns on him that he ain't alone."

Isaac blew on the end of his cigarette and shook his head. "I 'spect you ain't gonna believe this — not sure I do myself — but I can't help that, it's straight from Lester's mouth.

"He hears something on the other side of the tree where he's leanin'. Peeks around the tree and — there's this *thing*.

"He says it's got eyes like a big cat, like a lion's, only bigger. And it's a big animal otherwise, about the size of a lion, but no fur, just wrinkled hide like a rhino. It's got big shiny claws that it's usin' on the tree, and a mouthful of big teeth, which it displays at Lester and growls.

"Now Lester, he got nothin' for a weapon but about a quart of Dade County's finest — so he splashes that at the monster's face, hopin' to blind it, and takes off like a bat.

"He gets back to his box of booze, and stops for a second and looks back. He can see the critter against the light from the saucer. It's on its hind legs, weavin' back and forth with its paws out, just roarin'. Looks like the booze works, so Lester picks up the box, ammunition. But just then that saucer light goes out.

"Lester knows good and god damn well that that damn thing can see in the dark, with them big eyes. But Les can see our bonfire, a klick or so west, so he starts runnin' holdin' on to that box of corn for dear life.

"So he comes in on Eric's land and grabs the gun and all that happens. We pass the corn around a while and wash it down with good cold beer. Finally we got up enough Dutch courage to go out after the thing.

"We got a bunch of flashlights, but the only guns were Jommy's over-and-under and a pair of antique flintlock pistols that Eric got from his dad. Eric loaded 'em and give one to me, one to Midnight. Midnight, he was a sergeant in the Asia war, you know, and he was gonna lead us. Eric himself didn't think he could shoot a animal. Dirt farmer (good boy, though)."

"Still couldn't get the sheriff? What about the Guard?"

"Well, no. Truth to tell, everybody — even Lester — was halfway convinced we ain't seen nothin', nothin' real. Eric had got to tellin' us what went into that punch, pretty weird, and the general theory was that he'd whipped up a kind of halla, hallo — "

"Hallucinogen," John supplied.

"That's right. Like that windowpane the old folks take. No offense, Professor."

"Never touch the stuff."

"Anyhow, we figured that we was probably seein' things, but we'd go out an' check, just in case. Got a bunch of kitchen knives and farm tools, took the ladies along too.

"Got Midnight an' Lester up in the front, the rest of us stragglin' along behind, and we followed Lester's trail back to where he seen the thing."

Isaac took a long drink and was silent for a moment, brow furrowed in thought. "Well, hell. He took us straight to that tree and I'm a blind man if there weren't big ol' gouges all along the bark. And the place did smell like Lester's corn.

"Midnight, he shined a light down to where Lester'd said the saucer was, and sure enough, the bresh was all flat there. He walked down to take a closer look — all of us gettin' a little jumpy now — and God damn if he didn't bump right into it. That saucer was there but you flat couldn't see it.

"He let out one hell of a yelp and fired that ol' flintlock down at it, point-blank. Bounced off, you could hear the ball sing away. He come back up the rise just like a cat on fire; when he was clear I took a pot shot at the damn thing, and then Jommy he shot it four, six times. Then there was this kind of wind, and it was gone."

There was a long silence. "You ain't bullshittin' me," Leroy said.

"This ain't no story."

"No." John saw that the big man was pale under his heavy tan. "This ain't no story."

"Let me fix you a stiff one."

"No, I gotta stay straight. They got some newspaper boys comin' down this afternoon. How's your coffee today?"

"Cleaned the pot."

John stayed for one more beer and then started walking home. It was hot, and he stopped halfway to rest under a big willow, reading a few of the *Nature* articles. The one on the Ceres probe was fascinating; he reread it as he ambled the rest of the way home.

So his mind was a couple of hundred million miles away when he walked up the path to his door and saw that it was slightly ajar.

First it startled him, and then he remembered that it was Lester's delivery day. He always left the place unlocked (there were ridge-runners but they weren't interested in old books), and the moon-shiner probably just left his wares inside.

He checked his watch as he walked through the door: it was not quite three. Funny. Lester was usually late.

No Mason jar in sight. And from his library, a snuffling noise.

The year before, some kind of animal — the sheriff had said it was probably a bear — had gotten into his house and made a shambles of it. He eased open the end-table drawer and took out the Walther P-38 he had taken from a dead German officer, half a century before. And as he edged toward the library, the thought occurred to him that the 50-year-old ammunition might not fire.

It was about the size of a bear, a big bear.

Its skin was pebbly gray, with tufts of bristle. It had two arms, two legs, and a stiff tail to balance back on.

The tail had a serrated edge on top, that looked razor sharp. The feet and hands terminated in pointed black claws. The head was vaguely saurian, too many teeth and too large.

As he watched, the creature tore a page out of Fadeeva's *Computational Methods of Linear Algebra,* stuffed it in his mouth and chewed. Spat it out. Turned to see John standing at the door.

It's probably safe to say that any other resident of New Homestead, faced with this situation, would either have started blazing away at the apparition, or would have fainted. But John Taylor Taylor was nothing if not a cool and rational man, and had besides suffered a lifelong addiction to fantastic literature. So he measured what was left of his life against the possibility that this fearsome monster might be intelligent and humane.

He laid the gun on a writing desk and presented empty hands to the creature, palms out.

The thing regarded him for a minute. It opened its mouth, teeth beyond counting, and closed it. Translucent eyelids nictated up over huge yellow eyes, and slid back. Then it replaced the Fadeeva book and duplicated John's gesture.

In several of the stories John had read, humans had communicated with alien races through the medium of mathematics, a pure and supposedly universal language. Fortunately, his library sported a blackboard.

"Allow me to demonstrate," he said with a slightly quavering voice as he crossed to the board, "the Theorem of Pythagorus." The creature's eyes followed him, blinking. "A logical starting place. Perhaps. As good as any," he trailed off apologetically.

He drew a right triangle on the board, and then drew squares out from the sides that embraced the right angle. He held the chalk out to the alien.

The creature made a huffing sound, vaguely affirmative and swayed over to the blackboard. It retracted the claws on one hand and took the chalk from John.

It bit off one end of the chalk experimentally, and spit it out.

Then it reached over and casually sketched in the box representing the square of the hypotenuse. In the middle of the triangle it drew what had to be an equals sign: $\sim$

John was ecstatic. He took the chalk from the alien and repeated the curly line. He pointed at the alien and then at himself: equals.

The alien nodded enthusiastically and took the chalk. It put a slanted line through John's equal sign.

Not equals.

It stared at the blackboard, tapping it with the chalk; one universal gesture. Then, squeaking with every line, it rapidly wrote down:

$$1$$
$$\sim$$
$$- - - 1$$
$$\sim$$
$$1 \sim 1 - 1 \sim$$
$$\sim$$
$$1 \sim 1 - 1 \sim 1$$
$$\sim$$
$$1$$

John studied the message. Some sort of tree diagram? Perhaps a counting system. Or maybe not mathematical at all. He shrugged at the creature. It flinched at the sudden motion, and backed away growling.

"No, no." John held his palms out again. "Friends."

The alien shuffled slowly back to the blackboard and pointed to what it had just written down. Then it opened its terrible mouth and pointed at that. It repeated the pair of gestures twice.

"Oh." Eating the Fadeeva and the chalk. "Are you hungry?" It repeated the action more emphatically.

John motioned for it to follow him and walked toward the kitchen. The alien waddled slowly, its tail a swaying counterweight.

He opened the refrigerator and took out a cabbage, a package of catfish, an avocado, some cheese, an egg, and a chafing dish of leftover green beans, slightly dried out. He lined them up on the counter and demonstrated that they were food by elaborately eating a piece of cheese.

The alien sniffed at each item. When it got to the egg, it stared at John for a long time. It tasted a green bean but spat it out. It walked around the kitchen in a circle, then stopped and growled a couple of times.

It sighed and walked into the living room. John followed. It went out the front door and walked around behind the module. Sighed again and disappeared, from the feet up.

John noted that where the creature had disappeared, the grass was crushed in a large circle. That was consistent with Isaac's testimony: it had entered its invisible flying saucer.

The alien came back out with a garish medallion around its neck. It looked like it was made of rhinestones and bright magenta plastic.

It growled and a voice whispered inside his brain: "Hello? Hello? Can you hear me?"

"Uh, yes. I can hear you."

"Very well. This will cause trouble." It sighed. "One is not to use the translator with a Class 6 culture except under the most dire of emergency. But I am starve. If I do not eat soon the fires inside me will go out. Will have to fill out many forms, may they reek."

"Well . . . anything I can do to help . . ."

"Yes." It walked by him, back toward the front door. "A simple chemical is the basis for all my food. I have diagrammed it." He followed the alien back into the library.

"This is hard." He studied his diagram. "To translator is hard outside of basic words. This top mark is the number 'one.' It means a gas that burns in air."

"Hydrogen?"

"Perhaps. Yes, I think. Third mark is the number 'eight', which means a black rock that also burns, but harder. The mark between means that in very small they are joined together."

"A hydrogen-carbon bond?"

"This is only noise to me." Faint sound of a car door slamming, out on the dirt road.

"Oh, oh," John said. "Company coming. You wait here." He opened the door a crack and watched Lester stroll up the path.

"Hey, Perfesser! You ain't gonna believe what —"

"I know, Les. Isaac told me about it down at Leroy's." He had the door open about twelve centimeters.

Lester stood on the doormat, tried to look inside. "Somethin' goin' on in there?"

"Hard to explain, uh, I've got company."

Lester closed his mouth and gave John a broad wink. "Knew you had it in you, Doc." He passed the Mason jar to John. "Look, I come back later. Really do want yer 'pinion."

"Fine, we'll do that. I'll fix you a —"

A taloned hand snatched the Mason jar from John.

Lester turned white and staggered back. "Don't move a muscle, Doc. I'll git my gun."

"No, wait! It's friendly!"

"Food," the creature growled. "Yes, friend." The screw-top was unfamiliar but only presented a momentary difficulty. The alien snapped it off, glass and all, with a flick of the wrist. It dashed the quart of raw 'shine down its throat.

"Ah, fine. So good. Three parts food, one part water. Strange flavor, so good." It pushed John aside and waddled out the door.

"You have more good food?"

Lester backed away. "You talkin' to me?"

"Yes, yes. You have more of this what your mind calls 'corn'?"

"I be damned." Lester shook his head in wonder. "You are the ugliest sumbitch I ever did see."

"This is humor, yes. On my world, egg-eater, you would be in cage. To frighten children to their amusement." It looked left and right and pointed at Lester's beat-up old Pinto station wagon. "More corn in that animal?"

"Sure." He squinted at the creature. "You got somethin' to pay with?"

"Pay? What is this noise?"

Lester looked up at John. "Did he say what I thought he said?"

John laughed. "I'll get my checkbook. You let him have all he wants."

When John came back out, Lester was leaning on his station wagon, sipping from a jar, talking to the alien. The creature was resting back on its tail, consuming food at a rate of about a quart every thirty seconds. Lester had showed it how to unscrew the jars.

"I do not lie," he said. "This is the best food I have ever tasted."

Lester beamed. "That's what I tell ev'body. You can't *git* that in no store."

"I tasted only little last night. But could tell from even that. Have been seeking you."

It was obvious that the alien was going to drink all three cases. $25 per jar, John calculated, 36 jars. "Uh, Les, I'm going to have to owe you part of the money."

"That's okay, Doc. He just tickles the hell outa me."

The alien paused in mid-air. "No I am to understand, I think. You own this food. The Doc gives to you a writing of equal value."

"That's right," John said.

"You, the Les, think of things you value. I must be symmetry . . . I must have a thing you value." Lester's face wrinkled up in thought. "Ah, there is one thing, yes. I go." The alien waddled back to his ship.

"Gad," Lester said. "If this don't beat all."

(Traveling with the alien is his pet treblig. He carries it because it always emanates happiness. It is also a radioactive creature that can excrete any element. The alien gives it a telepathic command. With an effort that scrambles television reception for fifty miles, it produces a gold nugget weighing slightly less than one kilogram.)

The alien came back and handed the nugget to Lester. "I would take some of your corn back to my home world, yes? Is this sufficient?"

The alien had to wait a few days while Lester brewed up enough 'shine to fill up his auxiliary food tanks. He declined an invitation to go to Washington, but didn't mind talking to reporters.

Humankind learned that the universe was teeming with intelligent life. In this part of the Galaxy there was an organization called the Commonality — not really a government, more like a club. Club members were given such useful tools as faster-than-light travel and immortality.

All races were invited to join the Commonality once they had evolved morally above a certain level. Humankind, of course was only a Class 6. Certain individuals went as high as 5 or as low as 7 (equivalent to the moral state of an inanimate object), but it was the average that counted.

After a rather grim period of transition, the denizens of Earth settled down to concentrating on being good, trying to reach Class 3, the magic level.

It would take surprisingly few generations. Because humankind had a constant reminder of the heaven on Earth that awaited them, as ship after ship drifted down from the sky to settle by a still outside a little farm near New Homestead, Florida: for several races, the gourmet center of Sirius Sector.

Joseph Green

Joseph Green was born in the little hamlet of Compass Lake, Florida. He began his science fiction writing career in England, where his stories appeared in *New Worlds* in 1962, and where he published his first novel, *The Loafers Of Refuge*. He is a frequent contributor to the science fiction magazines ("Raccoon Reaction" is reprinted from *Analog),* and author of *Star Probe, The Horde, Conscience Interplanetary,* and other novels. He is employed by NASA at the Kennedy Space Center as a writer and editor.

Several years ago I gave some lectures on writing science fiction at some of the Florida Suncoast Writers' Conferences sponsored by the St. Petersburg campus of the University of South Florida. One year I needed an idea which had not been used before (to my personal knowledge) to illustrate the construction of the plot of a science fiction story. I created the basic idea used in "Raccoon Reaction" and used it in two lectures. At the end of each session I invited the attendees to make free use of the idea if they wished to do so.

A year or so later I was looking for a good story idea, decided it was unlikely anyone in my classes had used the one offered, and sat down to write the story myself. I used my own home island, the Kennedy Space Center, and Patrick AFB as backdrops, so we ended up with both the scene and the on-stage action occurring in Florida. Having the diplomat be a native of Florida who had grown up on Merritt Island prior to its space-age fame seemed a natural further development. As a native Floridian, raised in the hunting country of Northwest Florida as a child in the 1940s, I knew enough about 'coon hunting and animal behavior to make the comparison that is the heart of the story.

RACCOON REACTION

by Joseph Green

It was after 2 A.M. when the joint strategy session finally dragged to an end. For the past three nights he had slept only in brief catnaps, uncomfortably, in airplane or limousine seats. Commerce Jones was barely able to drag one leaden foot after the other as he walked slowly through the spacious lobby of the Kennedy Space Center Headquarters Building. He was tired to the marrow of his bones, so worn in body his mind was no longer functioning properly. And he felt he had not adequately defended the views of State against the relentless pressure of the military services.

The short walk to the VIP parking lot in front of HQ, through the mild coolness of a December night in Florida, helped shake the cobwebs out of Jones's brain. He started his Air Force car and headed out of the Center, following the Kennedy Parkway south toward the sprawling, unincorporated housing project called Merritt Island. Mildred had elected to stay in the old family home with her aging mother, rather than at the plush quarters available for senior government officials at nearby Patrick AFB.

It had been four days since the huge multi-mirrored spaceship had silently moved in from outer space and assumed a position in geosynchronous orbit over the Atlantic, a thousand miles west of Gabon. The world-wide panic that followed had barely crested, twenty-four hours later, when a message in artificial-sounding English had come crackling down in the lower radio frequencies. The aliens required some unknown amount of deuterium, which they would extract from the ocean themselves. They had no other designs on humanity's resources.

The brief message had done much to calm a fearful world, though it had not halted the extensive military preparations already underway. Then forty-eight hours ago, without warning or explanation, the aliens had started a giant waterspout in the ocean immediately below their ship. It rose in a misty cylinder over a thousand feet wide, speeding directly into space. In nine hours it reached the strange, undefinable vehicle, apparently undiminished in size, and emerged out the other side as water vapor.

And then the *real* panic began.

The President had decided to ignore the slow-moving United Nations, establishing a joint government task force instead. Undersecretary Jones, with extensive experience in dealing with some of the stranger cultures still unassimilated on Earth, had been designated to represent State. The Defense Department had already established an alien communications effort at Patrick AFB, using its Eastern Test Range. The latter stretched across the Atlantic from Florida to southern Africa, with a wide variety of antennas and instruments that could focus on the alien spaceship. The Task Force had set up shop at Patrick and started a two-pronged effort — extensive preparations to attack the aliens if necessary, and unceasing efforts to open a dialogue leading to negotiations.

Commerce Jones, his wife, and their youngest daughter returned home, to the island where the adults had been born, growing up black and poor in the shadows of the towering gantries of the Kennedy Space Center. . . .

The fatigue that dulled his mind had also slowed the reactions of the sixty-one-year-old body Jones tried hard to exercise into good health. His reflexes were slow when he started around a curve and saw the low dark form crossing the road ahead, his reach for the brake tentative.

The Kennedy Space Center was still largely open land, covered by trees, marsh, and orange groves. Wildlife, protected on government property, abounded here. The creature caught in the glare of his headlights was a raccoon, a large one, making his nightly prowl for food.

Jones saw the recognition of danger enter the animal mind as the lights suddenly exposed it: the instant, unthinking reaction. The raccoon whirled to face the oncoming attacker, lips drawn back over small fangs in a fighting snarl, tail up, the black mask across the bandit face wrinkling into menace.

Time seemed to slow for Jones as he found and pressed the

brake, not daring to turn the wheel on this curve. In clear, sharp focus he saw the small animal crouching, poised, ready to fight, responding in the only way it knew to imminent danger . . . and a second later felt the *thump!* of impact as the bumper caught the defiant raccoon and hurled it aside, crushed and mangled, dying before it hit the ground.

The car shuddered to a stop.

Jones sat there for a moment, gripping the wheel — then realized getting out was useless. He touched the accelerator again. If the stupid animal had been a street-wise dog, and had simply kept going . . . but that was not its nature. He should know. He had hunted 'coon many times on this island as a boy, almost half a century ago.

Shaken, regretful, thinking this was a bad ending to an already miserably long day, Jones drove on off the Center and the few miles to his mother-in-law's house on North Tropical Trail. His fatigue had returned, worse than before. But tomorrow, at least, he did not have to be at Patrick until eleven o'clock. He could get several hours of badly needed sleep.

At a late breakfast next morning with Mildred, Jones dawdled over his food. His mind was circling around the urgent problem of the aliens, probing, reexamining, shifting among the endless possibilities for a better solution. After this morning's meeting, he knew, the task force was going to recommend the military option to the President. And he had a terrified feeling this was the wrong answer, a deadly mistake that could have unthinkable repercussions. But he was in a minority.

Naomi came bouncing in from visiting friends in the neighborhood. She was a slim, dark-haired girl of thirteen, an accident that had happened after their first two children were almost grown. Mildred had been forty-one when the pregnancy was confirmed, but had refused to have an abortion. Over the years since they had both come to feel it was a happy decision.

Naomi danced across the room and hugged her father. She had

hardly seen him since they had arrived at her grandmother's house. She helped herself to a link of sausage off his plate and talked around it as she ate. "What's the latest, Dad? The kids are saying the Air Force is going to send up a space shuttle with three solid rockets tipped with tactical atomics, try attacking them from three sides at once. Anything to it?"

Jones tried to keep the startled look off his face. That had been one of the three possible military attack plans proposed by the Air Force last night. The NASA and Air Force space shuttle experts had ruled it out. The fastest possible time to prepare and launch such a cargo would be three weeks.

And by then, Jones knew, what the aliens did hardly mattered. The inescapable damage would have been done.

"Is it true that just one more week will throw the world into another ice age?" Naomi went on, her gamin face open and guileless, but the bright brown eyes watchful. Her father usually answered with nothing more than a brief smile if she touched on a sensitive area.

"The NOAA people have said that in the news, Naomi. The amount of vapor already up there will give us four or five bitterly cold winters."

"How can the scientists be sure of such a thing, dear?" asked Mildred, her deep, soothing voice now troubled and uncertain. "We've never had water vapor in space before."

"No, but when the Mexican volcano El Cinchón blew its top twice in one day, ten years ago, the amounts of ash and sulfur dioxide thrown into the upper atmosphere were carefully measured. The ash came down in about a year, but the gases lingered for several more. The cloud was thin, but it spread around the entire world in the northern hemisphere. There were a lot of temporary weather changes. For the next three years, until the gas naturally changed into sulfuric acid and came down as acid rain, the temperature under the cloud averaged being one or two degrees cooler, worldwide. That was the most-studied rapid change of that sort we've ever had, and it gave the atmospheric scientists a good data base. They claim their predictions on what the vapor cloud will do to the world climate are quite reliable."

"But won't that take thousands of years?" asked Mildred.

"Within Naomi's lifetime the ice will come marching down across Canada, Scandia, and Siberia, if the aliens continue spewing water into geosynchronous orbit for just one more week."

"Then why don't we just *give* them the deuterium from our own supply!" Naomi demanded. "Don't we have a lot of the stuff?"

"Honey, our physicists think that big ship uses the deuterium-deuterium fusion cycle in some way that supplies them with power while also producing tritium. We can't determine precisely how they apply their system, or why they need our deuterium. Our best guess is that they've had an accident of some kind that cost them their supply, and they have to have more to continue on their way — to home, or wherever they're going. But as best we can tell that's an awfully big ship, and if it's really hydrogen fusion-powered it will take maybe hundreds of millions of pounds of deuterium to get it up to relativistic speeds — you know, fast enough to get somewhere in under a thousand years. That means — and remember, these are just educated guesses — they'd need to run that column of water through their ship for another three weeks. We don't have a hundredth of that amount in stock, and the aliens obviously aren't willing to wait."

"So we're going to attack them, and maybe get blasted off the face of the Earth," said Naomi, with a look of angry resignation that made her seem older than her years.

"We're still searching for a peaceful solution, honey. That's my job. But I can't do anything if they won't talk to me, and they haven't responded to any of our messages except with that single announcement."

"Well, if all they need is the deuterium, why can't they just dump the water back in the ocean instead of letting it loose up there where it spreads out and hangs in orbit?" asked Naomi.

Jones automatically started to point out the idea wouldn't work — and realized he had closed his mouth again without speaking. The best guess of the physicists was that the aliens had a technology capable of creating localized fields of nullified gravity, or actual anti-gravity. It seemed reasonable that if they could pull the water up, they could also send it down again — if they wanted to go to the trouble.

"That's an interesting idea, my darling. And if the aliens ever return my calls, I'll certainly ask them about it." Jones was trying as always not to treat Naomi like a child. She was a very bright young lady with an I.Q. just below the genius level.

Naomi gave her father a chilly look, suddenly realized he wasn't making fun of her, hastily kissed him on the cheek, and left.

Jones hurried through the rest of his breakfast and finished dressing. He had just enough time to reach Patrick before the meeting. He hated leaving without brushing his teeth, but he had wasted too much time. And he had to be there. The President was pressing for a decision. If the State Department position of waiting and continuing to try to contact the aliens did not prevail — Jones did not like to think of the probable consequences.

Commerce Jones always drove his own car to work in Washington, though he was entitled to limousine service. Driving was an automatic function for him, something requiring little conscious attention. He had solved many a tough problem while driving to or from work, his mind free in the isolation of his slowly moving car to worry and twist, reexamine and weigh, until his special gift for synthesizing divergent facts and opinions enabled him, often, to come up with an answer acceptable to all parties.

The memory of the raccoon he had inadvertently killed last night returned, and he again saw the masked face, the gleaming white teeth, the crouching figure ready to charge or retreat. It was not a total fake, a show — 'coons would certainly fight when cornered — but a good 'coon dog could almost always kill its prey. Raccoons took to the water when they could, or left a false trail and doubled back. As a last resort, when nothing else had worked, they climbed a tree, from which they snarled defiance at the hated animals baying at them from the ground below.

There was something marvelous, an atavistic thrill deep in the soul of the hunter, in hearing the yapping barks of a trailing dog change to the deep, mellow baying of a hound who has treed his quarry.

Jones tried to pull his mind back out of the memories of his boyhood on this island. All of humanity was up a slim tree at the moment, and the limb was bending dangerously.

The news media were having a holiday — perhaps the last one before the ice formed on their presses and antennas — covering the most newsworthy event of the 20th century. The entire world was watching this small group at Patrick. The Soviet Union had sent the most angry message in recent history, direct from the Party chairman to the President, informing her that being left out of these deliberations was an intolerable affront. Their allies in NATO were pushing hard for representation on the negotiation committee. (They thought actual negotiations were going on?) An accident of geography and preeminence in space had placed the United States at the forefront here, and the President had chosen not to encumber the task force with innumerable second-guessers.

But they were not doing all that well at saving the world.

The main gate at Patrick AFB was open, but Jones had to flash his State Department I.D. to get past the guard at the temporary command center. He was two minutes late reaching his seat at the long and crowded table, and the meeting was just getting started.

"If you'll come to order, gentlemen." The chairman was a surprisingly young three-star general named Iverson, the commander of the North American Air Defense forces. "We have updates for you from NOAA, NASA, Air Force, and CIA representatives. Please keep your reports brief, executive summaries only."

Jones knew that frantically busy background groups had been organized to support every activity reported here, that what reached this room was the distilled essence of needed data. At this level no one read through detailed reports.

A gray-haired, wizened little man with a wrinkled brown face leaned forward in his chair, cleared his wattled throat, and said, "Briefly, then. We have refined the set of figures given to this task force when it first met. They are quite close to my agency's original estimates. At the present rate at which the water molecules are spreading both north and south of the equator and along the geosynchronous orbit circumference, NOAA's figures show the band will have enough mass in orbit after four more days to create a thin 'cloud' over four thousand miles wide. It will take several months to encircle the entire globe, at 22,000 miles altitude, but molecular action in a high vacuum will ensure it doing so."

The old meteorologist picked up a new piece of paper. He looked around the table, and his voice became so low Jones had to strain to hear him. "We estimate the shading effect of this cloud as sufficient to drop average world temperatures along the equatorial regions by as much as one point two degrees Fahrenheit for perhaps the next four years. Each day increases the expected temperature drop by point four degrees, in rough figures. If they stop tomorrow they will leave us a legacy of extremely bitter winters for at least five years. I have breakdowns for specific regions, but all you probably want to know is how this affects the grain belts of Canada, the United States, and Russia. The answer is, up to fifty percent crop loss each year. Seven more days of this will start the ice-sheets marching south again. Ten more will throw the world into a deep freeze such as we haven't seen since the last great glacial stage, the Wisconsin. Fifteen more and we have nothing with which to compare. It becomes possible for the oceans to freeze over entirely except for a band of unknown extent centered on the equator."

The tired little meteorologist leaned back in his chair, shuffling his papers into some mysterious but precise order. There was a moment of silent before Iverson said, "CIA?"

The CIA representative was a large, soft-looking man with white hands and a pink-skinned face, dressed in an excellent mohair suit. He wore thick glasses, which he kept taking off and holding briefly before putting them on again. In the soft light of the overhead fluorescents his almost bald head gleamed with a sweaty luster. He had a slow, measured way of speaking that lent weight to his words. He was no more than thirty-five years old.

"We have completed our psychological analysis of the aliens, and made best-guess projections as to their probable future actions and reactions. Our data base is slim, and conclusions somewhat speculative; please bear that in mind.

"We have made certain *a priori* assumptions — such as that the aliens are not only far more advanced than ourselves scientifically, but considerably more intelligent — or at least much better educated. We think they neither fear nor hate us, but are in fact indifferent to our fate. Their failure to respond to requests to stop drawing up our water is possibly explained by some cultural quirk in their — to us, completely unknown — background. We think they could do us great harm if they chose to do so, and that we provoke them at our peril.

"We think they will continue to siphon and mine our ocean water some unknown number of days — hopefully, less than a week more — and then leave with no more notice than they gave when they arrived. They are unlikely to do us any harm if we leave them alone — and that is what my study group strongly recommends. Leave them alone. Let them go in peace. We'll try to ameliorate the climatic problems they leave us after they've gone."

There was a small stirring around the table. Jones knew, when he saw the set, cold look on Iverson's face, that the CIA's view was in the minority here.

As was his own.

"NASA?" said Iverson. "No more than four minutes, please. The President, cabinet members, and congressional leaders are gathering in the war room now. I'm supposed to call them before twelve. They want our recommendations to open the meeting."

The man from NASA reported on what had been decided at the meeting Jones had attended the night before: that it was physically impossible to use the space shuttle as a weapons carrier in time to be effective.

Looking at the big-bellied, ruddy-faced NASA executive, Jones remembered for the first time in years how much he disliked the space agency. His parents had been poor, black, orange grove workers on Merritt Island in 1951, when the U.S. Air Force had first established the Cape Canaveral missile firing station. He had attended segregated schools before the great Supreme Court decision declared them "separate and unequal" in 1952. Somehow his parents had scraped up the money to start him at Howard, and he had worked his way through three more years to a student instructor's stipend and a chance for a master's. Back home with his degrees, he had taught in the slowly integrating local school system at ridiculously low pay, while he watched the prosperous engineers and technicians drive their large cars to work at "the Cape." . . . In the late fifties a labor relations job for the school system threw him into local prominence, and a chance for a job in the State Department. There, his ability to synthesize vast amounts of barely related data, and reach surely for the compromise that all parties to a dispute could unwillingly accept, had kept him moving steadily up the ladder. And his personal rise had been paralleled by a tremendous growth of consciousness among black people during the tumultous decade of the 60s, when the United States did the incredible in reaching the moon; while their society went to the brink of anarchy, the flames of revolt caught in the ghettos, and the inner cities began to burn. . . .

But somehow the country had survived, the fires had simmered down to a sustained glow, and the space program had lost its former glory. Now it launched an occasional scientific planetary explorer and a vast number of commercial satellites whose owners paid the bills. But Jones's dislike for the overpaid space workers had never faded, though he only thought about it upon returning home.

The NASA representative finished, having added nothing to what Jones knew, and he tried to concentrate on the next speaker. This was the Air Force general representing the Strategic Air Command, a two-star who seemed to feel nervous at being here. He gave a brief recital of SAC weapons capable of reaching geosynchronous orbit. Jones learned to his surprise that the old Minuteman and new MX missiles could be used only for sub-orbital "lobs" across the oceans, and were virtually useless here. But in approximately eighty hours the Air Force could prepare two Titan IV's at the Cape and one at Vandenberg, for simultaneous launches. In anticipation that the President would give the go-ahead, all three hydrogen warheads had already been loaded aboard and countdown preparations were underway. The general carefully emphasized the point that the launches could be stopped on a minute's notice, but could only occur after extensive preparations.

So a variation of the three-warhead attack becomes possible after all! The thought sent a cold fear spreading out from the pit of Jones's stomach. *And that's what they're going to recommend, and the President will do it!*

Jones glanced along the table at the grim, intent faces of men charged with saving their snug little world, and couldn't blame them. Billions dead of cold or hunger, the ferocious battles for the warm belts in Africa and South America, the abrupt descent into savagery and total anarchy when civilization failed. . . . Besides, men had always been fighters, holders of territory who unquestioningly defended their boundaries.

But Jones still felt that attacking the aliens was a suicidal move.

There was only one more report and a little discussion before General Iverson held up a quieting hand, looking around the table. The Air Force had presented the only specific plan of action. Their choices seemed limited to leaving the aliens alone and hoping they would stop their activity before much longer — or to attack.

And the president, an ex-military woman and a born fighter, would almost certainly use this task force recommendation to back up her own inclination to launch the warheads.

The bright, eager face of Naomi appeared in Jones's mind, and he saw death and destruction flaming down out of the depths of space, to end her young life. . . . he saw a raccoon snarling defiance, and something clicked into place and he was on his feet, demanding the floor.

Jones saw an angry expression flit briefly across General Iverson's lean face, but he ignored it. They at least had to listen to him.

Jones stood silent a moment, the only member to have risen to speak, trying to marshall his arguments. In his mind he saw the raccoon whirling to confront the onrushing light and noise, hair raised, mouth open, ready to fight. . . .

"I killed a wild animal as I was driving out of KSC last night," he began slowly, and saw the somewhat amazed looks of interest at this unexpected opening. He went on to tell them of the raccoon's defiant stand, of his slowness in reaching for the brake, the fighting instinct that had carried the brave animal to its death. "I was raised on Merritt Island. I hunted 'coons there as a boy. My father kept four dogs around the house. There's nothing quite like the baying of a hound when he has an animal treed — a lovely sound."

Jones saw that he had started to lose his audience. But it was necessary that they understand the fundamental point he was making, that animals reacted as their instincts dictated — and mankind had to rise above that primitiveness here.

"My point is that I think we're starting to react to imagined attack just like that raccoon," he said earnestly, looking around the table. "We're showing our teeth, taking a stand and rearing back to fight. And the assessment of State agrees with that of the CIA: that we'll be overwhelmed by a force so superior we don't even know how it functions, so powerful it can hurl us aside, crushed and dying. I think an attack will be writing our own death warrant."

"What would you do, then?" demanded General Iverson, a controlled anger in his voice. "Will you wait and let them shade our world with a cloud we have no way of removing? That's a big ship!" His voice rose slightly. "The CIA estimates agree with our own in regard to quantities needed to push such a mass. If they were quite low, which seems only logical, we're talking here of a minimum of two more weeks of that vapor pouring into orbit. That means it isn't just our children's future at stake here. Most of us will live to see those glaciers sliding down from the northlands."

"Oh, I quite agree; we have to stop them. But your way won't do it. I have a better suggestion." Jones looked around the table once more to gather his thoughts, wondering what these men of decision would think if they knew his idea for saving the world had come from an imaginative thirteen-year-old black girl, of sheltered upbringing.

"I propose we inform the aliens we are going to attack them unless they accede to our demand," Jones went on, lifting his voice slightly. "And that one demand is that they start returning the water that's now emerging from their ship as vapor, in a second column descending into the ocean. If their anti-gravity device allows them to control and lift the water, surely they can return it the same way. This may create considerable havoc in the Atlantic coastal regions, but our world can survive that."

Jones saw at once that he had gotten their interest. As the silent men were thinking through the implications, the beefy young CIA man suddenly spoke, without waiting for recognition. "You know, we really think the aliens haven't answered us because they don't want to be bothered. Like ignoring the squirrels in the tree you're stripping of pecans. Do we respond to their jabbering and squeaking?"

"Because there's nothing those squirrels can do to hurt us?" asked the SAC general. There was a deep-seated anger and frustration in his voice. "But if the squirrels actually threaten to attack us . . ."

"I recommend we let the launch preparations continue at full speed," said Jones, "but tell the President we're going to make a final effort to contact the aliens and ask them to send the water back down. And let the message we send up inform the invaders we intend to attack unless they accede to our very reasonable request. Maybe we can at least get their attention."

Jones and the other task force members who were not totally exhausted were in the mission operations room at Patrick when the new message was transmitted. It replaced one that had been in effect for the past thirty-six hours, simply demanding the aliens stop the waterspout.

The verbal statement, on the same frequencies on which the

aliens had originally transmitted, was sent out at five-minute intervals, and would continue until launch time. Jones was convinced they would hear from the hovering interstellar ship fairly quickly, or not at all. The first hour spent waiting in the ops room was the longest of his life. The second was even longer. And he had just started to relax during the third, having difficulty staying awake by then, when the answer came.

"Any hostile action against us will result in retaliation of a type you are not prepared to endure." The remote but now almost human-sounding voice filled the room with jarring abruptness. "We strongly advise against sending any form of force to attack our ship."

Jones felt suddenly sick to the stomach, the walls wavering as dizziness hit him like a physical blow. Their last real hope was gone: the missiles would be launched regardless of the threat, and the aliens would respond in dreadful kind. He remembered one of the oldest axioms of his trade, the code by which diplomats lived: *War is the last resort of the incompetent negotiator.* It had come down to that, and his failure to reach an agreement here might be the last negotiation conducted by mankind for untold millennia. *Again he had a vision of fire raining out of the sky, and the sad face of Naomi lifted to receive it. Around her the world burned.*

"It has taken some time to evaluate your request," the distant voice resumed. "We will require another nine of your hours to prepare the equipment to return the water to the ocean in a second column. We regret any disruption this has caused to your world and people."

There was a collective sigh throughout the small and somewhat crowded room. Jones felt that he would have fallen if not for the support of his hard-backed chair.

General Iverson rose from his seat near the front and looked back at the senior diplomat. His taut face slowly crinkled into a boyish grin of respect and triumph. But all he said was, "I'll call the President."

• • •

"I understand that descending column of water is digging out a giant hole in the bottom of the Atlantic," Mildred said, gazing out the plane window. True to their estimate, the aliens had suddenly started the second column of water descending just before midnight the previous day, and it had hit the Atlantic about six in the morning. The Joneses were on a 4 P.M. flight back to Washington.

"Yes, and creating some flooding in the closest coastal areas of South America." Jones was waiting for the plane to stop climbing so that his stomach could settle down again. "But the damage is relatively minor. Now that they are talking with us, the aliens have admitted they intend to keep the columns flowing for another three weeks. We'd have had a snowball for a world in ten years, and the devastation caused by the extremes of weather would have ruined us even sooner."

Naomi was sitting quietly in the row of seats ahead, watching the ground fall away. She had said very little about supplying her father with the idea that had saved the world, accepting the fact it had worked almost as a matter of course, as something not of great importance.

"And some of us got more credit out of the experience than we deserve, and some less," Jones added, glancing ahead at his daughter. He had been assured by a presidential assistant that he stood an excellent chance of becoming the first black Secretary of State, if the incumbent retired after recovering from the serious heart attack he had suffered in the War Room yesterday.

Mildred gave him a troubled look. "You aren't getting one bit more credit than you deserve, my darling."

But Jones was thinking of 'coon hunting as a boy, of baying hounds, and of wisdom learned from listening to bright children. . . . The aliens, apparently quite friendly now that they had decided to speak with humanity, had offered to leave an interstellar beacon capable of being heard by any ship passing within about six lightyears of Earth. There would be more contacts in the future. And the beacon would be sent to Earth on an antigravity platform, which they could also keep. . . .

Jones heaved a long sigh that he kept internal, and tried to rise above the prejudices and experiences of his youth. He promised himself that tomorrow he would ask the President to appoint him to the National Space Future Objectives Advisory Council. It was again time that he learned to see matters from another point of view.

Tilden Counts

Tilden Counts is an associate professor in the Department of Mass Communications at the University of South Florida. He has had short stories published in *Alfred Hitchcock's Mystery Magazine* and *Fiction Quarterly.* A resident of Florida since moving to the state from the mountains of Virginia as a child, he is married, with two children.

A few years after my parents moved me, my brother, and my sister to Hardee County, Hurricane Donna introduced me to the realities of Florida. Donna was not a big storm, I'm told, but it was impressive nonetheless. Impressive also, and instructive, was the acceptance of the hurricane by the people who had lived with the land there all their lives. To them, the hurricane was simply a fact, natural and necessary.

There are some Florida old-timers around still, but most Floridians are now displaced newcomers who think of something else when thoughts turn to weather. Just follow the developers along the beaches to see how little consideration is given to the hurricane, and follow them into the estuaries and the wetlands to grasp how little is understood of the delicate relationship between that which is natural in Florida, and that which survives.

When the next hurricane crosses the peninsula, we may very well be grateful that our diminishing water supply has been replenished; at the same time, we may regret not planning for its arrival with a little more care.

THE WEATHER AFTER THIS

by Tilden Counts

The light of a full moon fell on the weather map Kevin Robbins unfolded onto the hood of his Honda Civic. My Chevy was nose-to-nose with the Honda on a narrow country road about 10 miles outside Fort English. Pasture land receded into the distance on both sides, and flat-crowned pine trees here and there bent under the moonlight like old men frightened by something nearby.

Robbins, a history teacher at the local high school, had insisted we meet here because he said someone wanted to kill him. It was a strange comment from such a boyish young man. I told him he should have called a cop, not a newspaper reporter. Robbins agreed with me and said he had spoken to Sheriff Tom Hardester about it, but the sheriff had told him nothing could be done until a crime was committed. Anyway, he said, a cop wouldn't believe the story he had to tell.

I asked him why he thought I would. He said his story involved Pester Maak, a wealthy and eccentric Bethany County landowner, and that alone ought to interest my newspaper. I agreed to meet him and hear him out.

According to Robbins, he was going to be killed for the weather maps he had in his possession which, he said, were tracking charts of hurricanes crossing central Florida since the fifteenth century. I wondered out loud why anybody would kill for that. Because, he said, the maps weren't modern; they were very old maps, that told of hurricanes that were to come. Robbins said he had gotten them from Pester Maak's grandson, Justin, who had taken the maps from an attic trunk without his grandfather's knowledge. Justin, a freshman at the high school, had taken them to school to show Robbins.

"You don't believe me, do you?" Kevin Robbins said, leaning closer to me. I looked into his face for the madness that must have given birth to the story he was telling me, shoulders arching, fingers pointing to the pages he unfolded. But there was only fear in the shadowed eyes.

"Don't patronize me, Mr. Collins. There isn't time."

"All right, Kevin," I said. "Let me go over the easy parts. I can believe these maps are from a trunk in an attic belonging to Pester Maak. That's easy. I can believe Maak's grandson gave them to you and that the grandson hasn't been seen in the three days you've had them. High school freshmen sometimes skip school. And these maps . . ."

Unfolded like road maps were what looked like satellite photographs of the Florida-Caribbean area, 100 photos to a folded volume. Each photo represented a year, Robbins said, and each volume a hundred years. There were six volumes. The photos themselves looked like the kind you see on television weather programs, with several curving white lines. The lines looked artificially superimposed on each picture. They could have represented tracks of hurricanes, as Robbins said they did.

" . . . I can believe they're charts that track the paths of central Florida hurricanes since Christopher Columbus, although I'm not real sure there was anybody around here that far back to notice any passing through and I know that no one had a camera before sometime in the last century. And these photographs — they look like they were taken from something above the Earth, probably an Earth satellite. That's the way weather bureaus get the pictures they show us. But here's where I'm having difficulty with the story you're telling . . . I don't believe the photos were taken from a, well . . ."

"An alien space ship," he said for me.

"That's right. Or, like you just said, before Columbus arrived in Hispaniola 500 years ago. I also don't believe visitors from space gave the maps to a tribe of Indians as a gift. If all that were true, Kevin, I could turn to the final charts on the sixth volume and know, right now, standing here on this lonely road somewhere in Bethany County, exactly where the hurricanes for the coming years are going to strike and if we need to worry about them."

"There's a problem with that, Mr. Collins."

"Yes, there is," I agreed. "Finally, Kevin, I don't really believe someone is trying to kill you for hurricane tracking information the U.S. weather service in Miami or Channel 13 in Tampa could send you."

"I'm telling you the truth, Mr. Collins."

"Anything scientific to back you up?"

Robbins' shoulders slumped a little. "No, that's why I asked you to meet me. I want you to have the maps tested and dated, and then you'll know the truth."

"Why don't you do that yourself?"

"I already told you. Someone's going to kill me. You've got to take them and find out for sure if they're real."

It was the first indication that Robbins wasn't all that sure about the maps' authenticity. His tiny doubt didn't help me believe his story, but it helped me think that maybe Kevin Robbins wasn't a flake.

Robbins suddenly glanced left into the pasture, and for a moment he stared toward the dark bulk of the distant bayhead where an animal had cried out. Then he turned toward me. "We have to hurry," he said.

"Why do *you* believe what you're telling me, Kevin?"

"Because of Justin Maak," he said, speaking slowly, concentrating. "I taught a unit on Florida history last week and after class Justin got to talking about the Indians living on his grandfather's land. Justin says the Indians are descended from a tribe of Ocale. That would make them Timucuans, which history books say were assimilated a long time ago by other tribes, or killed or carried off by the Spaniards as slaves. Anyway, he told me about the maps. How old they were, how long the Indians had them. When I asked him if he could bring them and show them to me, he said OK. I had no clue that his bringing them would cause so much trouble."

"What kind of trouble?"

"His father, Gundy Maak, called me, mad as hell. He told me I'd better get those maps back right away, and I said I would, but Justin didn't show up at school to take them and he couldn't come to the phone when the guidance counselor called to find out why he wasn't there. Gundy probably beat the kid.

"That kind of trouble. I didn't need it, didn't want it anyway, for Justin's sake or mine. Gundy's phone call told me that he thinks the maps are important. Even so, I still didn't believe Justin's story."

"What changed your mind?"

"Wachutl. He's the cacique of the village of Indians living on Maak's land. I caught him stalking me, and I think he's searched my apartment and my stuff at school. That makes two people besides myself who think the maps are important."

"You think he's the one who wants you dead?" I asked because murder, even conspiracy to murder, was something real my paper could be interested in.

"Maybe. Because I think I know their secret now."

Robbins could see he was losing me.

"Look," he said, and spread the sixth volume over the first we'd been looking at and pointed to a photograph. "That's 1985. There's no date on it in any language I know, so you have to count photos to find the year you want. See that hurricane?"

He pointed to a white line that bent northward at the Yucatan Peninsula into the Gulf of Mexico. The line turned sharply eastward into Fort Myers and continued across the state.

"Yes, but it's not accurate," I said. "No hurricane — "

"That's right," Robbins said. "That storm didn't happen. It should have, but it didn't. No hurricane hit Fort Myers or central Florida in 1985, or any other year since 1960."

"And where is Elena?" he continued. "It followed a northwest track up the Gulf before it turned due east toward the Big Bend. You remember, it sat for a day off Cedar Key stirring up the water and battering the west coast beaches. It's not even on the map.

"Look here." He pointed to the last map on the fifth row. "That's 1960. Where's the line between Cuba and Key West that should curve north into Port Charlotte and head up the Peace River? Donna, it was called — it's not there either," he said, as if perplexed.

I was puzzled and I said so. "I don't get it, Robbins. You want me to believe these maps were made a long time ago by aliens in a space ship, and you want me to believe they predict hurricanes. But you're telling me they predicted storms that didn't happen and failed to predict one that did?"

I stopped talking, seeing no point in continuing. He edged closer to me, his face drawn with intensity.

"Look, Mr. Collins. You see for yourself what I'm talking about. I think I've got it figured out, but I need another view, someone used to sorting out the facts. You take these maps" — he pushed them toward me — "and you compare them with other charts of the known hurricanes of the past and you'll see why these maps almost have to be as I've told you they are." His eyes seemed to burn through the darkness.

A sharp sound from the left broke through the silence, startling Robbins. He abruptly straightened and looked toward the sound.

"Take these," he said, pushing the volumes into my hands. "See Dan Porter. He's been teaching at the school a long time, and remembers Justin's father talking about those maps in the sixties. He can tell you some things. And one more thing. The Indian. If he finds out you have the maps, he'll probably kill you."

"How will I know this Wachutl if I want to find him?"

Robbins shook his head, as if he had become exasperated with me. "He's taller than most, extremely thin, large head, sharp features, clear eyes. Colorless eyes, I'd say. You look into his eyes and you think you're looking into his brain. But don't worry about finding him, Collins. He'll find you."

A crack like a limb splitting echoed from the pasture. Robbins turned sharply and quickly got into his Honda. He cranked up and pulled around my car, stopped and stared up at me. "Work fast, it'll be too late to talk about what I've told you at my funeral — or yours," he said, and sped away.

More than a minute passed before Robbins' tail lights disappeared, leaving me alone on a deserted road, wondering what I was going to do with six volumes of useless hurricane tracking charts.

It was a simple ceremony. A local minister conducted the service at graveside, and close friends gathered around the casket holding Kevin Robbins' body.

Robbins had been discovered about dawn just two days after I talked to him, floating in the swimming pool of the apartment building where he had lived. I remembered Robbins saying he had told Sheriff Hardester about his fear for his life, but Hardester didn't appear to be treating Robbins' death as murder. Apparently there were no marks indicating foul play.

From the shade of a live oak tree I listened to the mourners and watched them as they left the cemetery. An attractive young woman who had looked my way several times from the grave site lingered until the others had left, then she walked toward me. She was fair, moderately tall, about Robbins' age, with long, reddish blonde hair. "I'm Eve Dalton, Mr. Collins," she said. "I'm a teacher. I knew Kevin."

"How well did you know him?"

"We didn't exactly live together," she answered, "but I knew him well enough to know that he gave you his weather maps. Do you believe him, now, Mr. Collins?"

"Do you, Ms. Dalton?" Her blue eyes were rimmed in red.

"Kevin was like a little boy in a lot of ways," she answered. "The kind who can break your heart with their wonder about all the things in this world. Do you understand?"

"You're saying I should believe him?"

"Yes," she said, glancing over her shoulder, "if for no other reason than to save your own life, now that you have the maps."

"You think he was murdered? And it was because of the maps?"

She nodded. "When Justin Maak gave them to Kevin, we looked at them for hours, wondering if they were real. It was the last time I saw Kevin. The next day his things were searched and he realized he was being followed. He called me and told me he was afraid of what would happen to me since I knew about the maps, and said he was going to give them to you."

"Do you know anybody who wanted him dead?"

"He talked about an Indian, but I really don't know, Mr. Collins. I only know that Kevin said he was going to die for having the maps and now he's dead."

There was fear mixed with the sorrow in Eve Dalton's face and I wanted to comfort her, but I couldn't think how.

"Kevin gave his life for those maps without a shred of evidence Justin Maak's story was true. He could have left town, but he gave them to you in a way no one would know so the maps would be safe. And then he was killed. You can't just forget about them now, even if you don't believe him. He's owed something for that."

Dan Porter put me off at first, but he finally agreed to see me at the high school during his planning period. The social studies teacher, in his fifties, looked tense when he talked about Robbins. He said Robbins had taught at the high school for about six years and was well liked by the students and his faculty colleagues. Porter had no idea that Robbins might have been murdered. I tried a different approach.

"Did he say anything to you about weather maps Justin Maak gave him?"

Porter's face blanched. "I have nothing to say to you."

"I'll keep it confidential, Mr. Porter. No attributions. Your name's out of it."

He hesitated but he agreed.

Robbins had told Porter Justin Maak's story, but Porter had heard about the maps before, about twenty-five years before, when Gundy Maak, Justin's father, was in high school. Porter said the class had been studying the contributions of the Seminole Indians to Florida history, when Gundy mentioned in class that there were mounds on his father's property, put there by tribes living before the Seminoles. Gundy had said there were burial mounds on the property but that five of the mounds had not been for burial, they were there for another purpose. Gundy had not elaborated and wouldn't say anything else about them.

"I told Gundy I thought it was terrible that archaeologists hadn't looked at the mounds. But Gundy said that would never happen. He said his father, Pester, wouldn't allow it, wouldn't permit anybody onto the property to look at them. Such ignorance is appalling, Collins. All that history lost to mankind owing to the stupidity of a backward old man."

"Did you follow up what Gundy told you? Do anything about it?"

"No," Porter replied, uncomfortable with the question.

I prodded. "Somebody could have called the university in Gainesville," I said. "If the mounds were historically important somebody could have gotten a court order to enter the property."

"You would have had to live here then to understand why I didn't say anything about what Gundy said in front of the whole class."

"I'd like to hear about it." Porter was visibly unhappy with the discussion. "This is confidential," I reminded him.

"About this time," Porter continued, "a teacher, a friend of mine who'd had an argument in class with Gundy, awoke one morning to find his car door full of holes. He said he thought he'd heard a tire blow out during the night, but what happened, somebody had used a 12-gauge shotgun to fire a round of double-aught shot into his car on a drive-by. A few students seemed to know who did it. I stupidly allowed talk of the shooting to come up in class and one kid blurted out that everybody knew Gundy did it. The room suddenly got very quiet, Mr. Collins, and I heard somebody tell the kid to shut up. So I turned to the chalkboard, changed the subject, and never mentioned it until now."

There was nothing Porter could really tell me about the murder so I left, but his confirmation of part of Robbins' story kept the matter of the weather maps alive. That and Eve Dalton's plea.

Next morning early, I drove to a small college not far away and searched the library for what I could learn about hurricanes. I'd heard of cycles of hurricanes — ten-year, twenty-five-year, one-hundred-year cycles — but the texts and government documents deposited there indicated patterns of activity, rather than cycles. Most of the Atlantic storms that touched Florida seemed to pass over extreme South Florida or curve northward over the Panhandle, if they didn't turn up the Atlantic. Gulf-born storms mostly passed over the Panhandle or turned westward.

Curiously, only ten hurricanes had passed inland over central

Florida between Cedar Key and Fort Myers in the 105 years between 1885 and 1990. And another pattern seemed to leap off the pages: there were many more hurricanes in the previous century than in the present one and fewer still affecting the peninsula, particularly central Florida, in the latter half of this century.

As I suspected, not much was known about the storms before the early 1800s. It was apparent that modern meteorology couldn't claim very much knowledge of hurricanes that might have happened before 1870, but the tracks on Kevin Robbins' maps looked precise back to the 1400s. Oddly, Robbins' maps began to diverge from reality early in this century, showing more hurricanes than actually occurred — and not showing most that did happen. If Robbins' maps were hoaxes, whoever phonied them began making critical errors at a time when the counterfeiter could have been most certain of the occurrence and paths of the storms.

That seemed to be that. Robbins had said I would understand why the maps were important if I would only look. Well, I had looked and I didn't understand.

I was back in Fort English by lunch time and stopped at Thelma's Mid-Town Café before going to the office. It was a quiet day so Thelma sat down at my table near the back where ceiling fans moved the air. I liked talking with Thelma because she made you think that what you said was important. I also liked to think it was me that brought that out of her, but I knew she was that way with all her customers. I felt lucky she was free at the moment. I ordered a pie à la mode but settled for the pie when Thelma told me her freezer was on the blink. I wanted to talk about Kevin Robbins' story so I eased into it by bringing up Robbins and Eve Dalton.

"Kevin and Eve liked to come in for breakfast together, as if nobody knew about them," Thelma said, a wistful look on her face. "Jessie would have had a heart attack if he'd known," she said smiling, referring to the loud and political school superintendent. Secrets were safe with Thelma so I told her about the maps, and about my trip to the college.

"He said he'd thought I would understand the importance of

the maps and why he believed what he told me, but I don't. I don't understand at all."

Thelma was looking toward the door leading into the café's kitchen, ignoring me, I thought, making me, her only customer, rate less interesting than a kitchen door.

"I can see his point, Whit," she said, bringing her eyes back to mine.

I looked back wondering, but pleased.

"Before my thermostat went bad, I knew the temperature in my freezer. I could set it for any temperature I wanted. I guess you could say I could predict the temperature in my freezer. Now I can't."

I stared at Thelma and thought about what she had just said. Machinery goes wrong sometimes. Kevin Robbins must have realized that, too.

I left Thelma's and went to my office. I cleaned up a couple of things that had come across my desk and put in a call to Pester Maak. I wanted to hear his ideas about the murder since the Indian Wachutl lived on his property and I'd need Maak's permission to go into their village. Gundy Maak answered and said they'd both see me at five o'clock.

The Maak place was even larger than I'd expected, situated on several thousand acres of land used in various sections as cattle pastures, citrus groves and vegetable fields. There was probably room in there for a small tribe.

Gundy Maak, not looking at all happy behind the mustache styled by the sixties, answered the door and took me to his father waiting in a rocking chair by a fireplace in the living room. A slight, blond teenager, probably Justin Maak, was sitting in an overstuffed chair. The boy had one of those pleasant faces with a slight smile built onto it. And clear, almost colorless eyes. He also had a bruise beside one eye.

When I was seated, Pester Maak got right down to business. He didn't appear to be the bumpkin I was led to believe he was.

"How can I help you, Mr. Collins?"

"I'm here to talk about Kevin Robbins."

"I thought you might be. What would you like to talk about?"

"His murder."

Maak seemed surprised. "Murder? I didn't know anybody said he was murdered. In any event, how can I possibly help?"

"There's a man who's said to live on your property who might've killed him. His name is Wachutl. I'd like your permission to talk to him."

Bushy white brows arched above long, craggy features. "That's absurd. Those people have never harmed anyone. I thought you were here to talk about the maps."

"OK," I said, a little unsettled by his directness, "let's talk about the maps."

"There's nothing to talk about — " Gundy started, but a look from the old man silenced him.

"We know you have them," Pester Maak continued, "and we'd like to have them back. They belong to Wachutl and his people. Ivan Maak promised a long time ago we'd keep them safe and we'd like to keep our word."

"Returning the maps is no problem as long as they're not evidence in a murder."

Maak sighed and eased back into his rocker. "Mr. Collins, understand this. Wachutl's people have lived in peace since Ivan came to settle in 1837. They've been content here and they've gone out of their way to avoid contact with other human beings, especially the white man. They've fought no wars and they've made no enemies. To think that Wachutl entered Fort English and killed a man is to think the impossible."

"Robbins said he saw the man in town."

"Wachutl did not kill that fellow Robbins. He could kill, but not for the maps, important as they are."

"That's enough," Gundy shouted, and stood facing his father, his anger unconcealed. Pester returned his look. I saw sorrow in Pester Maak's eyes and thought of Eve Dalton. There are people in this world who can break your heart, she had said.

"The early tribes," I said to Pester quietly, "the Timucuans, for one, they disappeared with the Spanish, didn't they? Aren't they considered extinct?"

"These survived. They had a reason to, a legacy to keep alive: those maps and their blood line."

Gundy cursed and left the room, slamming the door as he stalked out.

"Never mind my son," the old man said. "Gundy has never been the man I would like for him to be. Nor does he seem to know the importance of his own legacy."

Pester Maak was staring at the boy Justin. There was pride in the look. But there was more in his eyes than pride. Pester Maak was looking at his grandson with awe. It was then that I saw Justin, really saw him — saw the clear, almost colorless eyes, the slightly enlarged head and the smile that seemed now more intelligent than pleasant, and I guessed Pester Maak's secret. The maps were important, but Justin was the secret.

"Gundy killed the boy's mother, Mr. Collins. Oh, I don't mean he took a weapon and killed her. But he killed her just the same. She was the daughter of Wachutl," Maak said. Then he paused and looked directly into my eyes. "And she was a descendant of the people who gave the maps."

I didn't permit myself to show a response. I just looked at him, and he continued. "Gundy took her, made her pregnant and brought her to this house to live, away from her people, and she died. Justin is my grandson and the grandson of Wachutl. He is my biological link — and yours — to an extinct people and to their visitors who gave them the gift of the maps."

In the presence of the old man I finally began to believe the story Kevin Robbins had told me. And I could see why Robbins might have thought the maps were so important. They seemed to lead to a lost people and back to a time when there might have been visitors from another world. And isn't it possible, I thought. But shouldn't there be more than that for a young man like Robbins to have given up his life? More than just the knowledge of the maps?

"The maps might once have been a valuable gift, Mr. Maak, but now they're useless, utterly inaccurate. They predict nothing and nobody will believe the story now."

And that's when Maak finally made things clear for me.

"The maps were never intended to predict, Collins. They're not the product of a system that predicted storms. The maps are the guide to the system's creation. It's the system that generates the hurricane and directs its path to cross or avoid the peninsula's center."

He said the maps were more like a blueprint for a planned outcome than a prediction in an almanac. The visitors seemed to know there would always be a need for water. And with the arrival of the Europeans, the need would ultimately be even greater. So hurricanes in central Florida from the fifteenth century had been made to happen at particular times and in specific paths by an alien technology that was meant to be friendly but that had just stopped working — like the thermostat in Thelma's freezer. I almost laughed. That was what Robbins had wanted me to see.

"Nothing lasts forever," I said.

Maak gave me a funny look. "Unfortunately, Collins, that is not quite accurate. As my father explained it to me, the weather sub-station here is still emitting signals, as always, creating weather patterns according to instructions it is probably still receiving. That, regrettably, could go on forever. The problem is that imprecision has found its way into the control device. There's error in the system."

Maak read my confusion.

"The visitors built several sub-stations around the world like the one they built here. And they built a master station somewhere out there" — he waved a hand upward — "that could read signals from the sub-stations down here and transmit back down coded signals to produce a hurricane or a snowstorm, or whatever. But now, something's wrong — the greenhouse effect, the floods, the droughts all over the world — the system must be sending random signals." Maak seemed to stare off, lost in the thought.

"Wouldn't it need a power supply?" I asked. "And that would eventually have to run down."

Maak shook his head. "The source of its power is the sun. The thing could run forever. It is most unfortunate for us that the controls in the sub-stations are like any other set of controls. They need maintenance, calibration, and the visitors haven't returned to see to it."

It wasn't just the trouble with the weather control system that worried Maak. He said there was something wrong in the village. The tribe was now only half the size it had been when he was a boy. The villagers were dying and not reproducing sufficiently. Maak saw the fate of the villagers to be like that of the Dusky Seaside Sparrow, made extinct by an artificially altered environment it could not adapt to.

Maak loaned me a truck to drive the dirt road into the tiny village. He said the sub-station was a series of mounds camouflaged to look like the burial mounds of the period. He said Wachutl's English was broken but that he would speak to me and probably answer any questions I might have about Kevin Robbins' murder.

It was a beautiful day, the kind of day you might expect in late January. The sun was low in a sky cleared by a cold front that had passed over the day before. It was difficult to think of all this somehow influenced by a technology gone awry.

The road entered a hammock and began weaving, following the drier ground and avoiding older, more impressive trees. I saw Gundy by the road ahead. He waved me down and told me it would be better to walk the rest of the way because the road got muddier and the village was just ahead. I got out of the truck.

Gundy led us into a pristine Florida jungle. My shoes sank into the moist, rich ground.

"Did you believe the old man?" Gundy asked.

I thought about it. The story was improbable, but the people telling it and the circumstances made it compelling. "I don't know. Do you?"

"Yes. But you should never have been told about it. If the story gets out, it'll ruin everything."

Gundy held aside a branch of a tree that had fallen across a creek of brackish swamp water. I climbed onto the water-slickened trunk. My leather-soled street shoes were already wet and muddy so when Gundy pushed me, I easily fell into the water.

The creek was shallow, about knee deep, but Gundy locked onto the back of my neck with a powerful grip and my arms sank elbow deep into the muck as I pushed against his fist holding me under. I couldn't raise my head out of the water. I was going to drown, much as Kevin Robbins had drowned, without a suspicious mark to suggest it wasn't an accident.

My lungs had emptied when I belly-flopped in, so there was nothing I could do to prevent an instinctive inhalation about to take place against all the will I had left in me.

But then Gundy released his grip on me. I tried to push myself above the water, but couldn't. My arms were mired deeply into the creek's bottom. Suddenly I was jerked free of the water and pulled to the bank next to the roots of the tree I had fallen from. I turned and looked up into an old face with clear, colorless eyes, and I lost consciousness.

When I awoke there was still light. I couldn't have been out for more than a few minutes. Neither Gundy nor the face I had seen was anywhere about. When I could walk steadily, I went to the truck and returned to Maak's house.

Pester Maak, standing with the help of a walker, met me on the front porch. He was visibly upset, the sorrow I had seen earlier now much deeper. "I know what happened, Collins. Wachutl told me, and my son has left, run away. Gundy tried to kill you, like he must have killed that school teacher."

"I'll have to tell the police."

Maak hesitated then indicated a telephone inside in the hallway. But when I raised the receiver, Maak spoke from the doorway, his voice whispering his grief.

"Gundy's dead, Mr. Collins. Wachutl's people are burying the body now. I can take you there if you want, but it will be better for Wachutl if the authorities believe that it is Gundy who is the fugitive from justice."

"Where is Wachutl?" I asked.

"I don't know. I told him it would be a mistake if he ran, but he's never killed before. I assured him I would protect him. His people need him. He is their strength."

I tried to think how a man who had lived his life in the natural habitat I had seen a few minutes earlier could survive in the urban sprawl just beyond Fort English.

"I hope you will not reveal the death of my son," Pester Maak said, "but the story of the maps and the weather station must now be told. The world has to know in order to begin some action to save these people, and perhaps even to save itself."

My involvement was now topsy-turvy. It all seemed reasonable to me that I should not write about the story that any newspaper would cover — the facts surrounding Kevin Robbins' murder and the suspicion that a member of a prominent local family was the killer — and yet write the story nobody would believe — a story about aliens controlling the weather, all of it based on Indian myth and the word of a dead school teacher and an old man. But the maps were tangible. They could yet be scientifically tested for their content and dated.

Standing before Maak, who seemed to be waiting for a response, I pondered an angle to the story of the maps and the visitors, searched for a lead sentence that could be convincing. I drew a blank. "How do you tell a story like this?" I asked.

"How, indeed, Collins. As truth, to be scorned? As myth merely to be enjoyed by your readers one Sunday morning? And just who would you tell? News reporters, who will pursue you and these people into the very eye of a hurricane for a publishable quote? The military, who will classify you, these people, and the maps for no reason a sane man can fathom? A politician, perhaps, who wants votes? A scientist? Yes. A scientist. But in which science? In which field of knowledge? That, Collins, has been my burden, why I have allowed myself to be considered an eccentric, uneducated, isolated old fool. Help me. Help me protect Wachutl and his people. And help these people survive."

I turned away from Pester Maak and went to my car, my clothes and shoes ruined, my nose and throat burning. I decided that I'd go to my apartment and clean up, maybe call in sick in case something had come up at the office. For the next couple of days, I thought, I'd do my job, ask, beg my editor for normal assignments, look for facts I could count on, and report them, and try not to think about Kevin Robbins or about Gundy Maak's murderer out there somewhere trying to stay alive. And then, maybe in a couple of days, I would take the maps to a scientist at the university, a chemist, maybe. I would ask that the maps be tested, without commenting about what might be expected. But if in testing the maps, the analyst happened to come across something unusual, not of this Earth, I would do as Pester Maak finally did. I would ask for help. And I would take it from there.

I switched on my Chevy's headlights. The sun had set.

Martin Caidin

Martin Caidin, whose books inspired the television creations of "The Six Million Dollar Man" and "The Bionic Woman," has ten motion picture and television movies released or under production, and is the author of more than one hundred books, including thirty novels. His first science fiction novel was *The Long Night* in 1956. A very successful 1964 novel, *Marooned,* became his first major film success, starring Gregory Peck. This selection is excerpted from a recent novel, *Prison Ship.* Caidin is an expert pilot, and the only civilian to fly as a member of the famed USAF Thunderbirds. His long association with NASA, beginning with his work with Dr. Wernher von Braun and a small research group at Cape Canaveral in the 1950s, continues.

This piece is one of my favorite episodes in Prison Ship. *The main alien character, Arbok, is a space-jockey of some note and has flown through many solar systems — but on none of those planets has he encountered the clear atmosphere of Earth. I've tried to convey the glory and the challenge, as well as the majesty of what it might be like for an interplanetary rocket pilot to encounter* our *atmospheric flight for the first time.*

And what better place to meet this experience than in the glorious Florida skies! Here I hope the readers will respond with my character to our Earth's atmosphere known fully for the first time as a fluid medium, with the resistance you would expect from a fluid medium — and the silky response.

NEW WINGS

by Martin Caidin

They sat within the cockpit of the slim jet fighter-bomber, still behind closed doors, the dual Plexiglass canopies raised above them to bring in the cold feel of the air-conditioned hangar. Jake sat in the forward seat of the tandem cockpit. Behind him, Arbok had "disappeared" as an alien with the brain bucket, the jet helmet, fitted securely to his head. His helmet visor was down, almost completely obscuring his face, and with the lip mike so close to his mouth he was no different from any other pilot in a Magister. She was low and sleek with a great Vee tail, an old but magnificent French jet with all the flight characteristics endearing to a pilot. Jake wanted more than simply flight. He wanted Arbok to gain, even if quickly and at times overwhelmingly, the elements of numbers and gauges and controls.

They went over and worked the dual controls. The sticks between their legs for pitch control that would let them ascend or dive or, when eased either left or right, would bank the machine with deceptive smoothness and speed. Arbok had flown atmospheric aircraft before and he understood the basic principles of ailerons, elevators, and rudder, the latter operated through foot pedals. Jake went over each control individually, from the spoiler boards to the throttle and the engine and flight gauges.

"I'll handle the power until you feel her out," he told Arbok. "You forget the engine instruments. I'll take care of those. See the airspeed indicator? I've got the critical speeds marked off in white, yellow, green, and red. Once we're airborne we'll keep her within the green, although being in the yellow band won't hurt."

Arbok took it in swiftly and with as much professionalism as Jake had ever experienced in another pilot just stepping into a new ship. "We'll be using the metric system for the numbers," Jake explained.

"That is curious," Arbok came back immediately. "In this country, from everything I've seen, you use miles per hour or knots for your speeds, right?"

"Yes."

"But here everything is, as you said, in kilometers. Why?"

"This ship was built in France. A European country. They use the metric system. It wasn't worth changing everything. Doesn't take much to shift from one to the other, and since it's all marked off in both the color bands and in kilometers, that's the way we fly her. Oh, one major change. To your left: the rate of climb gauge that tells us our vertical speed up or down. That's in feet. The French gauge crapped out and since it's a barometric instrument we just put in an American system."

"Barometric?"

"It operates off the pressure of the air at any altitude we may be flying."

Arbok sounded doubtful, but he acknowledged with a simple "Okay," a phrase he'd adopted quickly from Jake.

"If you want, Arbok, I'll call off the numbers and what we're doing as we go through the flight."

"Please. That is how we taught our new pilots. It provides for good anticipation."

Jake smiled to himself. "It doesn't much matter, I suppose, what country or planet you're from," he said. "Not when it comes to flying. Okay, bring in your arms and watch your head. I'm going to lower the canopies and then we'll have them tow us outside to start up. Your harness feel comfortable?"

"Yes. I'm ready."

Jack closed the canopies on the power from the battery cart. He signalled the line crew waiting at the work station across the hangar. The doors opened wide and a tow cart pulled the low-bellied fighter onto the ramp and turned the ship so the jet exhaust would blow away from the building. Within the closed canopies and wearing their helmets, Jake knew they remained almost totally obscured. He locked the brakes and ran the two Turbomeca engines to start, eased in the power and heard and felt the tremendous shrill scream of the jets running up to power. A hand signal and the battery cart cables were removed. They were free.

Jake ran the power up with the twin throttles. The temps went to five twenty Centigrade at twenty thousand RPM and everything checked out in the money. He thumbed the speed boards in the wings up and back down to check them visually, went through the full control check, ran the flaps up and down and went quickly through their checklist. *It's been a long time but you never forget the touch of a sweetheart . . .*

He thumbed the radio from intercom to outside transceive; he'd arranged Arbok's radio so he could hear both intercom and outside radio work, and his own voice would remain strictly on intercom between himself and Jake.

"Gainesville Tower, November Five Zero Four Delta Mike, Kenn Air, ready to taxi. Over."

Gainesville Tower came back with taxi instructions and they rolled steadily away from the ramp, stopped at the runup area short of Runway One Zero where Jake did another quick but thorough scan and check of the gauges. The tower cleared them to taxi into position and hold on the runway; moments later they had their "Cleared for takeoff and cleared for left turn . . ."

Jake stood on the brakes, rechecked the flaps, stick forward, eased the throttles to their stop. He had just under six forty Centigrade for his temps and the engines spooled up to twenty two thousand five hundred RPM; he released the brakes and they kicked free and accelerated swiftly down the runway. At a hundred and eighty kilometers per hour, he called out "Okay, we've got one eighty clicks," on the intercom, following immediately with a call of "Unstick," gentled back on the stick and lifted her free. For a few moments it was all slick business. He climbed at two twenty indicated, brought up the gear and then the flaps, let her speed up to four hundred clicks and they went upstairs like a magic carpet, Arbok's hands and feet caressing his own controls as he followed through on Jake's movements.

Jake had intended to run through the full drill with Arbok, calling out the numbers and the maneuvers. He glanced in his rear-view mirror. Arbok had pushed up his helmet visor; Jake could see his eyes and his facial expression and only that one glance changed his mind about rattling conversation with numbers.

Wherever he had come from in that vast black well of space and distances so great they were meaningless to Jake, the alien enjoined with him in the magic of flight was *home*. The numbers at this moment would largely go unheard. Arbok had no need for them to *fly*. The details of pressures and temperatures were all within the grasp of Jake. Arbok threw his full receptors into flight itself, a world of different sky and alien clouds and extraordinary landscape.

Jake needed only to feel the whisper touch of Arbok to recognize immediately that this man, this alien, *was a flier*. Jake kept turning until they headed just south of west, past the northern rim of Gainesville, climbing steadily. They whipped through some scattered clouds, the Magister trembling deliciously with the merest touches of turbulent air, a brush with gentle invisible forces, but that gave them a sense of great speed. And then they were above the scattered clouds stretching in all directions about them. The clouds rested along the plateau of a thin haze layer, but created their own visual impact of another world — men and prosaic everyday beneath, and the great castles and freedom of flight above. In the distance, far south, rose the battlements of isolated thunderstorm cells; from this distance they were rounded and splendid in the midday sun, glorious and pink-golden.

"Arbok, I'm going to go through some maneuvers. I'll call them out first, go through what control motions I'll use. Follow me through on each one until you've got the feel of this thing."

A mere touch on the stick: he knew Arbok's fingers had applied the barest additional authority to the stick to comply with Jake's directions. "Okay, level left turn, left rudder and left stick together and keep the nose level with the horizon. Got it? On my count of three."

"Got it. Okay."

"One, two, three," and Jake brought the stick over hard left and tramped down on the rudder pedal, brought in the barest back pressure on the stick to keep up the nose, and the Magister hauled around in a g-force-punishing tight left turn. Jake kept her in the turn for two complete swings and as they neared the end of the second turn he sang out, "All right, coming up on rollout, reverse the controls, *now*," and snapped the ship back into level flight.

"Take it," Jake said, and he was amazed with what happened next. Immediately after his words he felt the stick move barely left and right. The unspoken signal pilots used to denote they had the controls from another pilot, but Jake had never mentioned this to Arbok. Was it possible this same reflex motion was used by pilots *anywhere* in the whole damned universe?

"Try some turns left and right," Jake said. "Keep a westerly heading."

"Numbers?"

"You recognize the directional gyro? What we also call the DG?"

"Yes."

"Two seven zero is west. That's your general heading. I'll watch for other aircraft. Have fun."

Arbok had fun. He went through gentle turns, climbing and diving turns, hard-racking turns, feeling out the Magister, playing the old tune of "getting to know you" through his controls. In those few minutes they crossed the last of the land edging the Gulf of Mexico. Before them towered great cumulonimbus clouds, many of them pouring avalanches of water oceanward. But these storms were isolated and of no danger to a machine cavorting between the battlements at four hundred miles an hour. Arbok sped through ravines, lifted the nose and dashed within narrow cloud canyons, and they found themselves within a great bowl of sky, an arena perhaps ten miles on all sides within the circular walling of the clouds.

"I've got it," Jake said, and Arbok relinquished the controls. All this time he hadn't said a word. The man was lost in reverie, inebriated with the glory and wonder of flight through an air ocean and above a liquid ocean the likes of which he'd never before encountered. Jake had wondered long and deep what might be this alien man's reaction to such flight, if he would find it tame after handling metal monsters weighing tens of thousands of tons down through gravity wells to the surfaces of different worlds.

Then he realized it might not be so. He had his own nation's astronauts by which to judge the true nature of a pilot. Back in the old days of early manned space flight, when Mercury, Gemini, and Apollo were the latest marvels of engineering and science, the government decreed that flying airplanes was a waste of time and money by the astronauts and grounded all the pilots. The same day that decree came down, so did the mass resignations of the astronauts. *Every* astronaut.

The moon might beckon and starlight might shine, but *nothing* could replace the touch of the man against the elemental forces of *flying*.

And Jake Marden had been flying since he was a kid. He had grown up in the heady world of flight in every kind and type of aircraft on which he could place his hands. He'd flown single-engine and multi-engine, seaplanes and landplanes, piston jobs and turboprops and jets. He few sailplanes and ultralights and the great old warbirds of wars gone by, and then he'd climb into replicas of World War One fighters and go out to throw himself and his machine all over the sky. He flew hang-gliders and he threw himself from airplanes to skydive. He spent pensive and relaxed moments in hotter-than-air balloons. The sky was his element. He earned his commercial rating and got himself type-rated in a dozen different machines, and his greatest fun came in air racing and flying different warbirds and aerobatic ships at airshows before a hundred thousand people or more.

Jake, like the others of his breed, wasn't the kind of commercial pilot who earned his bread-and-butter from a flying *job*. He considered himself an amateur pilot, but the amateurs of his class handled heavy four-engined bombers with the easy aplomb of chunking about the sky in an old Piper cub or whirling madcap maneuvers in a Pitts or a Christian Eagle.

Now, he had shared with this man from across a galaxy, and the bond was as close as if they'd grown up next door to one another. Jake finally broke the silence that had wrapped about him.

"Arbok?"

"Go ahead."

"I'd like to cut this thing loose. But I don't want you hit with any sudden surprises, and if you don't feel like — "

"You mean maneuvering? Aerobatics?"

"Yeah. Sort of. Not the hard competition stuff. Nice and easy. *Feel.* Not work."

"Please. I had hoped you would. I am ready."

Jake smiled. The son of a bitch had wanted it all the time!

"You got it, friend," he told Arbok.

He cleared the sky about them and eased forward on the stick. The Magister trembled again, that delicious embrace of wind and sky as speed built swiftly and then ran the rapids of mild turbulence and chop in the air, and then Jake came back steadily on the stick, back, back and he held her back and the nose came up and the little jet soared skyward with astonishing ease and smoothness, the nose came up through the vertical and they were on their backs, an instant of level inverted flight, still soaring skyward, the sun reflecting dancing shards of light as Jake rolled her along the high arc of the loop. Sun and sky and ocean and horizon and clouds whirled marvelously about them, and then they were inverted again. He gave her a touch of forward stick while they were inverted to round out the comedown slide of the loop, and down they went, wind speed carrying into the cockpit, and he let her round out at the bottom. He came back a touch harder on the stick and the g-forces planted them solidly into their seats and now he went straight up, rolling swiftly through six full turns, and as the speed bled off and she began to shudder from spilled airflow, he tramped in the left rudder to bring the nose about in a perfect hammerhead and with their speed laughingly slow, hanging in the sky, the nose dropped and then they were going straight down and he was rolling again. Back on the stick and a soaring, turning ascent to come around in a swallow-graceful chandelle.

A single thunderhead loomed before them and Jake cut a tight turning corner around the sheer wall of the dark cloud, the Fouga punching and banging from sudden touches of vertical wind shear. Everything *flowed;* Jake's hands and feet moved almost of their own accord, and it was the kind of flight even the birds might dream of in whatever passed for bird dreams. He went down around the cloud and a great shaft of sunlight speckled the gulf waters and he saw a freighter on the water, moving laboriously through her course. Jake took the Fouga down to barely six feet high, full power, and they flashed alongside the ship, the crew waving from high above them, and then Jake hauled her high and let her speed play off in the climb and without effort they eased to level flight at six thousand feet.

Jake sighed. He'd brought heaven into the cockpit.

Regretfully, he turned back toward land, his fuel gauges reminding him with a glance that all such miracles of flight are limited by the go-juice in the tanks. They had been easing their way southward off the coastline. Jake pushed the nose forward and they arrowed toward the south of Ocala, descending steadily, feeling the ship rock and tremble in the heated disturbed air of lower altitude. Jake swung south of Ocala Airport and soon he sped just above the smooth grass strip of the Leeward Air Ranch, six thousand feet of billiard-table grass with a hundred private homes alongside the runway, each home with its own taxiway and hangar. His pass down the runway did more than signal other aircraft of his intent to land; it notified the men in the large private home at the south end of the Ranch of their arrival. Jake brought up the nose and kicked her hard over into a vertical left bank for his pitchout. He punched up to twelve hundred feet and reversed course to slip into his downwind leg.

He ran the numbers aloud, an old habit he followed whether or not anyone else was in an airplane with him. "Two hundred fifty clicks, eighteen thousand in the bucket, okay now for gear down, fifteen degrees of flaps, and a touch of the dive boards, and we're in the money." The Magister rumbled loudly now with the dive boards, gear and flaps whipping air into turbulence, but it was a welcome and familiar sensation. "Here we go, around into base, get the boards up slow to two twenty, confirm three in the green and flaps down to thirty, neat-o, and rollout onto final with one ninety and we're a quarter mile out, full flaps to forty five, play the boards, very good, we've got her made, flaps, one sixty clicks, keep the boards at half, whisper back on the stick and — "

She feathered in like a princess on the mains. Jake let her bleed off speed with full boards and a test of brakes, and he let her run to the south end where the huge hangar door of the grey-and-blue home yawned wide, and he rolled in smoothly, a touch of power to make sure the tail cleared the doors and he killed the engines. They wound down from their shrill scream and the moment power was off the hangar door came down, baffles open to slip free any unexpected jet thrust, and then the baffles closed and there was no sight of the Magister.

Exactly three minutes later a grey-and-burgundy GMC van with Jake at the wheel and Arbok by his side drove from the air ranch into Ocala and headed for the I-75 highway going north.

Eighteen minutes later the Magister emerged from the hangar. In the two seats were two pilots, the man up front sporting a thick salt-and-pepper beard, and the pilot in back a shaved skull. Both men wore the flight suits and helmets that not long before had been worn by Jake Marden and Arbok. The Magister took the runway, boomed into the air, and six minutes later was in the pattern for Gainesville Airport.

"They" were a hell of a lot closer than even Jake had ever expected. The Magister rolled from Runway One Zero to the taxiway and turned off at Kenn Air Aviation. Neither pilot missed the fire trucks that blocked the taxiway behind them or the other trucks that moved in to prevent the airplane from turning left or right. They shut down, opened the canopies, removed their helmets and climbed from the aircraft to face four FBI agents.

No problem. Their papers were in order, they flew as charter pilots for Magnum Aviation, and they'd gone off for a post-maintenance flight check of the Magister.

The FBI agents never did tell them *why* the extra precautions to block the Magister off from moving before the questioning began. They just looked puzzled and frustrated.

Dead-end.

The lead agent called in to his operations office in Atlanta to report on their investigation. Tom Wheeler sat with his feet on his desk in Atlanta, cursing an ulcer silently as he listened to Ben Jamieson in Gainesville.

"You didn't get even the first hint?" Wheeler pressed.

"Sir, *nothing*. Absolutely nothing."

"I thought that goddamn airplane landed in that ritzy field south of Ocala. Wasn't there anything *there?*"

"Sir, that house has been there three years. It belongs to Magnum Aviation. They often bring their pilots there for training and meetings. That jet landed, went into the hangar, apparently refueled — we're not sure about that — and then it went back to Gainesville. I guess the pilots had to take a leak or something. We can't find *anything* out of line."

Wheeler dropped his shoes heavily to the floor. "All right. How's the schedule for checking out the prisons?"

Ben Jamieson didn't respond immediately. Of all the dumb things he'd ever done in his life, going through every prison in Florida and Georgia looking for aliens from outer space was about the dumbest. "Uh, that's next on our schedule, sir. Raiford and then Old Millford."

"Okay, go to it. And when you get to Old Millford and meet the warden, count your fingers if you shake hands with him. That'll be Herbert Spunt. Crookedest son of a bitch in the whole state system. He'll steal the rings from your fingers."

"That's terrific, sir," Jamieson said, not concealing the sarcasm in his voice.

Wheeler hung up.

Joe Taylor

Joe Taylor has lived in Florida for ten years. He is a married college teacher with a Ph.D. in creative writing from Florida State University. His stories have appeared in a variety of literary magazines, including *Triquarterly,* the *Virginia Quarterly Review* and the *South Carolina Review.* His novel-in-progress, *Persephone's Escalator,* is a horror genre work set in Florida.

Florida has a history filled with colorful characters, yet most people seem content with the glitter of beachfronts, shopping malls, and amusement attractions — all of which have a place, certainly. After all, Walt Disney himself was a colorful enough character. But a barefoot postman, a celestial railway, a defiant Indian tribe refusing to sign a treaty with the government, a town full of retired carnival people, another full of psychics — all these should certainly pique curiosity, too. But just the word 'history' seems equivalent to 'irrelevant' these days. Hence the projections of this story and a 'land without history.' Enjoy your pizza.

WELCOME TO THE PLEISTOCENE AND LAND

by Joe Taylor

"Protein!"

Someone yelled this as a beer can bounced off the poster of Picasso's *Don Quixote*. Truth be known, Peter felt more like the windmill than any sentient thing on the poster — except maybe a yeast now threading the foam oozing down.

"Protein!"

How many times can someone yell this in — he saw that the face of his watch was cracked from the party's roughhousing — in not long. Two beautiful L'Egg legs — long, tan, reptilian — were weaving up the stairs. A figure hunched behind, either nipping or licking at them. Peter turned from that to a young woman with butterscotch eyes you could stir forever. She managed the mall's chain bookstore and was one of 312 mall workers his brother had invited to the Diehl Brother Importorium's "Try Something New Party."

She bit her catfish pizza. Fish flakes drizzled, but Peter focused on those butterscotch eyes, envisioning progeny romping on a warm marital bed. Her eyes were so satiny, so . . . new. He grimaced at the word, at himself for using it. His brother had mesmerized him as surely as Tituba had the poor Salem girls, as surely as the tragic emperors did Rome. A history teacher's privilege, mixing similes. Rather, an ex-history teacher's.

"Have you ever tried a history section? Besides war, I mean."

"Mystery? Right between our romance and fantasy. War's in the corner — this is a kinky idea." She indicated the pizza.

The party was loud, so he nodded agreeably at her eyes. "There's been fifty already — all different, all new. Like my brother Tom's business philosophy. He's got these phrases: 'Bought in the New S.A.' That's one of a million." He cleared his throat, bared his teeth in Tom's salesman smile. " 'Inalienable credit is the pursuit of happiness.' " As an ex-history teacher, Peter regarded the last with bemusement and nausea, but the woman just sniffled. He tried again.

"Yeah, if my brother'd been alive in Florida during the Pleistocene Epoch he would've planted a glittery fish scale sign on Treasure Island as its beach formed, to await the first legged animal crawling ashore and beat Disney to the punch: 'Welcome to the Pleistocene and land. Herd drivers eat free.'"

She sniffled again and pinched his cheek. "Epic — is that the new mall?"

Someone stopped the 4,398-dollar (and 27 cents!) sound system mid-stream to put on a newer, faster song. Her hips quivered, then changed beat. He bobbed once in sympathy, then returned to those eyes. "No, epoch, a geologic time period. The Pleistocene Epoch was twenty thousand years ago, when Florida first became land. There were mammoths, saber-tooth tigers, and giant sloths. Malls are the Holocene Epoch, now. Who knows what Floridians were like in the Pleistocene?"

His throat was sore from talking so loudly, and he rubbed it. She shook her honey hair and blinked her butterscotch eyes like she'd encountered a moldy copy of Machiavelli in the romance section. A young man passed and she jammed the last bite of catfish pizza into his mouth. He licked her fingers with an amazingly long, pink tongue. Four, five inches, Peter could swear. Was that possible? "I need to get to know you," she said, grabbing the boy and bouncing away.

"Squid!"

Peter's shoulders fell as he looked from her designer jeans to his brother yelling into a phone. Tom's bulk wedged between two partyers like a quarter-pounder between sesame seed buns. So much for butterscotch eyes. The burger, barely interrupting its yells over the phone, motioned Peter over by slinging some grease or sweat.

"You said anything we wanted, Tina. We want squid pizza. Squid. That's new. We haven't tried that yet. That's the whole point: a new deal at Diehl. Can't you keep up with modern merchandising? . . . No, I don't care how long it takes. Squid." As the burger sweated and dripped, the buns rubbed. Peter watched them, but Tom grabbed his shoulders and spun him around, nodding toward the kitchen, toward smoke slipping out the door to wisp around the genuine Moroccan drums (imported by Diehl Importorium) hung over the door.

Peter dutifully worked through the crowded dining room, enduring spilt beer and poked ribs as if he were being marinated. He tripped over beer cans, hearing them pop. Was he imagining it, or were the cans taking on life of their own like a stereo's luminous sound level indicators? Or like swamp gas bubbling life. The archway to the kitchen was clear of people for a circle five feet in diameter; it was, however, littered like some prehistoric cave dig, which made it a cave entrance. A potbellied, bearded man grunted, stepped from the crowd in the kitchen, and swayed under the genuine drums. Peter didn't recognize him, but the party had been on since noon, and new faces appeared as quickly as old ones disappeared — like dinosaurs, in then out.

"You should run for president; you look like Ulysses S. Grant." In fact the man did, and Peter thought he might as well get a laugh.

"Who-p?" The man crushed his half-full beer, sloshing foam onto the dirt-brown carpet. Behind him, Peter could see the kitchen table piled with pizza boxes: a drunk was trying to burn them with a lighter. He squeezed by Grant's tomb with an apology and slapped out the fire that had caught — harder to do than he figured, because of the grease soaking the boxes. Then he grabbed the drunk, the manager of Fame Video.

"New," the man said for no discernible reason, pointing to his face with the lighter. Flame shot up a nostril, sending him to the floor in a spasm of shouting and sneezing.

"New!" the onlookers hurrahed, one stumbling to knock an empty box onto Fame Video's pyro-hero. Peter kicked the lighter through a chance clearing of feet to under the refrigerator and left, glad the potbellied man was gone.

"We need more garlic pizza," he whispered on reaching his brother, who was still quibbling with Tina on the phone. As Peter then bent to pick off a beer can that had stuck on his shoe, Tom whirled and smacked a fat palm on his back, hippo crushing a troublesome native. Hacking, Peter realized he'd forgotten the party's whole point: try something new. He again fought the can, but someone else jabbed him exactly where Tom had; he looked to see only a shirt with a large alligator on it slink through the crowd toward the kitchen, where for a brief instant he saw people gathered near the piled pizza boxes, sniffing the char and smoke, giving an occasional tenuous touch. One jumped, perhaps brushing an ember. Then the clearing closed with large rear ends; at the same time, the beer can came off his shoe and popped from his hand onto his brother's foot.

"Hey Tina, what about a pepper pizza to tide us over? Yeah, black pepper. No one thought of that. Sometimes you got to look in front of your own peeper-doos." Tom gave Peter a scowl and unbuttoned his shirt. Breasts rolled out so heavily they defied the word *vestigial*. "One pepper and one salt pizza, hey? Check your list just in case though, Tina. My brother's taking care of ours, so who knows."

"Ours" was the master list kept by the front door; Tina kept a duplicate. Elected "court jester" by his brother, Peter had the job of looking after the master list. For entertainment he'd scribbled the new pizza ingredients like a student trying to hide bad spelling or ignorance. Or did he scribble for job security? If no one could read the court notes but himself. . . . Court jester at twenty-five grand per annum was nothing to scoff.

When he first started teaching, he thought his enthusiasm would infect the students. He told them of Juan Ponce de León and his Fountain of Youth, of Flagler's two wives and his Celestial Railroad, of the barefoot mailman walking (yes, walking!) from West Palm to Miami, of Teddy Roosevelt and the Rough Riders leaving Port Tampa, of Walt Disney and twenty thousand acres of swamp. History's the best soap opera going, he argued. All those examples from just one state, your own Florida.

Instead of seeing surprised looks, he heard a fingernail file scrape, car keys flip. Years passed; and as more drugs came to school, files screaked; keys dug into desks; knives and guns surfaced like reptilian sharks. A teacher — a friend of his — was killed: shot down in the cafeteria. Two others were hurt — one hospitalized — by an irate student with a brown belt in something or other. Enough was enough. "New," his brother told him. "America doesn't need history; that's what those kids are telling you. America needs new." So he began work for his brother as court jester. Better than court historian, he was often reminded. Probably so, even tonight: as each new type of pizza arrived, he marked it so there'd be no duplication. He was a scribe of sorts, in a monkish cell of sorts. He'd bury the list in the back yard in the full of the moon and imagine some future historian's master's thesis over the find: *Deviant Behavior in Fin de Siècle Twentieth Century.* But who'd read it? Space invaders? America was The Land Without History, like his brother said.

He heard retching on the front lawn. "New!" a voice outside shouted amid laughter. More retching. He worried that he'd not marked down catfish pizza. And now a black pepper pizza, too. Suddenly his brother belly-bumped him, sending him into the bookstore girl he'd previously talked to.

"Have we met?" she asked, wobbling on a high heel. He looked from her plastic heels with embedded goldfish and her tight jeans to see her rub her nose and titter. The boy with the pink lizard tongue walked up with two drinks. "What's that?" she snapped, taking off her heels. "Here-o-she-ma," the boy answered. "It means 'let's get doped.' The bartender's mixing new drinks to keep up with the new pizzas."

"Here *O*-shima," the girl called, giving her own emphasis to the syllables. "It sounds like some prissy poodle's name." She gave a whistle at the lizard-tongued boy, whose tongue darted obediently.

Tom gave his brother another punch. When Peter turned, Tom pointed to the head of a woman sitting on the couch before him and sporting a plastic bird from India in her hair, another trinket from Diehl's Importorium. Then he rubbed his belly against the bird. The woman chirped and reached back to clasp folds of sweaty fat underneath those vestigial breasts. She suddenly twisted about to nibble a fold. Peter had never seen her before, though she had on a Sporting Universe golf shirt from the mall.

"I love eating new men," she said. "MEETING!" she corrected with a shout.

"New! New!" The room began to lurch in ritual refrain that had begun at the party's start; each time the delivery boy came, the chant was taken up again. Peter left the woman sticking her nose against his brother's belly and snorting, and made his way to the list near the door, still fearful he hadn't marked down *catfish*.

"New! New!" People from the kitchen and upstairs and all the bedrooms were pounding walls and stamping their feet until Peter could feel hot breath steam. On the living room table he saw the cattails someone had brought sway in their vase. There was a sharp noise — the delivery boy, unnerved, had lurched to crack his head against the door's frame. Much laughter.

Peter was close to the list now and saw the boy trying not to drop the boxes while he attempted to rub his head with his arm. He'd just taken over deliveries, and Peter assumed he was related to Tina or he'd never have landed a job dealing with the public — not with that zit-face: he looked like a leprous two-toed sloth, whatever that looked like. The din subsided but only temporarily as the book-store girl with butterscotch eyes began banging wildly on the stairway bannister with both high heels. Peter felt a jab: his brother.

"Write, Your Gobbledygook Highness! Write, don't gawk. It's his-tory."

Peter wrote *catfish*, then looked to the delivery boy, who told him to put down red snapper, chicken livers, and flounder. The black pepper pizza was coming next. Peter wrote. When he looked from the list, the stairway was empty except for a high heel on the bottom step. The goldfish inside seemed to frown. How had the SPCA ever let that pass? Peter wondered. A drunk passed gas. The Picasso poster was spattered with pizza sauce. Peter felt ridiculously sad, as if watching a fallen civilization crumble in air.

He and the boy fought their way through a gauntlet of spilling beers and mauling hands, the kid stupidly trying to protect the three pizzas and the box they were in. From somewhere, Peter heard someone shout, "New pizza! New! New!"

New. New. Florida, in the guise of Modernity Mall, supplying eternal youth. Drink the waters. What would Juan Ponce de León think? He wouldn't care. For him, the Fountain of Youth had been a public relations ploy to finance his exploration — and, alas, his slave trade: history would out the truth, however painful. What would history out about malls? *New. New.* The dialect of evil and good gobbled by the snort of consumption.

They were nearly at the dining room table when a saleswoman from the Femme Fatale lingerie boutique dove to snap at the delivery boy's ankle. He fell forward, but two muscle boys from the mall's spa caught him and the pizza box.

"New! New!" was cawed again.

The spa boys twisted their arms so their biceps showed, then took the box to the kitchen table, knocking its charred litter to the floor. The boy reached for the box's cover when a man Peter recognized as the maitre d'hotel of Six Seas Restaurant intervened.

"Why don't you just leave it with us so we can keep the pizzas warm?"

"We gotta use the box at work to keep the pizzas warm."

"That's what I just told you, son. You've got more boxes, don't you?"

The boy didn't respond.

"Don't you?" The man's voice had taken on a nasty edge.

The boy looked around. The spa boys laughed; others in the kitchen fretted, animals confused by a sudden temperature shift. Peter saw, peripherally, a thin man with an amazing long snout — what else could it be called? — watching the pizzas from the side of the refrigerator that was close to the kitchen wall. The man was framed by the cattails (here too? almost as if they'd grown — no, this is another vase). That snout — if you saw it in the Everglades you'd shiver *genetic throwback,* rev your airboat, and glide.

"My mom would kill me if I left it here."

So he really is Tina's son.

The maitre d' rapped his knuckles against the obviously home-made construction. "Your dad built this, right? What'd it cost?

Twenty bucks? Here, I can manage that just to rent it till you get back." As the man stuck a bill in the boy's pocket, someone sent Peter sprawling into the boy. There was a hiss, and the thin, snoutish man tumbled the pizza box onto the floor. The kitchen filled with shouts. Peter rubbed his kidney and asked the boy if he was okay.

"He's fine," a voice said. It was his brother, no shirt at all now, patting his belly as the woman with the plastic bird lifted a beer over their heads. She turned it upside down; they lapped loudly.

"Damn! Hot!" someone yelled. A man jumped up from the floor, shaking his head and blowing in short gasps. Mozzarella whipped in strings on both his cheeks, but he persistently bit again. "Hot!"

"There, you see?" The maitre d' grabbed the delivery boy by the shoulders. "You keep that twenty. Here. You ever see a fifty?" He pulled out another bill. "Bring back more pizzas — as long as they got something new on them — and you might get a closer look. Something new, that's the rules. *Nouveau bien!*" he shouted to Peter's brother. But Tom and the bird woman were kneeling, lapping beer from one another's faces. Peter saw the owner of the sporting goods shop stand over them, huge and red-faced, cracking his knuckles.

Screams of "New! New!" came like grunts over rutting ground, and the delivery boy broke away from the maitre d'. Peter led him to the front door.

"I'll call your mom about the box."

The outside air was fresh and tempting, but Peter thought he heard his brother shout. He went back, bending to look for him under a table or chair. Where could he have gone already? Disappeared like the woolly mammoth. He heard a thump on the ceiling from his brother's upstairs bedroom and smiled. Like a mammoth, all right, and tusked, too — or horned: he was in the middle of his fourth divorce. *New.* Peter noticed the maitre d' chewing a slice of flounder pizza. "Good party," the man said mid-bite. Peter nodded. The bird woman who'd nibbled his brother's belly and licked his face offered Peter a slice.

"Chicken liver. New."

He looked to the ceiling with surprise. "Have you seen my brother?"

She ran her lips along the pizza's crust. He repeated the question, getting no answer.

"I thought you were with him. I have to see him — about the delivery boy."

"A woman can't wait like she used to. A woman needs food and love. Shelter, protein." She grabbed Peter's belt and held the pizza near his cheek until he could smell her scent and the food.

The maitre d' walked over. "Your brother's in the kitchen."

Peter felt his belt being unbuckled.

"Protein," the woman repeated.

The maitre d' smiled and pulled her hands away. Freed, Peter worked his way toward the doorway. The potbellied man was slumped in it, his face gashed, blood dried on his Ulysses S. Grant beard and neck. Peter was so surprised that he actually hopped over him, accidentally kicking an unnaturally stiff arm.

He looked back in shock, but the snoutish man was on the floor with a can of beer, nudging Grant's tomb drunkenly, so Peter convinced himself it was okay. Meanwhile, the muscle boys whimpered in unison at the kitchen sink as they looked out the window. It was evening. Where had time gone? The watch again, its crystal blurred. "Have you seen my brother?" The muscle boys whimpered: he watched the sunset, heavy and ochre.

There was a stirring, a steady beat filling the house like lapping, cooling swamp water creating fog. New. New." The refrain came from upstairs where the street could be seen, so the delivery boy was back already. Peter suddenly remembered the Grant look-alike and pushed to the archway to find it empty. The man must have gotten up, he told himself. Flakes fell from his watch crystal to tickle the back of his palm. He turned on a lamp and people scampered. This was life without history, life for the Neanderthal: always hoarding gnawed bones and wood artifacts, always shivering from a peripheral glance — of incisor or claw? Someone dove, a woman, to scrap with two others over what appeared to be the Grant's shredded trousers. Their motions were blurred in a henna haze. The doorbell rang. They skittered to some darker corner and the crowd jumped, then milled as if no one remembered how door-knobs worked. Life: in and out, back and forth, he used to tell students. Love the past, you'll love the future; love the future, you'll love life. He felt his homily thin as he edged through the room to open the door. Tina was there with her son.

"I got your squid pizza. But I got to have my box back. And tell the man who pushed my son and gave him the twenty if he wants to hit on my boy again, it'll cost more than that."

She shoved past Peter, who turned on another light. She stopped short as she looked at the circle of people. Her boy tugged her like a kitten on a nipple.

"Don't be afraid. That's just good honest hunger you see," she told him.

"Protein!"

This came from the top of the stairs. Peter turned, but there was nothing other than a thumping.

"You're running out of ideas, aren't you?" Tina snorted. "You'll barely make it past sunset. Where's that brother of yours?"

"I don't know."

"Who's going to pay me — you?"

Peter reached for his billfold, but the maitre d' who'd poked at the delivery boy stopped him. "My treat," he said, handing Tina a fifty. "Keep the change and bring us an armadillo pizza."

"That's not enough for that," she said.

The man smiled and took out three more fifties. Tina reached, but he held them back. "For this much, we keep the boy."

"No one'll be able to deliver the pizzas then," Peter pleaded.

"I'll take care of it," Tina said. She took the bills and directed her son to remove the pizzas from the box. When he did, she left, slamming the door.

Peter thought he saw a tiger's tail hanging below the banisters.

"What's the matter?" the maitre d' asked.

Peter watched a woman creep down the steps in a tiger-striped bikini and claw at the door, yowling sadly. She'd tied a tail on. Something jabbed him and he turned, hoping it was his brother, but it was Jean, their store manager, a set of keys dangling from her waist. She pressed with her hips until the keys dug like awls.

"Have you seen Tom?" he asked.

She moved closer. Peter hit against something and turned to see the delivery boy. They both were being herded into a corner of the dining room. Hot sauce spurted onto his neck; it was Jean, close enough for a kiss, biting into squid pizza she'd nabbed from the air like a saber-tooth might catch a bird. Behind her were faces, huge with night eyes. "New," one started, his voice warbling deeply. The rest were too busy eating pizza to take up the chant. Their eyes were unblinking and watchful.

"Has anyone seen my brother?" Peter asked, leaning back.

Jean smiled. The pizza box was being passed overhead, and it knocked hollowly against the dining room's chandelier to land with a bounce on Peter and the boy, further wedging them into the corner.

"Isn't this party awesome?" someone asked.

No one answered.

"We need to try something new."

"New, new" was taken up timidly.

The doorbell rang. Peter could hear Tina's voice over the chant. Had that much time passed? He didn't even bother with his watch. The delivery boy began to cry.

"New, new," voices said as hands pushed his face.

Peter heard the maitre d' bargain with Tina and tried to move, but the box pushed against him. "Tom?" he called. Ridiculous. It was the age of communication, documentation, not the Pleistocene. How could a man disappear without trace or question? Even in The Land Without History there was too much history for that. Even in The Land Without History people formed too many bonds, remembered too many good and bad times for that. Even in The Land Without History there remained fads of morality: the healing power of crystals, the channeling of Cro-Magnons.

"New!"

Something bumped his head. He looked up and was bashed in the nose. As he coughed from pain, he heard Tina shout out to be careful with the box.

"So whadya want next?" she then asked.

"Tom!" He called, feeling the urge to sneeze as blood bubbled in his nose. He squeezed his stinging eyes shut.

"New! New!"

"Protein!" a voice yelled.

There was an odd quiet. Something wet began suctioning his upper lip where blood oozed: he opened his eyes but saw only a peripheral flash — then the room staring hungrily at him and the boy.

Jack C. Haldeman

Jack Haldeman has worked as a research scientist in parasitology and veterinary medicine, conducted field studies of whales in the Canadian Arctic, and spent three years as part of a research team investigating the greenhouse effect for the United States Department of Agriculture. He is the author of ten novels, and has published over one hundred short stories and novellas in major science fiction magazines including *Omni, Analog, Amazing, Galaxy, Twilight Zone* and *Fantasy and Science Fiction.* Two of his stories have been finalists on the Nebula Award ballot. In addition to science fiction and fantasy, he is an accomplished mainstream poet and has also published articles in scientific journals. He lives and works on a farm in rural Florida with his wife, Vol, and daughter Lori.

Most writers, whether they will admit it or not, have a favorite story. "Quartet" is mine. Born of a day when life took a sudden shift, it is a retelling of that day in an attempt to make it turn out differently. It is retold four times, maybe five, but there is no escape from the patterns and details that lead to the preordained end. There are no rocket ships in this narrative, but it could be interpreted as an alternate universe story, and therefore science fiction of sorts. It's a Florida story to its heart, echoing what my friend Rotten Robert told me years ago: Everything falls apart down here.

"Quartet" was born in a cypress cabin on a salt marsh outside of Bayport, Florida. The events that the story mirrors played themselves out on Redington Beach and passed through Dade City and Largo a few times before finding a relatively safe haven in Key West. The story has sand between its toes, and even after fifteen years I can close my eyes and still hear the pool balls clicking against each other in the dark bar where we sat trying to make sense out of a senseless world. It seems like yesterday.

QUARTET FOR STRINGS AND AN OCCASIONAL CLARINET

by Jack C. Haldeman

STRING ONE

Waves frame the scene: an open door, a movie screen where the setting sun and orange sand play their roles to an audience of one.

It's time to go, I know, I don't have to be reminded. The stage is set and as the moon chases the sun down into the water I really should leave. It's all there in the scenario, carefully plotted out by a pipe-smoking, cardigan-sweatered screenwriter in an overstuffed chair in Burbank. But it's all too pat, don't you see? The total structuredness of the situation patterns it for all time. Forever I'll sit here in *this* bar reaching for *this* warm beer, watching *that* sun, feeling *these* same emotions with *that* bartender always bringing me *that* greasy hamburger that I'll always take that one bite out of and pull out *those* onions and lay them on the side of *that* paper plate along with *those* forgotten pickles and then I'll get up and walk through *that* door and into the next scene, *that* scene. The next few minutes of my life run past my eyes at 24 frames per second.

My own indecision holds things up. It is necessary that there be no pauses or blank spots, so the time sequence slows down, the sun takes a little longer to set. A cast of extras come on the stage from somewhere in the wings, their whole lives a river of branches that take them to *this* spot at *this* time to intersect with the patterns of my life that brought me *here* to see them playing in the Florida sand, framed by the door, drinking beer, laughing, loving-living and dying in order that they may pass by *that* door at *this* instant.

This is why I nurse my beer.

I am anxious to see how they will handle this. A temperamental actor. Perhaps the director will come out in Bermuda shorts, flower print shirt, cigarette in an ivory holder, megaphone and sunglasses. Perhaps he will yell at me to get my ass in gear. "Get your ass in gear," he would shout. "We haven't got all day you know." Perhaps. Maybe not. Maybe he will humor me, play with my emotions like puppet strings to get his desired effect.

But maybe I'm selling him short. Perhaps he considers himself an artist, a painter of human emotions across a silver screen; a little more love here, a little less hate there. Perhaps. I have never met him, which may explain my ambivalence.

It's really a rare day, you know. One of those days locked forever in amber for my future. Each scene crystal clear, frozen. Each movement, word, action laid down unchanged, unchangeable. I will play it back a thousand times. I have played it back a thousand times. It is always the same, a closed loop in space and time turning over and over again, starting and ending like a snake eating its tail.

I nurse my beer and try to break the pattern.

But it is the pattern that is breaking me. How long does it take a sun to set? How long does it take to fall in love? How long is a life? There are variables involved here, problems to the questions. If a question isn't framed right, the answer, although correct, is worthless. It is necessary to give considerable thought to the framework of the question.

I nurse my beer and the pattern breaks.

It may be that the pattern has not been broken at all but only that it has taken a new turn, one that I was not prepared for. It happens that way sometimes.

What has broken it is a small extra brought on the scene for just this moment. A little something extra, I think that's what they call him. About two years old and a young bearded man wearing cut-off jeans and no shirt picks him up and blows in his belly-button, inflating him. They both laugh and in spite of myself I feel the corners of my mouth trying hard to start a grin, an unusual feeling — I had given up smiling for Lent.

They walk into the bar through the open door, shedding sand and setting sun as they trade salt spray for semi-darkness. It is definitely a bad trade, but one they make of their own free will, so who am I to say? The young man props the boy up in the middle of a battered pool table as he walks to the bar to get a beer. The boy, mirroring the old man he will soon grow into, plays with the loose balls on the table, dropping them one-by-one into the corner pocket until there are no more left.

(It was fun to watch him play because his interest in the game was directly proportional to the number of balls remaining on the table. At first he was very excited, making two-year-old noises as he gathered up the balls and rolled them all to one corner. Then one by one, a little at a time, his interest flagged as the balls disappeared. By the time he got to the last ball, I wasn't sure he could summon up enough involvement to drop it in, but he did. It was almost as if there were rules for the game, set down in black print on white pages in some two-year-old Hoyle.

RULES FOR PLAYING ON TOP OF POOL TABLES

1) You must be two years old and have a reasonable number of balls on the playing surface.
2) The number of balls = n.
3) Your interest at the beginning of the game is calculated by the formula: Interest (I) = n/x, where x, of course, is a constant.
4) As n decreases, (I) decreases until there are no balls remaining on the playing surface and interest will cease.
5) This game will prepare you to function adequately in your upcoming adult life, which will be outlined in chapter 16.

As I said, it was fun to watch him.)

But the sun is still setting. How long can they keep this up, this continued prolonging of the setting sun? Just long enough, I decide as I finish my beer and you come out of the ladies room, a shadow silhouette sitting down beside me.

We talk and make casual conversation, carefully avoiding what we really want to say, making the exchange a Chinese puzzle to unravel, pulling apart the extraneous nouns, verbs, adjectives and supportive clauses until we get to what's on each other's mind.

At just the right time we get up from the table to leave. It's a long walk back down the beach to the car, the others, the rest of the real world. We had better get started. I half expect the director to come out. "Finally," he would say. "It's about time we got this show on the road." Maybe he would pat me on the back, shake your hand for getting me moving. But he doesn't show up so I can only conclude that things are taking their natural course.

Sitting on the picnic table outside the back door of the bar, we watch the orange-pink horizon frame a long line of pelicans as they dip and rise above the water in regular formation. Somewhere a dolphin is breaking the surface of the water, although neither of us can see it. It is enough that we are aware of it. I want to sit and think and unravel some more of the puzzle, so I do and you do and we do and the swirls of cloudy color provide the backdrop.

But sitting here is awkward; in my short-sleeve shirt I am cold, shivering. It is easier to walk along the beach, quietly turning shells over with our toes, than it is to sit forming verbal complexities.

The water seems a lot warmer than it was earlier, almost as if while we were in the bar someone turned up the thermostat. But as we run and fix your cut foot I feel momentarily younger than my 32 years and I guess that's an okay feeling.

The gathering darkness chases us up the beach past all the dead jellyfish in the world to the car where they wait, caught up in their own branching lives.

It's your movie, you know. The lines are all there, you laid them out. All I have to do is walk through the part, make all the right moves. But that's okay too, I've turned down worse roles.

Somewhere out on the horizon they are packing away the ocean, saving the sun for another day.

I turn and brush the last tear from your cheek.

STRING TWO

Waves frame the scene; the palmetto fronds nailed to the wall form the backdrop to it all; we actors simply project the shadows of our lives against the wall for the entertainment of those on the other side. Perhaps they sit and eat popcorn and occasionally comment on the reflections of our lives. It would go like this:

"Look at him, Sharon. Isn't he ever going to get up from that table? Won't he ever finish that beer?"

"He's waiting for her, you know."

"How long is he going to sit there? Isn't there something else on?"

"The *Times* gave this four stars and we're going to see it through. The bridge club meets next Thursday and I've got to have something to talk about."

"I hope they haven't taken the sex out of this. It's not at all like the book."

It would go like that. It is always like that. I can almost hear the popcorn-crunch on the other side of the wall.

I don't mind waiting, really I don't. The setting sun reminds me somehow of the color television I left behind with the mortgage in Baltimore so long ago, a life ago.

But the sun is so much more *real, substantial*. So many movies end with the setting sun and yet our movie always begins with it. There is something here, a concept to grasp. Surely this must mean something. Anything. Perhaps I am grasping at straws.

How long can you stay in there? I mean, even if the ladies room *does* have two doors, there ought to be a limited number of things you can do in there. Perhaps there is a library in there, books with soft leather covers and gold-leaf titles stamped on their spines. Perhaps you have started reading — starting, let us say, with Aachen, a city in West Germany captured by the U.S. Army in October of 1944 (maybe you grieve for all those lost in the battle, a battle, any battle, not our battle), and you are slowly working your way to zymurgy and are even now heavily engrossed in the chemistry of fermentation. The thought makes me thirsty and I raise my near-empty glass and catch the bartender's eye and he makes motions to draw me another warm beer.

Perhaps there is a television in there and you are watching an hour-long special on wood carving and you are too involved with the program to leave. I couldn't blame you. There is something definite in wood carving, the act of making something out of something else.

I really don't know what's in there. I can guess. I've never been in there, but I can imagine. And since I will never be in there, whatever I imagine will be the image I will hold forever, thus becoming as real — or even more real — than the actual room. At least to me.

The room has walls that appear to be flimsy quarter-inch masonite panels and they are crumbly and old. The sink is dirty, with a jagged crack running through it and brown stains where the leaky faucets have dripped for a thousand years or so since the last plumber (lately retired from a successful practice in Hoboken and searching, like all of us, for a place in the sun; his children visited him during the winter months until he became so senile they found it an emotional burden — *we can't expose the children to this, I don't care if he is your father, we have our own lives to lead* — and finally he died and they shipped his body back to be buried in Hoboken, a town that he hated (except for one bar and a girl he had slept with twice a long time ago), to be shuttled into the ground next to a wife he had laughed with on occasion and had had truly ambivalent feelings toward for the last forty years or so) had been in the rest room with a large metal box full of tools. The floor is wet, the seat on the commode is cracked. There is an empty sanitary napkin dispenser on the wall, covered with telephone numbers written in magic markers. There is a window boarded up; it faces west, out onto the Gulf of Mexico and there are cracks in the boards so that you can see small slits of the setting sun.

That's the way it is now. There! See how easy it was? That's the image that will stay with me unless you come out as you are doing now and tell me what you saw.

But our conversation winds its way around warm beer and greasy hamburgers and all the things inside me remain unsaid and inside me as we build our verbal walls to hide what hurts from each other.

I reach down and touch your fingers. Instinctively you close your hand around mine. I look into your eyes and I find it hard to see past the pain, the turmoil. Your tinted glasses are a filter, trying and failing to keep out the unpleasant scenes. I want to take them off, clean them, take you out into the setting sun. The beer comes, one for me and one for you, a hamburger for me (too many onions, I have already forgotten the pickles). You detach your hand, a sense of loss overwhelms me, the beer a trivial consolation.

Now it is your turn to pause. I can't help but wonder if they have more patience with you. After all, you are younger, more attractive, and it *is* possible they predict great things from you. Perhaps they have typed you in the role of minor stardom. Perhaps you will play the role to completion. Perhaps you will tire of their constant pulling of puppet strings. Perhaps you desire to pull them yourself. I conjecture too much, it is a minor fault of which I am well aware, thank you. It should be easier to play it as it rolls.

"Play it as it rolls," they would coach from the wings. "Quit trying to gain control of the situation. What the hell do you think you're getting paid for?"

So I return to the relative security of my hamburger, finding comfort in the arrangement of the seeds on top of the bun. The seeds are all alike, made from the same seed machine. The hamburger is too greasy and one bite is all I can manage.

You are still quiet, beer untouched. Someone is playing pool and you are not reacting to anything, a solid rock sitting beside me. I ask you something and you don't answer, choosing instead to stare out the door at the setting sun.

I ask you again and you don't reply, you don't react at all. Tears run down your face, drop to your shirt. The tears have nothing to do with me, I'm just here, an innocent bystander. It could be that I'm wrong, however. It has been known to happen before.

So I say it again, three time's a charm. No reaction. I pick up my hamburger and throw it against the juke box. I brush the twin beers off the table with a wet sweep of my arm. I grab you by the shoulder and turn you to me, forcing you to look at me. You stand up, turn your head away and I take my cue, it's time to go.

We walk through the door into the setting sun. It is colder now than it was when we came in. You shiver. I take off my shirt and drape it over your shoulders. They're waiting for us, you know. It is only a matter of time.

We have to face it. You have to face it. I have to face it. It won't go away if we ignore it. It won't look any better in the morning sun.

We walk down the beach to the car, the others. Perhaps it will rain tomorrow. Maybe I'll get a job, cut my hair, sell my typewriter. Do you really think we could've gotten tickets to the Dylan concert?

The car, the others, are just a few jellyfish away. I turn to you, start to say something, think better of it, pause uncomfortably, look for the words, fail to find them. The film is winding down, going slower now. The wind sweeps through your hair.

I turn and brush the last tear from your cheek.

STRING THREE

Waves frame the scene; the dice are tossed and in their preordained way they land, sometimes face up, often face down, always an infinity of black dots mirroring the complex patterns of our lives.

I can't help it, you know. Pillow talk, bar talk; I can't seem to leave well enough alone. Drink your beer, I know it's warm, I can't do anything about that. Let's just sit here awhile. I have things to say before the sun sets. If you would listen, it would make it easier.

I stare at the cigarette in my hand, turning it around and around between my fingers, brushing the dead ash off against the pile of butts that sleep together in the sea shell sitting between us, between our beers so carefully arranged on the table, a tableau, a still-life awaiting only the photographer to come out with his Nikon and say "Wait a minute. Hold it *just like that.* Don't move." Perhaps he will take one shot, two. Then again, it could be that this is his calling, that the dice have been rolled and he will spend the rest of his life photographing two warm beers and a sea shell ashtray full of used and abused cigarettes, their filters giving *just* the right amount of color.

But it is not the photographer who arrives, but the bearded bartender who reaches down and grabs the sea shell from between us. He is setting a new one down, one I've never met, one I don't care to be on intimate terms with. My stomach tightens up. I don't want him to take the old one, I had just gotten to the point where I felt relaxed around it, where it no longer intimidated me with its strangeness. But I don't know how to tell him this without seeming to be uptight about the whole situation. But I *am* uptight. Why can't I let him see this? Would it be giving away too much of myself to an unreciprocating stranger? Would he then sit down and tell me his problems, his fears, his secret fantasies? I don't think I could handle that. "For fifteen years I have hated my sister," he would start. "And for much of that time I have had mixed feeling towards my brother who married above his class and is having a terrible time trying to keep pace. His daughter committed suicide in their bedroom with one shot from a thirty-eight caliber revolver that tore off the side of her head. Things have not been comfortable since that happened." He would probably go on with his story if I didn't interrupt him, something I would find myself totally incapable of doing. "My feelings towards my parents," he would continue, "are a mixture of love and hate and so on and so on and so on until his life, like the structure of this sentence, becomes a linear stream of words and emotions that stretch from where it started to where it will logically go, winding down to its appointed conclusion, facts spread out neatly so that one is able to pick and choose at will those events that happen to strike a responsive chord. It is possible to take these events and rearrange them, discarding some, inventing others, until we have taken the shards of his life and made someone else's life out of them.

Perhaps it will be my life. Perhaps yours.

I can tell by the way you are staring out through the door to the sea that you are locked in your own head, rolling dice around in your mind, working your own things out, things I can't touch, can't feel; things I have only a passing knowledge of, things you like, things you fear, things that hurt you or make you happy. Things I would like to get to know. Things you always hide from me.

Perhaps I can learn from all this. Become a better citizen, well known in my community for my charitable work and the fact that I am kind to small children and dumb animals. I can see it now, it's very clear. They will give me an award, it will be a holiday and the town will be dressed in bright and dancing banners, a festive occasion, full of good feelings, everybody smiling. The mayor will be there on the podium, giving the introduction. It will go like this: "This man, whose name has momentarily slipped my mind, is well known in our fine community for lots of things, the majority of which I can't seem to recall at the moment. It is because of, or maybe in spite of, these *deeds* I believe you call them, that we honor him today. Ladies and gentlemen, I give you *him*." He waves his arm in a grand gesture, marred only by the fact that he is pointing at the wrong person, the county mail clerk who is squirming uncomfortably. I stand and clear my throat. I want to tell you, I begin, about a movie I'm doing right now. It's not a bad movie, though most of the action is yet to come. However, I continue, I have read the working script and the end, while somewhat complex, does manage to bring together most of the loose ends. I seem to have let my cigarette burn down to my fingers and still you sit staring out through the door, through the sea, through the sun, through the cloud of emotion I am surrounding you with, through it all to that special place where you are alone, totally alone, unbothered, unfettered by ties with me. You sob. I hold your hand. We breathe at each other for a moment, struck by it all. Somewhere the car is parked and they are waiting, but the juke box is playing and the dice turn over and over in your eyes, sliding around on your tears.

The juke box is playing a song we have heard before, one that we both know, a relatively new song, recently fallen from near the top of the charts. It is almost by necessity that it be a new song, our lives don't mingle back far enough for us to share old songs, although undoubtedly there are many we have common knowledge of, ones that we may have heard during the prolonged period of time before we met. It could develop into a trivia session: Have you heard _____? Do you remember _____? What did you think of _____? Who were you loving when _____ was popular? Were you happy? Did you smile a lot? Would you like to talk about it? No, I didn't think so. You'll have to excuse me, I don't mean to pry. Well, yes, I *do* mean to pry, to intrude. It is a habit I have, you see, of trying to get to know a few things about the people I am involved with, people who mean something to me. If it makes you uncomfortable, I'm sorry.

The juke box is playing a song we have heard before, somebody put in a quarter, rolled the dice and up came a record we know, one written for a girl named Toni. Doesn't it strike you strange, even just a little bit, that they should play one we know? There must be over two hundred records in the juke box, most of them strangers to us, maybe four hundred if you count flip sides — written by all the desperate flipside songwriters — that will never be hits, destined to be thrown away with the other side, perhaps only played once or twice by mistake, a wrong button hit, a malfunction in the machine, played to beer-sodden customers who sit up as the flip side plays, accusing each other of bad judgment in the choosing of songs to provide the background for the games they're playing, to fill in the embarrassing silences when they run out of things to say. Perhaps all the flip sides in the world were made for just such moments. Perhaps our little scenario is a flip side, written for much the same reason.

The juke box is playing a song we have heard before, it comes at just the wrong moment. I was about to say something, but it seems inappropriate now. My mood and the record's mood clash and the record is louder, better orchestrated. After all, they spent weeks practicing, getting all the sounds *just right* and I am only one person, sitting here alone in my thoughts, trying hard to see how the dice are rolling. It is only natural the song should get the upper hand, the odds are heavily weighted in its favor.

The juke box is playing a song we have heard before, I resent the intrusion. It had been so nice, so quiet just sitting here with you, watching the sun sparkle on the water, watching the shadows creep along the floor. I cannot keep the record out of my head, it keeps going around and around, playing itself again and again, always the same, never changing, frozen forever when they pressed the master, all the work that had gone into it finished, cast in concrete. The instant after the record was recorded the performers went their own ways, living, breathing, dying and all we have of them is this three-minute slice out of their lives set down unchanged, unchangeable, never getting any better, never getting any worse, never growing, never anything except *just there* for us to react to, bounce off of like dice against a wall, coming up with different reactions and emotions that are preordained in a complicated formula dependent heavily upon the people involved, their state of mind at the time and the possible imperfections in the dice.

It grows late. We really should go. The car and the people and the rest of our branching lives are waiting in the wings. I can hear the rattle of the dice and soft cursing of a male voice distracted, diffuse, almost inaudible what with the record and the surf and all this heavy breathing going on around us, between us, inside us.

Order another beer. I think I might have a hamburger. It will probably be greasy, so I don't think I'll eat much of it, but I haven't had anything to eat in quite a while, haven't felt much like eating, to tell the truth, and I really should make the effort.

It's important to make the effort, you see, any effort. Success and failure are relative terms, meaningless in the long run. The significant thing is that we make the effort, any effort, some effort. It will undoubtedly improve our state of mind, even if it doesn't solve anything. If, indeed, there is anything left to solve. I happen to believe there is, but then again I'm just one person, only human, often wrong, sometimes mistaken, always misunderstood by those around me, just trying to get through life without hurting anyone.

So the hamburger comes and, as I expected, I can only manage one bite, piling onions on top of onions, pickles on top of pickles on the side of my paper plate like so many cords of firewood or bodies in a concentration camp or after some natural disaster, mud-slide, earthquake, prison riot. The cook will take offense and mutter under his breath as he slides them off the plate into their common grave.

So we stand at the appointed hour and walk once more through the eternally open door, up the unpaved beach, pausing to comment on the sun, the birds, the surf, your cut toe, the sea shells and the jellyfish — all items common to our limited, mutual experience. We walk the sandy middle road, the dividing line, swaying first one way and then the other, never going too far in either direction. The dice sit poised in their cardboard container.

We are about to run out of beach. The end of this road is in sight. Nothing has been decided, everything has been decided, the dice are falling in slow motion, clicking against each other like two thin people making love. There's the car, still parked. There are the others, still waiting. And still the sun sets as you hold my arm for one last time. There are words lost in the wind, phrases drowned in the pounding surf. There is you.

I am torn, twisted by the widening gulf between us. There should be something to say, but there isn't.

Instead, I turn and brush the last tear from your cheek.

STRING FOUR

Waves frame the scene. I am alone at last, sitting at the end of a long pier. There is water all around me, just below my feet. I wonder if the tide is in, if the fish are biting. Perhaps I should have brought along the fishing pole Bill left at my house, the one without any line, without any hooks. It would justify my appearance here to those curious people walking up and down the beach.

The film is winding down forever. I can hear the people gathering up their coats, looking for their shoes. It's strange to be in the last act alone, without you. But then again, I've always been without you, without anyone, really. We go through life touching and being touched and in the end we walk off stage, essentially ourselves.

There! Look! The dolphin a brief black slash in the darkening water.

Life teems under the surface of the water, unseen and for the most part unnoticed, yet every bit as important, maybe even more so, than those lives that walk around on the surface.

"You mean I paid good money for this?"

"Shut up! Let's watch the end. Will you help me with my coat?

Can you find my other shoe?"

"I don't care if this is the last act. I'm going to walk out now."

Some are leaving, some will stay. Some will like it, some won't. I can't get too terribly excited about that. It's just here, that's all.

The world still goes on, people still walk their shadow lives, tiny mirrors of each other. I just can't feel anything anymore. I'm all reacted out.

So I sit here with my legs over the edge of the pier, my toes touching the tops of the waves. The car is still waiting, just up the road from the setting sun. I guess I'm ready for that now. I am thinking of you.

I brush the last tear from my eye.

THE OCCASIONAL CLARINET

Waves frame the scene, crashing forever outside an open door. A solitary figure makes his way through the deserted bar. He is wearing Bermuda shorts and is carrying a clipboard. He stops at one of the tables, the one facing the door, the one I am familiar with. He examines the ashtray, picks up a loose cigarette, brushes stray ashes onto the floor. He picks up the jean jacket covered with patches, the one I left on the seat, and he carefully lays it across the bar, always directing, even after the movie is finished.

An intense young man walks into the bar, goes up to him. It is an intrusion, he resents it. The young man is full of facts, figures, questions. These are the last things the director wants to get involved in. He wishes to be alone on the set. It is his prerogative and he enforces it with a curt shake of his head. Alone again.

The juke box provides the only illumination, a flashing, dancing sense of unreality. The director walks over to it, examines the selections in a detached manner. The names of the songs mean nothing to him, they are young songs, songs for another age; they are fossils of the future to him. He unplugs the juke box and its slight hum stops. The bar is nearly dark now, except for the small amount of moonlight bouncing off the water, creeping in through the always open door. He walks by the pool table.

And in doing so, he picks up a ball off the table, holds it close to his face, brushes his cheek with it. It is like all the others, with small imperfections where perhaps it had flown off the table after being hit too hard and at the wrong angle. Perhaps it hit the concrete floor, perhaps another table. He rolls it across the dark surface to a corner pocket. It moves slowly in the quiet bar, missing the pocket, bouncing back into the middle of the table, clicking quietly up against another ball. He leaves it there, walks around to the door, steps outside.

The moon is nearly full, the beach quite bright. The stars, beach and moon are only backdrops to him, things to be manipulated, things to be used for effect.

Does he think of you? Of me? Does he wonder about the car and the waiting people and what is happening to us now?

More things to be manipulated.

He sighs and I sigh and you are warm lying next to me, keeping the cold away.

There. I have it now. Your face across the pillow, scene framed by your hair, your smile, the wooden beads around your neck. How close and warm you look without your glasses. It is something I hold on to. There is sand in the sheets.

Your face is flushed, your touch gentle. I'm glad; it's what I need, what you need. There are soft questions answered in quiet whispers.

Yet even now as I look at you and hold you I can feel you growing farther away, your presence receding into the distance, dice clicking, endlessly clicking as miles and miles of movie film run through the broken projector and pile in loose loops on the floor.

Gone. I never had the chance to say good-bye.

James B. Johnson

James B. Johnson is a graduate of Florida State University and a U.S. Air Force veteran. His novels *Habu, Mindhopper, Treckmaster,* and *Daystar and Shadow* have been published by Daw Books. *Mindhopper* takes place in a future Florida. His short stories have been published in *Fantasy and Science Fiction, Analog, Swallow's Tale,* and other magazines.

The genesis of "Flankspeed" is a dream I had one night about getting drunk with a dolphin. The concept was fascinating and I enjoyed figuring out why someone would drink booze with a dolphin. Mote Marine Lab in Sarasota was a natural. I wrote the story and added a shark tank. Shortly thereafter, Mote built a shark tank. Because of the choreography I've slightly rearranged the physical layout of the facility, but since the story's projected into the future, the differences are possible.

FLANKSPEED

by James B. Johnson

The images were fuzzy until Elrod started feeding beer to the grizzled old bull dolphin, Flankspeed.

Out of the Gulf of Mexico Flankspeed would lead his school of bottlenosed dolphins through New Pass, or sometimes Big Pass, into Sarasota Bay. They'd round City Island Park and head straight for Mote Marine Laboratory just off Lido Key, newly rehabbed after being closed since '98 and the mysterious murder.

Elrod Truman would open the gates and the dolphins would romp in, leaping and clowning, doing tricks, raising hell. Elrod, or whoever had the duty, would feed them fish, and some of the scientists would don masks and fins and mingle with the dolphins, checking their transmitters, replacing any that had stopped their recording or broadcasting functions. The dolphins would always put on performances, delighting the crowds that gathered during the day.

But whatever the dolphins did, they would instantly obey the dictates of their leader, Flankspeed. If he tired of the games and headed out, the other forty or fifty dolphins would dutifully follow; their sleek grey bodies pretty well filled up the bay as they seemed to move together like a well-trained unit. Half a hundred! The sheer numbers were impressive. Though the exact count varied, Elrod knew that a school of bottled-nosed dolphins usually numbered only a dozen or so. Flankspeed's leadership had certainly changed that. He commanded respect from the masses. And on the rare occasions when a follower angered the leader, that dolphin would become an immediate victim of Flankspeed's swift discipline — bites, tail-slaps, nose-rams.

Elrod didn't know why, but he liked the grizzled old dolphin. Nobody knew who had named him Flankspeed, but the name struck a responsive and romantic chord in Elrod's core. He began to save pompano, his own favorite, for Flankspeed, while the other dolphins got whatever else was available — blues, mackerel, whiting.

"Say, Elrod," Doc Ambersson would repeat at least once a week, "it amuses me, the juxtaposition of you and Flankspeed."

What she clearly meant was that Elrod was timid, not at all a match for the dolphin in terms of leadership ability. Doc had to go and get that word "juxtaposition" in practically every conversation; it was her favorite word, in this case meaning something like, "It's funny how you and that bull are such good friends — the two of you having such opposite personalities."

Elrod would rub his hand through his salt-and-pepper hair and demurely blink his hazel eyes. "Gee, Doc. Thanks, I think."

Not to mention that Flankspeed was huge, ugly, dark, scarred, and marred. And Elrod was slight and fair with totally unremarkable features and the lingering look of innocence still worn by those who have not yet fully taken on the world.

Even though he was relatively new at this job, Elrod already blended in like a permanent fixture in his uniform of cut-off jeans and clean T-shirt. Before this he had worked on the Tambay estate over on Siesta Key until the grande dame died off and it was finally clear he didn't have any future there. Working for the Tambays he had risen from dockhand, helping out with their yachts, cabin cruisers, powerboats, sailboats, fishing boats, to assistant manager of the whole estate, with direct supervisory responsibilities over the docks, channels, beaches, even the golf course. But the general manager had seniority on Elrod and Elrod knew he was at the end of the line. Without a college degree these days, you were nobody. Mitchell Tambay had said as much when he took over as administrator of his mother's estate.

"Elrod," Mitchell Tambay had told him, "you have the ability. Get a college degree and you might go far. We could use a man with the right education."

"But I'm thirty-six," Elrod had objected.

"So?"

Elrod had dodged the question. In the end, Mitch had found him a new job, as facilities manager at the reopening of Mote Marine Lab, obviously hoping that the association with scientists and students might encourage him to attend a university somewhere. And, if not, well, at least Mitch would be in a position to find someone else with the right education to work on his estate.

The laboratory was doing well now, thriving as an extension of the Florida State University oceanography program. A wily old woman, Professor Charlotte Ambersson, had been named director just shortly before she took on Elrod. Between her and Elrod, they'd whipped the place into shape, and that was no small feat. For three years after the murder, Mote had floundered and fallen into disrepair.

The lab had begun about mid-century, over on Siesta Key, as Cape Haze Marine Lab. Then it moved to City Island, and became two things, Mote Marine Lab and Mote Marine Foundation, specializing in marine science and ichthyological research, with specific emphasis on southwest Florida and the Gulf of Mexico. In 1995, Florida State University had acquired Mote. Fidel Wickett became the director and ran the lab successfully for three years, until he was murdered. Wickett had seemed eminently qualified to direct scientific work at Mote, though his distinguished career as a neurosurgeon was an odd match for the marine institute. He had acquired the directorship by dint of huge donations to the university and its oceanography program, generous funding which made that department rival even the football team in budget and scope.

The only picture Elrod could remember seeing of him made the man look like a stuffed-shirt jerk, and Elrod had heard that Wickett was autocratic and intolerant. Then one night in '98 somebody murdered Dr. Wickett. The body had been found mutilated and beheaded in the shark tank. Police forensics established that Wickett had been beheaded before he had been dragged into the tank, probably in an attempt to make the death look like an accident. It was all very grisly. The resulting scandal and investigations forced FSU to shut the program down and close the lab. The murder was never solved and the lab fell into disrepair.

The local bigwigs finally realized the sad state of the institution which had once commanded such civic pride. Subject to local political pressure, FSU was at last prevailed upon to send in Charlotte

Ambersson and reopen the facility.

It wasn't long before Elrod and Dr. Ambersson had the place running well. Research was under way. The public willingly paid for the dolphin performances and tours of the facilities, and the museum, shark tank, and other aquatic exhibits more than paid their way. Elrod was happy with the way the funds balanced every month — though he was glad he didn't have to account for the scientists' salaries. Dr. Ambersson and the university took care of that, and Doc, determined to regain the facility's former excellent reputation, made the scientific side run professionally.

Elrod was rather fond of Doc Ambersson. She had a strong, some-times pushy, way about her that led everyone to think of her as highly competent — which Elrod had come to realize she was. In time Doc Ambersson even came to like the quiet and timid Elrod, tacitly acknowledging he had his strengths as well.

Every morning she'd come in and Elrod would already be on the job — he lived in a small house on the grounds. She'd ask him, "Elrod, what's the marine weather forecast today?"

"Two infantry corporals, a captain, and a parade in review," he'd answer quietly, or, "A colonel, a first sergeant, and a pilot."

She'd smile and know there were no immediate problems and go about her daily business.

This day, Elrod was sitting on the dock dangling his feet in the water and holding out a six-pound pompano in his right hand. It was still early and only a thin stream of tourists wandered through the bleachers to watch. Flankspeed hovered in the water right there in front of Elrod. They had their daily battle of wits going: Who would win? Would Elrod's arm tire first? Or would Flankspeed become bored with the game and snatch the fish?

Then another dolphin swam in close, entranced by the pompano. Suddenly, Flankspeed turned in the water and Elrod swore he could hear the growl as Flankspeed showed his teeth. The other dolphin veered off and Flankspeed turned his attention back to Elrod and the pompano. Flankspeed was strong — though weighing close to four hundred pounds and stretching maybe twelve feet in length, he could leap twenty feet in the air to ring a bell or snatch a fish; he could "walk" backward over the surface of the water by powerful strokes of his fluke.

He reminded Elrod of a weathered Doberman: mouth and snout low and squat and wide; when his teeth showed menacingly, Flankspeed's eyes would seem to come closer together. Behind the eyes the dolphin's head wore a cicatrix of scars that might have come from a tangle with a shark or barracuda. At least that's what Elrod wanted to think, but deep down he knew the wound was more than likely the result of an encounter with a propellor churning so fast that the blades would have sliced into the dolphin's head a dozen times in the fraction of a second it had taken the animal to react or the boat to skate over him.

The scarred area was behind the blowhole and the melon. The melon! Elrod smiled to find himself using the word the scientists had taught him. There was nothing about Flankspeed which even remotely reminded him of a cantalope, but melon was the proper term for the organ on top of the dolphin's head that directed sounds forward and enabled the animal to use its natural sonar system for what they called "echolocation." Flankspeed's melon looked undamaged and efficient and Elrod wondered whether it might have undiscovered functions. Then the train of thought was lost as he noticed that a little girl had gotten out of the bleachers and was leaning precariously over the edge of the giant pool. He started to get up to shoo her back to her seat, but a panicked mother beat him to it.

Suddenly, Elrod's arm jerked upward, no longer required to counter the weight of the pompano. Flankspeed had taken advantage of the split-second distraction and nabbed the fish. Under their unspoken, but nonetheless established, rules of the game, Flankspeed's action was fair, and thus the dolphin won the contest that day.

Flankspeed had one eye cocked out of the water, bobbing on the surface which was riled by the continuing antics of the other dolphins. Elrod knew the dolphin was waiting for him to acknowledge the final result of the game. Elrod slapped his hand into the water and splashed the dolphin's eye.

Just when things seemed to be running smoothly and Elrod seemed to be doing so well with the dolphins, he started to get his tension headaches. It was the only thing he could think of to call them. Something would vaguely disturb his mind, the painful confusion would sweep over him, and he'd have to withdraw.

He'd had plenty of experience withdrawing. His mother had been a domineering woman, loud and demanding. She'd run his father off even before Elrod made it to kindergarten. Elrod never had friends because his mother disapproved or was too demanding, dictating what he could do and when he could do it. She smothered him, made all his decisions for him, chose his clothing every day even into his high school years, kept constant track of him when he wasn't in school — in short, she ran his life. When he was ready to graduate from high school she had up and died of heart failure one day at the local Florida Power and Light office raising hell about her latest bill. Elrod knew how hard she'd made things for him, but he didn't hate her. He didn't love her a lot, but it wasn't in him to detest her either. During the bad times, he'd simply withdrawn into himself, like a turtle into its shell.

After she died, there seemed to be no particular reason to go on to college, so he went to work on the Tambay docks, and things went on from there. He suspected the reason he'd worked so long at the Tambay estate was that he was afraid of change. He'd found a niche, a comfortable, nonthreatening place to be. He'd learned there was some enjoyment to life. However, even there during some minor crisis or other when stress levels were high, the tension headaches rolled in and he would have to practice his withdrawal technique again. He knew all of this was why he'd never go to college, this and the fact he was now thirty-six, almost thirty-seven, and he wasn't apt to change. He'd actually been surprised at himself for handling the stress of the change to facilities manager at Mote. For a time he'd thought he was getting better. Now the headaches were returning.

And with them now, vague images.

He told no one. They'd think he was crazy — and his history as a recluse would back them up.

However, Elrod Truman was no dummy. After a while, he came to associate his mental pain with the presence of the dolphins. Jesus, if he told anyone he thought that, they'd *know* he was crazy. But there was something happening inside his head. He was beginning to suspect that somehow the dolphins were trying to communicate with him with . . . with their minds.

Communicating, he thought, might be too strong a word. Using auras? Showing feelings as people do with their faces, hands, body language? Were they somehow bombarding him with melon impulses the way they did for echolocation? Something. Those dolphins were doing something the scientists didn't know anything about.

Maybe it was just the electronic transmitters and recorders the scientists had attached to the dolphins, maybe he was somehow able to pick up the signals. He'd heard there were freak instances of people receiving radio broadcasts through their metal dental work. But Elrod eventually discounted this idea. Scientists used the same equipment tracking and recording the big loggerhead sea turtles and he felt nothing from them.

When he'd finally identified his problem as emanating only from the dolphins, Elrod thought it might be an allergy he was developing, perhaps some pheromone they exuded to which he'd become allergic. Then the headaches phased into fuzzy images, and Elrod became frightened. No allergy, this.

Each day the images continued, indistinct but compelling in their own way, and eventually the fright eroded from him, which, in turn, lowered the stress of the situation and allowed him to feel more comfortable. This, in turn, allowed him to receive the images a shade more clearly.

Colors and shadows. Strong emotions binding with snatches of whirling lights and, occasionally, some actual figures.

Was he seeing what the dolphins saw?

He paid attention, and this wasn't the case.

One evening Elrod was sitting on the sea wall drinking a Stroh's from a longneck bottle. The sun was setting on the far side of Lido Key and the tide was in. Bay water lapped the top of the sea wall and Elrod worried about the effects of a storm. He'd have to get the engineers to look at this; the lab would be particularly vulnerable.

A swift wind off the mainland blew mosquitoes and traffic smells over the bay. A fuzzy image snaked into his mind and almost immediately Flankspeed popped into view in front of him. There was no mistaking Flankspeed: the scar on top of his head, and a crusty-looking dorsal fin.

Elrod looked for other dolphins, but none appeared.

"It's you!" he said wonderingly.

The big dolphin stretched his mouth and his jaws parodied a grin while he blew spume through his blowhole.

The fuzzy images boiled behind Elrod's eyes, around their perimeters, came forward and went back like fragments caught by a zoom lens trying to focus. Elrod took a long pull at his beer. Then, irritated, he spat some at Flankspeed.

Flankspeed finned himself closer, mouth open, and Elrod could've sworn that the dolphin was actually trying to ingest the foaming froth from the mouthful of beer.

The images receded and the dolphin swam closer to the sea wall. Flankspeed lodged his head upon the wall and looked longingly at Elrod. The bull's mouth opened invitingly.

"No pompano today, good buddy," Elrod said conversationally. "If I feed you at the wrong time and for the wrong reasons, it screws up the scientists, hear?"

The dolphin seemed to nod and pant at the same time. He blew, a sudden and clearly taunting gesture.

Elrod stuck out his tongue at the dolphin. "Damn *fish*. Whatcha doin' to my mind?"

Flankspeed turned his body slightly and blew spume at Elrod, turned back, and opened and shut his mouth quickly, squeaking like he had rubber balls in his jaws.

And Elrod knew what he wanted. He never knew how he knew, but he knew. As if under some kind of compulsion, Elrod reached out with his longneck Stroh's and upended the bottle into the dolphin's mouth. He was rewarded with a satisfied croak from Flankspeed's throat as the dolphin swallowed the beer. Then Flankspeed slid slowly back into Sarasota Bay. Lazily, he swam to and fro for a few minutes.

Elrod had no knowledge about a dolphin's metabolism, and he wondered if the animal would feel the effects of the alcohol. Would it impact the dolphin's balance or judgment like it would a person's? If so, the damn fool could drown himself.

Elrod watched with growing interest. He felt for a moment that he could understand what the scientists would feel like as they studied these creatures. Flankspeed gradually increased the pace of his swimming, then rolled on his back and porpoised upside down for a moment, one of the behaviors the tourists loved to watch. Then the dolphin swam back toward Elrod on the sea wall.

An image came unbidden into Elrod's mind. The dolphin's eyes seemed to lock onto his and the image cleared somewhat. The fuzziness swirled away.

"A train! A goddamn locomotive!" Elrod blurted aloud, then sheepishly looked around, relieved to find he was alone. The sun was gone, dusk was flaring over the bay, and the water's edge was deserted.

The vivid image faded as Flankspeed roiled the water with his fluke and heaved himself halfway up on the seawall to rest his head in the crux of Elrod's crossed legs.

The full import of this uncharacteristic maneuver didn't hit Elrod at first: he registered the solid power of that dolphin flesh and wondered, if the dolphin took a bite, would he have to pee through a catheter for the rest of his life? But when Flankspeed showed no inclination toward castrating him, Elrod relaxed and lapsed into scolding amusement at the face before him.

"A train? You? What do you know about trains?"

The dolphin simply looked up at him. Elrod smelled Gulf water and seaweed from the dolphin's open mouth.

"I don't recall there being any train bridges over water hereabouts — well, maybe up in Tampa Bay somewhere, but you couldn't prove it by me." He looked into the dolphin's eyes. "How do you know about trains, old boy?" His voice was gentle, his curiosity genuine.

The dolphin didn't move.

Unconsciously, Elrod rotated the top of his cooler and pulled out another Stroh's. He twisted off the cap and took a long drink. He burped slightly. " 'Scuse me, hear?" Then he felt embarrassed talking to a fish. He looked around uneasily. Nobody. Dark was almost upon them. Lights winked on across the bay. Condos, hotels, waterfront. The big marina.

Flankspeed moved his head and nudged Elrod's stomach with his snout. Elrod didn't know what to make of it at first. "Hey. Don't spill my beer."

In a few seconds, the dolphin repeated the movement. "Awright, awright, you don't gotta draw me a picture." Elrod tipped the beer and liquid disappeared down Flankspeed's throat.

The dolphin rested his head gently on Elrod's right ankle. He kept swishing his fluke slowly to maintain his position half on the sea wall. He turned his head slightly, appearing to rest, so that Elrod could see only one great eye.

With his left hand, Elrod reached out and rubbed his knuckles on the rubbery surface of the dolphin's head. Even with the slick of water on the surface, the scars were evident to Elrod's touch. With the slight buzz that the beer had given him, Elrod transformed Flankspeed's head scars into woven olive branches or whatever the hell the old Greek gods wore around their heads on Mount Olympus drinking nectar and all.

An emotion formed in Elrod's mind, visually formless but nonetheless definite, a deep sense of emotional relief, and he thought of scratching behind a dog's ears. He took another sip of beer and poured the rest into Flankspeed's mouth. The smell of beer overpowered the smell of the sea. With the fish smell lost in the familiar yeasty aroma of the beer, Elrod could almost imagine himself with a friend in a local bar. He opened another Stroh's and shared that with Flankspeed.

It was dark now, and Elrod watched a pelican speed by oblivious to the sight of a dolphin half out of the water with his head in the lap of a man.

Few lights were on up at the lab, almost everybody having gone home by now. Elrod was the only one who actually lived on the grounds, just as he had at the Tambay estate. It gave him a sense of proprietorship and a relaxed confidence that he was in familiar surroundings.

"You gotta be shittin' me, Jack!" he said involuntarily as a sharp, clear picture leaped into his brain. He didn't know where the scene was, but he'd seen it before. In Tampa, sixty-five miles north. The intersection of interstate highways 4 and 275. "Malfunction junction," they called it.

"Ohmigod," he whispered. This wasn't just a snapshot. Those fuzzy lines were cars moving along the roads. The image wavered and changed perspective. The picture in Elrod's mind showed — what was it? Like the underside of a culvert, sort of . . . like an open place beneath a great roadway spanning a creek maybe? Elrod suddenly realized the image was clear. Only his failure to recognize what he was looking at prevented his complete understanding.

His mind was reeling. He drained the beer and was startled out of his reverie by a squeaking complaint from Flankspeed. He opened another bottle and poured the whole thing down the dolphin's throat. Then he tossed the empty into the bay, something else he'd never done before. Then he firmly pushed Flankspeed's head away, lurched to his feet, and staggered dumbly away through some longleaf pines toward his house.

(Later, when he remembered to retrieve his cooler, it wasn't on the ground near the seawall where he'd left it. Instead, he found it bobbing gently in the water, nudging against the wall. There were several great gashes across the white cover. But Flankspeed had been unable to manipulate the push-button to open it.)

Elrod's sleep that night was disturbed. He dreamed weird dreams and had nightmares. He tossed and turned. He awoke in the morning half-convinced the night's experience had been merely the result of too much beer, too much sun, and too little sleep — in short, a dream.

He went into the kitchen for his morning glass of V-8 with a squeeze of lime. There on the counter next to the microwave was his battered cooler with the gash marks unchanged — bearing their mute witness to the truth.

"Oh, Jesus Flippin' Pizzas," he said.

Somehow Elrod managed to get through the day. Should he tell Doc or someone what was going on? They'd think he was crazy — crazier than they already thought he was. And he had no real proof. A gashed styrofoam cooler was no evidence for mental images transmitted by a dolphin.

That evening, after everyone had left, Elrod was coiling a hose at the main tanks when he felt a compulsion to go to the seawall. He wondered if Flankspeed would show up again. The dolphin had learned to come on regular occasions to the tanks and pools for fish and fun or just to show off, hadn't he? Well, in that case, surely the animal could train himself to come for a beer if he wanted, couldn't he?

It was getting too dark for any more chores when he heard a commotion near the gates to the bay. A fuzzy image crept into his mind, one he couldn't decipher. Flankspeed. It had to be. Determined to assert his control of the situation, Elrod ignored the dolphin.

Soon he heard mighty slams upon the bay waters just outside the gates. Flankspeed was smacking his fluke on the water to get attention, a characteristic macho gesture delivered with perhaps more power than usual. These moves were followed by a series of powerful jaw claps. The sounds conveyed such power that it briefly passed through Elrod's mind that the dolphin might actually do itself damage if this didn't stop soon.

The noise died and then suddenly the gates and even the shoreline trembled from an underwater blow.

"I give up," Elrod said aloud and went to the gates. He punched the right sequence on the control computer and one of the underwater entrances opened.

In a flash, Flankspeed was in the tank, his torpedo shape tearing around, ripping through the water like a dog who'd been caged too long. Then the dolphin went to the hydrophone, a device which monitored and amplified the dolphin calls and was automatically turned on each time the gates were opened.

Flankspeed evidently had a lot he wanted to say, but the racket was so loud and annoying that Elrod turned the damn thing off.

Shortly, almost as though he knew the plug had been pulled, Flankspeed abandoned the hydrophone and appeared in front of Elrod. The dolphin squeaked at Elrod demandingly.

"Want a beer, eh?" Elrod went to the holding tank and scooped out a pompano with a net. He took the fish by the tail and held it out above the water. Elrod braced himself for the long hold and fixed his attention on the dolphin, thinking their traditional game had begun. But Flankspeed tailed his way up to Elrod's outstretched arm and, with his bottle-nose, knocked the pompano from his grip. The dolphin ignored the fish and continued to stare at Elrod.

When Elrod failed to move, Flankspeed hustled himself up on the perimeter of the tank and pushed Elrod's ankle with his snout. Then the animal backed off and an image came uninvited into Elrod's mind, more clear than fuzzy, almost within the grasp of his mind's eye: Golden arches? MacDonald's?

Elrod needed a drink. He turned abruptly and strode off toward his quarters. He found his bottle of Jim Beam, tipped it up, and swallowed, savoring the familiar warmth of the whiskey as it found its way inside. For a few moments he almost felt normal, but he then sensed again the demanding presence of Flankspeed churning the waters of his mind as deftly as he maneuvered every inch of the main tank.

Resignedly, Elrod replaced the Jim Beam and got six bottles of

Stroh's out of his refrigerator. He put them mechanically in the cooler and walked out, feeling like he was going to the scaffold and the waiting hangman. Instead he arrived back at the tank to find Flankspeed fairly dancing on his fluke, triumphant, waiting.

Elrod let out a long sigh and opened a beer. Then he poured, conscious of the picture he was part of: a slight man standing with an upturned bottle pouring beer down the gullet of a *Tursiops truncatus* who was dancing yet another mocking victory dance on his powerful fluke. When the bottle was emptied and Elrod stepped back, Flankspeed let himself slam back into the tank, spraying Elrod and most of the bleachers.

Elrod moved over and sat on the platform where the show's emcee would stand tomorrow above the tank and hold hoops for the more compliant dolphins to jump through, to be rewarded with the cheap bait fish they had been trained to take out his hand. Elrod let his legs dangle beneath the platform. He drank his own beer while below him, Flankspeed lounged lazily in the water.

An image materialized in Elrod's mind, and he concentrated: *An enclosed place. Cars and a lift. A socket wrench and hot, spurting oil. Grit, grime, dirt, oil, stuffy when cold — snow outside! An old and rounded and faded Coke machine. Tires on the back wall. Cars coming and going infrequently.*

Water splashed on Elrod and he realized his insides were cold enough to skate on. Flankspeed slapped the water again, obviously demanding another beer.

Elrod obediently climbed off the overhanging platform and went back to the bleachers for another Stroh's. When he turned around with the beer, he found Flankspeed almost completely out of the water resting on the concrete lip of the tank. Elrod spilled the beer into Flankspeed's gasping mouth. When the bottle was empty, the dolphin abruptly wormed his way back into the water.

Visions flooded Elrod's mind again: *undersides of cars, engines, bellhousings, transmissions, valve cover gaskets, spark plugs, electronic ignitions, fuel pumps, water pumps, wheel bearings.*

The visions gradually changed from the stark inanimate close-ups:

people showing only as shadows against blizzards and snow and then green to summer dry.

In the back of his mind, Elrod was starting to ascribe the images — visions, now — to mental thievery. Somehow, Flankspeed had stolen these visions from some human person, or persons. Or perhaps he was even somehow able to manipulate the store of images trapped over a lifetime deep within Elrod's own little braincells.

What the hell could a dolphin know about transmissions and Ford fuel pumps?

Not a damn thing, Elrod answered himself.

However, while the images changed, the perspective always seemed the same. Not just because of the angle of vision, about from eye level, but also the gut-level tacit interpretation of what was seen, which gave each vision its contrast, color, emotional impact.

Elrod came back to his own senses as he became aware of the strange tableau he'd been too involved in enacting to notice. He was sitting just off center in the first row of bleacher seats, leaning back with his elbows resting on the second row. At his feet lay Flankspeed, completely out of the tank.

Elrod was not surprised to find that they were out of beer. "That's it for tonight," he told the dolphin.

Flankspeed squeaked at him and fishtailed himself back into the tank. With a wave of the tail he disappeared, and Elrod had enough presence of mind to close the bay-access gate behind him.

This went on for a week. Every night at sundown, the dolphin would appear at the bayside tank gates. Elrod would let him in and together they would share a six-pack. Then the visions would appear. But the images changed. They weren't confined to the garage. There were views of different places, different times. The perspective was on the move. Aimlessly, Elrod thought. But the images and visions were strikingly clear. The more the alcohol-induced empathy flowed between Elrod and Flankspeed, the clearer the visions became.

Once — and he didn't think Flankspeed was even aware of it — Elrod got a glimpse of the perspective character, probably the one whose mind the dolphin picked. It was a gray day, somewhere so generic to the American countryside that, as usual, Elrod couldn't determine the location. Or even guess at it. The perspective character walked in front of a Kmart window. His eyes were riveted somewhere inside, glued to a flashing blue light. Elrod could imagine the intrusive voice saying, "Attention, Kmart Shoppers." But the view showed the person through whose eyes Elrod was seeing: a quick glimpse of a reflection in the glass of the window. *Disheveled straw-colored hair topped by a soiled Atlanta Braves baseball cap. Shaggy straw-colored beard with flecks of gray. In between, a rigid nose and a loose mouth, and knowing but resigned eyes. Upper torso only. Gray long-sleeved work shirt, Elrod somehow knew, hanging out of the pants. A ragged, dirty jacket covering the shirt, cuffs frayed. Held just above the waist in a trembling hand was a paper bag obviously containing a bottle of some kind.*

The vision faded as the perspective character shambled ahead, dodging a three-horse merry-go-round. Elrod now thought of the man as the "Wanderer." Elrod shivered. He'd brought along his bottle of Jim Beam and he took a long swallow.

Flankspeed took renewed interest in Elrod and squirmed out of the tank immediately, worming his way across the concrete like a GI on an obstacle course. Urgently, he nosed Elrod's knee.

"Sure, Speedy," Elrod said, still shaken. What in the *hell* was going on? He poured a dollop down Flankspeed's demanding gullet. Their shared empathy told Elrod that the dolphin was deeply satisfied.

The next day, Flankspeed did not appear at showtime. A dozen or so of the other dolphins did, but their performances were not up to standard.

The following day, Flankspeed showed up again, bringing with him his entire school. The others performed, but again it was a ragged production. Flankspeed ate the pompano Elrod gave him.

The following day there were fewer dolphins, and one young bull continuously challenged Flankspeed. Elrod had never seen

Flankspeed so passive and indifferent, and he also noticed, in the light of day, that Flankspeed's color seemed to have changed. The dolphin simply did not look as healthy as he had weeks before.

Late one afternoon, Elrod was on the phone in his cubicle-sized office arranging a fuel contract when Dr. Ambersson walked in and perched on the edge of his desk. Elrod licked the point of his pencil, anticipating the fuel figures forthcoming when his party returned; he'd been on hold for a while. He knew Dr. Ambersson disliked dealing over telephones; she didn't like the power technology held over people. She always complained that phone calls got priority over personal visits, and that bothered her.

Right now, she started talking, knowing Elrod was on hold, forcing him to shift his attention from the apparatus to the live individual before him. Maybe she liked to pull his chain, too, Elrod thought.

"Elrod, we've got a problem." Elrod smiled indulgently at her. "The dolphin school's disintegrating," she went on. "And our people cannot determine the cause. Something like this can jeopardize all our studies." She looked at Elrod expectantly. "The tracking screen shows several individuals have already gone their own way."

Elrod nervously shifted the telephone receiver in its cradle. "I'm facilities, Doc. The onliest degrees I got are Fahrenheit."

Dr. Ambersson smiled. "*You* are going to encounter facilities problems, budget-wise, Elrod. What's our main attraction? Right. Wild dolphins doing tame fish tricks. The juxtaposition of wild creatures in our theater performing — earning their keep and getting paid, so to speak — is what draws the audiences. Those audiences generate revenues, which you use. Am I getting through to you?"

Elrod nodded. "What can I do?"

She shrugged. "Beats the hell out of me. However, it has not escaped my notice that you have a particular relationship with Flankspeed, the leader . . ."

Elrod flushed, suppressing a panic reaction. Could she know? Did she suspect? If he were caught giving alcohol to Flankspeed it could mean the end of his job. But could he face the prospect of losing the only drinking buddy he'd ever really gotten close to?

She must have misinterpreted his look of consternation. She held up a hand. "Now, now, I know you're not a handler or trainer or scientist. I just thought you might have observed something. Dissension in the ranks could be indicative of some kind of territorial fight; perhaps some young bull is challenging Flankspeed for a cow or for the leader's role. I don't know. Do you?"

Elrod fought to keep his composure. He managed a sickly grin. "Want me to ask him?"

"Sure, Elrod, sure. You don't have any more of an idea what's going on than the rest of us, do you?"

Elrod found it difficult to lie. It was always awkward, so he usually didn't. However, in his job he was sort of a bureaucrat and had learned how to use weasel-words in official statements and letters. "If I did have the answer, I'd expect to get a scientist's pay scale and perks, Doc. Are you willing to provide me with same?"

She made a face at him.

He pressed his advantage, turning the subject. "It occurs — to me," he said in his best professorial tones, "that the *juxtaposition* of me, a mere high school graduate, trying to solve this problem that's baffled a whole staff of highly educated scientists, would be . . ."

Doc's mouth curved briefly into a wry smile before she stuck out her tongue at him and walked out.

But the reality of what was happening bore down on him like the assault of a tension headache. The pressure was on. The equation was changing. Would his and Flankspeed's nightly drinking parties be endangered? And if they were, so what?

That was the question he'd been dodging for days. So what? Beyond the comfort of their shared and secret ritual and a strange but deep companionship, he was feeling a compulsion to continue to find out more about the strange visions emanating from the dolphin. He had a sense that they were leading somewhere. And that he was being led for a reason, though he couldn't imagine what that reason was. He found himself caught up in something he could not articulate even to himself, nor did he know if he wanted to articulate it, he told himself. If you don't want to know the answer to the question, don't ask that question.

Elrod tried the scientific method. That night, he refused to give Flankspeed any beer or booze. The creature begged him as much as an animal could be said to do such a thing. The squeaking pleadings got to Elrod. But he stuck with his plan. He went swimming with the dolphin, but Flankspeed simply ignored him.

Elrod got no visions: no clear images, no fuzzy images. Nothing. The trade-off was clear. Flankspeed had only one thing to sell — the visions. And alcohol was the only currency he'd accept.

Elrod's compulsion to continue grew with his perplexity and his ineffectual gestures toward breaking off. A raging curiosity had replaced his initial reluctance to be a part of the bizarre transaction with the dolphin. Now he knew full well that for the first time in his life he was participating in something absolutely unique. There was a secret pleasure in circumventing his mother and the Tambays, even science and education. He, Elrod Truman, was involved in something maybe monumental.

And, he realized, this relationship was strangely intimate. Elrod deeply *liked* Flankspeed, even though the dolphin seemed to have a terribly fatalistic outlook upon life. Elrod enjoyed the nightly encounters more than he could say. He had a buddy, a friend. His occasional hangovers reminded him that he was in a dangerous cycle, one he might not be able to break free from. But the visions had some sort of narcotic effect on him and he didn't want to break free. He didn't think he was a slave to the alcohol, but he admitted he was a slave to the strange visions. And he knew the only way they would continue was if he provided the dolphin with the alcohol demanded. And, of course, he had to drink himself.

Which led him to admit to himself that it was probably wrong to feed a dolphin alcohol, but what the hell? Flankspeed was old enough (twenty? twenty-five?) and smart enough to know what he wanted. That is, Elrod decided that he was not *morally* in error to give a fellow being what that being craved.

And Elrod was being paid, so well, for doing so.

So be it.

That night, Elrod set up Flankspeed's own drinking apparatus. He got an empty gallon plastic jug and hung it from a tripod they used sometimes to mount cameras. At the mouth of the bottle he inserted a rubber stopper and some surgical tubing, which he ran to a demand valve. He'd gotten the idea from watching a baby in the crowd that day, sucking on her bottle. From the demand valve, he ran more tubing to a rubber bulb. He filled the container with beer and squeezed the bulb. The bulb filled with beer and the action squirted the liquid through the airhole of the bulb. Just to be sure, he enlarged the airhole.

Flankspeed figured out the contraption immediately. The bulb rested in his throat where his jaw action would squeeze the thing. When he wanted a drink, he simply worked his jaws and squirted beer down his throat.

Before long, it became habit that when Flankspeed finished a gallon, he would leave. Elrod noticed that he was arriving earlier and earlier for their evening binges. He'd swim impatiently in the bay outside the compound waiting for nightfall and Elrod. The other dolphins sometimes followed him in, but he'd run them off.

Elrod began feeding Flankspeed fish while they drank, afraid that the dolphin wasn't getting enough food. Sometimes Elrod brought out his portable quadraphonic disc machine and played old Bruce Springsteen and Elvis Presley music. When the two of them got really high, Elrod would lip-synch using a beer bottle for a mike and Flankspeed would dance on his fluke. Flankspeed seemed to like the Boss's "Jersey Girl" the best. Elrod thought maybe this was because of Bruce's vocal range and the building rhythm in the song.

One week Elrod experimented with different drinks for the dolphin each night. He tried bourbon and coke, gin and tonic, and then vodka and orange juice in Flankspeed's dispenser. He discovered that the dolphin's affinity for alcohol had increased, as had his tolerance. One hundred proof liquor was Flankspeed's preference. But he didn't seem too fond of manmade chasers such as Coke or tonic, nor did he like orange juice. Elrod checked with a marine biologist and discovered dolphins have no sense of smell and little, if any, sense of taste.

Finally, Elrod settled on the "dolphin dispenser drink": one part of the cheapest vodka mixed with four parts water. Personally, Elrod couldn't stomach the stuff, but Flankspeed seemed to like it.

Dr. Ambersson's concern grew as the dolphins' daily performances became weekly and then stopped altogether. She told Elrod she was arranging to bring in some trained dolphins from Sea World over near Orlando. "Our school here is almost totally dispersed. The scientists don't understand. A school that large was an anomaly in itself; now the dissolution of that school is worthy of study as well."

That plan worried Elrod. Permanent dolphin residents would invade his and Flankspeed's privacy.

Flankspeed consumed his gallon more quickly nowadays. In response, Elrod increased the strength of the mixture to three parts water and one part vodka, using one hundred proof vodka only. The change seemed to satisfy Flankspeed for a while.

The visions began to alter with the stronger blend. They had started to reflect a quiet desperation. The Wanderer continued wandering, clearer yet, and easier to recognize. Small clues told Elrod that the Wanderer was heading south. Perhaps not by design, but heading south nonetheless. He could tell because the Wanderer was on odd-numbered highways. Elrod knew that federal highways were even east-west and odd north-south, and as he wandered deeper down the odd-numbered roads the people he encountered were wearing lighter, scanter clothing. Also occasionally he would glimpse a sign or a run of auto license tags which suggested a location.

There was one constant thread: a drabness. Never a lot of color or life. Downtowns, underpasses. Rough accommodations — though through the visions Elrod wasn't generally privy to the personal information.

Trains and buses. Cheap booze for sustenance. Hunger sometimes, but blunted by the booze. Elrod didn't want to admit to any parallels, so he ignored the similarity between his current circumstances and the visions.

One day Elrod was surprised to notice orange groves in the visions. Florida. Then the recognizable front of the John Ringling Museum, right across the bay from Lido Key. A feeling of dread overcame Elrod. He was afraid of what he'd find out once the journey was complete.

The visions were often somewhat blurry now, a factor Elrod attributed to the constant drunkenness of the perspective character.

One day, the visions stopped.

"What the hell, Speedy?"

The dolphin fixed Elrod briefly with his eyes from his favorite resting place on Elrod's lap, then rolled himself over off the cement lip into the tank, drenching Elrod. Flankspeed raced through the water, circling the pool, swimming faster and faster. With their developed empathy, Elrod knew Flankspeed was working off psychic energy, gaining confidence to continue with some particularly bad part of the journey. Was it coming to an end? It had to be.

Flankspeed raced off at the same frenzied pace, out through the access panel, and Elrod didn't see him for two days. Elrod was getting worried, since the new trained dolphins were due any day. Sea World stock. Must be a profitable business, he reflected. Maybe he and Flankspeed could train other dolphins and sell them to places that needed them. Goddamn, he thought, that's slavery! Elrod knew he identified too much with the dolphin now; his reaction had just proven it.

It was on Saturday night that Flankspeed returned. Once again he nosed up on the lip of the tank and grinned at Elrod. Elrod stroked the scars on the dolphin's head. Then he prepared Flankspeed's mixture. The dolphin drank long and fast, finishing a quart of the vodka on his first draft.

Elrod poured himself a Tanqueray tonic. He had the process down pat now. A bottle of gin, ice in his cooler, a couple of bottles of Alta Springs sugar-free tonic. A short glass because he was a gulper.

He stretched out in the webbed lawn chair he'd brought along for the occasion and drank his first drink while Flankspeed was slaking his initial thirst.

The dolphin lolled alongside him on the concrete. Elrod worried that there might be some sort of physiological problem indicated by the dolphin's inclination to remain so long out of water. He used a hose that was connected to the pump house and occasionally hosed Flankspeed down, keeping the dolphin's skin moist. But he knew dolphins were designed for the sea; the water supported them so they didn't need a body fit for land. Would the dolphin's weight on land crush some sensitive organ? Elrod didn't know, but he guessed Flankspeed wouldn't do what he was doing if he were terribly uncomfortable.

As Elrod contemplated these scientific matters and gulped his gin, the visions hit him again.

Night. Where? There. Downtown Sarasota, no doubt about it. Park bench, bottle upended in front of eyes, level decreasing. Bottle finished. Aimless wandering for some obscure purpose. A place to sleep? Dozing. A face, an actual face, right there in the image. Hand holds out bottle. "His" hand accepting, tilting. Deep pulls from the bottle.

The face was somehow familiar, but the growing energy of the visions blurred that fact to Elrod, who was having trouble separating himself from the Wanderer.

World going dark. Awakening, strange. JesusohmigodIknewit. Strange room. Same man. Trolley with an arm and a giant sling. Big mutherfuckin' fish in sling. Sling settles fish into coffinlike tank next to Wanderer's/Elrod's resting place. Dolphin flipper wags listlessly. Long goddamn needle slides into dolphin. Several times in body, twice behind eyes. Dolphin turns quiet, immobile in small tank. Inevitability of the thing overwhelms Elrod/Wanderer. Like a surging wave. Electronic machine against dolphin's head. Lines drawn with some kind of marker. Dolphin frozen with horror. Man working feverishly. Incisions. Man consulting viewscreen of equipment as if it showed the inside of the dolphin's head. Man noticing

Wanderer/Elrod awake. Angrily moves toward him/them. Ohmi-godohmigodohmigodohsweetjesus — Mask slaps down. Creeping lethargy. Blackness. Awakening, Ohjesusdon'ttellmeIknewit — Pleasedon'tletitbe — All bleary, choking. Water. How the fuck do these goddamn fish breathe underwater? Move arms and legs, try to swim. Phantom pain. Limbs no longer working. Burst through to surface, giant intake. Hunger. Light. Air.

A man is standing above a small tank. The view is really weird, like the camera's squeezed but still recording. Hangover — terrible headache.

The wave crested and crashed and he was Flankspeed.

His head is a maze of confused memories, views. He is moved to the tank, the man observing all the time. He is gradually learning how to swim, feed, everything. Later, someone punches a wrong sequence and Wanderer/Flankspeed is able to move to another tank, and then out into the bay.

Fright.

Then realization: he is able to soar in the water. Wonderful power in body. Enjoyment. Later, strange mating, biology and body in control, need, unable to register disgust, orgasm negating revulsion. He is a slave to his body.

Time meaning nothing.

Eventually the plan emerges. Return with school to Sarasota Bay. Enter tanks. Do tricks. Earn food for these services. Introduce the barter system to dolphin life. Difficult to communicate as other dolphins do. Makes him odd. Human belligerence and cunning make him leader. Unconsciously communicates with others. Combination of body language, aura, snorting, whistling, clicking, underwater sounds. Plan fixed in mind, determined to carry out. Not worried about changing dolphins' habits forever. Visit the bay frequently, plan.

Then at last finds bad man alone in evening. Man's curiosity makes him open access. Man squats a way back from lip of tank, observing. Flankspeed grins, climbs on top of water, "walking" with frantic fluke activity. So absorbing to watch, no care taken.

Flankspeed at edge of tank grinning widely. Suddenly lunges at man, striking out at least one body length. Great, strong jaws close satisfyingly on man's head, severing it.

Almost chokes him. Slam to concrete, head expelled into next tank, sharks attack it voraciously. With powerful nose, push body to shark tank, flippers scraping concrete, a compulsion to do this, to wreak final vengeance.

"Jesus, Jesus, Jesus," Elrod whispered, tearing himself from the vision. He felt drained, as if he'd actually gone through the whole terrible ordeal. Well, he had, hadn't he?

He discovered he'd finished most of the bottle of Tanqueray. Flankspeed lay beside him, looking at him. Elrod couldn't read anything in the dolphin's expression. But he said "I understand" anyway, repeated it softly several times while they just lay there looking at each other.

Flankspeed's drink dispenser was empty and Elrod knew he had to refill it. He did so and the two of them drank together, silently for them, with no exchange of vision. Just a comfortable feeling between them. The barter was complete. No rock music this night.

But Elrod kept on thinking. The Wanderer had gone down down down. He looked at Flankspeed and thought about the dolphin's behavior lately. Flankspeed had gone down down down. Not without cause, Elrod amended. Dr. Wickett too had gone down down down, terribly, degradingly, rottenly down down down.

Elrod Truman resolved to go up up up. Why was he wasting time in dead-end jobs? Life was a one-time affair. Strive, reach out and touch someone, grab all the gusto, do something. Be someone special.

He looked down at Flankspeed. The dispenser was empty again and the dolphin was nudging the webbed lawn chair.

"You've had two quarts of vodka already, Speedy." The dolphin looked at him. "Or is it liters? I can never keep track of them damn metrics." Still the dolphin looked at him.

Realization hit Elrod and it felt immensely sad. He mixed another batch of the dolphin's drink, this time using a one to-one ratio. Meanwhile, he drank straight gin himself. Maybe Doc Ambersson could arrange for him to get a scholarship up there at FSU in Tallahassee. She was important enough to be able to do that or she wouldn't have this job. Elrod thought these things so he wouldn't have to think of the sadness to come, the other thoughts.

Elrod found himself crying silently when the dolphin, having emptied the dispenser, somehow propped his head on Elrod's knee. Elrod reached out and scratched the cicatrix of scars on the dolphin's head. He was weeping openly now.

The dolphin dropped his head to the concrete and wiggled ineffectively. Elrod helped the dolphin back into the pool. Flankspeed surfaced one time, looked at Elrod, and dove. Elrod saw the dolphin's shadow against the bottom of the channel near the access panel.

Elrod didn't close the panel that night. He sat in the lawn chair and drank vodka and water and wept and then was glad. It was finally over.

The next afternoon, somebody over on Longboat Key called, as somebody always does when there are "marine biology" things people don't know how to deal with. A dead dolphin. Did Mote Marine Lab want it?

Doc Ambersson recognized Flankspeed from the description. But she checked the screen. "It's Flankspeed all right." She and two other scientists took a pickup over the bridge and drove to the condominium where Flankspeed's body had washed up.

They brought the dolphin's body back to Mote. Later, Doc Ambersson told Elrod gently, "Poor thing drowned, Elrod. You know, dolphins get old, they have problems just like people. They drown just like people."

They commit suicide just like people, Elrod said to himself.

"Elrod?" she said, face dead serious. He raised his eyelids. "Elrod, I ran a chemical analysis, just like they do in autopsies on those old "Quincy" reruns you love to watch so much. A couple of the readings are passing strange."

"Oh?"

"I did a minor autopsy, also. It's not really my thing, you know. I was always a marine geologist, but administration is my strong suit and they sent me down here."

"Oh? "

"I stopped the autopsy when I got to the brain."

"Oh?"

"A dolphin the size of Flankspeed would have a brain weighing perhaps three and a half or closer to four pounds." Doc's eyes bored into Elrod's. "A one hundred and fifty pound man's brain weighs in the neighborhood of three pounds."

Elrod couldn't look at her any longer.

But Doc continued talking, standing there, looking between Elrod and the floor. "Dolphin laminar differentiation varies widely from the human brain — some use it as a measure of intelligence. An opposing argument is that the highly convoluted dolphin cortex and great surface area provide the intelligence. A lot of theories have been put forward. Elrod?"

He looked up at her.

"Elrod, I vomited, and then I burned Flankspeed's brain — or spliced brain. Whatever it was."

Elrod nodded approvingly. Good old Doc.

"Can you tell me about it?"

He wondered whether, if he didn't tell her, would she still help him get into the university. He was thinking in terms of marine biology, specializing in dolphin psychology. He suspected there were going to be some startling changes in that area. Plus he had a headstart and a special insight.

He felt drained, more than he had in his entire life.

"Not now," he said.

She nodded. Did she understand? She touched his shoulder with her hand. "Maybe one day soon?" A small amount of residual empathy passed between them.

"Maybe one day."

Don F. Briggs

Don F. Briggs retired from upper-level management of an international publishing corporation in 1977 and returned to writing. He has been a newspaper reporter, the managing editor of one weekly newspaper, and copublisher of another, and a public relations consultant. A member of the Science Fiction Writers of America since 1966, he has written and edited two book-length biographies as well as numerous short stories and articles. Briggs and his wife, Gerre, live in St. Petersburg Beach. They have two married daughters and five grandchildren. He is currently completing a novel and some shorter fiction.

I chose St. Petersburg and Pinellas County as the setting for "Miss Molly and the Alien" because of the availability of boarding houses, fairgrounds, and major hotels with live entertainment, all essential to the story.

Having lived occasionally in a number of theatrical boarding houses during periods when my brother and I traveled with our parents on the road with various plays, I have a warm spot in my heart for boarding houses where show people congregate. I am certain that I had fondly in mind a number of the fine actors, actresses, and performers with whom I once shared many a roof and so many dog-eat-dog boarding house meals. Whether intentionally or not, my story is in a small way a tribute to the many interesting people — some good, some not so good, some successful, some not — that I recall from long ago.

MISS MOLLY AND THE ALIEN

by Don F. Briggs

1

It was 11:45 last night when Sommersett of Defense and someone who may have been Mrs. Sommersett came into the Starlight Roof of The Mansions luxury hotel on St. Pete Beach. I was sitting out the remaining quarter hour before our last show with the three other guys from my group when a well-padded hip brushed my arm on its way to the crowded dance floor.

I dabbed the Scotch off my costume and looked around for the owner of the hip, who turned out to be Sommersett. By then he was dancing with the bosomy blonde to the offerings of the fill-in combo. I hadn't seen him in more than sixteen years, after I got back from Nam, but I recognized him at once. I was tempted to get up and speak to him but thought better of it. There were already too many links with the past, and I figured it was better to let sleeping aliens lie.

Seeing him again reminded me that I was lucky to be where I was. As a headliner whose live performances could fill Madison Square Garden and whose recordings and videos were at the top of the charts, I was right where I'd wanted to be ever since I was knee-high to a heron. The others at our table were arguing about something, but I was no longer tuned in. I was back at Miss Molly's boarding house for entertainers in downtown St. Petersburg, Florida, where my acquaintance with the irrepressible Molly began.

It was a large house, a rambling four-storied blemish in a section of the city that had known better days. Miss Molly's place was like many others on the street, a drab weather-worn structure victimized by time and awaiting a major hurricane to put it mercifully out of existence. At least that was the way I remembered it, and also the way I first remembered its owner, Miss Molly, then my landlady and the bane of my existence. There were other memories of her, too — quite, quite different.

That boarding house may not have been paradise, but it was all

I could afford in those days. I had come to St. Pete shortly after getting out of the army and discovering that Jacksonville, Florida, didn't fully appreciate my talents. The Suncoast hadn't proved to be any more perceptive.

I said Miss Molly's was all I could afford, but in fact, Miss Molly's was more than I could afford. That was why Molly was in the process of throwing me out that afternoon when it all began. She had tossed one of my suitcases down the last flight of stairs, and I remember watching the second as it sailed out and down to land with a shattering crash on the lower landing. It tumbled end over end, almost to my feet. Miss Molly was small but wiry, agile, and remarkably formidable for her age. I'd tackled a few rough customers in Nam, but I didn't relish taking on this tough old woman. Besides, I never had the urge to test my martial arts, such as they were, on elderly women — unless of course they were trying to kill me, which actually had happened once.

I looked up at her helplessly. "Have a heart, Miss Molly," I said, realizing with disgust that there was an unaccustomed whine in my voice. "You know I don't have anyplace else to go." And that was a fact; I didn't. I knew that unless I could hang on there, I would have no choice but to swallow whatever pride I had left and go back to Jacksonville and a routine job on my father's charter fishing boat.

St. Petersburg had been my one hope, but the kind of job I was seeking had not materialized. My voice and routines appeared to be good enough for a few Gulf beach dives but little else. Still, though nearly broke, I wasn't quite ready to give up. If I had any chance of making a last-ditch stand it had to be there and then. There was another reason why I didn't want to leave: Alice. She had been living at Miss Molly's for only five weeks, but we were beginning to reach a most interesting understanding.

Miss Molly laughed. It was a dirty sort of laugh, and I knew that she was enjoying herself. "No place to go?" she asked, mocking my tone. "Well, well, well. And I suppose you would like the 'old witch' to extend more credit?"

I shuddered. I should never have allowed myself the pleasure of calling her that. From the foot of the stairs, I surveyed the woman who stood between me and a night's sleep in a bed, rather than on the streets. She was eighty-one, I'd heard, but she looked twice that age. If only half the rumors about her were true, she had packed enough living into those eight decades to fill a dozen lifetimes. She had had it all. A beautiful heiress with a scorn for money and love for men, she had quickly squandered her inheritance and without breaking stride had become a beautiful mistress with a scorn for men and a love for money. And in the end she had kept neither. She had never married nor had children. But she had lived (how she had lived!) wildly, extravagantly, uncontrollably — a leaping, soaring flame that had in time consumed even itself, leaving only this cinder.

Looking at her, I could scarcely reconcile that caricature with the portrait hanging in the living room. She must have been really something when the great Derriksen, Florida's premier portrait painter and later the world's, in what they said was a last labor of love just before he killed himself, had captured her on canvas. Now, some six decades later, she resembled something left over from a special effects studio specializing in horror flicks.

I probably would have felt guilty thinking that about anyone else, but not Miss Molly. She had scourged people all her life to satisfy her appetite for her own pleasure and others' misery. And now her malevolence was directed at me. But I knew she represented the only possibility of regaining the lost sanctuary of my room. She blocked the stairway as effectively as a Russian tank. It looked hopeless. That was the route I must travel if I were to sleep indoors that night. "Have a heart," I repeated.

She laughed again, reading the pleading in my tone. "Well, that's better. Singing a different tune now, aren't you, Buster?"

She knew how I hated being called Buster. I ran a shaking hand through my hair, feeling uncertain of myself, young and immature. She had a way of making me doubt my own ability. Maybe I just didn't want to be reminded that I was only Jeff MacNeil, a twenty-three-year-old failure between two-bit engagements, who couldn't quite make up his mind whether or not he actually had any talent.

"Old witch," she mumbled again.

"I said I was sorry about that. It just slipped out."

"Well, you can just slip out right along with it." She sat down at the head of the stairs, pulled a pint of vodka from her apron pocket, and upended it. Then she returned it, patted it affectionately, and waited.

I steadied my voice. "How about another week?"

"Not on your life, Buster. You haven't paid your last month's rent." Getting up, she started down the stairs.

"What are you going to do?" I must have outweighed her by fifty pounds, but nevertheless I retreated a step or two.

"Why, not a thing," she grinned toothlessly. "I'm just going to help you get your suitcases down to the sidewalk."

I picked up one of the bags. "You don't have to. I'll go."

"Well," she said, "isn't that nice?"

"But I'll have to get my instruments."

"Oh, did I forget to tell you? I'm keeping them."

"You are like hell! You've got no — "

"Just until you settle your bill, Buster, that's all. Don't get your privates hot. That is, if you have any worth considering."

"I'll be back for those instruments tomorrow," I snapped, "and they'd better be here. I could have paid you tonight if it weren't too late to cash my bond."

"What bond?"

"I tried to tell you, but you wouldn't listen. I've been saving it for an emergency, and I guess this is it. It's the last one."

The old woman's eyes glistened moistly in the semidarkness of the hallway. I could almost hear her thinking. "How much is it for, son?" she asked sweetly.

"The name's still Buster," I said, beginning to breathe easier. "And it's enough."

"But how much?"

"It'll pay my bill in full tomorrow, if that's what you want to know."

Okay," she said, making a quick gesture over her shoulder with her thumb. "You can stay."

"I'm not sure I want to anymore."

"Suit yourself."

"However," I added hastily, "since I'm already here, I'll go on up to my room." I picked up my other bag.

"Not your old room."

I turned, surprised, setting the suitcases back down. "Why not?"

"I'm giving you another room."

"But why?"

"Because your room is rented," she said. "You'll take the room on the top floor."

"You mean the attic room?"

"I said the room on the top floor," she repeated testily. "Do I have to draw you a diagram? It's a nice room."

"It's a garret."

"It's a nice room." Her tone was icy.

"I won't do it! What do you mean? My room isn't rented. It can't be."

"I rented it this morning."

I looked at her blankly. "Do you mean to say," I sputtered, "that you rented my room without even waiting to see whether or not I was going to pay the rent?"

"And why not? You couldn't pay it, could you?" She looked at me triumphantly.

"But I told you I'd pay you tomorrow."

"It was due today."

"And you rented my room this morning?"

She nodded.

"That's a fine thing!" I said. "Now what am I supposed to do?"

"I said you could have the room on the top floor."

"And if I don't take it?"

"Suit yourself." She shrugged her shoulders. "If you can do better someplace else, go ahead. I never stood in the way of a young man trying to get ahead."

I almost laughed at that. She had probably broken more men than all of the racks of the Inquisition.

"Well?" She stood with her hands on her bony hips.

"I'll take it." I picked up my bags for the second time and started up the stairs but stopped when a thought occurred to me. "You started this argument as an excuse to get me out of my room, didn't you?"

She laughed lustily. "Did I, Buster? But I didn't need an excuse. You didn't pay your rent."

Her laughter followed me up the stairwell as I carried my bags slowly to the room on the top floor. Then suddenly I was chuckling to myself. I hadn't lost that round entirely. At least she hadn't asked to see the bond.

2

That was how the alien happened to get my room. He moved in the next morning, although I didn't meet him until lunch. He certainly didn't look like an alien, or anything else spectacular for that matter. But that was how Miss Molly introduced him when she brought him into the dining room at mealtime. "Meet Rxll, folks," she said, "the man from — where did you say it was? He's an actual alien from a distant star."

"Arazenza," the stranger said quietly. "A planet near the center of our galaxy. Our suns are not visible from Earth."

"Did you get his name?" Miss Molly asked. "Rxll. Sounds like a drugstore." She laughed loudly.

Nobody else laughed. There was a momentary hush as everyone surveyed the stranger and the food on the table, trying to decide which afforded the greater attraction. It was no choice for me. The stew that day was an unsavory mess. I got up. "Hi!" I said, putting out my hand.

He was a big man, about six-three and probably in his late forties. "My name's Frank Whetlow," he said, winking and nodding his head in the direction of Miss Molly. "She's quite a character.

'I don't believe I've ever seen her in such a good humor," I said, to have something to say.

"Pay no attention to that alien stuff," he said. "That's my business. I'm putting on a show at the Pinellas County Fair here. Do it all over the country."

"Oh — " I couldn't think of anything else to say.

"A guy's got to eat," he added apologetically.

"Don't apologize to me," I said. "I'm barely eating, myself. If I got a chance at a job as a singing busboy, I'd probably grab it."

"You're a singer, then?"

I felt the redness gathering about my ears. "I work at it," I said. "Nobody else seems to think so."

He closed his eyes a little. "I'd like to hear you sing sometime." I could tell that he meant it, and it made me feel good.

Then the rest of them were around us, pumping his hand and asking him questions. They were pretty good about that at Miss Molly's, making a stranger feel at home. I stepped back out of the way. Miss Molly was beaming, and I remember thinking that there was some life in the old girl yet. Obviously, Whetlow had made a hit with her. With his height and all, he was a very distinguished-looking fellow. It puzzled me how a guy like that could wind up as a carnie working county fairs. More puzzling was how in certain lights his skin was a funny color, sort of bronzed, not tanned but more like actually bronzed, and when he stood up straight he had a strange stance, almost as if he mistrusted Earth's gravity. But there the resemblance to any imagined alien ended.

3

After lunch and a brief conversation with Whetlow, I left for an audition. I didn't get the job, but the effort did take most of the day. Consequently, I didn't see either Miss Molly or Whetlow again until dinner. I had met with one small success that day, however. I had been able to pawn my watch and a few other things and had enough money by the time I returned to ensure my continued residence at Miss Molly's, at least for another week or two.

Miss Molly was her insulting self once more. The novelty of a new boarder disappeared fast at her place. As far as Whetlow was concerned, I had liked him from the beginning. From our brief discussion at dinner, I gathered he was well-read and far more intelligent than the run-of-the-mill transients who passed through the boarding house, except Alice of course, with whom much of my free time was spent.

I was surprised along about the third evening after Whetlow arrived when he asked me if I'd like to go to the fair with him and catch his show. I agreed, having suddenly found myself with nothing to do. Alice had informed me that she already had a date for that evening and in the future I would have to get my bid in earlier. It was just curiosity, I guess, that prompted me to go.

His performance at the Largo fairgrounds was about what he'd led me to expect, really cheap science fiction stuff. The saucer inside the tent was a ludicrous monstrosity. He gave four performances, like he did every night. The audiences were small and generally derisive about the show except for two special stunts, but everyone seemed to go away satisfied and probably feeling a bit superior. After his last performance, Whetlow and I walked for a while under the stars talking about a number of things, but mostly about his act and how he might be able to improve it. "Anything," he told me laughingly, "would be an improvement."

"Dim the lights more," I suggested, "and replace that saucer with something that looks halfway real."

"I thought of that," he said, "but it all costs money."

"Anyway, your monologue's not bad. Where'd you get the idea for that stuff?"

"I've studied a little astronomy and read a ton of science fiction."

"And those stars of yours and this planet Arazenza?"

His voice was soft. "A binary and planet I once dreamed about. I like to think of Arazenza as the center of a small, peace-loving federation of planets."

"So I gathered. Tell me, how do you pull that levitation stunt? And the vanishing act? Wires? Mirrors?"

"Trade secret," he said. "I used to understudy a pretty good magician. While I'm here on the Suncoast, I'm teaching a weekly course at the University of South Florida over in Tampa. Once in a while, I instruct a class at the St. Pete campus. In neither case, however, do I demonstrate the routines that require our advanced technology. That would be giving too much away."

"You bet!" I glanced at a clock in a store window. "Getting late," I said, "and we're a long way from home. Anyway, I'd leave that part in and try to add other magic stunts if you can. That was the only part the customers really seemed to go for." I hesitated. "Listen to me!" I said. "I can't even get a job. Who am I to give advice?"

The alien smiled. "Let's grab a cab, okay? And after the boring evening I've given you, I'll pay."

"Sounds good," I said, "if I can buy us a nightcap first." He nodded and we headed toward the nearest bar.

We talked about a lot of things over that drink and in the cab on the way hack to Miss Molly's, mostly about me, I'm afraid. I told him about my last audition, which was still sticking in my craw. The manager I'd sung for, a bald little man, had not been very polite. "Not too bad," he'd said, "but not commercial. You're not good enough to sing straight and not dramatic enough, or if you prefer, not far-out enough, to sustain interest. No pizazz! You need a group — or a gimmick. Probably both. And better material." He'd paused, and my heart had sunk into my shoes when he added, "On second thought, maybe you ought to try driving a truck or parking cars for a while — at least until you can put together something good." Reading my disappointment, he'd said, "Anyway, you wouldn't starve."

Frank listened sympathetically. "You'll be a singer yet," he said. "I'm sure of it."

4

The bed felt good as I settled into it a half-hour later. Another day wasted, I thought. I got up again and opened the window. The attic room had two advantages: free ventilation and an excellent view of the top of a palm tree. I crawled back between the sheets.

At least I had a bed. Maybe tomorrow would be my lucky day. I was just dozing off when I heard a gentle rapping on my door. At first I thought I was mistaken, but the tapping was quickly repeated. Cursing quietly under my breath, I opened the door. It was Whetlow. He was still fully dressed and looked worried.

"I need your help," he whispered huskily.

"Come in." I switched on the light. "What's up?"

"Something is missing from my room."

"Oh, I'm sorry. Is it something important?"

"Very."

I sat down on the edge of the bed and watched him pace up and down the length of the room. "Do you want to tell me about it?"

"I can't," he said, looking at me with a sort of helpless expression. I felt sorry for him.

"Then I don't see how I can help."

He stopped pacing. "You're right," he said. "I've got to tell you part of it at least. How are you at keeping secrets?"

"Try me."

"The thing that's missing could be very dangerous if it is misused," he said. "I've got to find it."

"What does it look like?"

"Like a ring," he said. "But it's not."

"Was the room locked?"

He nodded.

"Does it look valuable — this ring, I mean?"

"It might," he said thoughtfully, "to someone who didn't know what it really was."

"I think I know where we can find it."

"Where?"

"Miss Molly's room. She has a master key. Does the cleaning herself, such as it is, since she's too cheap to hire a maid. She's crazy about jewelry and must have seen it when she was cleaning your room." I hesitated. "On second thought," I said, "why don't we just wait until tomorrow?"

He shook his head. "Tomorrow may be too late. Already it may be too late. It depends on how long she's had it."

"All right," I said. "I'm game if you are."

"No," he said. "There's no reason for you to become further involved."

"Forget it, man!" I snorted. "Do you think I could sleep now? Besides, if we're mistaken about Miss Molly's having your whatever it is, it may take two of us to control the old girl when we break in on her at this time of night. She's ancient and tiny, but don't let that fool you. She may be toothless, but she has plenty of claws. Even an old tigress is still a lot of cat."

5

I don't know what I expected to find when the light finally came on under her door and then the door swung open in response to our repeated knocking, but it was certainly not what we found. I stared in disbelief, but there she was. This is where you're going to doubt me anyhow, so I might as well give it to you straight.

The woman who stood blinking in the doorway was not the Miss Molly I knew, except as a painting on the living room wall. She was radiantly lovely, surely not more than twenty-two years old. Her long auburn hair fell in gentle waves, breaking against the creamy whiteness of her throat and shoulders. All I could think of in that first moment was that she was what talent scouts have always searched for and never quite found.

I was dazzled by her beauty and, in the same instant, overcome with the provocative nature of that beauty. Her face was perfect and yet mischievous, her nose just saucy enough, her mouth ripe, her teeth flashing. And her eyes. What half-hidden invitations and unspoken messages lurked in those indescribable violet eyes! Her figure was hidden beneath a loose white garment that made her look like an angel in an old-fashioned nightgown.

As she put her hands on her hips, I could see for an instant the outline of her perfect breasts against the fabric. Her eyes flashed, and I knew that anger was building up in them.

I could hear Whetlow's voice next to me saying, "I was afraid of this. In another hour or two we'd have been altogether too late."

Even then I didn't get it. I started to stammer something about not knowing that Miss Molly had relatives visiting her, when she turned those violet eyes on me and said, "What in the devil are you talking about, Buster?"

I clutched at Whetlow for support. Something was going clang in my head, and I felt very sick all of a sudden. Somewhere in the background I could hear him saying, "If we may come in for a moment or two, Miss Molly, we'll discuss this."

But Molly wasn't listening. The look of anger on her beautiful face had faded and been replaced by an expression of shocked amazement which must have matched my own. "My voice!" she said. "What's wrong with my voice?"

"Not a thing," I said huskily.

Then she was gone away from the door, back into the room. We followed her. She was standing before the full-length mirror, barefoot, and I could hear her saying in a small voice, "Oh. Oh. Oh." She seemed oblivious to our presence as she ran her hands through her hair and along arms that had not been that slim for half a century. "I'm young again!" she cried. Then, in a cascade of white she divested herself of the nightgown and stood naked and shameless before the mirror, her gaze riveted upon her slender figure.

I felt my face growing crimson. I'd seen naked women before, but never a goddess. Her expression was enraptured. I glanced at Whetlow and saw that his bronzed face was growing whiter even as mine grew more red. Picking up her robe which she must have thrown over a chair earlier, I slipped it over her bare, white shoulders. She didn't struggle as I turned her around and guided her to a chair; she sat there dumbly looking at us with big, searching eyes.

"Well," I said to Whetlow, "I think now you're going to have to explain."

He nodded gravely. "The fat's in the fire all right, to use one of your Earth expressions." He smiled.

"*Our* expressions!" I exclaimed.

"That's right. As you've probably guessed, I *am* from Arazenza, just like the spiel goes."

"Oh, brother," I said, "wake me up. I'll sleep this one off some other time."

He smiled, a bit sadly. "I wish I could."

"But it's unbelievable!"

"Not as unbelievable as if there were not life out there. In a universe teeming with every variety of life, a planet like the one I come from would be something of a curiosity only if it bore no life at all."

"But what about her? What happened? How long will it last?"

"What?" He looked at Miss Molly. "Oh, I see what you mean." He sighed. "It's permanent, or at least as permanent as youth ever is." He reached out and took her hand. She was still too dazed to resist as he removed something that looked like a ring from her finger and stuffed it into his pocket. "She'll grow old again just like anyone else."

"No, I won't!" Molly stood up. "Not like anybody else."

I couldn't take my eyes off her.

"Sit down," Whetlow said. "We might as well discuss this now. We're in this thing together."

"Can you make me old again?" she asked.

"No," he said, "not physically. But in every other respect you're no younger than you were a few hours ago."

She seemed relieved. "Well," she said, a smile illuminating her face, "I feel young." She threw her head back and laughed, a beautiful throaty laugh that made my scalp tingle. "And look at Buster, here." She pointed to me. "He thinks I'm young, too, don't you, Buster?"

Her juvenescence hadn't robbed her of the power to make me feel inferior. I concentrated on Whetlow. "What was that thing anyhow?"

"It's nothing, " he said modestly. "In my world we use it to keep ourselves young. Doesn't work indefinitely, of course, but it does prolong life by rejuvenating worn-out tissue."

"But what's it all about? Why are you here?"

He smiled. "That's a long story, but we've been on Earth for a long time as observers. In a way, I guess you might say I'm a caretaker. We sort of look after things. Unlike yours, our civilization is not warlike. One of the things we try to do here is prevent wars and help your civilization develop to the point where it will be ready to receive us as friends."

Well, I'll be damned! What'll happen now when everyone knows Earth's been visited by an alien?"

'That's the problem." He looked downcast. "We'll probably be withdrawn. Earth's people aren't ready to accept us yet."

"I'm sorry," I said.

"I am, too, especially for your people. It has only been the work of the caretakers that has prevented the outbreak of World War III at least a dozen times during the past four decades. With the weapons you've already stockpiled, another war would set Earth's civilization back ten thousand years — if indeed it survived at all."

"Drivel!" Miss Molly said.

We turned to her. "What was that?" the alien asked.

She stood with her hands on her hips. "I said that it was drivel. If you play your cards right, there's no problem at all."

"What are you talking about?" Whetlow looked puzzled.

Who has to know about it?" she said. "Just the three of us know so far — you, me — " she jerked a thumb in my direction — "and Buster here."

The light began to dawn for both of us. "Yes," Whetlow said, "we could do that."

"But how would we explain —?" I began.

"I can pretend to be my grandniece or somebody. We could just say the old witch" — she looked meaningfully at me — "went away for a while. Later on, we could say she'd finally bought the farm and was being buried up North."

"It could work," I told Whetlow excitedly.

Hope had returned to him. "Sure," he exclaimed. "What's to stop us?"

Miss Molly had walked back a few paces and stood teetering on the balls of her bare feet, her hands on her provocative hips. She was smiling. "That's right," she said. "There's only one thing that can stop us."

"And what's that?" I asked.

"Me." And with that, she began to laugh, that same dirty laugh she had always had since I'd known her, only it sounded a lot younger now.

Uh-oh, I thought. Here it comes, and indeed it did. She didn't want much to keep her mouth shut about the incident: only five million dollars a year for life. There was nothing smalltime about Miss Molly. I was only just beginning to realize that. She had first extended to Whetlow the solution to his problem and then thrown up a barrier that kept him from reaching it.

"Blackmail?" Whetlow asked coldly.

And Miss Molly just smiled prettily at him and said, "Of course."

Well, that was the beginning of it. The alien twisted and wheedled and coaxed and cajoled, but in the end, all she did was raise the price to seven million a year and demand that she also be given a "ring" for herself. In vain I pointed out that if the caretakers withdrew it might mean the end of our civilization.

"Don't be an ass!" she told me. "They're not here for their health — or ours either. Everyone has an ax to grind."

Whetlow denied that there was any ulterior motive, but he was finally forced to agree to contact his Federation to determine whether or not Molly's demands would be met.

At that, she yawned. "Well, don't wait too long," she said. "I may up the ante."

6

By the next morning, I had been prepared to find that it was all a dream, but it hadn't been, and it wasn't a dream that sat across the living room from me that afternoon either. It was a vision. The rejuvenated Miss Molly had done some shopping and looked stunning in a cute little suit.

Everyone had accepted her as Polly, Miss Molly's grandniece, and had taken her to heart. Especially the men. But most of the women seemed to like her, too, as though they thought some of her beauty might rub off on them. Only Alice was reserved. I caught her casting appraising glances at Miss Molly from beneath long lashes. I wasn't surprised. Alice was the only young woman in the group, and until now she had been considered pretty much the belle of the parlor.

"It's surprising," Alice was saying, "that we haven't heard Miss Molly speak of you."

"I'm not sure that my great-aunt approves of me," Miss Molly purred. "She's led such a sheltered life, so I understand — " She went on pouring tea while the boarders exchanged covert glances.

Whetlow was sitting quietly in the corner. I motioned to him, and he followed me outside. "Did you get in touch with the Federation yet?" I asked.

"The conditions won't be right until tonight. I'll use the ship transmitter."

"Oh, you have a ship?"

He glanced sharply at me and then apparently decided that I knew so much already that I might as well know the rest. "Just a small one. A scout. At the fairgrounds. It's the 'monstrosity,' I believe you called it, which you criticized so constructively."

"I feel sort of silly about that."

His lips twisted into a smile. "Don't. You should hear some of my people who have never visited your planet describe an airplane or a submarine."

"When will you try to make contact?"

He glanced at his watch. "A few hours yet. Want to come along?"

Of course I did. I had been set down right in the middle of the biggest adventure of my life and didn't intend to miss a minute of it.

As we passed the open living room door on our way out, I heard Alice's voice. "Twenty-two you say? Why, dear, I would have sworn you were older."

"You'd be surprised," said Miss Molly.

7

Frank and I spent the remainder of the day talking about everything under two suns — his, not ours. By showtime, I felt I knew the guy pretty well. What's more, I trusted him fully. I watched his four performances again with renewed interest generated by a vastly different perspective. After the last of the cash customers had departed, he took me inside the saucer.

Whetlow set to work immediately. The interior of the ship was small and unprepossessing. In fact, I was disappointed. Had I not already experienced the miraculous occurrence of the preceding evening, I would have still doubted the authenticity of the tiny craft.

Whetlow draped his frame over a type of bucket seat and stroked a few levers on the control board in front of him. No lights flashed. No sound traveled up the scale from the lower register to almost supersonic wailing as it did in low-budget science fiction movies of that day. But a voice came out of the air just over our heads and said, "Ready here," and with that Whetlow began to tell what had happened. He told the full story, not concealing anything. At any moment, I expected a stinging reprimand to come sizzling out of wherever the voice was coming from. But if he was to be chastized for blundering, apparently that would be reserved for a later date.

When he had finished with his story, he asked simply, "What should I do next?"

"Do you think she will he silent if you pay her off? Money is the least of our concerns."

"Yes, but only for a while. She'll come back for more if she needs it."

"Will not this sudden wealth arouse suspicions?

"That is a risk we shall have to take. It may, but she is so eccentric it would probably go unnoticed. But what about the life giver? She demands one for herself."

"Impossible. You must talk her out of it."

"And if I can't?"

"You have no choice. Her fingerprints are the same now as they were when she was an old woman in appearance. With her past, the prints are undoubtedly on file with the police. She has definite proof of her story. If she is believed, all of our plans will be disrupted. If you cannot dissuade her, you must remove her."

"Hey, now," I interrupted. "I'm not going to get mixed up in — "

Whetlow flashed a smile in my direction. "My young friend is alarmed."

"We kill nothing," the voice said. It sounded sincere.

"Okay, then." I relaxed.

"Our friend can be trusted," Whetlow continued. "He realizes what we are trying to accomplish and how much depends upon our success."

"Good."

There was silence.

Whetlow got up.

"Where will you get the money she asked for?" I inquired.

"We have billions in every form of Earth currency. We long since recognized the value of money in dealing in human relations. Making the payment will be no problem. What concerns me is whether or not she will settle for wealth alone. She's been old once. She may regard the life giver portion of her terms as more important."

And so it proved to be when we met Miss Molly that evening in her bedroom after the rest of the house had retired. Whetlow had told her she could have the money but not the "ring."

She stalked up and down in the big room, her dress swishing against the furniture, her hips swaying. "Well, we'll see about that."

"There is nothing more I can do."

"Well, I can. I can go to the government. I read in tonight's paper where a certain Phillip Sommersett of the Defense Department is here, over on St. Pete Beach. He's staying at The Mansions. Suppose I go to him and tell him what I know?"

"He'll never believe you."

"He's a man." She smiled provocatively. "He'll believe *anything* I tell him."

Whetlow sighed. "I suppose you're right."

"Besides, I have proof. Right here." She had thought of it, too. She held up her two small hands. "Ten witnesses, any one of which can prove my case."

"But what do you hope to gain by this?" I asked her. "All they have to do is go away, and then how would you ever get your precious ring?"

She laughed loudly. "Listen to Buster! He still believes your fairy-tale." She jabbed a forefinger at Whetlow. "You can't afford to leave. I don't know why yet, but I'll find out. You'll meet my terms. Other-wise the United States government will meet you. They'll pay my price and more to get you into custody, I can assure you."

"I've told you the truth," the alien said. "But perhaps I have been too naive in dealing with you." He reflected a moment. "Yes, I believe I have."

"What do you mean?" she asked.

Whetlow looked at me. "Do you mind leaving us?"

I was surprised, and a little hurt. "All right," I said.

"Thank you," he said. "I think Molly and I can reach a better understanding if we talk this out man to woman, so to speak."

I stepped out into the hallway, closing the door quietly behind me.

"Well!" said Alice, pausing on her way to the bathroom with her towel draped over her arm and her toothbrush clutched tightly in her hand. "What a pleasant surprise!"

"I was just — I was only — " I began.

"I can imagine," she said as she swept past.

8

After breakfast the following morning, Whetlow took me aside. "I'm afraid I'll have to remove her after all."

"Oh?" I had hoped that he would be able to persuade her.

He shook his head gloomily. "She plays for keeps."

"Where will you take her?"

"Arazenza, of course."

I hesitated a moment before asking, "What happened last night?"

He looked at the ceiling. "When?"

"You know when."

"Nothing," he said. "She's a very beautiful woman." He smiled at me, but that was all he would say on the subject.

"When do you plan to take her away?" I asked him at last.

"Tonight. After she retires. We can't risk waiting too long. Will you help me?"

"You can count on it," I said.

I spent a good part of the day trying to explain to Alice. But since there were far more things that I could not tell her than things that I could, my efforts in that direction were wholly unsuccessful. In the end I succeeded only in getting my face slapped, which hurt my pride as much as anything. Although I was not yet certain that I was in love with Alice, I still thought enough of her not to want her to think that I'd spent the night being entertained by Polly in Miss Molly's bedroom.

After Alice had stamped off, a voice behind me said, "You don't do any better at singing love's sweet song than any of your pop junk, do you, Buster?" I didn't have to turn around to know who it was. Molly had been eavesdropping.

"I get by."

"You could take a few lessons from your friend, the caretaker. He has the technique but is unwilling to pay the price."

"What do you mean?" I said, coloring.

"Not a thing." She smiled invitingly. "But I've had an idea all along that he could take care of things just fine." She looked more pleased with herself than I had ever seen her before.

She walked off, leaving me speculating.

9

I awoke to the sound of pounding on my door. It was very loud. "Come in!" I shouted.

The door opened and closed, but nobody came in. I sat up in bed abruptly, my eyes staring, hackles rising. "It's me," Whetlow's voice said close beside me.

"Where?"

"Right here." The springs creaked as something heavy sat down on the bed. "I'm wearing space garb," he explained. "Naturally, I can't be seen looking like this."

"You're telling me!"

A laugh came out of the air. "I mean I shouldn't be seen."

"How do you do it?" I asked, still searching the air for even a hint of his presence. Between me and the far wall I could see nothing but emptiness.

"It's nothing really. Just a method of diverting light around an object. Very simple when you know how."

"Yeah?"

"Anyway, it works."

"What does it?"

A tube appeared magically and dropped to the bed. I picked it up. It looked like a pocket penlight.

"We try to disguise everything as something that will appear natural to Earth's inhabitants. It is the unusual that attracts attention." Something took the tube out of my hand and it disappeared once more. "Are you ready?"

"In a minute." While I dressed, we talked. "You aren't planning to whisk me off, too, are you?" I asked.

"No," he answered immediately. "We don't think that's necessary. In the first place, we believe that your aims are the same as our own: to keep your planet safe. And even if you should try to give away our secret, no one would believe you without proof. In fact, after we've gone, we're not even going to ask you to keep it a secret."

"Will you be back?"

"Perhaps some day, though probably not in your generation, and not here. But don't worry, there will be others here always, on the job and ready to do what's necessary to help keep your people moving in the right direction."

We went out together, but visibly there was only one of us. Downstairs, I rapped softly on Miss Molly's door. There was no answer. "Knock again," the alien whispered close by my ear. I did, but still there was no reply. "Try the door." The knob twisted in my hand and we went in. As I closed it behind me, I caught a glimpse of Alice's piquant features peering at me from her doorway almost directly across the hall. To her eyes I was alone and surreptitiously letting myself into Polly's room. It was too late to retreat. I closed the door.

"Come here," Whetlow said. Even though I couldn't see him, I could sense the distress in his voice. "She's gone."

"Where?"

"To see Sommersett."

On her mirror she had drawn her own profile with lipstick, and a good likeness it was, too. There was a hand also, fingers spread and thumb to nose. Underneath was a message: "Sorry, young man, we couldn't do business. A year or two with an alien lover might have been amusing. But business is business. Tell Buster I gave his worthless instruments to the Salvation Army as an act of charity. The sooner he's put out of his misery the better. Love, Polly."

"She gave away my instruments!" I said, stunned. "She gave them — "

But Whetlow wasn't really listening. "She called me a young man," he snorted. "I'm old enough to be her father."

That got my attention. "Older? You?"

"And then some." He groaned. "I guess this finishes us."

"Not yet," I told him. "Feel this ashtray. Still warm. She couldn't have had much of a head start." There was a half-filled bottle of vodka standing on the dresser. "If we're lucky, she drank that before she left. Could slow her down."

"Do you think we might be able to catch her before she gets to The Mansions?" Whetlow asked. There was renewed hope in his voice.

"Come on!" I cried. "What are we waiting for?"

10

We caught a taxi, and for the promise of an extra twenty dollars (supplied to me by Whetlow) succeeded in getting probably one of the speediest rides through St. Pete ever recorded. Shortly after we got under way, I was certain that the driver of the cab was convinced that I was slightly insane. Several times in the excitement of the chase, I made remarks to Whetlow who was, of course, invisible, and once, he answered. The driver turned halfway around in his seat on that one, but thought better of it when as a result he almost piled up the taxi at the next intersection. Even at that hour, the traffic was more noticeably congested once we hit First Avenue North and headed toward the beach.

"This ought to help," whispered Whetlow, and another penlight appeared miraculously in midair. He sprayed the beam quickly over the entire cab. I didn't notice anything at first, until I glanced out the window. A few late-night pedestrians we passed were frozen in midstride. Automobiles were halted on and off the avenue. As we flashed by a small section of park, I caught a glimpse of a flock of sea birds frightened into flight by the sound of the speeding taxi, silhouetted against the moon and arrested on the wing, as it were, their pinions motionless, suspended a hundred feet above the tallest unwavering palms.

"What the hell!" yelled the cabbie hoarsely as he swerved the careening taxi in and out of the motionless traffic. He echoed my own thoughts exactly."

I've speeded up our time sense and the cab's, too," Whetlow whispered. "Tell him to tend to business."

I did, and the driver did, though neither one of us liked it.

"Can't keep it up too long," Whetlow said, and the penlight disappeared again as we left First and headed south on Pasadena toward St. Pete Beach. Everything outside suddenly returned to normal. Shortly after crossing the causeway, with brakes squealing, we drew up in front of The Mansions just in time to catch a glimpse of the trim figure of the new Miss Molly disappearing through the main lobby door.

"Quickly," I said, tossing the fare and the twenty-dollar bribe to the dazed driver. We darted out of the cab and into the lobby. But we were too late. The doors of one of the elevators were closing, and I saw Molly's face just for a moment before they snapped shut. In that instant I realized that she had recognized me. Now she was on guard.

"She saw us," I told Whetlow.

"You, at least," he said.

"Who are you talking to?" asked a bellman. He edged away from me when I didn't answer.

"She must have known the floor," I said, when we had put a little distance between ourselves and the inquisitive bellhop. The lobby was crowded. "That's going to set us back."

I crossed the spacious lobby to the main desk, the invisible alien close on my heels, or so I hoped. It only took a minute, plus another of Whetlow's twenties, to get Sommersett's suite number from the obliging clerk.

In the elevator, Whetlow sneezed. The other elevator riders darted apprehensive glances in my direction all the way up.

We burst into the corridor just in time to see Miss Molly round a corner. I caught a glimpse of a small automatic in her hand and a look of consternation on the face of a small man who was flattened up against one wall trying to make himself even smaller.

"She must have taken a wrong turn," said the alien. "We're in luck."

"Come on," I cried. The corridor beyond the bend was long and thickly carpeted. Our feet made soft thudding sounds as we ran swiftly down the long hall. Turning another corner, we caught sight of Miss Molly some fifty feet away. She was pounding on a door. An elderly man and woman were standing chatting together some ten feet further down the hall.

"Wait!" Whetlow tugged at my arm. I stopped, breathing hard. "She's seen you," he whispered. Miss Molly was glaring at me and hammering frantically at the door. She raised the automatic. "I can paralyze her temporarily," he said. "It won't hurt her. Then we can stroll down there and pick her up, if somebody doesn't answer that door first."

"Hurry," I said. "She can't see you. I'm the one she's going to shoot."

Another tube appeared magically and pointed in her direction. A pencil ray of light emanated from it. I'd expected to see her freeze, but instead a shot whined down the corridor, and she continued pounding on the door even more desperately. There was only one difference. Now she wasn't wearing any clothes.

"Good heavens!" the alien said.

"What happened?"

"I got the wrong tube. That's the invisibility ray."

"But I can still see her."

"The range was too long. It just permeated the garments she was wearing. The effect was transmitted to all parts of the material through its molecular structure."

Just then the door opened, and Miss Molly dashed inside. Except for us the corridor was deserted, the old lady having dragged the old gentleman by the lapels into their room when the shooting began and Molly's clothing disappeared.

"What do we do now?"

"Go on with it, I suppose. She won't dare use the gun now and unless I miss my guess, Sommersett has got his hands full with a naked lady dashing into his room. He's probably not going to be too inclined to listen to what she has to say — at least for a few moments."

We approached and without knocking turned the knob and stepped inside.

Whetlow had been right. We found the portly, balding Sommersett cowering in a big chair in front of a television set, a highball glass in his hand and an energetic Miss Molly standing beside him trying to make him understand. But it was obvious by the look in his eyes that he was not absorbing too much of the conversation.

She whirled as we entered and cut loose with as colorful a string of profanity as I had ever heard — even in Nam. All of it was directed toward me since she was unable to see Whetlow and was completely unaware of his presence. She finished with, "Unless you tell him what I'm saying is the truth, Buster, I'll claw you into mincemeat."

And I knew she would try it, too. I took a deep breath and steeled myself. "Now, now, calm down, young lady. What are you telling the nice man?" I was using my most soothing tone. "Are you telling him about your Lady Godiva act at the sanitarium or all about you,

Adam, and that big snake in the Garden of Eden?"

"Oh!" She stamped her foot, furiously.

"Here, put this on," I suggested, whipping off my jacket with a gallant flourish.

"I am fully dressed!" she said.

"So I noticed." I smiled at Sommersett, but his eyes were too busy elsewhere. "Tch, tch," I clucked, "and you've been drinking again. I see you've taken off *all* your clothes this time."

"Yes, indeed," said Sommersett. It was the first peep I had heard out of him.

"I think you'd better come with me," I told her. "It's a long trip back to the sanitarium and I forgot your nice comfy straitjacket. We'd better get started."

"I'm not leaving here until I've told Mr. Sommersett what I came to tell him," she said.

I took her by the arm and wrenched the gun from her hand. "Come on now, I'd hate to have to use force," I said, grabbing her invisible purse away from her. Then to Sommersett I explained, "We're trained for this. She's not the violent type, ordinarily — just a bit deluded. Thinks she sees men from outer space, sometimes even when she's doing her strip routine."

"Oh," said Sommersett. "What a pity. Really a beautiful girl, too." He looked her over again, as though to verify the accuracy of his appraisal.

Whetlow had taken hold of Miss Molly's other arm.

She shook it violently. "Let go of me!" she cried. But the alien held on.

"Now she probably thinks someone has grabbed her other arm," I told Sommersett. "Persecution complex."

"Tch, tch, tch," said the man from the Defense Department, echoing my earlier remark.

Just then the sleepy voice of a woman sounded from the next room. "Phillip, is that you in there? What is all that racket?"

"Great Scott!" Sommersett exploded into action. "That's my wife. I'll never be able to explain this. Take her out of here!"

Together, Whetlow and I managed to half-carry the shouting Miss Molly from the apartment. Getting her downstairs and out of the hotel was another problem. Once, she almost broke away, and for an agonizing moment I had visions of myself chasing a naked Miss Molly through the crowded lobby of the hotel with the security guards hot on my heels. But we finally managed to get her down to the basement in the freight elevator and out through the rear entrance.

11

It was as though fortune were truly on our side. I rented a car with more of Whetlow's money, and forty-five minutes later we were driving along toward the fairgrounds where the county fair was closed for the night. Miss Molly was trussed up like a huge sack of grapefruit in the back seat.

Whetlow and I were both exhausted by the time we got her aboard his ship.

"How will you get it away?" I asked Whetlow, who had become visible once he was safely inside the tent where his vehicle was housed.

"No one will see it," he told me. "Invisibility, remember?"

"Won't there be questions asked? About your disappearance, I mean?"

"None whatever. Things will be managed, just as it was arranged for me to have tonight free from the side show."

"What about Miss Molly's disappearance? Now that there's no Polly either — "

"That will be arranged, also. Many things are possible when you have unlimited capital."

"I imagine."

He put out his hand. "Well, I suppose this is farewell."

"Goodbye," I said, "and good luck. Or break a leg, if you prefer."

He looked toward the saucer where Miss Molly had been safely stowed away. Just before he'd put her aboard he had kissed her once, hard, then used the paralysis beam on her. He got it right this time.

It had seemed to me that she had stopped struggling even before the beam took effect.

"Thanks," he said to me. "I may need a bit of luck."

I rubbed a two-inch gash in my cheek that Miss Molly had torn with her fingernails. "I'm sure you will."

"But you know," he went on, "it may be fun at that. Your Earth's playwright Shakespeare once wrote about the taming of a shrew. Maybe it *can* be done." He smiled. "Might almost be worth it."

"I suspect others have tried it without much success," I told him. "I'm glad it's your job, not mine. Did you see the way she looked at me when we locked her in? She would have killed me."

"I'm sure she would have, gladly." Smiling, he reached out to shake my hand. "Well, I guess this is it. I can't thank you enough," he said. "You've done us a great service — and served your own planet, too, of course. The sad part of it is no one will ever know."

"I wasn't looking for any reward."

"But still," he said, "there's no reason why you shouldn't have one. You deserve it. Some money perhaps? Name the amount. A million? Two? Three?"

I gulped. "No, I couldn't," I said. "Not for what I did. Consider it a patriotic gesture — not only for the U.S. but for all of us."

He shrugged his shoulders. "If you're sure." He thought a moment. "But wait. At least I can do this much." He reached into his jacket and took out the "ring" I had seen before, what he had called the life giver. He twisted the top of it, then put it on. Reaching out he passed it across my neck. I felt a tingle in my throat! "Hold still," he said, "for just a moment." Then he massaged my neck with his strong fingers. He made a further adjustment to the life giver and then passed it over my entire body. "There," he said at last. "You said you needed a gimmick. Now you've got one."

"What did you do?"

"You'll find out," he said. "Just do what comes naturally."

12

There wasn't much I had to do after that. I watched the saucer become invisible and then felt the gentle whoosh as it lifted and left the tent through an opening that magically appeared overhead. I stepped outside and looked up at the stars, but there was nothing further to see. The scout ship, my alien friend Whetlow, and Miss Molly were gone from my life forever.

Everything was as Whetlow said it would be. Somehow his disappearance and that of Miss Molly and her grandniece Polly were hushed up. After a time, Alice forgave me. We were married. Oddly enough, when I later told her the full story, she believed every word of it. She was the only one who ever did. "But you know," she said, "right from the first I thought there was something peculiar about that girl."

"How right you were," I told her.

Sometimes I kick myself for not taking the money Whetlow offered me. Alice thinks I should have and says so sometimes when we quarrel, which isn't too often. We're happier than most couples, I believe. We have two children, Jeff junior, who is a preteen, and a daughter, Ann, just two years younger.

As far as the money is concerned, in the long run I guess I'm happier this way. I've made plenty and will make far more. And I've done it the way I always wanted to do it: performing. Because now, as a result of something my friend Whetlow did to my throat, I'm a pretty good singer. Hell, let's face it, I'm sensational — or at least different.

It's like the man said, you've got to have a voice and a gimmick. And there's no question that I do. Unless you've heard me sing, I can't describe my voice. It's unearthly — alien, you might say — with a range that astounds audiences. If you've ever heard any old records of Yma Sumac or seen the few movies she made, you'll get the idea. But her incredible vocal range was minor league compared to what I can do. Of course, my trick of levitating and then floating out high over the paying customers while I'm performing drives the audiences into frenzies. In short, our group, The Alien Planetbusters (it was Alice who dreamed up the name), is doing better than all right.

Someday, maybe in fifty or a hundred years, there will be real alien singers here on Earth. It all depends on how soon we here on Earth get ready to receive them. Until then, I've got the market cornered.

Now and then after the last show, I go for a walk before going home to Alice and the kids. Every so often, I stop and gaze up at the Milky Way, across the immense distances toward the blazing bright center of our galaxy, and I wonder how Miss Molly is doing there — Miss Molly, young in body and ageless in mind and spirit.

How long, I wonder, did it take her to subdue poor Arazenza and the Federation? Do the aliens regret they took her there? Is it still, as Whetlow said it was, a peaceful civilization?

Alice says that someday Miss Molly will come back, but I don't believe it. Maybe on Arazenza she's found what she was searching for throughout the first of her lifetimes. I think that on Earth Miss Molly never found a man who was a match for her. But out there maybe it will be different. Whetlow just might be the one, though heaven help him if he is. With Miss Molly, his life will be exciting and anything but peaceful. She's out there — somewhere — right now charging every moment of whatever she is doing with every fiber of her inextinguishable being.

Charles L. Fontenay

Charles L. Fontenay is a science fiction author who drifted away from the field after publishing several novels in the 1950s. After a distinguished career in newspaper journalism, which included many years at the *Nashville Tennessean* and, more recently, *USA Today*, Fontenay has returned to science fiction and now lives in St. Petersburg. His novels include *Twice Upon a Time*, *Rebels of the Red Planet*, and *The Day the Oceans Overflowed*. He has also published nonfiction, including a biography of Estes Kefauver.

"Savior" is based on the early consequences of the greenhouse effect, primarily a rise in sea level, which I extrapolate somewhat beyond more conservative estimates. It's one of my major themes currently, and the novella Fredeya *(recently published in Robert Adams'* Barbarians II *anthology) and other novels I am working on are also based on it.*

Florida's a good place for a story on early phenomena of the greenhouse effect, because it will feel the effects of a rise in sea level much more quickly and severely than other areas. The kind of chaos that will result from even a minor sea level rise, tacked onto our current problems such as drugs and gang violence, will change society radically, with those who don't flee inland necessarily barricading themselves and their possessions into fortified homes with armed guards to protect them. I used topographical maps from the U.S. Geological Survey to set my scene appropriately in St. Petersburg.

SAVIOR

by Charles L. Fontenay

The armored truck turned right some seven blocks from where 4th Street eased gently into Tampa Bay. The truck then threaded its way through a complex of deep potholes and pulled up left to the curb in front of a high brick wall that fronted at least a hundred feet on the street, only another half-block from the shoreline.

Jigger Penrod got out of the truck's front seat, shifting his submachine gun to a more comfortable position on his shoulder. In a moment Flower, a huge young man similarly armed, joined him from the back of the truck.

Jigger surveyed the length of the ten-foot-high wall. How far back from the street it extended at its ends he didn't know. He never had seen Fort Cardwell, as it was called, except when passing it on the street.

"Fishface," said Jigger to the driver, "hold it here till we come back out. If any druggies sneak up looking to sniggle stuff for selling, the slikes in back are to shoot to kill. That'll be that many less to deal with later."

He and Flower went to the iron-barred gate that provided entrance to the brick wall and after a moment Jigger found a lever that evidently rang a bell or gave some other signal inside. He pulled it down, twice. Shortly a metallic voice issued from behind the barred gate: "Who are you and what do you want here?"

"Jigger Penrod and Lieutenant France de Lilac of the Saints," replied Jigger. "I have an appointment with Miss Cardwell."

There was a brief silence, then the gates swung open. Jigger and Flower stepped into the cool, shadowy vestibule which extended some eight feet inward to another barred gate. They were the focus of half a dozen full-fledged machine guns, each manned by an alert gunner with hand on trigger.

"ID," said a youth standing beside the gate through which they had entered. Jigger and Flower produced cards and the young man studied them briefly.

Something scratched the surface of Jigger's mind, irritating. It was the subtle contrast. Jigger's garb was somewhat neater than the nondescript clothing Flower and the others wore, but it was rough, acquired variously. Only the red berets both wore identified them as members of the St. Petersburg Saints. This young man was dressed in designer jeans and sports shirt, and even the gunners, obviously his subordinates and probably servants, were trimmer in their attire than the newcomers.

"Forgeries are possible, of course," said the youth, in an accent that conveyed good breeding and education. "What's the distance from the Earth to the Moon?"

"Five miles," answered Jigger promptly.

The young man grinned and signaled the gunners, who relaxed.

"Stupid damn password," he commented. "But effective, I suppose, since most would struggle to come up with the real distance. You can go in, and one of the maids'll take you to Miss Cardwell. Leave your weapons here."

Without protest, Jigger and Flower divested themselves of their submachine guns, the pair of automatic pistols each carried and their fighting knives. The young guard searched each perfunctorily but missed Jigger's private, ultimate weapons: the half dozen syringes, filled with lethal fluid, attached to the inside hem of his loose shirt.

The outer gate closed, the inner one opened, and Jigger and Flower stepped into a large garden, scattered with ornamental trees and filled with brilliant flowers between its winding walks. Jigger blinked. There were still flowers scattered around, of course, in this climate, but he had not seen anything this orderly since he was a young boy, before the waters rose and what was left of St. Petersburg became an island.

The two Saints made their way along the walks of the garden to the arched and columned entrance of the large stone building, three stories high, that was the center of Fort Cardwell. As they approached, the door swung open. They entered, to be greeted by a young woman in her late teens or early twenties, clad in traditional maid's costume — short full skirt, frilly apron and one of those lacy things in her hair. Flower glanced at Jigger and Jigger winked and nodded slightly.

"If you gentlemen will follow me, I'll take you to Miss Cardwell," said the girl, with a slight curtsy.

They were led down a short hall and into a large room in which seven or eight people of varying ages sat around, talking, drinking liquids that Jigger identified as tea and wine, some of them smoking cigarettes. The room was one of those that used to be called a sunroom, its walls on three sides consisting mostly of tall windows, curtained and draped, that overlooked a terrace and the garden.

These were people such as Jigger had seen rarely, for they seldom went abroad, then only in the daytime and well guarded. They were all expensively dressed, though informally so. All of them were neatly groomed, the men clean-shaven and the women with hair meticulously cared for, so that it conveyed that careless, natural look.

And the room astonished him. The sofas were overstuffed, the furniture polished and unmarred; there were lamps and vases of flowers about. He had heard that many folk had lived this way before the rising of the waters, and perhaps many still did, inland, but it was beyond anything he had seen. He himself had never lived in total poverty but the home in which he had been reared had been simple, a little shabby, most of the furniture and other things always in need of repair.

"The Saints, Miss," announced the maid, and a woman who was talking with a smooth young man arose and turned to them.

She was blonde, blue-eyed and beautiful, her yellow hair hanging in two braids down her back. Her calf-length white skirt and translucent white blouse complemented her figure in a way that set Jigger's blood to burning.

"You're Mr. Penrod, positive?" she asked, coming across the room to them. "I'm Fascina Cardwell."

"Yes, ma'am," answered Jigger politely. "This is my chief lieutenant, France de Lilac."

"Would you like to go out on the terrace where we can discuss this privately?" asked Fascina Cardwell.

"Whatever you wish, ma'am," said Jigger.

"No, Fascina," said a gray-haired man, getting up from a captain's chair and laying aside his pipe. "Not everybody in here's interested in hearing the young man's proposals, I suppose, but some of us are."

"All right, Father," said Fascina. "Mr. Penrod, you and Mr. . . . your lieutenant . . . please do sit down. Can I have you served some wine? Or something stronger?"

"I don't drink when I'm working, Miss Cardwell," replied Jigger. "I'll have some of your tea if you don't think it negative on my asking."

"I'm not much on wine, but if you've got the harder stuff I'd gopher a snort," said Flower.

Fascina smiled at them.

"Tea for Mr. Penrod and Chivas Regal for Mr. . . . French, is it?" she instructed a hovering maid.

"Call me Flower, dossie . . . Miss," said Flower somewhat awkwardly. "That's what the slikes call me . . . because of my last name, you scan it, not because I'm . . . well, anything else."

"I understand," said Fascina.

Jigger, relaxing in a marvelously comfortable chair, surveyed the room and its people. Again, the contrast with what was familiar to him . . . with what he was.

Jigger Penrod was at twenty-four the undisputed boss of the approximately three dozen tough-fibered members of the St. Petersburg Saints. He ran the Saints like the martial arts school in which he had been trained for a time. His discipline had raised them in a few years to primacy among the half dozen similar organizations in the area.

Here, in this richly appointed room, the comely people behind their protective wall chatted amiably, drinking their wine and their tea, untouched by the constant, cynical tension that kept the Saints and their women always alert. Except for the periodic inconvenience of overseeing the male servants on guard duty, they could live as though there were nothing wrong with the world and it was still back in the 1970s or 1980s.

Two of the men and the other two women here were comparable in age to Mr. Cardwell, Fascina's father — fifties or early sixties — and these four seemed unconcerned enough about the implications of Jigger's appearance to continue their conversation among themselves. The other two men, nattily attired, were younger, though considerably older than the youth at the gate and appeared a few years older than Fascina. Jigger gained the impression from their glances and expressions that they were competitors for her favor.

"Mr. Penrod," said Fascina, "the reason I got in touch with you is that we've become quite concerned about our security here, and I was told the St. Petersburg Saints are the best on the island in this field."

"Yes, ma'am. Since we decided to make a business of it we've persuaded quite a few people to use our services," said Jigger gravely. For some reason, Flower chuckled. "I can see why you're worried about your security."

"Why?" asked Fascina, surprised. "As you saw when you came here, we keep that front gate well guarded at all times. The back one, too."

"The machine guns? A bomb or a bazooka could take care of them, right through that gate, if you had a serious attack by an organized force — and this is the kind of place that would draw that kind of an attack if there were any forces like that on the Island. The kind of punks you must have to worry about wouldn't be trying to come through the *gate.*"

"That's what got us thinking about more expert help," she said. "Several times recently we've had groups try to climb the walls, and the other night half a dozen of them made it over in spite of the barbed wire along the top. I hate to see the men shoot down those kids, but they have to. We know 'those kids' would make a wreck of this place if they got in."

"They'd do worse than that," said Jigger. "They'd strip the place of everything they could sell, to buy drugs, and kill all of you who stood in their way. If you didn't have your wall you'd have been wiped out long ago, because those men at the gate may be brave enough but I could tell as soon as we came in that they aren't fighters."

The two younger men had drifted up to listen, and one of them spoke now.

"In other words," he drawled superciliously, "you're recommending that we employ mercenaries. That's what you so-called 'Saints' are, isn't it? Mercenaries?"

The other young man simpered. "That's what the Romans had to do in their final days, isn't it?" he asked. "I told you, Gaylord, the ongoing collapse of the country's strictly analogous to the fall of Rome."

"These are two of my friends, Mr. Penrod, members of our little community of convenience." Fascina introduced them: "Gaylord Paragon and Leon Ghest."

"Call me Jigger, Miss Cardwell," suggested Jigger. "You'll scan it for natural after a time and I'm not used to this 'mister' business." He turned toward one of the men. "Leon, I believe she said you are, I'm not too sharp on ancient history but Rome did have walls, didn't it? That didn't do them much good in the long haul."

Leon only nodded but Gaylord, a dark-haired young man of patrician features and a physique that proclaimed considerable athletic activity, said, "True, true. The downfall of Rome, brought about by some of its own mercenaries, occurred because the once-invincible legions . . ."

"We've had the wall for a long time, Mr. . . . Jigger," interrupted Fascina, brushing Gaylord's comment aside. "Father and I lived in St. Petersburg Beach before it was flooded. When everybody who could afford it was panicking and moving north, he chose to stay here and bought this place on higher ground. But the greenhouse effect made the seas rise farther and faster than anyone thought . . . I think they'd predicted about sixteen feet. So Father thought it had reached maximum several years ago when the shoreline was a block farther east than it is now and Gulfport hadn't yet gone under."

"Only a small error in clairvoyance, for scientists," said Gaylord sardonically. "They overlooked the tectonic disturbances that followed the melting of the polar ice caps. I say it's a long way from finished yet."

"You mean your father had the luck to find a house with a wall around it?" Jigger asked Fascina.

"No, Father had the wall built after we moved in. With the social disruption and people crowding to higher ground, he saw that gang violence would just get worse and he felt that with a strong wall around us we could ride it out until things settled down at a different level. After all, when we moved the city hadn't become an island yet."

"It's going to get worse," predicted Gaylord with a kind of perverse relish. He pulled a monogrammed case from his pocket, extracted a cigarette from it and lit it with a monogrammed lighter. "Another five feet and *this* place will be flooded. And it may be slower than it has been but when the water gets twice as high as it is now the island of St. Petersburg will stretch only from about 8th Street to Disston Street and a few blocks north and south."

"I'm afraid you may be right, Gaylord," conceded Mr. Cardwell. "I'm already reconciled to the necessity of leaving the island within another few years and finding some place farther north, beyond any possibility of flooding."

A sudden burst of music caused Jigger to start and Flower came up halfway from his seat on the sofa, slopping his drink. One of the older women had turned on a compact disc player on the other side of the room and the strains of Wagner's *Das Rheingold* blared forth. She turned the volume down.

"You haven't had much to say in all this forecasting, Leon," Jigger remarked to the slight, blond young man sardonically. Leon shrugged.

"Nothing I can do about it, one way or another," he answered. "I watch the telly, mercenary, and I see what's happening to the people fleeing inland to be 'safe' from the rise of the seas and the scum it dredges up in the coastal cities. Besides being unwelcome there, they're preyed on both by the wolves who follow them in their flight and the wolves already laired in the places to which they go. When there's no escape, the sensible man enjoys what's left as long as he can."

"That's just giving up," responded Jigger scornfully. "*Somebody's* going to survive, so why not us? The Saints have outfought gangs as tough as any you'll find inland."

"Oh, the mercenaries?" countered Leon with a chuckle. "You're suggesting you be our mercenaries when we trek inland? Bully for you, Saint. I had no idea you people were so altruistic."

"I didn't suggest we ward you folk when you leave here," replied Jigger. "We might, at that. But we aren't altru . . . what you called it. We get paid for our warding."

"I'm sure you do," said Gaylord. "And one thing you neglect to mention in your erudite exposition of late Roman history, Leon, is that the mercenaries the Romans brought in to save the empire from the barbarians were the very barbarians who eventually destroyed the empire."

Jigger waved a hand and turned to Fascina.

"Thing is," he said, "you folk aren't Romans and you're not thinking on sliding north right away. What we're here for is the upgrading of your security system."

"That's correct," agreed Fascina with a smile. "And, before we begin, the question of bringing your men in as guards isn't under discussion."

"No mercenaries, positive?" said Jigger with a grin. "I hadn't figured on it, Miss Cardwell. I'm not saying it you wouldn't be safer if we did come in and take over from your amateurs, but what I came here figuring on, from the way you talked it, is inspecting your place and telling you how you can make it stronger."

"Then we'd better go," she said, arising.

Jigger lifted an eyebrow, but gestured to Flower, and the two men followed her out of the room. Only when they were in the hall did he ask, "You're going to show us around yourself, Miss?"

"If you want to learn about our defenses, I'd better," she answered with a little laugh. "Father could show you, but at his age he tires easily, climbing around the place. As for the others . . . the older couples know nothing about it and I'm afraid Gaylord and Leon aren't a great deal better. Especially Leon. They do their stint at supervising the guards but I think both of them consider the whole business a little beneath them."

"They're not members of your family, I scan it," said Jigger.

"No, Father and I are the only 'family' here. Other than the servants, they're all friends from back in St. Petersburg Beach we took in when we moved here."

She laughed ruefully.

"I suppose I'll marry Gaylord, eventually," she said. "He wants to, and so does Leon. Of the two, I'll take Gaylord."

"I'd think it a dossie like you'd gopher a strong slike," suggested Jigger. "A slike who's his own man."

"I'm afraid that's a lost breed, in my class," Fascina answered with a shrug. "As you probably observed, that arrogance of Gaylord's grates a little but he's really not a bad person — and when I put my foot down I can control him. Besides, he does come of good family."

"I guess it that's what's important," remarked Jigger drily. "How many servants?"

"Fifteen men. They worked for us before and came with us here. It's a considerable strain on them, alternating their guard duty with their regular chores, but they've held up well so far."

"Dossies?" asked Flower abruptly. "I spotted two maids."

"There are about a dozen of them," answered Fascina. "Three are older women, but most of them are young like the two maids you saw. We have three married couples among our servants."

Their tour took several hours. It was a big place.

"Barbed wire can't stop those druggies," commented Jigger as they inspected the wall. "The wall itself is really your only barrier but when they get to the top they can get over the barbed wire."

"It's electrified," said Fascina.

"What about power failures?"

"There *have* been some since we've been here — more frequent lately than before," she conceded. "It messes things up but we have plenty of electric lanterns and an auxiliary generator. Of course that doesn't provide enough power to keep the barbed wire electrified but we've been fortunate in not being attacked while the power was off — except that one time I mentioned when several of them got over the wall."

"There's only one way of guarding a wall and that's with guns," said Jigger.

"Unfortunately, we simply don't have enough people for that," she said.

"I spotted that. Now I'd gopher taking a scan at the mechanism that opens the gates. Likely it could be made safer."

Late that afternoon the St. Petersburg Saints, fully armed, were amassed at their headquarters and communal domicile, an abandoned supermarket on 34th Street North near 22nd Avenue, ready to climb into the trucks lined up outside. Their near-equal number of women (along with a few unintended children) were already in the trucks.

"You're sliding it today?" asked Flower as the two of them emerged from the building, the last to leave.

"That's positive," replied Jigger. "I don't gopher them thinking on it too long. I told that dossie, Fascina, that we'd boost the security on opening that front gate and there's no better time for such than now."

Flower chuckled.

"I'm thinking on that maid, the one that took us back when we first got there," he said. "Said it her name was Daisy."

"Business first," said Jigger. "Daisies bloom all summer."

He went up to the lead truck.

"Fishface," he said to the trooper behind the wheel, "you halt the caravan at Twenty-second and Fourth and sit tight while Flower and I go in. If nothing more happens, keep on sitting tight and wait for us. Be ready to move on up if one of us comes back out and signals to you."

He and Flower got in the armored car, pulled out of the former shopping center and turned right onto 22nd Avenue. The cavalcade of trucks followed at a distance. Jigger drove straight east on 22nd, eventually crossed 4th Street, and pulled up in front of Fort Cardwell. He and Flower got out and went up to the barred gate.

"Who are you and what's your business here?" asked the metallic voice when he rang the bell.

"Jigger Penrod and French de Lilac," answered Jigger. "We're back to boost up the front gate security."

"Oh, the mercenary," said the metallic voice. The outer gate swung creakingly open. Jigger and Flower entered, to be confronted by the half dozen machine gunners and their supervisor, now the man Gaylord.

"I didn't expect you back so soon, mercenary," said Gaylord. "Fascina assumed you'd return tomorrow sometime."

"Thought you might as well be protected for the night, " replied Jigger mildly. The gunners relaxed and took their hands from the triggers of their weapons. "I'll be here tomorrow with counsel for better general security but I brought a little gadget with me to boost security on this gate for tonight."

Shifting his submachine gun from his shoulder, he laid it down carefully on the floor. Flower also unshipped his weapon as though to follow suit. Jigger straightened and reached inside his jacket. He brought forth a syringe and in a single smooth movement drove the point into Gaylord's arm and pressed the plunger. At the same time Flower swung his gun in an arc, spraying the half dozen surprised gunners in a burst of fire.

"They'll wonder about that firing, inside," said Jigger calmly, surveying the six corpses and Gaylord, writhing on the floor in his death throes. "Slide out and signal Fishface to bring the slikes on up, while I open this inner gate with the combination Fascina gave me."

By the time Flower had stepped outside, signaled Fishface and returned, Jigger had the inner gate open.

"If I were you, I'd set claim to your dossie, Daisy, before the slikes get here and start picking and choosing," Jigger advised his lieutenant. "I'm taking that blonde dossie Fascina for personal winnings, and as quick as this place is secured I'm thinking on it to sample her . . . before suppertime."

"You don't think on it to let the slikes free at her for a few days first, like usual?" asked Flower curiously. "She's a fair-shaped dossie and a pocketful of the slikes'll have a pecker up for her."

"I don't share this one unless she gets uppity," replied Jigger firmly. "Then I might turn her over to the slikes for a night, to prove it to her how lucky she is to be the leader's private dossie and warded from being passed around among the slikes. Anything besides that'll be just lending her to one of the slikes as reward for some special service."

He peered through the open inner gate. Beyond the garden, several armed servants had emerged from the front door past the garden and were looking around nervously. Sitting ducks.

"Those slikes that choose it to lay down their guns and not get blown out can work for us," he decreed with satisfaction. The trucks were pulling up to the front of the wall outside. "You scan it now, Flower, how smart it was to play it legitimate with those business folk we talked into hiring us for protection, and not take advantage and sniggle their stuff. With this walled place we can be top dogs on St. Pete island without any flak — and if we decide it later to shed this place and slide north to the inland, we're a clear strong ward force, with our own weapons and our own trucks, strong enough to take a town and hold it and power its folk to work for us."

He grinned and flexed his muscles. He had caught sight of Fascina, standing in the arched and columned front door trying to assess what was going on outside. The competent young mistress taking charge, still in that white skirt and blouse; so translucent it had been easy to see she wore no brassiere under it.

"That Fascina," he added, almost fondly. "She's a smart dossie, for swearing, and it won't take her long to see it clear how things slide these times and get over her high-class ways. I'm thinking it I'm just the strong slike she's been looking for without knowing it."

Clark Perry

Clark Perry graduated from the University of Tampa as a writing major in 1988. His work has appeared in the anthology *Bringing Down the Moon* as well as the magazines *Starlog* and *The Horror Show*. He is a freelance writer, recipient of a Florida Individual Artist Fellowship Award for 1990-91 from the Florida Division of Cultural Affairs, and is at work on a novel. Perry is the winner of the *Subtropical Speculations* contest for new writers. "Killing Time" was chosen by author Joe Haldeman as the best from dozens of submissions. Haldeman praised the manuscript for "its unrelenting pace, and the way the author handled slipping from one environment to another. It's a fast and exciting story."

"Killing Time" is the first of a series I have planned set in alternate worlds — specifically alternate Floridas. It seems that wherever I am living becomes the setting for my stories. Florida is where I am living now, and it's too colorful, too vast, and too threatened to ignore. When most Floridians think about the destruction of their waters and lands, they do so with much concern — but also with no small amount of inevitability, like there's nothing that can really be done. Maybe there's some answer to be found through the fictional exploration of alternate worlds.

Neither Hale's nor Carlos' people really understand the portals in "Killing Time," and it is how their cultures perceive them that intrigues me. For one it is a kind of salvation; for the other, a damnation. Like the duality that currently pervades environmental thinking in Florida, both views are correct in their way.

KILLING TIME

by Clark Perry

Hale came through the portal half-crazy and dripping wet, clutching his right shoulder. His boots hit the ground and he almost collapsed, but the faceplate of his helmet showed him green grass, blue sky, and half a dozen strange men in a semi-circle, all glaring fearfully in his direction.

Hale crouched low and took a breath. They couldn't see him clearly, he knew, not in this dead black pressure suit with the equally dark portal behind him. Perhaps they had seen his silhouette as he leapt through, but the blue glow of transference had faded by now, and he was almost invisible to the men.

At least they looked like men. Superimposed over Hale's vision through the faceplate was an atmospheric analysis showing they breathed oxygen. Hale's tanks were dangerously low; he needed a recharge before he could go on. He looked at the men a moment more, taking in their simple brown and green clothing, the wide-brimmed hats that nearly hid those sharp, bearded faces. Then he unhooked a small flash charge from his belt, squeezed its bulb tip and tossed it into the air above their heads.

Even with the helmet's protection, the blast made him wince. The faceplate caught the bright flash and toned it down. The six men stumbled back, gasping and shouting incoherently. One of them must have caught a good glimpse of Hale in the explosion; he let loose a tortured cry and shot past the others as if they were statues on the hillside. The rest contracted his fright and followed him down the gentle slope. Hale relaxed as he watched them make for a dirt road across the field before him.

When they had disappeared into the forest, he slipped heavily to his knees and dug his finders into the earth, tearing loose handfuls of dirt, clumps of grass. Thank God, he thought. Oh, thank you.

The last one had been water, too much water, a huge ocean made of stuff he couldn't even peg. He had come tumbling from the portal in free-fall, slamming into the water, faceplate going rainbow crazy with colors and symbols, trying to decipher the liquid's composition. But the "smart" helmets only knew what was programmed into them, and this silent, green ocean had racked up columns of UNKNOWNs on his readout.

He remembered surfacing, fear flooding his thoughts when he saw that the steel gray cylinder was suspended a full three or four feet above the ocean. He had kicked hard for the distant black portal, pushing away with both arms, but his first grasp had fallen short. He'd fought off nightmare thoughts of never reaching it, of fighting hard against the slow pull of this alien ocean and losing, sinking below its surface until his air ran out.

But the fingers of his right hand had caught on the next try, and he'd damn near pulled that arm from its socket getting up to the portal. There the cold blue light had enveloped his body, and he had fallen through.

Fallen here. That's all that matters, he said to himself. Put that fear in your back pocket and survey the area. Do your job, Hale.

This time the cylinder sat on a small hill, a low rise much like those of the Florida he had known. Hale stared past the numerics and text the faceplate offered. Everything was being recorded; he could study the data later if he ever cared to. Hell, he could study them all, data from seven hundred and eighty-six different worlds. But after passing through each, he never cared to look at them again.

There was one sun here, close to normal gravity. He had realized not long into his mission that this could be expected. The scale of interstellar objects was just too large to be affected by the changes. It was the minute stuff, the details that he had to look for. Details, he thought to himself. Like an ocean replacing a land mass, right? The fear rose in him again, the memory of panic, and he shot it back down his spine, where it stayed.

A dim shape, almost hidden in a stand of large trees not fifty yards away, caught his eye. He squinted and clicked his back teeth together twice. The helmet felt his command, and Hale fought against the brief vertigo as his faceplate zoomed in for him, covering the distance in two seconds. Staring him in the face was a young boy of perhaps ten or twelve, dark brown hair, eyes and mouth propped open in disbelief. Hale released his squint, and when the faceplate receded to normal vision, he burst into a sprint, making for the trees where the boy stood. He could see the kid pulling something over his shoulder and turning to disappear into the trees. Hale thought he heard him cry out as he ran.

Hale easily crossed the field separating them but almost broke his leg as he tore through the trees, which were big cypress. Their thick roots rose from the ground in gnarled loops, just the thing to catch your foot and bring you down hard. He slowed his pace, sidestepping roots, plunging through the trees and across a smaller field. Ahead he could see the boy entering the outskirts of a deep green forest.

The child shot through the cypress easily, but kept glancing back to check Hale's distance. One of the roots tripped him up and Hale grimaced as the boy went cartwheeling through the air and was slammed into the base of a large oak. When Hale reached him, seconds later, the boy was motionless and blood trickled from his nose.

He knelt at the boy's side and lifted his head to stop the bleeding. Wiping a streak of dirt from the boy's face, Hale got a good look at him: pug nose, sallow cheeks, thick lips. He placed a palm on the boy's forehead and his suit snapped into medic mode. The readout showed him that the boy was just unconscious, nothing serious. Poor kid just had his brain sloshed around in his skull, Hale thought. Would probably awaken soon with a nasty headache. Hale told the suit to synthesize some aspirin.

The boy wore the same simple clothes as the men, plain trousers and shirt and leather shoes. Hale searched the pockets and found a small knife and some pencils. The knife's blade was too small for any practical purpose. He figured the boy used it to sharpen his pencils, which were thin wooden sticks with shafts of dried ink pressed through the center. A leather satchel had flown from the boy's arm and lay in some tall grass nearby. Hale opened it and withdrew a large leather book. He ran his fingers across the pebbled surface and saw that it was alligator hide, or something very close to it.

He popped the seal around his neck and tugged off the helmet, placed it at his side. The air was pungent with a sour-green stench, that of a swamp going dry beneath an oppressive sun. He knew this smell: its sharp odor wormed its way deep within his memories, and for a few moments he sat there, remembering. He allowed himself this brief interlude, then, after running his fingers through his thick gray hair, turned his attention to the book. He had hoped for some clue to the language spoken here, since the unintelligible shouting of the frightened men hadn't helped much. But he got something else entirely.

Pictures. The boy was an artist, not a writer. The first page showed a two-story wooden house, built from logs, rendered on the white page in rough, sparse lines. Both the design of the house and the boy's drawing style were utterly simple but effective.

He took off his gloves and turned the page, feeling the heavy paper's coarseness against his fingertips. Here was the face of an old woman, black hair pulled back tightly over her skull. Behind her some sort of oil lamp hung from a wall. He stared at her narrow eyes and pug nose, noting the wrinkles the boy had chosen to draw. He flipped the page.

A man. Hale looked hard for a moment and realized this was one of the men who had been standing outside the portal when he came through. Why had those men been there, as if they were waiting for him to come out? He turned the page: a newborn infant wrapped in cloth, snug in a wooden rocking cradle.

Then, a group of black-clad people clustered around a hole in the ground, their downcast eyes drawn as sad, horizontal slits. Hale flipped forward a few pages and looked, then a few more. This was more than a sketch pad, though there were practice pages where the boy had doodled, repeating some technique or shape to get it right. Hale wondered if this were some sort of record book where important events were drawn.

Hale flipped faster now, trying to get some general sense of these people. He saw them at work in fields and groves, or in the woods and swamps. They were agrarians and hunters. Some were fishermen, and others walked wooden planks laid out over ponds, using poles to herd dark shapes that swam below. Alligators, maybe manatees down there, Hale couldn't be sure. They lived like early American settlers, and their features weren't Indian. He skipped the details, hoping that he would be able to snap pictures of each page before he left this place. Still, he saw enough to admire the boy's eye and hand.

The book's pages were about two-thirds full of drawings, and when Hale came to the very last one, his fingers froze on the page.

He was still staring at it when the boy moaned and rolled over, facing away from him. Hale watched. The boy rubbed at his temples and pushed himself up, grunting with the effort. He gingerly touched his foot, the one caught by the cypress root, and his thin shoulders jerked up to a point with the pain. He hissed like a snake and surely would have wept, but Hale softly cleared his throat.

The boy's face snapped around, eyes glazed with fear. He opened his mouth as if to cry out, but Hale calmly said, "It's okay." Even if he couldn't understand the language, there were other ways of communication. Hale repeated himself a few times, making no move at all.

The boy stared, transfixed in his fear. Slowly, gently, Hale extended a finger and pointed to the picture in the book. The boy saw the book in his lap and cautiously craned his neck forward to see the picture. And his expression grew pained. He took in quick breaths and blinked rapidly. Hale lay the book on the ground between them and held out his hands, palms up, trying his best to project a soothing countenance.

Hale gestured to the boy's foot. The top of the leather shoe had bitten lightly into the boy's shin, and there was a crust of dried blood around the tiny wound. The boy studied the wound, never really taking his eyes off Hale, and a new drop of blood fell from his nose onto his white shirt. The boy raised an index finger to his nostril and caught the next drop, held it up for Hale to see.

"I'm bleeding," said the boy. In Spanish.

Hale sat back in disbelief and managed a grin. Relief washed over him — he knew some Spanish, you had to where he came from — but he had not used it in a very long time. He eased his mind back into it slowly. "I am bleeding," he repeated after the boy a couple of times. Then: "You are bleeding. He is bleeding. We are bleeding, you are bleeding, they are bleeding."

The boy frowned. "*I* am bleeding," he said hesitantly.

Hale nodded, ransacking his brain for the words and verbs he wanted. He cursed the suit for not having a translator program. But who had expected Spanish? The pressure suit was an Air Force prototype designed to keep you alive, and the smart helmet had no audio pickup for language translation, anyway. Hale struggled for a moment. "I understand — the words," he finally stammered.

The boy nodded, then fired back a quick statement. Hale pointed to his ear and shook his head. The boy repeated slowly: "A demon should not wear the head of a man."

Either Hale had forgotten more than he thought, or in this world Spanish had taken some strange turns. It took him a moment. "I am not a . . . demon," he said. "My name is Hale, Victor Eugene Hale. I am from the United States of America." The last bit had been required learning in the government's foreign language class, and rolled off his tongue effortlessly.

The boy said, "I am called Carlos-who-draws. And you are from the devil."

Hale shook his head. "This is . . . clothing. Like your . . . shirt. I take them off, I am like you."

Carlos pointed back towards the direction of the portal. "You came from the devil box. I saw you. The leaders could not, but I could."

Hale was puzzled, and then it hit him. The boy had seen it all in profile, Hale realized. I stood out clearly from that angle. "The leaders," he said. "Your father?"

The boy nodded grimly. "My father."

"What were the leaders . . . uh, why were they before the devil box?" Carlos looked away, lips tight. Hale pointed to the book between them again. "Tell me of this picture please. What . . . happens?"

The drawing was unfinished. It showed the six men standing before the cylinder, as they had been when Hale leapt through. But there was another man there, a seventh, his hands bound behind his back. Carlos had drawn his mouth open in a scream or shout, and two of the other men had him by the arms and were dragging him toward the portal.

"They executed him," Carlos whispered, shaken. "They caught him worshiping it and they executed him."

"They threw him in?" Hale exclaimed in English. Carlos was startled by the gibberish. Hale calmed himself and repeated it in Spanish.

Carlos nodded. "And then the devil came."

"It is not a devil box," Hale told him plainly. "I am not a devil. And that man is not dead." Unless, of course, he lands someplace where an ocean has replaced a land mass. For an instant Hale thought of that, the poor man falling free to the water, smacking into its surface and sinking, hands forever tied behind his back, kicking his legs. . . .

He fought it down. Come on, back pocket, he thought. He probably got through okay, no sweat. Hale closed the book and slid it into its satchel. "Your head hurts," he said, raising an eyebrow. Carlos nodded warily. "Take me someplace safe, Carlos-who-draws, and you will feel better. Then I will show you *my* pictures, for they too have a story to tell."

The swamp was indeed dry. They ventured into it, shoes crunching on its cracked bed where a tiny rotlike moss grew in pale webs through the earth. Carlos limped but made no fuss. Hale admired him for that. The kid was obviously scared to death.

Maybe death had already been accepted in his wide eyes when he had turned to face Hale.

Hale had a grip here. In previous places, there had been no sign of humanity at all, merely harsh landscapes, alien terrain that chilled him to the bone simply because there was no place for him. They were mostly environments where, were it not for the pressure suit, he would have perished. The places that could support life were few and far between, and he had no idea how far removed he was from his own place and time.

But suddenly he was surrounded by familiar elements. He watched Carlos as he walked. It had been so long since he'd seen another person. He had recorded various other life forms, but they were either of low intelligence or they had attacked him on sight before he could find out. Strange hybrid creatures, and then some that may as well have been extraterrestrial.

Carlos led him out of the swamp to a fresh-water spring that collected in a tree-shaded pool. He wanted Carlos to trust him, but he wasn't yet sure he could trust Carlos. So he unhooked his own backpack and withdrew his coiled utility cord. The boy was still as Hale knotted it around a small tree and fastened the other end to an adjustable alloy bracelet. The ring had been originally designed to hold a small flexpistol, but Hale's supply of ammunition had run out long ago. He had driven the gun's barrel into the sand of a world that was endless desert, a solitary landmark for any subsequent travelers.

The boy's thin wrist fit snugly in the silver ring. He locked it shut and went to the other side of the pool where the sun shone down through a break in the trees. There he peeled the suit from his body. Carlos-who-draws averted his eyes, gave him his privacy. Hale lay it out in the shape of a man and from the backpack unfolded a small array of flat solar panels. These he connected to the helmet and the suit. A quick glance through the faceplate told him the charge would be sufficient. The tiny air bladders in the suit were refilling, as well. With this done, Hale walked quickly to the pool and dove in.

The water was cool and clean and bit through the grime that had built up on his skin. He rubbed at himself vigorously, clawed at his scalp, and climbed out. Hale sat across from Carlos with the backpack in his lap and proudly held up his flat plastic view screen. "My pictures," he said. Along the right edge of the screen was a row of tiny buttons. He pressed the top one.

The screen flashed white, then was filled with a photograph of a gleaming metal tower — the Harris Bank Plaza in downtown Tampa. Built after Hurricane Lydia flattened the city back in '98, it easily dwarfed the other buildings that stood in its shadow. But this was only a test picture taken from a magazine photograph, and had reproduced with a flat dull finish. "You make a picture this way," he said, showing Carlos the eyepiece in the upper right corner. "Look at something through here, then press this red button. See?" Carlos nodded unsurely as Hale snapped a picture of the pool. Hale advanced the frame.

Here was the portable hangar at the old Air Force base, abandoned for years because of leakage from the underground fuel tanks, but suddenly the military hotspot once the portal materialized there. Some armed soldiers patrolled in the foreground, and Hale pointed them out to Carlos to give him some perspective. The clarity was much better on this one.

The next shot was of the cylinder itself, identical to the one that sat on the hill. Carlos gaped in recognition, turned to Hale, then looked again at the picture. The cylinders were all the same: ten feet and three inches tall, with a circumference of eight feet even. The doorway was so black you couldn't see into it.

Hale punched up the next picture, the one he looked at often: the eight-member team standing before the cylinder, not smiling, just standing there impatiently, their work obviously interrupted. Hale pointed himself out to Carlos. The boy had not said a word the whole time. "It is no devil box," Hale explained quietly. "It is a doorway. My home has one, too."

He advanced the pictures rapidly now, pausing only to show Carlos the shots of Air Force volunteers suiting up in the pressure outfits. The first volunteers. Never heard from again. They were still out here, somewhere, like Hale. And he envied them, because they had gone of their own volition. Hale and Vance and the others had had no choice. They would have died had they not donned the last few suits and jumped through.

He showed Carlos his pictorial studies of the alternate worlds. But there were a lot of pictures — though the screen's memory was not even half full yet — so Hale gave it to Carlos and showed him how to advance the frames. The boy sat hypnotized, not even blinking, his only movements the rise and fall of his chest and his right forefinger as it pressed the button. Hale watched him, studied his bewildered expression, and thought of what he should tell the boy.

"The suit keeps me alive. It scares you, but I need it or I die. Each time I go through, something . . . bad may wait for me. The suit helps."

Carlos paused and looked up at him. "Why?"

Hale considered. There was no way to answer the boy's question. He was not asking about the suit. Hale believed the boy understood about that now. He was questioning the doorway itself — as Hale and his fellow researchers had done for months, before the missiles came down like huge red-hot nails.

Thanks to his forced experience, Hale had more answers now, but he still wasn't sure. What do I say? he thought. Do I even know the correct words and concepts?

In the end, Hale just shrugged. He was exhausted. The sun had slid away to reveal the faint but familiar patterns of constellations in the darkening sky. Yes, he thought, depending on the time of year, this is one of many Floridas. "Vance, this guy I worked with, suspected a lot of things, but even now I'm not sure of the answer.

"What we didn't suspect was that our research would be cut short by a war — *the* war. Christ, Carlos, I might not even have been at work that day, let alone the fact that we had less than ten minutes to decide what we were gonna do. At least I was there to make that choice, though, huh?" He shook his head back and forth lazily. Sleep was near, and the tapping of Carlos' finger was strangely soothing because it reminded him of the clacking of keyboards in the portable hangar back home. He could almost see the others there with him, peering into terminals, testing new equipment, running new probes through the portal, praying that just one would come back.

His latest theory blazed in his head as sleep took him: go through enough times, and you come out where you began. Perhaps earlier, he hoped. Maybe I could get back in time with all this information. Wouldn't it be enough to stop a war? Just pop right out of the portal, say, the Tuesday before, walk right past myself and deliver a presentation to the president . . . that would do it.

"I think it's a time machine," he said, sleep slurring his words. "Something to do with temporal displacement, anyway. Only . . . only it doesn't lead to *my* past or future . . . it must skip time streams randomly . . . alternate worlds . . ."

Carlos was busy clicking past the pictures. He glanced over at Hale and nudged him awake one final time. "We should not stay here long," he said. "My father will see I am missing from the house. Even if they have given up looking for you, they will come for me."

Hale opened one bleary eye and smiled. "What are they gonna do? Execute me?" He chuckled and his head fell back against the grass.

Carlos stared blankly. He had understood nothing the strange man had said for a long time, now. This Hale had gone back to speaking in his own gibbering tongue, and Carlos had not even bothered to correct him. He had been so taken by these magnificent pictures that it had not even mattered.

But now he watched the sleeping man and wished he had understood those meaningless words. Perhaps he could ask again tomorrow, and the man would speak in a tongue he could understand. Carlos-who-draws knew this was no devil. This man had made the pain in his head disappear with his white powder, and now he thrilled Carlos with the unbelievable pictures on the book of one page. After a while he turned back to the screen and began clicking the button again.

The men came at night.

Carlos awoke when someone pressed a hand across his mouth. His eyes jerked open and he saw his father crouching before him, using his own blade to saw through the black rope that bound him to the tree. His father's fierce expression told him to be quiet. He tried to speak but his father muffled it and stared him down with quiet rage as he jimmied his blade into the metal ring. After a few moments it popped open.

As Carlos' wrist was freed, he heard scuffling nearby. Men's voices shouted to each other and a lamp was lit and brought near. His father's hand came away from his face and Carlos stood to see that Hale had been bound with heavy grass rope. The other town leaders stood around him, prodding him with their boots, making quiet comments. Then they saw Carlos and looked at him impassively. "The boy is all right," his father told them. They stared a moment more, just to be sure, then returned their gaze to Hale as he rolled back and forth, struggling against the ropes.

Hale was saying something through clenched teeth. "My clothes! Give me my clothes — I will go!"

Carlos darted forward. "Leave him alone!" he said, but his father caught him by the arms and jerked him back angrily.

"You listen to me," he snapped at his son. "I know you were there today. I know you disobeyed me! This demon has held you here all day, and you want us to leave him alone." The grip tightened and Carlos wanted to cry but he bit it back. His father continued: "You get back to the house this instant. We have things to do here and this is no place for you. And if you have drawn anything that happened today, I'll tear out the pages and make you swallow them." With that, he shoved Carlos away and waited for him to disappear.

Carlos took a step backward but screamed, "He's not a demon, you've all been wrong! You didn't kill Jose this morning, he's still alive in there!"

His father never used his full strength against Carlos, but this was the exception. It shamed and terrified and angered him to have his son say these horrible things in front of the town leaders. Without thinking, he whipped around, backhanding his son as hard as he could to stop the evil filth spilling from his lips. Carlos spun, face bloody, and fell into the pool.

The water was a cold shock to him, like falling into another world. Eyes wide, he swam to the far side and raised his head above the water. His father and the others were watching to make sure Carlos was not drowning, and when he climbed up, they all turned back to Hale and spoke quietly to one another. Carlos stared at his father's back with so much hatred he thought he would scream.

But he stayed quiet. His nose had started bleeding again, and he held up his shirt to stop the flow. His father glanced back at him one last time, and Carlos pretended to leave, but when his father turned back, he quietly crept into some thick bushes where he knew he could not be seen.

Hale was on the ground laughing at them, calling them names, sometimes in the language they could understand. "Listen to me," he was shouting. "I won't hurt you! Just untie me and let me get my suit first!" The men watched him curiously and Carlos could no longer hear what they were saying to each other. All he could hear were Hale's hoarse shouts of "Please, don't throw me back in yet!" over and over.

The town leaders withdrew for a moment and whispered together, heads down. The lamp was held low, and Carlos could see their faces lit ominously, features exaggerated. For a moment, they looked exactly like the demons he had imagined living in the devil box — long noses, deep hollow eyes, terrible expressions on those dark faces.

Then, without further discussion, Carlos' father pulled something from his belt and stood over Hale. Hale looked up and screamed and shook his head. Carlos watched his father grab Hale by his gray hair, bend down, and slowly pull his blade across Hale's throat.

Hale tried to speak, but his voice was a wet gurgle. He fought even harder against the ropes. Carlos watched the line of blood open and close as Hale breathed through it. The men stepped back and watched him bleed to death. It seemed to last forever.

When his naked, blood-drenched body was still and unmoving, two of the town leaders lifted Hale by his feet and shoulders, and the person with the lamp led the way back to town, where Hale's body would be presented the next morning in public for all to see. Carlos' father and the others followed them out of the dry swamp bed, and soon the lantern light was a tiny glow through the thick trees.

Carlos had not moved, not even to wipe away his tears. He did not know why he had cried: whether it was more for this strange man Hale, or for the fact that his father and the other leaders were capable of such hatred, such violence. Against his father's will, Carlos had hidden and watched them throw Jose into the box. That had been nothing compared to the shock of seeing this. After a long moment he stood from the bushes and went to see if Hale's picture box had been found by the men.

The screen was still there, tossed into some nearby grass by his father, who did not understand what it was. Carlos had gone to sleep with a picture on its surface, but now the picture was gone. He pressed the buttons in the way Hale had shown him and the screen flickered, showing him the picture of Hale and his friends standing before the portal. He looked at it for a long time, then tucked it beneath his arm and began his long walk home, planning shortcuts so he could beat his father there.

He did not get far. On the other side of the pool his foot snagged on something and he almost fell for the second time that day. He bent down and in the light from the picture box, he found Hale's demon suit. It was almost impossible to see in the dark. The black outfit was still spread out where Hale had left it. Carlos ran his hand up and down its slick fabric. He remembered how Hale had unfolded the shiny panels, and Carlos managed to fold them back up so they would fit in the backpack. He found the helmet, too, and put it on. Nothing happened. He would play with it later and see how it worked.

Before he rolled up the suit, Carlos saw how the arms and legs were pulled out flat on the ground. It was laid out in the shape of a man, in the shape of Hale. He dropped his belongings and lay down on it to see how he fit. His arms and legs were not long enough to fill the suit yet, but there was time. He knew he was small, he knew he was young, but he knew he would grow.

He took everything Hale had left behind, and hid it all carefully on his way home.

Damon Knight

In the 1950s, Damon Knight established himself as one of the first outstanding critics in science fiction as well as a distinguished short-story writer and novelist. His collected essays, *In Search of Wonder,* won him the Hugo Award in 1956. He also began the Milford Science Fiction Writers' Conference in 1956, and was largely responsible for the founding of the Science Fiction Writers of America, serving as the group's first president. He began editing a series of influential anthologies in the 1960s, including the famed Orbit series, first produced in 1966. As a writer, he is widely admired for his short stories, collected in volumes including *Far Out, In Deep, Off Center,* and *Turning On.* His other books include *Hell's Pavement, The People Maker, The Sun Saboteurs, Beyond the Barrier, The Rithian Terror,* and most recently, *A for Anything,* and *The Observers.* He and his wife, Kate Wilhelm, lived in Florida for the better part of ten years, from the mid-sixties to the mid-seventies.

I wrote "Down There" in Madeira Beach, in the little cottage we rented while we were house hunting. The story still has memories for me of the beach and the ocean, the slatted glass windows, and the salami on rye I had for lunch every day. Although it is partly about a future New York City, I think you can see inverted images of Florida in it, like photographic negatives of a better world.

DOWN THERE

by Damon Knight

The hard gray tile of the corridor rang under his feet, bare gray corridor like a squared-off gun barrel, bright ceiling overhead, and he thought bore, shaft, tunnel, tube. His door, 913. He turned the bright key in the lock, the door slid aside, hissed shut behind him. He heard the blowers begin; faint current of fresh cool air, sanitized, impersonal. The clock over the console blinked from 10:58 to 10:59.

He leaned over the chair, punched the "Ready" button. The dark screen came to life, displayed the symbols "R. A. NORBERT CG190533170 4/11/2012 10:59:04." The information blinked and vanished, recorded, memorized, somewhere in the guts of the computer nine stories down.

Norbert removed his brown corduroy jacket, hung it up. He sat down in front of the console, loosened the foulard around his throat, combed his neat little goatee. He sighed, rubbed his hands together, then punched the music and coffee buttons.

The music drifted out, the coffee spurted into the cup, fragrant brew, invigorating beverage, rich brown fluid. He sipped it, set it down, filled his pipe with burley from a silk pouch and lit it.

The screen was patiently blank. He leaned forward, punched "Start." Bright characters blinked across the screen, the printer clattered, a sheet curled out into the tray.

The first one was "WORLDBOOK MOD FEM MAR 5, SET OPT," and the other two were just the same except for length — one four thousand, the other three.

He thought discontentedly of novels, something there a man could get his teeth into, a week just setting up the parameters; but then a whole month on the job, that could be a bore: and Markwich had told him, "You've got a touch with the short story, Bob." A flair, a certain aptitude, a *je ne sais quoi*. He drank more coffee, put it down. He sighed again, pinched his nose reflectively, touched the "Start" button.

The screen said "2122084 WORLDBOOK MOD FEM MAR SET OPT 5," then

"THEME: COME TO REALIZE
VICTORY OVER RIVAL
ADJUSTMENT WITH GROUP"

He picked up the light pen, touched the first of the three choices. The other two disappeared, then the whole array, and the screen said:

"SETTING: NEW YORK
PARIS
LONDON
SAN FRANCISCO
DALLAS
BOSTON
DISNEYWORLD
ANTWERP
OCEAN TOWERS"

He hesitated, waving the light pen at the screen. He paused at "Antwerp" — he'd never done that one — but no; too exotic. New York, Paris, London . . . He frowned, clenched the bit of the pipe in his teeth, and plunged for "Ocean Towers." It was a hunch; he felt a little thrill of an idea there.

He called for pictures, and the screen displayed them: first a long shot of the Towers rising like a fabulous castle-crowned mountain out of the sea; then a series of interiors, and Norbert stopped it almost at once: there, that was what he wanted, the central vault, with the sunlight pouring down.

Sunlight, he wrote, and the screen added promptly *fell from the ceiling as* — and here Norbert's plunging finger stopped it; the words remained frozen on the screen while he frowned and sucked on his pipe, his gurgling briar. *Fell* wouldn't do, to begin with, sunlight didn't fall like a flowerpot. *Streamed?* Well, perhaps — No, wait, he had it. He touched the word with the light pen, then tapped out *spilled.* Good-oh. Now the next part was too abrupt; there was your computer for you every time, hopeless when it came to expanding an idea; and he touched the space before *ceiling* and wrote, *huge panes of the.*

The text now read:

Sunlight spilled from the huge panes of the ceiling as

Norbert punched "Start" again and watched the sentence grow . . . *as Inez Trevelyan crossed the plaza among the hurrying throngs.* End of sentence, and he stopped it there. Trevelyan was all right, but he didn't like Inez, too spinsterish. What about Theodora — no, too many syllables — or Georgette? No. Oh, hell, let the computer do it; that's what it was for. He touched the name, then the try-again button, and got *Jean Joan Joanna Judith Karan Karla Laura.* There. That had got her — Laura Trevelyan. Now then, *crossed the plaza* — well, a plaza was what it was, but why be so obvious? He touched the offending word with the light pen, wrote in *floor*; and then *murmuring* instead of *hurrying,* appeal to another sense there; and now, hmm, something really subtle — he deleted the period and wrote in *of morning.*

Sunlight spilled from the huge panes of the ceiling as Laura Trevelyan crossed the floor among the murmuring throngs of morning.

Not bad — not bad at all. He sipped coffee, then wrote, *The light.* You had to keep the computer at it, or it would change the subject every time. The sentence prolonged itself: *was so brilliant and sparkling,* and he stopped it and revised, and in a moment he had: *The light was so yellow and pure, even where it reflected from the floor amid the feet of the passersby, that it reminded Laura of a field of yellow daisies. The real sun was up there somewhere, she knew, but it was so long since she had seen it . . .*

Good. Now a little back-look.

Her first day in Ocean Towers, she remembered unexpectedly, it had been gray outside and the great hall had been full of pearly light. It had seemed so wonderful and thrilling then. It had taken some pluck for her to come here at all — cutting her ties with County Clare, leaving all her family and friends to go and live in this strange echoing place, not even on land but built on pylons sunk into the ocean floor. But Eric's and Henry's career was here, and where they went she must go.

She had married Eric Trevelyan when she was nineteen; he was a talented and impetuous man who was making a name for himself as a professional table tennis player. (A mental note: jai-alai might be better, but did they have jai-alai in Ocean Towers? Check it in a moment.) *He had the easy charm and bluff good humor of the English, and an insatiable appetite for living — more parties, more sex, more everything. His teammate, Henry Ricardo, who had joined the marriage two years later, was everything that Eric was not — solid, dependable, a little slow, but with a rare warmth in his infrequent smiles.*

So much for that. Norbert punched the query button and typed out his question about jai-alai in Ocean Towers. He found they had it, all right, but on thinking it over he decided to make it chess instead: there was something a little wonky about the idea of a slow jai-alai player, or for that matter table tennis either. And besides he himself loathed sports, and it would be a bore looking up rules and so on.

Anyhow, now for a touch of plot. Eric and Henry, it appeared, were rising in their field and had less and less time for Laura. An interesting older man approached her, but she repulsed him, and took the transpolar jet back to County Clare (using Eric's travel permit).

The computer displayed a map of Ireland, and Norbert picked a town called Newmarket-on-Fergus, avoiding names like Kilrush, Lissycasey and Doonbeg that were too obviously quaint. Besides, Newmarket was not far from Shannon Airport, and that made it plausible that Laura had met Eric there in the first place.

Laura was rapturous to be home again (the daisies were in bloom), and although the Clancy cottages seemed crowded and smelly to her now, it didn't matter; but after a few weeks she grew tired of watching the cows every day and the telly every night, and went over to Limerick for a party. But Limerick was not what she was seeking, either, and she finally admitted to herself that she was homesick for Ocean Towers. The register stood at 4,031 words.

Laura took the next jet back to Ocean Towers, had an emotional reconciliation with Eric (but Henry was a little cool), only to learn that they had been offered a three-year contract in Buenos Aires. Walking the promenade over the Pacific that night, unable to sleep, she met the older man again (Harlow Moore) and wept in his arms. The next morning she called Eric and Henry together and told them her news. "You must go on to the wonderful things and far places that are waiting for you," she said. "But I — " and her eyes were suddenly misty as the dawn over Killarney — "I know now that my yellow daisies are here."

Five thousand, two hundred and fifteen words: pretty close. He became aware that he was hungry and that his legs ached from sitting so long. The clock above the console stood at 2:36.

No point in starting on the next one now, he would only go stale on it over the weekend. He got up and stretched until his joints cracked, walked back and forth a little to get the stiffness out, then sat down again and relit his pipe. When he had it drawing to his satisfaction, he leaned forward and punched the retrieval code for a thing of his own he had been working on, the one that began, "Chirurging down the blodstrom, gneiss atween his tief," and so on. He read it as far as it went, added a few words half-heartedly and deleted them again. *Ficciones* would probably send it back with a rejection slip as usual, the bastards, although it was exactly like the stuff they printed all the time; if you weren't in their clique, you didn't have a chance. He tapped out, "THANK HEAVEN IT'S THURSDAY," and blanked the screen.

At 2:58 the screen lit up again: a summary of his weekly earnings and deductions. The printer clattered; a sheet fell into the tray. Norbert picked it up, glanced at the total, then folded the sheet and put it into his breast pocket, thinking absently that he really had better cut down this week and pay back some of his debit. He remembered the music and turned it off. The soothing strains. He punched the "Finished" button and the screen came to life once more, displaying the symbols "R. A. NORBERT CG190533170 4/11/2012 3:01:44." Then it blinked and went dark. Norbert waited a moment to see it there was anything else, a message from Markwich for instance, but there wasn't. He straightened his foulard, took down his jacket and put it on. The door hissed shut behind him and he heard the wards of the lock snick home. Down the gunmetal corridor. He gave his key to the putty-faced security guard, a crippled veteran of the Race War who had never spoken a word in Norbert's memory. In the public corridor, a few people were hurrying past, but not many; it was still early. That was how Norbert liked it. If you could choose your own hours, why work when everybody else did? He punched for twenty, and the elevator whisked him up. Here the traffic was a little brisker. Norbert got into line at the mono stop, looking over the vending machine while he waited. There were new issues of *Madame, Chatelain, Worldbook* and *After Four.* He punched for all of them and put his card into the slot. The machine blinked, chugged, slammed the copies into the receptacle. Moving away, he could hear the whirring of the fax machines.

After Four had nothing of his, as he had expected — he did very little men's stuff. But *Madame* and *Chatelaine* had one of his stories apiece, and *Worldbook* two. He checked the indicia to make sure his name was there: " 'Every Sunday,' by IBM and R. A. Norbert," the only recognition he would get. The stories themselves were unsigned, although occasionally one of them would say, "By the author of 'White Magic,' " or whatever. He boarded the shuttle and sat down, leafing through the magazines idly. "Making Do with Abundance," by Mayor Antonio, illustrated by a cornucopia dribbling out watches, cigar lighters, bottles of perfume, packages tied with blue satin bows. A garish full-page ad, "Be Thoroughly You — *Use Vaginal Gloss.* The best way to give it to you is with a brush." "Q Fever — the Unknown Killer." "Race Suicide — Is It Happening to Us?" by Sherwood M. Sibley. The medical article had an IBM house name for a by-line, but the others were genuine. He had met Sibley once or twice at house parties — a popeyed, nervous man with a damp handshake, but judging by the clothes he wore, he must be making plenty. And it was really unfair how much better non-fic writers were treated, but as Markwich said, that was the public taste for you and the pendulum would swing.

He got off at Fifth Avenue and changed to the uptown mono. The lights in the car were beginning to make his head ache. As the car pulled up at the 50th Street stop, he looked back and saw something curious: a sprawled black figure hanging in midair in the canyon of the avenue. Then the car pulled in, other people were getting up, and by the time he could see in that direction again, it was gone: but he knew somehow that it had been too big and the wrong shape for anything but a man falling. He wondered briefly how on earth the man had got outside the building. All the balconies were roofed and glassed-in. The fellow must have been a workman or something.

The farther uptown they went, the more crowded the mono cars were on the other side of the avenue, going south; it was getting on toward the dinner hour. The crowds he could see on the balconies were mostly touristy-looking people in Chicagoland suits and West Coast freak outfits, white-haired and swag-bellied. Some of the women, old as they were, had smooth Gordonized faces. A few Pakistanis, a little younger. Really, he told himself, he was lucky to have such a good job, young as he was, and let's face it, he didn't have the temperament for going out and interviewing people, gathering information and all that.

The man beside him, getting off at 76th Street, dropped his newspaper on the seat and Norbert picked it up. MORE KIDNAP-MURDER VICTIMS FOUND. WILL MARRY KEN, ORVILLE: ELLA MAE. UNIVERSE LESS THAN 2 BILLION YEARS OLD, SAYS COLUMBIA PROF. The usual thing. At 125th Street, a glimpse of the sky as he stepped out onto the platform: it was faintly greenish beyond the dome. He crossed the public corridor to the bright chrome and plastic lobby of Bank-America. At the exchange window, he presented his card to the blond young woman. "Another twenty-five, Mr. Norbert?"

"That's right, yes, twenty-five."

"You must really like currency." She made a note on a pad, put his card into her machine and tapped keys.

"No, I don't really — I travel a good deal, you see. It isn't safe to carry credit cards any more." She glanced up at him silently, withdrew his card from the machine. "They kidnap you and make you buy things," he said.

Her beautiful Gordonized face did not change. She counted out the bills, pushed them across the counter. Norbert took them hastily, sure that his cheeks were flushed. It was no use, he would have to change banks; she knew there was no legitimate reason to draw twenty-five dollars in cash every week . . . "Thank you, good-bye."

"Good-bye, Mr. Norbert. Have a good trip."

In the public corridor of his level a few minutes later, he ran into Art and Ellen Whitney heading for the elevators. Art and he had been roommates at one time, and then when they got married, Art and Ellen moved up to one of the garden apartments on the fiftieth floor. They looked stiff and dressed up in identical orange plastiques. "Why, here he is now," said Art. "Bob, this is real luck. We were just trying to get you on the phone, then we went and banged on your door. This is Phyllis McManus — " he turned to a slight, pale blonde Norbert had not noticed until now. "And her date stood her up. Well, you know, ah, his mother is sick. Anyhow, we've got tickets to the ice opera at the Garden, and we're going to Yorty's afterward. What do you say, would you like to come along?" Phyllis McManus smiled faintly, not quite looking at Norbert. Her virginal charm. "You will come, won't you, Bob?" said Ellen, speaking for the first time. She gave his arm a squeeze.

"I'm *terribly* sorry," said Norbert, letting his eyes glaze and bulge a little with sincerity. "I promised my sister I'd have dinner with her tonight — it's her birthday, and, you know . . ." He shrugged, smiled. "I would have loved it, Miss McManus, really I can't say how sorry I am."

"Oh. Well, that's really a shame," said Art. "You're sure you couldn't call her up — tell her something — "

"Sorry . . . just can't be done. Hope you have a good time, anyhow — good-bye, Miss McManus, nice to have met you. . . ."

They drifted apart, with regretful calls and gestures. When they were safely gone, Norbert headed for the private corridor. His room, 2073; the telltales showed it was all right. He unlocked the door, closed and barred it behind him with a shudder of relief. The little green room was quiet and cool. He rolled up the closet blind, undressed and hung his clothes up with care. Before he stepped into the minishower, he punched for a Martini and a burger-bits casserole, his favorite. Then the refreshing spray. Air-dried and out again, he ate leisurely, watching the 3D and leafing through the magazines he had bought. By now Art and Ellen and what's-her-name would be sitting in a row at the Garden under the lights, watching the mannequins cavort on the ice-covered arena below. Norbert's thighs were beginning to tremble. He dressed again, quickly, in his "street clothes" — dirty denim pants, a faded turtleneck, cracked vinyl jacket. He retrieved the wad of bills from his weskit, pulled the closet blind down again. He locked and secured the door behind him. Once out of the building, he took the shuttle crosstown to Broadway, down two levels, then north again to 168th Street. The dingy concourse was echoing, almost empty. Two or three dopes, twitching and mumbling, rode the escalator down with him. He came out into the gray street, slick and shiny under the glare of dusty light panels. Streaks of rust down the gray walls. The spattered pavement, here since LaGuardia; globs of sputum, puddles of degradable plastic. Posters on the walls: PARENTHOOD MAY BE HAZARDOUS TO YOUR HEALTH. DRIP, DON'T DROP. WHAT DID KIDS EVER DO FOR *YOU?* Rumble of semis and vans on the expressway just overhead; electrics sliding by on the avenue. Hallucinatory red and blue of 3D signs, the faint sound of music. Norbert went into the Peachtree and had a quick shot at the bar; he wanted another, but was too nervous and walked out again. In the window of Eddie's, three or four good old boys were tucking into a platter of pork and mustard greens. Norbert crossed the avenue and turned west on 169th. The doorways were full of 'billies and their girls lounging and spitting; one or two of them gave him a knowing look as he went by. "Hey, yonky," called a mocking voice, just barely audible. Norbert kept walking, past a few closed storefronts into an area of crumbling apartment houses built in the sixties. The front windows were all dark, the hallways lit only by naked yellow bulbs. At the remembered entry, he stopped, looked around. On the sidewalk, beside an arrangement of numbered squares, someone had written in yellow chalk, "Lucy is a Hoka." He went in, under the sick yellow light. The hallway stank of boiled greens and vomit. The door at the end was ajar.

"Well, come awn in," said the lanky old man in the armchair. His blue eyes stared at Norbert without apparent recognition. "Don' knock, nobody else does, walk right in." Norbert tried to smile. The others at the card table looked up briefly and went back to their game. The red drapes at the courtyard window were pulled back as if to catch a breeze. Somewhere up there in the blackness a voice burst out furiously, "You cocksucker, if I catch you . . ."

"Hello, Buddy," said Norbert. "Flo here?"

"Flo?" said the old man. "No sir, she sho' ain't."

Norbert's insides went hollow. "She's not? I mean — where'd she go?"

The old man waved his arm in a vague gesture. "Down home, I reckon." He stood up slowly. "Got us a new gal, just up from the country this mornin'." He put one hand casually between Norbert's shoulder blades and pushed him toward one of the bedroom doors.

"Well, I don't know," said Norbert, trying to hang back.

"Come on," said the old man in his ear. "She do innythang. You wait now."

They were standing in front of the door, pressed so tightly together that Norbert could smell the old man's stale underwear. Swollen knuckles rapped the door. "Betty Lou?"

After a frozen moment, the door began to open. A woman was standing there, monstrous in a flowered housedress. Norbert's heart jumped. She was olive-skinned, almost Latin-looking; the folds of her heavy face were so dark that they seemed grimy. She looked at him steadily from under brows like black caterpillars; her eyes were evil, weary and compassionate. She took his hand. The old man said something which he did not hear. Then the door had closed behind him and they were alone.

Rick Wilber

Rick Wilber's short stories and poetry have appeared in a variety of magazines and anthologies, including *Analog, Isaac Asimov's Science Fiction Magazine, Cencrastus, Fantasy & Science Fiction, Aboriginal, Pulphouse, Alien Sex, Whisper of Blood,* and others. He edits "Fiction Quarterly," the *Tampa Tribune's* short story and poetry supplement, and teaches journalism at the University of South Florida. He has written hundreds of feature articles for a wide variety of newspapers and magazines, and lives in Tampa with his wife, Robin, and son, R.A.

I've lived in Florida full-time since 1979, and have been a regular visitor since I was seven months old, so I feel practically like a native. My father was a major league baseball player, and the whole family spent spring training in Florida each year. My brothers and sisters and I would drop out of elementary school for six weeks each spring to head south, and our mother would force us through workbooks to keep up with the classes back in St. Louis.

That Florida of my youth, with its clean air and water, is mostly gone now, and what remains is in real danger from the classic threats — growth, lack of planning, the destruction of the state's rather fragile environment — and also from the more speculative disasters of the greenhouse effect and the state's social woes.

A local, slick city magazine planned an issue devoted to what Tampa would be like in fifty years, and asked me to contribute a short story. The editor expected a rather rosier prediction, but "Finals" is how it came out, and the editor, to his great credit, went with it despite its dismal view. I hope I'm wrong.

FINALS

by Rick Wilber

The sun was shining on the sea
Shining with all his might;
He did his very best to make
The billows smooth and bright —
And this was odd, because it was
The middle of the night.

— Lewis Carroll

Sean-Tomas Kyoshi Miller wants to go to university today, but it's been closed again. His European Finals are next week, and he's still a little shaky in conversational German, so he could use the lab time. He's OK, he figures, in Italian, French and Spanish, and he's got the Contemporary Society part sussed all the way around. But the conversational German, for some reason, still has him worried. And if he doesn't pass that test. . . .

He doesn't want to think about that, about failing. His future rests on passing that test, so he can make probationary. Next year there'll be the Asian Finals. Pass them and he's in full. But for now, he thinks, focus it in. First things first. Get that German down.

Still, he sighs, there's nothing he can do about it today. When university's closed, it's closed tight. Power outages, gunfights, bombs and bomb threats — it's always one of those, sometimes all three. It's a wonder he's managed to learn anything at all under the circumstances.

He is lying on his back in his too-small bed, staring vacantly at the ceiling. He notices the diagonal crack that has lengthened by another few inches in its march across the room. The ceiling needs to be fixed up, no doubt about that. The ceiling, the room, the house, the whole neighborhood, hell, the whole damn country — it all needs to be fixed up somehow.

Won't happen, though, he thinks. Just won't happen, no matter what Grandpa thinks. Instead it'll be the same slow slide, the long slow slide.

And Sean-Tomas wants out of it, at least as far out as he can get — out of Tampa and its slow death and its decay and its violence. He shakes his head to think of it, about how it's supposed to be better here than most places in the country. He shakes his head, takes a deep breath, tries to concentrate as he looks up at that cracked ceiling and tries to recite his German verbs. These little verbs, after all, are his maglev route out of here, right into the Zone.

The Zone, that's what he wants. The Tourist Zone, where he'll have a chance to make something out of all this. That's what next week's, next year's, test is all about. Getting into the Zone.

There is a sudden banging on the door, it's Grandpa with that heavy cane he uses to take the weight off his arthritic left knee. And he hits the door hard, like he always does, announcing himself to his grandson, his favorite grandson, his only one, now, since Raffy was killed in the food riots four, no, five years ago.

"Sean-Tomas, what you doing lying here staring at that ceiling, boy? I thought you had a test coming up on Monday. Gonna get that Tourist Card, right? Gonna get out of here. Why aren't you off at that school?"

"Hi, Grandpa. I'm working on my German. The university's closed again and I can't get into the language lab, so I'm just doing what I can here."

He sits up, reaches over to the pressed wood desk that is falling apart already, despite how much it cost him and how proud he was to get it, and grabs the old German textbook.

He opens it at random, tries to pay attention to the verbs, figuring that's what Grandpa wants, that must be why he came banging into the room. Grandpa really wants him to get that card, get into the Zone.

But then the cane slaps down hard right onto the open spine of the book and Grandpa, gravelly-voiced but with that hint of gentleness that sneaks through so often, says, "You need a break, son. You been at that for weeks. You're ready. You know it."

Sean-Tomas smiles. "I know, Grandpa, I know. But I wanted to run through the conversational exercises one more time. It might help."

Grandpa looks at the boy — eighteen, put together right, could've played ball back in the old days. Got a fullback's body, thick but tight, with wide shoulders, trim waist, powerful calves and thighs. Could've played, been a Gator, maybe, like his Grandpa. Famous, maybe.

But no, no more of that nonsense. All that's long over with. And the boy looks tired, too. Been studying too damn much, worrying all the time about those Finals. Boy can use a day off.

"You come with me, Sean-Tomas," Grandpa says gruffly, putting his plan into action. "I got us a little excursion figured out. You're gonna like this, we're going into the Zone, see that sub-orbital come in with all them Japanese. It'll be good for you, show you what you got coming when you ace those Finals.

"C'mon, put some good clothes on and get yourself ready. I got us permits, ration cards to get us there and back on the 'rail, everything, even some spending money in Eurocoin."

Sean-Tomas looks up at his grandfather. He doesn't believe this, doesn't believe what he's hearing. Into the Zone? Ration cards? Permits? The new sub-orbital? What's got into Grandpa? Why's he doing this? How is he doing this? Sean-Tomas is speechless.

"It's true, boy. I got the permits, the cards, everything. Let's go." They go.

II

The maglev 'rail runs on time. Everything for the tourists and the wallys runs on time, works right, gets proper maintenance. The Euros expect it, and they get it or they won't come back. And now, with the sub-orbital, the Japanese will be here, too, and they're even crazier than the Euros about things working right, about things being, you know, tight, on-time. And then the Wallys, of course, the lucky few living behind the walled-in, safely suburban neighborhoods,' they just benefit, reap the profits, from all this touristic perfection.

Grandpa's thinking all this as he and Sean-Tomas waltz coolly onto the 'rail at The Busch Gardens station, right there at the theme park with its rides and shows and little pocket Serengeti for all the Euros who are happy getting a mock Africa thrown into their Florida holiday. Grandpa took Sean-Tomas and his brother there once, fifteen years ago, back when locals could still afford to go.

As they enter the station, Sean-Tomas is remembering little snatches from that day — a giraffe eating leaves, some performing monkeys, a thrilling triple-loop roller coaster, and all the people, the happy, smiling people.

Grandpa's already a little tired. It took the two of them an hour just to get to the glossy, top-techie station with its holo ads and its gift shops full of authentic Florida handicrafts and its fancy restaurant with authentic Florida seafood and its indoor waterfall.

The rackety beat-up local bus seemed to stop at every corner on the way, and the ride was a little risky, too, getting through the neighborhoods in this part of town. But nobody much is gonna mess with somebody the size of Sean-Tomas, Grandpa figures, and here they are, big as life, just like the tourists, riding on out to the Zone in real style, impressive as hell.

Grandpa's dressed in his best — the brown slacks that are twenty, no twenty-five years old now but still look good, and his favorite yellow shirt, and the string tie with the Bucs clasp from the Superbowl back in '98. Some times they had back then, Grandpa thinks. Some times.

Sean-Tomas is dressed up, too, and nervous. It's his first time on the high-speed maglev monorail. This pod is almost empty, but he's listening in on a conversation that four French tourists are having over on the other side. They're having a good time, "bon temps," but they'd like to find a decent meal. And it's too bad, they're saying, that they can't really travel around and see the way people live here. One, the oldest one, with gray hair and a tattered gray beret, can recall when you still could, when the roads were safe enough and everything wasn't yet all closed off for security.

Sean-Tomas can recall those days. But, like his memories of the Gardens, they're all in bits and pieces. He was just a kid when the subdivisions went to hiring the armed guards full-time and putting the broken glass into the concrete walls they were building to shelter themselves from the growing collapse and even, in some places, the rising water.

He can remember walking by a place like that with Raffy. The wall went on forever, and then there was a black steel gate. Two kids, a boy and girl, were on the inside, looking out. Sean and Raffy just walked on by them. Nobody said anything.

Those insiders, the Wallys, still got to live a good reproduction of the good life. The rest, the vast majority, had to deal with reality's decline.

Sean-Tomas can even recall how the attacks finally came. Too few seemed to have too much and the outsiders got upset about it enough to storm OakHaven up in the fancy Carrollwood area and The Trace in comfortable Temple Terrace, not far from where Sean-Tomas lives now. OakHaven fell and was looted, thirty people died. The Trace held and later built a statue to the victory.

But all that was awhile ago. Years. Things are stable now. The adjustment's been made. Violent, deadly sometimes, but stable. Sean-Tomas hasn't really known it any other way.

But Grandpa has. Grandpa remembers how it was and how it all came to be this miserable.

"The price we've all paid," he mumbles to himself as he sits next to Sean-Tomas and stares out the window as the hovels and the occasional high-walled tracts stream by.

"What did you say, Grandpa?" Sean-Tomas asks, only half paying attention. He can't get over how fast they're getting to the Zone. He's walked to it before, just up to the main gate so he could say he'd seen it, and it took him all day. Even on the buses it takes hours. The 'rail is getting them there in maybe fifteen minutes. Amazing. And the tourists consider it all just the normal kit, business as usual.

Downtown Tampa slips by. To Sean-Tomas the water halfway up the first story of downtown's aging skyscrapers is normal. The water taxis get the job done, and there are skyways between buildings. No big deal.

There's never been any trouble handling the water unless there's a big storm. More of those, of course, what with the Greenhouse warming up the water. Sean-Tomas has studied all this, how the storms are forty percent stronger than they used to be, how there's more of them, and how the icecaps are melting and all of that. The gutted old bank building is proof of what the storms can do when they sweep up the coast.

They haven't started rebuilding the thirty-story building, and it's been four years since Miriam roared through. None of the Euros want to fund it; they're in a recession right now and Eurocoin is tight. The city is hoping the Japanese will want to buy in a little more now. The sub-orbital makes Tampa so handy to them, just three and a half hours and they're here.

". . . way it used to be," Grandpa is saying. Sean-Tomas hasn't been listening, he's been gawking. He looks away from his own reflection in the tinted glass of the window and smiles at Grandpa.

"The way it used to be," Grandpa says to him again. "It was, well . . . hell, we were a great country back then, back before it all fell apart, before the oil dried up and the damn water rose and the Japanese bought everything up and the Euros got together and then went to damn Mars . . . "

Sean-Tomas pats his grandfather's arm, stops him. He's seen him get like this before, get all wound up. A lot of the older folks do this, remember how it was and how it all got thrown away and how fast it all came tumbling down when the debts got called in. Sean-Tomas has studied it all, dry and boring, in university.

So what, he figures. Assyria, Egypt, Greece, Rome, Islam, Spain, the French and the British and the Dutch and the Germans and Russians and all the rest. And now us. Empires fall. That's the way it is. Boring dates. Boring names.

All that matters, all that really matters, is passing the European Finals, getting into the Zone where life serving the tourists is easy and you're well fed and taken care of. Sean-Tomas wants to keep the focus narrow, he needs to. Now is not the time for a broad perspective on the national decline and how it could have been stopped or eased. Now is not even the time to worry about

Grandpa's whole generation and how they're going to survive with the collapsing empty sack of Social Security. They're sixty-five percent of the population now, they'll figure something out.

Sean-Tomas figures those kind of solutions are out of his control. The Finals, those he can worry about, do something about. The Finals.

They reach the station, arcing in over a lower class hotel that caters to the U.S. trade and then shooting by the remnants of the old interstate bridge. From their height Sean-Tomas can see the whole area better than he ever has before — the hotels stretching north and south into the distance, the huge filter pumps and the barrier booms offshore to clarify the water, the reverse osmosis plant right inside the gate where they make their own fresh water for the tourists, the broken pieces of the interstate bridge marching so visibly across the bay that he thinks it must be low tide.

And there, in the distance, the scattered Pinellas islands, some of them really big. A dozen different tourist boats are in the bay, all of them either heading toward the islands or coming from them. Great fishing over there in the underwater ruins, and the snorkeling in the shallow water is world famous.

Then the 'rail dips down into the station and clicks smoothly into the receiving tube with a gentle bump.

"We're here, boy," says Grandpa, smiling. "The Tourist Zone. Let's go."

They rise, they go, Sean-Tomas almost in a trance. He's actually getting inside.

III

And he's disneyed, absolutely disneyed, by it all. Even the holo ads that flow by in the breeze are new to him. He's fractaled, wiped, burned and blown — every word he can think of to describe it. It's wonderful.

He and Grandpa are getting some stares. No, a lot of stares. Must be the way they're dressed or something. No matter.

They get a bowl of soup, which is all they can really afford, at a restaurant near the docks where the tour boats tie up. Sean-Tomas orders in French and chats with the couple at the next table in Italian. He's in heaven. It's all worth it. He can't wait to really get here.

The couple smiles condescendingly. Yes, they're having a good time. No, they're not sure who they're voting for now that the government has fallen again in Italy. They're Romans, and they don't really care about such matters. Yes, he does speak excellent Italian, something of a northern accent, his teacher must have been from Torino, perhaps. One can hear the mountains in the way he says his "E's."

Then, later, Sean-Tomas and his grandfather walk along the beach. The gurgle of the filter pumps sounds comforting, somehow, Sean-Tomas thinks. They sound like prosperity, like jobs and money and a future.

The beach is narrow, and the Zone Commission will have to bring in more sand from the central part of the state again to widen it out. This happens every year now, Grandpa is thinking as he pokes at a shell with the cane. He does have to wonder how long it can all go on.

Grandpa is really feeling tired now, and something else, too. There's something nagging at him, something he can't quite define yet. There's a feeling, somehow, that he's been here before. But, of course, he hasn't, not since it was zoned for the tourists anyway, and that's been fifteen years now.

It's been a good day for the boy, Grandpa thinks, and worth all the trouble to make it happen. It cost Grandpa what money he had, plus calling in old favors, hocking the Sugar Bowl ring, some begging, some cajoling.

But worth it. Here they are, looking for a good spot on this beach to see the sun-orbital landing. The boy has a future here, a real chance. It's been worth it.

Still, there is this disquieting feeling. Grandpa shakes it off, angrily stabs the cane down onto another shell. The shell shatters.

There is a distant whine. Sean-Tomas hears it first, stops, looks up, scanning the deepening blue of the late afternoon sky for the sub-orbital. Can't see it yet.

Grandpa doesn't look up, he just looks at the boy. Could've been a Gator, maybe.

The whine grows louder. Grandpa finally does look. There, over there, is a glint of sun off those new top-techie tiles that coat the thing. A planeload of Japanese. From there to here in three and one half hours. The next wave of tourists, with pockets full of yen. Spendable yen. Eurocoin and yen, keeping Florida afloat.

A little group of Euros is walking by. Germans. They stop, look up, too, and point.

"Guten tag," says Sean-Tomas, smiling.

The Germans just look back, then look at one another. They smile tightly and begin to move away. Sean-Tomas and his grandfather worry them. They've heard what the locals are like. They're surprised that any of them are allowed on this beach. They'll rob you, they'll beg, they're violent, mean and stupid. Best just to walk calmly away. Show no fear.

And Grandpa realizes what the feeling is that he's having. He's remembering how it was when he was Sean-Tomas' age or a bit older, when he and Kyoshi were newly married.

They traveled back then, back when you still could, back when there was money for it. The Caribbean, mainly. Jamaica, the Yucatan. Good times, happy times, walking along the beaches, drinks in hand.

And he remembers how they felt about the locals, about the Mexicans, the Jamaicans, about how he and Kyo mainly stayed right in the resort area. What did they call it in Cancun? The Hotel Zone, that was it. And the warning signs in Negril about leaving the resort's beach. "Beware peddlers."

The whine is a roar now. Sean-Tomas is speechless, stunned by the sight and sound of the sub-orbital heading for the runway, retractable wings fully extended, landing gear down, scramjets silent as the propfans ease the huge thing toward the ground.

Grandpa stares as it passes by, its huge shadow going right over them. He just stares, and then turns to leave.

Sean-Tomas is excited. He doesn't understand why Grandpa's

gotten so quiet, sullen almost. The older folks, Sean-Tomas thinks sadly to himself. It's tough on them.

And then he turns his thoughts again to the Finals, to his German verbs, to his future as he watches the sub-orbital gently touch down.

Kate Wilhelm

Kate Wilhelm began her science fiction career in 1956 with a short story, "The Pint-Size Genie," in *Amazing* magazine. She published a mystery novel, *More Bitter Than Death,* in 1963 and her first science fiction novel, *The Clone,* written in collaboration with Theodore L. Thomas, appeared in 1965. Her short story "The Planners" won the Nebula Award for best short story in 1968, and she achieved major critical and popular success with her 1976 novel, *Where Late The Sweet Birds Sang,* which won the Hugo Award for best novel. Other novels include *The Clewiston Test, Fault Lines, The Nevermore Affair, Let the Fire Fall, Juniper Time, The Dark Door, Huysman's Pets,* and *Crazy Time.* She and her husband, Damon Knight, are principal lecturers at the annual Clarion Science Fiction and Fantasy Workshop.

I first visited Florida in 1946 when I drove into the interior of the state on a two-lane road with no other traffic and saw a flock of turkey vultures at the carcass of a pig on the side of the road. They ambled out of range with such disdain that I never forgot the image. This was their domain, that was clear, and I was the intruder. The swampy woods pressed hard against the clearing for the road, and again it seemed that the road was out of place, the woods would prevail in time.

It was more than twenty years before I moved to Florida for a time. The road had become a major highway, the swamps drained in part, no sign of the vultures. But the feeling persisted. All of this concrete was temporary; Florida gave me the impression of waiting presence. Then, house hunting, we saw the dance of the herons on a seawall, and the story emerged from a recess into a whole, ready to be written almost, with very little tinkering.

So I got the nuance of the story ten years before I began to write, and thirty years before a story was created from it. The feeling persisted all those years — waiting.

THE SCREAM

by Kate Wilhelm

The sea had turned to copper; it rose and fell gently, the motion starting so deep that no ripple broke the surface of the slow swells. The sky was darkening to a deep blue-violet with rose streaks in the west and a high cirrocumulus formation in the east that was a dazzling white mountain crowned with brilliant reds and touches of green. No wind stirred. The irregular dark strip that was Miami Beach separated the metallic sea from the fiery sky. We were at anchor eight miles offshore aboard the catamaran *Loretta*. She was a forty-foot, single-masted, inboard motorboat.

Evinson wanted to go on in, but Trainor, whose boat it was, said no. Too dangerous: sand, silt, wrecks, God knew what we might hit. We waited until morning.

We had to go in at Biscayne Bay; the Bal Harbour inlet was clogged with the remains of the bridge on old A1A. Trainor put in at the Port of Miami. All the while J.P. kept taking his water samples, not once glancing at the ruined city; Delia kept a running check for radiation, and Bernard took pictures. Corrie and I tried to keep out of the way, and Evinson didn't. The ancient catamaran was clumsy and Trainor was kept busy until we were tied up, then he bowed sarcastically to Evinson and went below.

Rusting ships were in the harbor, some of them on their sides half in water, half out. Some of them seemed afloat, but then we saw that without the constant dredging that had kept the port open, silt and sand had entered, and the bottom was no more than ten to fifteen feet down. The water was very clear. Some catfish lay unmoving on the bottom, and a school of big-eyed mullet circled at the surface, the first marine life we had seen. The terns were diving here, and sandpipers ran with the waves. J.P.'s eyes were shining as he watched the birds. We all had been afraid that there would be no life of any kind.

Our plan was to reconnoiter the first day, try to find transportation: bicycles, which none of us had ridden before, skates, canoes, anything. Miami and the beaches covered a lot of miles, and we had a lot of work; without transportation the work would be less valuable — if it had any value to begin with.

Bernard and Delia went ahead to find a place to set up our base, and the rest of us started to unload the boat. In half an hour we were drenched with sweat. At first glance the city had seemed perfectly habitable, just empty of people, but as we carried the boxes to the hotel that Bernard had found, the ruins dominated the scene. Walls were down, streets vanished under sand and palmettos and sea grapes. The hotel was five stories, the first floor covered with sand and junk: shells, driftwood, an aluminum oar eaten through with corrosion. Furniture was piled against walls haphazardly, like heaps of rotting compost. The water had risen and fallen more than once, rearranging floatables. It was hellishly hot, and the hotel stank of ocean and decay and dry rot and heat. No one talked much as we all worked, all but Trainor, who had worked to get us here, and now guzzled beer with his feet up. Evinson cursed him monotonously. We carried our stuff to the hotel, then to the second floor where we put mosquito netting at the windows of three connecting rooms that would be used jointly. We separated to select our private rooms and clear them and secure them against the mosquitoes that would appear by the millions as soon as the sun went down.

After a quick lunch of soy wafers and beer we went out singly to get the feel of the city and try to locate any transportation we could.

I started with a map in my hand, and the first thing I did was put it back inside my pack. Except for the general areas, the map was worthless. This had been a seawalled city, and the seawalls had gone: a little break here, a crack somewhere else, a trickle of water during high tide, a flood during a storm, the pressure building behind the walls, on the land side, and inevitably the surrender to the sea. The water had undermined the road system, and eaten away at foundations of buildings, and hurricane winds had done the rest. Some streets were completely filled in with rubble, others were pitted and undercut until shelves of concrete had shifted and slid and now rested crazily tilted. The white sand had claimed some streets so thoroughly that growth had had a chance to naturalize and there were strip-forests of palm trees, straggly bushes with pink and yellow flowers, and sea grapes. I saw a mangrove copse claiming the water's edge and stopped to stare at it for a long time, with curious thoughts flitting through my brain about the land and the sea in a survival struggle in which man was no more than an incidental observer, here, then gone. The afternoon storm broke abruptly and I took shelter in a building that seemed to have been a warehouse.

The stench of mold and decay drove me out again as soon as the storm abated. Outside, the sun had baked everything, the sun and rain sterilizing, neutralizing, keeping the mold at bay, but inside the cavernous buildings the soggy air was a culture for mold spores, and thirty years, forty, had not been long enough to deplete the rich source of nutrients. There was food available on the shelves, the shelves were food, the wood construction materials, the glues and grouts, the tiles and vinyls, the papers neatly filed, the folders that held them, pencils, everything finally was food for the mold.

I entered two more buildings, same thing, except that one of them had become a bat cave. They were the large fruit bats, not dangerous, and I knew they were not, but I left them the building without contest.

At the end of the first day we had three bicycles, and a flat-bottomed rowboat with two oars. I hadn't found anything of value. The boat was aluminum, and although badly corroded, it seemed intact enough. Trainor slouched in while J.P. was cooking dinner, and the rest of us were planning our excursions for the next day.

"You folks want boats? Found a storehouse full of them."

He joined us for dinner and drew a map showing the warehouse he had found. His freehand map was more reliable than the printed ones we had brought with us. I suspected that he was salvaging what he could for his own boat. Unless he was a fool that was what he was doing. When Evinson asked him what else he had seen that day, he simply shrugged.

"How's chances of a swim?" I asked Delia after we ate.

"No radiation. But you'd better wait for Corrie to run some analyses. Too much that we don't know about it to chance it yet."

"No swimming, damn it!" Evinson said sharply. "For God's sake, Sax." He issued orders rapidly for the next day, in effect telling everyone to do what he had come to do.

Strut and puff, you little bastard, I thought at him. No one protested.

The same ruins lay everywhere in the city. After the first hour it was simply boring. My bicycle was more awkward than going on foot, since I had to carry it over rubble as much as I got to ride it. I abandoned it finally. I found the Miami River and dutifully got a sample. It was the color of tea, very clear. I followed the river a long time, stopped for my lunch, and followed it some more. Ruins, sand, junk, palm trees. Heat. Silence. Especially silence. I was not aware of when I began to listen to the silence, but I caught myself walking cautiously, trying to be as quiet as the city, not to intrude in any way. The wind in the dry fronds was the only thing I heard. It stopped, then started again, and I jerked around. I went inside a building now and then, but they were worse than the ruined streets. Rusty toys, appliances, moldering furniture, or piles of dust where the termites had been, chairs that crumbled when I touched them, and the heat and silence.

I got bored with the river and turned in to what had been a garden park. Here the vegetation was different. A banyan tree had spread unchecked and filled more than a city block. A flock of blackbirds arose from it as I approached. The suddenness of their flight startled me and I whirled around, certain that someone was behind me. Nothing. Vines and bushes had grown wild in the park, and were competing with trees for space — a minijungle. There were thousands of parakeets, emerald green, darting, making a cacophony that was worse than the silence. I retraced my steps after a few minutes. There might have been water in there, but I didn't care. I circled the park and kept walking.

The feeling that I was being followed grew stronger, and I stopped as if to look more closely at a weed, listening for steps. Nothing. The wind in some pampas grass, the louder rustle of palm fronds, the return of the blackbirds. And in the distance the raucous cries of gulls. The feeling didn't go away, and I walked faster, and sweated harder.

I got out my kit and finished the last of the beer in the shade of a live oak with branches eighty feet long spreading out sideways in all directions. Whatever had poisoned Miami and reduced its population to zero hadn't affected the flora. The wind started, the daily storm. I sat in the doorway of a stinking apartment building and watched sheets of water race down the street. After the storm passed I decided to go back and try to get Corrie to bed with me. It never occurred to me to snuggle up to Delia, who seemed totally asexual. Delia and J.P., I thought.

Corrie was alone, and she said no curtly. She was as hot as I was and as tired. But she had a working lab set up, complete with microscopes and test tubes and flasks of things over Bunsen burners. She glanced contemptuously at the collecting bottle that I handed her. They knew about me, all of them.

"What did I do wrong?"

"Label it, please. Location, depth, source, time of day. Anything else you can think of that might be helpful."

Her tone said, and leave me alone because I have real work to do. She turned back to her microscope.

"So I'm not a hydrologist. I'm a pamphlet writer for Health, Education and Welfare."

"I know." She glanced at me again. "But why didn't they send a real hydrologist?"

"Because we don't have one."

She stood up and walked to the window netting and looked out. Her shirt was wet under her sleeves and down her back, her hair clung to her cheeks and the nape of her neck. "Why?" she whispered. "Why? Why? Why?"

"If they knew that we wouldn't be here."

She walked back to her chair and sat down again, drawing the microscope toward her once more.

"Is the bay all right?"

"Yes." She adjusted the focus and forgot about me. I left.

The warehouse where Trainor had found the boats was half a dozen blocks up the waterfront. I walked and sweated. Trainor had dragged some small boats outside, and I chose the smallest of them and took it down to the water. I rowed out into the bay, undressed and swam for half an hour; then I started to row, going no place in particular.

The water was marvelously calm, and I felt cooler and less tense after the swim. I stopped to drive a couple of times around a sunken yacht; it had been stripped. I stopped again, this time ashore at what looked like a copy of the Parthenon. It had been a museum. The water lapped about the foundation; marble stairs and massive fountains indicated that it had been a grandiose thing. A statue had toppled and I considered it. A female form — vaguely female, anyway. Rounded, curving, voluptuous-looking, roughly hewn out of granite, it was touching somehow. The eye-hollows were facing out to sea, waiting, watching the water, waiting. The essence of woman as childbearer, woman as nourisher, woman as man's sexual necessity. Her flesh would be warm and yielding. She would be passive, accept his seed and let it come to life within her. Those great round arms would hold a child, let it suckle at the massive breasts. I wished I could stand the statue upright again. When it fell one of the arms had broken, it lay apart from the bulk of the work. I tried to lift it: too heavy. I ran my hand over the rough rock and I wanted to sit on the floor by the woman and talk to her, cry a little, rest my cheek against that breast. I began to feel suffocated suddenly and I turned and ran from the museum without looking for anything else. The sun was setting, the sky crimson and blue and green, incredible colors that looked like cheap art.

It was dark when I got back to headquarters. All the others were there already, even Trainor. Delia was cooking. I watched her as she added water to the dehydrated stew and stirred it over canned heat. She was angular, with firm muscles and hardly any breasts at all. Her hips were slim, boyish, her legs all muscle and bone. I wondered again about her sexuality. I had seen her studying Trainor speculatively once, but nothing had come of it, and I had seen almost the same expression on her face a time or two when she had been looking at Corrie.

I turned my attention to Corrie — a little better, but still not really woman, not as the statue had signified woman. Corrie was softer than Delia, her hips a bit rounder, her breasts bouncier, not much, but Delia's never moved at all. Corrie had more of a waistline. My thoughts were confusing to me, and I tried to think of something else, but that damn statue kept intruding. I should have talked to her, I found myself thinking. And, she would have looked at me with contempt. She would have looked at any of our men with contempt — except, possibly, Trainor.

I watched and listened to Trainor then, speaking with Bernard. Trainor was tall and broad-shouldered, his hair white, face browned by the sun, very lean and very muscular.

"Have you ever seen any wild animals as far north as the cape?" Bernard asked, sketching. His fingers were swift and sure: That characterized him all the way, actually. He was soft-looking, but he moved with a sureness always. A dilettante artist, photographer, in his mid-thirties, rich enough not to work. There had been a mild affair with Corrie, but nothing serious. I didn't know why he was here.

"Deer," Trainor said in answer to his question. "There's a lot of things up in the brush. Foxes, rabbits, muskrats, possum."

"Anything big? I heard that lions were let loose, or escaped around West Palm Beach. Did they live, multiply?"

"Can't say."

"Heard there were panthers."

"Can't say."

"How about Indians? You must know if any of them are left in the swamps." Bernard's pencil stopped, but he didn't look at Trainor.

"Could be. Don't go inland much. No way to get inland, hard going by boat, hyacinths, thick enough to walk on. Too much stuff in the water everywhere. St. John's River used to be open, but not now."

"How about fish then? See any porpoises?"

"They come and go. Don't stay around long. Hear they're thick down around South America and in the Caribbean. Might be."

I watched Bernard for a long time. What was he after? And Trainor? I had a feeling that the seven people who had come to the city had seven different reasons, and that mine was the only simple one. Orders. When you work for the government and an undersecretary says go, you go. Why were the others here?

In bed later, I couldn't sleep. The odors all came back in triple strength after dark. I could feel the mold growing around me, on me, in my bedroll. The humidity was a weight on my chest. I finally got up again, drenched with sweat, my bed soaked through, and I went back to the second floor where I interrupted Delia and Bernard in a quiet conversation. I got a beer and sat down near the window, my back to them both. After a moment Delia yawned and got up.

At the doorway she paused and said, "Why don't you take him?"

I looked at her then. Bernard made a snorting sound and didn't answer. I turned back to the window. The silence was coming in along with the night-time humidity, and I realized that I had chosen my room on the wrong side of the building. The night air blew from the land to the sea. There was a faint breeze at the window. The oil lamp was feeble against the pressure of the darkness beyond the netting.

"Night," Delia said at the door, and I looked at her again, nodded, and she started through, then stopped. A high, uncanny, inhuman scream sounded once, from a long way off. It echoed through the empty city. The silent that followed it made me understand that what I had thought to be quiet before had not been stillness. Now the silence was profound, no insect, no rustling, no whir of small wings, nothing. The the night sounds began to return. The three of us had remained frozen, now Bernard moved. He turned to Delia.

"I knew it," he said. "I knew!"

She was very pale. "What was it?" she cried shrilly.

"Panther. Either in the city or awfully close."

Panther? It might have been. I had no idea what a panther sounded like. The others were coming down again, Evinson in the lead, Corrie and J.P. close behind him. Corrie looked less frightened than Delia, but rattled and pale.

'For heaven's sake, Bernard!" J.P. said. "Was that you?"

"Don't you know?" Corrie cried. At the same time Delia said, "It was a panther."

"No! Don't be a fool!" Corrie said.

Evinson interrupted them both. "Everyone, just be quiet. It was some sort of bird. We've seen birds for three days now. Some of them make cries like that."

"No bird ever made a sound like that," Corrie said. Her voice was too high and excited.

"It was a panther," Bernard repeated. "I heard one before. In Mexico I heard one just like that, twenty years ago. I've never forgotten." He nodded toward the net-covered window. "Out there. Maybe in one of the city parks. Think what it means, Evinson. I was right! Wild life out there. Naturalized, probably." He took a breath. His hands were trembling, and he spoke with an intensity that was almost embarrassing. Corrie shook her head stubbornly, but Bernard went on. "I'm going to find it. Tomorrow. I'll take Sax with me, and our gear, and plan to stay out there for a day or two. We'll see if we can find a trace of it, get a shot. Proof of some kind."

Evinson started to protest. If it wasn't his plan, he hated it. "We need Sax to find water for us," he said. "It's too dangerous. We don't know what the beast is, it might attack at sight."

I was watching Bernard. His face tightened, became older, harsher. He was going. "Drop it, Evinson," I said. "They know about me. The only water I'll find is the river, which I already stumbled across, remember. And Bernard is right. If there's anything, we should go out and try to find it."

Evinson grumbled some more, but he couldn't really forbid it, since this was what the expedition was all about. Besides, he knew damn well there was no way on earth that he could enforce any silly edict. Sulkily he left us to plan our foray.

It was impossible to tell how the waterways had been laid out in many places. The water had spread, making marshes, and had changed its course, sometimes flowing down streets, again vanishing entirely, leaving dry beds as devoid of life as the Martian canals. Ruined concrete and sand lay there now. And the ruins went on and on. No frame houses remained; they had caved in, or had been blown down, or burned. A trailer court looked as if someone had taken one corner of the area and lifted it, tipping the chrome and gaudy colored cans to one side. Creepers and shrubs were making a hill of greenery over them. We rowed and carried the boat and our stuff all day, stopped for the storms, then found shelter in a school building when it grew dark. The mosquitoes were worse the farther we went; their whining drowned out all other noises; we were both a mass of swollen bites that itched without letup. We saw nothing bigger than a squirrel. Bernard thought he glimpsed a manatee once, but it disappeared in the water plants and didn't show again. I didn't see it. There were many birds.

We were rowing late in the afternoon of the second day when Bernard motioned me to stop. We drifted and I looked where he pointed. On the bank was a great grey heron, its head stretched upward in a strange but curiously graceful position. Its wings were spread slightly, and it looked like nothing so much as a ballerina, poised, holding out her tutu. With painful slowness it lifted one leg and flexed its toes, then took a dainty, almost mincing step. Bernard pointed again, and I saw the second bird, in the same pose, silent, following a ritual that had been choreographed incalculable ages ago. We watched the dance of the birds in silence, until without warning Bernard shouted in a hoarse, strange voice, "Get out of here! You fucking birds! Get out of here!" He hit the water with his oar, making an explosive noise, and continued to scream at them as they lifted in panicked flight and vanished into the growth behind them, trailing their long legs, ungainly now and no longer beautiful.

"Bastard," I muttered at him and started to row again. We were out of synch for a long time as he chopped at the water ineffectually.

We watched the rain later, not talking. We hadn't talked since seeing the birds' courtship dance. I had a sunburn that was painful and peeling; I was tired, and hungry for some real food. "Tomorrow morning we start back," I said. I didn't look at him. We were in a small house while the rain and wind howled and pounded and turned the world grey. Lightning flashed and thunder rocked us almost simultaneously. The house shook and I tensed, ready to run. Bernard laughed. He waited for the wind to let up before he spoke.

"Sax, we have until the end of the week and then back to Washington for you, back to New York for me. When do you think you'll ever get out of the city again?"

"If I get back to it, what makes you think I'll ever want out again?"

"You will. This trip will haunt you. You'll begin to think of those parakeets, the terns wheeling and diving for fish. You'll dream of swimming in clean water. You'll dream of the trees and the skies and the waves on the beach. And no matter how much you want to get it back, there won't be any way at all."

"There's a way if you want it bad enough."

"No way." He shook his head. "I tried. For years I tried. No way. Unless you're willing to walk crosscountry, and take the risks. No one ever makes it to anywhere, you know."

I knew he was right. In Health and Education you learn about things like public transportation: there isn't any. You learn about travel: there isn't any, not that's safe. The people who know how to salvage and make-do get more and more desperate for parts to use, more and more deadly in the ways they get those parts. Also, travel permits were about as plentiful as unicorns.

"You wanted to go back to Mexico?" I asked.

"Yeah. For twenty years I wanted to go back. The women there are different."

"You were younger. They were younger."

"No, it isn't just that. They were different. Something in the air. You could feel it, sniff it, almost see it. The smells were . . ." He stood up suddenly. "Anyway, I tried to get back, and this is as close as I could get. Maybe I'll go ahead and walk after all." He faced the west where the sky had cleared and the low sun looked three times as big as it should have.

"Look, Bernard, I could quote you statistics; that's my job, you know. But I won't. Just take my word for it. That's what I'm good at. What I read, I remember. The birth rate has dropped to two per thousand there. As of six years ago. It might be lower now. They're having a hell of a time with communications. And they had plague."

"I don't believe that."

"What? The birth rate?"

"Plague." He looked at me with a strange smile.

I didn't know what he was driving at. I was the one with access to government records, while he was just a photographer. "Right," I said. "People just died of nothing."

"It's a lie, Sax! A goddamn fucking lie! No plague!" He stopped as suddenly as he had started, and sat down. "Forget it, Sax. Just forget it."

"If it wasn't the plague, what?"

"I said to let it drop."

"What was it, Bernard? You're crazy, you know that? You're talking crazy."

"Yeah, I'm crazy." He was looking westward again.

During the night I wakened to hear him walking back and forth. I hoped that if he decided to start that night, he'd leave me the canoe. I went back to sleep. He was still there in the morning.

"Look, Sax, you go back. I'll come along in a day or two."

"Bernard, you can't live off nothing. There won't be any food after tomorrow. We'll both go back, stock up, and come out again. I couldn't go off and leave you. How would you get back?"

"When I was a boy," he said, "my father and mother were rather famous photographers. They taught me. We traveled all over the world. Getting pictures of all the vanishing species, for one last glorious book." I nodded. They had produced two of the most beautiful books I had ever seen. "Then something happened," he said, after a slight hesitation. "You know all about that, I guess. Your department. They went away and left me in Mexico. I wasn't a kid, you see, but I'd always been with them. Then I wasn't with them anymore. No note. No letter. Nothing. They searched for them, of course. Rich gringos aren't — weren't — allowed to simply vanish. Nothing. Before that my father had taken me into the hills, for a hunt. This time with guns. We shot — God, we shot everything that moved! Deer. Rabbits. Birds. A couple of snakes. There was a troop of monkeys. I remember them most of all. Seven monkeys. He took the left side and I took the right and we wiped them out. Just like that. They shrieked and screamed and tried to run away, and tried to shield each other, and we got every last one. Then we went back to my mother and the next day they were gone. I was fifteen. I stayed there for five years. Me and the girls of Mexico. They sent me home just before the border was closed. All North Americans out. I got permission to go back to New York, and for seventeen years I never left again. Until now. I won't go back again, Sax."

He leaned over and picked up a rifle. He had had it with his photographic equipment. "I have ammunition. I've had it for years. I'm pretty good with it. I'd demonstrate, but I don't want to waste the shell. Now, you just pick up your gear, and toss it in the boat, and get the hell out of here."

I suddenly remembered watching television as a child, when they had programs that went on around the clock — stories, movies. A man with a rifle stalking a deer. That's all I could remember of that program, but it was very clear and I didn't want to go away and let Bernard be that man. I stared at the rifle, until it began to rise and I was looking down the barrel of it.

"I'll kill you, Sax. I really will," he said, and I knew he would.

I turned and tossed my pack into the boat and then climbed in. "How will you get back, if you decide to come back?" I felt only bitterness. I was going back and he was going to be the man with the rifle.

"I'll find a way. If I'm not there by Friday, don't wait. Tell Evinson I said that, Sax."

"Bernard . . ." I let it hang there as I pushed off and started to paddle. There wasn't a thing that I could say to him.

I heard a shot about an hour later, then another in the afternoon, after that nothing. I got back to headquarters during the night. No one was up, so I raided the food and beer and went to bed. The next morning Evinson was livid with rage.

"He wouldn't have stayed like that! You left him! You did something to him, didn't you? You'll be tried, Sax. I'll see you in prison for this." Color flooded back into his face, leaving him looking as unnaturally flushed as he had been pale only a moment before. His hand trembled as he wiped his forehead that was flaky with peeling skin.

"Sax is telling the truth," Delia said. She had circles under her eyes and seemed depressed. "Bernard wanted me to go away with him to hunt. I refused. He needed someone to help him get as far away as possible."

Evinson turned his back on her. "You'll go back for him," he said to me, snapping the words. I shook my head. "I'll report you, Sax. I don't believe a word of what you've said. I'll report you. You did something, didn't you? All his work for this project! You go get him!"

"Oh, shut up." I turned to Corrie. "Anything new while I was gone?"

She looked tired too. Evinson must have applied the whip. "Not much. We've decided to take back samples of everything. We can't do much with the equipment we brought. Just not enough time. Not enough of us for the work."

"If you knew your business you could do it!" Evinson said. "Incompetents! All of you! This is treason! You know that, don't you? You're sabotaging this project. You don't want me to prove my theory. Obstacles every step of the way. That's all you've been good for. And now this! I'm warning you, Sax, if you don't bring Bernard back today, I'll press charges against you." His voice had been high-pitched always, but it became shriller and shriller until he sounded like a hysterical woman.

I spun to face him. "What theory, you crazy old man? There is no theory! There are a hundred theories. You think those records weren't sifted a thousand times before they were abandoned? Everything there was microfilmed and studied again and again and again. You think you can poke about in this muck and filth and come up with something that hasn't been noted and discarded a dozen times? They don't give a damn about your theories, you bloody fool! They hope that Delia can come up with a radiation study they can use. That Bernard will find wild life, plant life that will prove the pollution has abated here. That J.P. will report the marine life has reestablished itself. Who do you think will even read your theories about what happened here? Who gives a damn? All they want now is to try to save the rest." I was out of breath and more furious than I had been in years. I wanted to kill the bastard, and it didn't help at all to realize that it was Bernard that I really wanted to strangle. The man with the gun. Evinson backed away from me, and for the first time I saw that one of his hands had been bandaged.

Corrie caught my glance and shrugged. "Something bit him. He thinks I should be able to analyze his blood and come up with everything from what did it to a foolproof antidote. In fact, we have no idea what bit him."

"Isn't Trainor any help with something like that?"

"He might be if he were around. We haven't seen him since the night we heard the scream."

Evinson flung down his plastic cup. It bounced from the table to the floor. He stamped out.

"It's bad," Corrie said. "He's feverish, and his hand is infected. I've done what I can. I just don't have anything to work with."

Delia picked up the cup and put it back on the table. "This whole thing is an abysmal failure," she said dully. "None of us is able to get any real work done. We don't know enough, or we don't have the right equipment, or enough manpower, or time. I don't even know why we're here."

"The Turkey Point plant?"

"I don't know a damn thing about it, except that it isn't hot. The people who built that plant knew more than we're being taught today." She bit her lip hard enough to leave marks on it. Her voice was steady when she went on. "It's like that in every field. We're losing everything that we had twenty-five years ago, thirty years ago. I'm one of the best, and I don't understand that plant."

I looked at Corrie and she nodded. "I haven't seen a transplant in my life. No one is doing them now. I read about dialysis, but no one knows how to do it. In my books there are techniques and procedures that are as alien as acupuncture. Evinson is furious with us, and with himself. He can't come up with anything that he couldn't have presented as theory without ever leaving the city. It's a failure, and he's afraid he'll be blamed personally."

We sat in silence for several minutes until J.P. entered. He looked completely normal. His bald head was very red; the rest of his skin had tanned to a deep brown. He looked like he was wearing a gaudy skullcap.

"You're back." Not a word about Bernard, or to ask what we had done, what we had seen. "Delia, you coming with me again today? I'd like to get started soon."

Delia laughed and stood up. "Sure, J.P. All the way." They left together.

"Is he getting anything done?"

"Who knows? He works sixteen hours a day doing something.

I don't know what." Corrie drummed her fingers on the table, watching them. Then she said, "Was that a panther the other night, Davidson? Did you see a panther, or anything else?"

"Nothing. And I don't know what it was. I never heard a panther."

"I don't think it was. I think it was a human being."

"A woman?"

"Yes. In childbirth."

I stared at her until she met my gaze. She nodded. "I've heard it before. I am a doctor, you know. I specialized in obstetrics until the field became obsolete."

I found that I couldn't stop shaking my head. "You're as crazy as Bernard."

"No. That's what I came for, Davidson. There has to be life that's viable, out there in the Everglades. The Indians. They can stick it out, back in the swamps where they always lived. Probably nothing much has changed for them. Except that there's more game now. That has to be it."

"Have you talked to Evinson about this?"

"Yes, of course. He thinks it was Trainor who screamed. He thinks Trainor was killed by a snake, or something. After he got bitten himself, he became convinced of it."

"J.P.? Delia?"

"J.P. thinks it's a mystery. Since it has nothing to do with marine biology, he has no opinion, no interest. Delia thought Bernard was right, an animal, maybe a panther, maybe something else. She is afraid it's a mutated animal. She began to collect strange plants, and insects, things like that after you left. She even has a couple of fruit bats that she says are mutations."

I took a deep breath. "Corrie, why are we here? Why did the government send this expedition here?"

She shrugged. "What you told Evinson makes as much sense as anything else. The government didn't mount this expedition, you know. They simply permitted it. And sent an observer. It was Bernard's scheme from the start. He convinced Evinson that he would become famous through the proofs for his schoolboy theory. Bernard's money, Evinson's pull with those in power. And now we know why Bernard wanted to come. He's impotent, you know." She looked thoughtful, then smiled faintly at me. "A lot of impotent men feel the need to go out and shoot things, you know. And many, perhaps most men are impotent now, you know. Don't look like that. At least you're all right."

I backed away from that. "What about Evinson? Does he believe a leak or an explosion brought all this about?"

"Bernard planted that in his mind," she said. "He doesn't really believe it now. But it leaves him with no alternative theory to fall back on. You can't tell anything by looking at these rotten buildings."

I shook my head. "I know that was the popular explanation, but they did investigate, you know. Didn't he get to any of the old reports? Why did he buy that particular theory?"

"All those reports are absolutely meaningless. Each new administration doctors them to fit its current platforms and promises." She shrugged again. "That's propaganda from another source, right? So what did happen, according to the official reports?"

"Plague, brought in by Haitian smugglers. And the water was going bad, salt intrusion destroyed the whole system. Four years of drought had aggravated everything. Then the biggest hurricane of the century hit and that was just too bloody much. Thirty thousand deaths. They never recovered."

She was shaking her head now. "You have the chronology all mixed up. First the drop in population, the exodus, then the plague. It was like that everywhere. First the population began to sag, and in industrialized nations that spelled disaster. Then flu strains that no one had ever seen before, and plague. There weren't enough doctors; plants had closed down because of a labor shortage. There was no defense. In the ten years before the epidemics, the population had dropped by twenty percent."

I didn't believe her, and she must have known it from my expression. She stood up. "I don't know what's in the water, Sax. It's crawling with things that I can't identify, but we pretend that they belong and they're benign. And God help us, we're the ones teaching the new generation. Let's swim."

Lying on my back under the broiling sun, I tried again to replay the scene with my boss. Nothing came of it. He hadn't told me why he was sending me to Miami. Report back. On what? Everything you see and hear, everything they all do. For the record. Period.

Miami hadn't been the first city to be evacuated. It had been the largest up to that time. Throughout the Midwest, the far west, one town, one city after another had been left to the winds and rains and the transients. No one had thought it strange enough to investigate. The people were going to the big cities where they could find work. The young refused to work the land. Or agribusiness had bought them out. No mystery. Then larger cities had been emptied. But that was because of epidemics: plague, flu, hepatitis. Or because of government policies: busing or open housing; or the loss of government contracts for defense work. Always a logical explanation. Then Miami. And the revelation that population zero had been reached and passed. But that had to be because of the plagues. Nothing else made any sense at all. I looked at Corrie resentfully. She was dozing after our swim. Her body was gold brown now, with highlights of red on her shoulders, her nose, her thighs. It was too easy to reject the official reasons, especially if you weren't responsible for coming up with alternative explanations.

"I think they sent you because they thought you would come back," Corrie said, without opening her eyes. "I think that's it." She rolled on her side and looked at me.

"You know with Trainor gone, maybe none of us will get back," I said.

"If we hug the shore we should make it, except that we have no gas."

I looked blank, I suppose. She laughed. "No one told you? He took the gas when he left. Or the snake that killed him drank it. I think he found a boat that would get him to the Bahamas, and he went. I supposed that's why he came, to get enough gas to cruise the islands. That's why he insisted on getting down by sail, to save what gas Evinson had requisitioned for this trip. There's no one left on the islands, of course."

I had said it lightly, that we might not get back, but with no gas, it became a statement of fact. None of us could operate the sail, and the boat was too unwieldly to paddle. The first storm would capsize us, or we would run aground. "Didn't Trainor say anything about coming back?"

"He didn't even say anything about leaving." She closed her eyes and repeated, "There's no one there at all."

"Maybe," I said. But I didn't believe there was, either. Suddenly, looking at Corrie, I wanted her, and I reached for her arm. She drew away, startled. They said that sunspot activity had caused a decrease in sexual activity. Sporadically, with some of us. I grabbed Corrie's arm hard and pulled her toward me. She didn't fight, but her face became strained, almost haggard.

"Wait until tomorrow, Davidson. Please. I'll ovulate tomorrow. Maybe you and I . . ." I saw the desperation then, and the fear — worse, terror. I saw the void in her eyes, pupils the size of pinpricks in the brilliant light, the irises the color of the endless water beyond us. I pushed her away and stood up.

Don't bring me your fear, I wanted to say. All my life I had been avoiding the fear and now she would thrust it upon me. I left her lying on the beach.

Evinson was sick that night. He vomited repeatedly, and toward dawn he became delirious.

J.P. and I took turns sitting with him because the women weren't strong enough to restrain him when he began to thrash about. He flung Corrie against the wall before we realized his strength and his dementia.

"He's dying, isn't he?" J.P. said, looking at him coolly. He was making a study of death, I thought.

"I don't know."

"He's dying. It might take a while, but this is the start of it." He looked at me fixedly for a long time. "None of us is going back, Sax. You realize that, don't you?"

"I don't know about the rest of you, but I'm going back. You're all a bunch of creepies, crazy as bedbugs, all of you. But I'm going back!"

"Don't yell." His voice remained mild, neutral, an androgynous voice without overtones of anything human at all.

I stamped from the room to get a beer, and when I got back, J.P. was writing in his notebook. He didn't look up again. Evinson got much worse, louder, more violent, then his strength began to ebb and he subsided, moaning fitfully now and then, murmuring unintelligibly. Corrie check him from time to time. She changed the dressing on his hand; it was swollen to twice its normal size, the swelling extending to his shoulder. She looked at him as dispassionately as J.P. did.

"A few more hours," she said. "Do you want me to stay up with you?"

"What for?" I asked coldly. "I must say you're taking this well."

"Don't be sarcastic. What good would it do if I put on an act and wept for him?"

"You might care because he's a man who didn't deserve to die in this stinking city."

She shrugged. "I'll go on to bed. Call me if there's any change." At the doorway she turned and said, "I'll weep for myself, maybe even for you, Sax, but not for him. He knew what this would be like. We all did, except possibly you."

"You won't have to waste any tears for me. Go on to bed." She left and I said to J.P., "You all hate him, don't you? Why?"

J.P. picked up his pen again, but he hesitated. "I hadn't thought of it as hating him," he said thoughtfully. "I just never wanted to be near him. He's been trying to climb onto the glory train for years. Special adviser to presidents about urban affairs, that sort of thing. Absolutely no good at it, but very good at politics. He made them all think there was still hope. He lied and he knew he lied. They used to say those that can do; those that can't teach.

Now the saying goes, those that can't become sociologists." He put his pen down again and began to worry at a hangnail. His hands were very long and narrow, brown, bony with prominent knuckles. "A real scientist despises the pseudo-scientist who passes. Something unclean about him, the fact that he could get permission for this when his part of it was certain to be negligible from the start."

"And yours was important from the start, I suppose?"

"For fifteen years I've wanted to get back into field research. Every year the funds dwindled more. People like me were put into classrooms, or let go. It really isn't fair to the students, you understand. I'm a rotten teacher. I hate them all without exception. I crammed and worked around the clock to get as good a background as I could, and when I was ready, I forced myself on Albert Lanier." He looked at me expectantly and I shook my head. Only later did I recall the name. Lanier had written many of the books on marine biology that were in the libraries. J.P. looked at me with contempt. "He was a great man and a greater scientist. During his last years when he was crippled with rheumatoid arthritis, I was his eyes, his legs, his hands. When he died all field research died with him. Until now."

"So you're qualified for this work."

"Yes, I'm qualified. More than that fool." He glanced at Evinson who was breathing very shallowly. "More than anyone here. If only my work is made known, this farce will be worth ten of him, of all of you."

"If?"

"If. Would any one of my own students know what I'm doing? My own students!" He bit the hangnail and a spot of blood appeared on his thumb. He started to scribble again.

At daybreak Evinson's fever started to climb, and it rose steadily until noon. We kept him in wet sheets, we fanned him, Corrie gave him cool enemas. Nothing helped. He died at one thirty. I was alone with him. Corrie and Delia were both asleep.

J.P. knew when he looked at my face. He nodded. I saw his pack then. "Where the hell are you going?"

"Down the coast. Maybe down the Keys, as far as I can get. I'd like to see if the coral is coming back again."

"We leave here Saturday morning at dawn. I don't give a damn who's here and who isn't. At dawn."

He smiled mockingly and shook his head. He didn't say good-bye to anyone, just heaved his pack onto his back and walked away.

I rummaged on the *Loretta* and found a long-handled small-bladed shovel, and I buried Evinson high on the beach, above the high-water mark.

When I got back Corrie was up, eating a yellow fruit with a thick rind. I knocked it out of her hand reflexively. "Are you out of your mind! You know the local fruits might kill us." She had juice on her chin.

"I don't know anything anymore. That's a mango, and it's delicious. I've been eating the fruits for three days. A touch of diarrhea the first day, that's all." She spoke lightly, and didn't look at me. She began to cut another one.

"Evinson died. I buried him. J.P. left."

She didn't comment. The aromatic odor from the fruit seemed to fill the room. She handed me a slice and I threw it back at her.

Delia came down then looking better than she had in days. Her cheeks were pink and her eyes livelier than I had seen them. She looked at Corrie, and while she didn't smile, or do anything at all, I knew.

"Bitch," I said to Corrie bitterly. "Wait until tomorrow. Right. Bitch!"

"Take a walk, Sax," Delia said sharply.

"Let's not fight," Corrie said. "He's dead and J.P.'s gone." Delia shrugged and sat down at the table. Corrie handed her a piece of the mango. "Sax, you knew about me, about us. Whether or not you wanted to know, you did. Sometimes I tried to pretend that maybe I could conceive, but I won't. So forget it. What are you going to do?"

"Get the hell out of here. Go home."

"For what?" Delia asked. She tasted the slice of mango curiously, then bit into it. She frowned critically. "I like the oranges better."

"These grow on you," Corrie said. "I've developed an absolute craving for them in the past three days. You'll see."

"I don't know about you," I said furiously, "but I'm leaving Saturday. I have things to do that I like doing. I like to read. To see a show now and then. I have friends."

"Are you married? Do you live with a woman? Or a man?" Delia asked.

I looked at Corrie. "We're in trouble. It'll take the three of us to manage the boat to get back. We have to make plans."

"We aren't going back," Corrie said softly. "We're going to the Seminoles."

"Corrie, listen to me. I've been out farther than either of you. There's nothing. Ruins. Rot. Decay. No roads. Nothing. Even if they existed, you'd never find them."

"There's the remains of the road. Enough for us to follow west."

"Why didn't you try a little bribery with me?" I yelled at her. "Maybe I would have changed my mind and gone with you."

"I didn't want you, Sax. I didn't think the Seminoles would want to take in a white man."

I left them alone for the rest of the day. I checked the *Loretta* again, swam, fished, gloomed. That night I pretended that nothing had been said about Seminoles. We ate silently.

Outside was the blackness and the silence, and somewhere in the silence a scream waited. The silence seemed to be sifting in through the mosquito netting. The wind had stopped completely. The air was close and very hot inside the building. "I'm going out," I said as soon as I finished eating.

Delia's question played through my mind as I walked. Did I live with a woman? Or a man? I stopped at the edge of the water. There were no waves on the bay, no sound except a gentle water murmur. Of all the people I knew, I could think of only three that I would like to see again, two of them because I had lived with them in the past, and our relationships had been exciting, or at least not abrasive, while they had lasted. And when they were finished, the ending hadn't been shattering. Two women, both gone from my life completely. One man, a co-worker in my department. We did things together, bowled, swapped books, saw shows together. Not recently, I reminded myself. He had dropped out of sight.

A gust of wind shook me and I started back. A storm was coming up fast. The wind became erratic and strong, and as suddenly as the wind had started, the rain began. It was a deluge that blinded me, soaked me, and was ankle deep in the street almost instantly. Then, over the rain, I heard a roar that shook me through and through, that left me vibrating. A tornado, I knew, although I had never seen or heard one. The roar increased, like a plane bearing down on me. I threw myself flat, and the noise rocked the ground under me, and a building crashed to my left, then another, and another. It ended as abruptly as it had started.

I stumbled back to our building, shaking, chilled and very frightened. I was terrified that our building would be demolished, the women gone, dead, and that I would be alone with the silence and the black of the night.

Corrie opened the door on the first floor and I stumbled in. "Are you all right? It was a tornado, wasn't it?"

She and Delia were both afraid. That was reassuring. Maybe now they would be frightened enough to give up the nonsense about staying here. The storm abated and the silence returned. It didn't seem quite so ominous now.

"Corrie, don't you see how dangerous it would be to stay? There could be a hurricane. Storms every day. Come back with me."

"The cities will die, Sax. They'll run out of food. More epidemics. I can help the Seminoles."

Friday I got the *Loretta* ready for the return trip. I packed as much fruit as it would hold. Enough for three, I kept telling myself. Forbidden fruit. For three. I avoided Corrie and Delia as much as I could and they seemed to be keeping busy, but what they were doing I couldn't guess.

That night I came wide awake suddenly and sat up listening hard.

Something had rattled or fallen. And now it was too quiet. It had been the outside door slamming, I realized, and jumped up from my bedroll and raced downstairs. No one was there, anywhere. They had left, taking with them Corrie's medical supplies, Delia's radiation kit, most of the food, most of the beer. I went outside, but it was hopeless. I hadn't expected this. I had thought they would try to talk me into going into the swamps with them, not that they would try it alone.

I cursed and threw things around, then another thought hit me. The *Loretta*! I ran to the dock in a frenzy of fear that they had scuttled her. But she was there, swaying and bobbing in the changing tide. I went aboard and decided not to leave her again. In the morning I saw that the sail was gone.

I stared at the mast and the empty deck. Why? Why for God's sake had they taken the sail?

They'll be back, I kept thinking all morning. And, I'll kill them both. Gradually the thought changed. They would beg me to go with them inland, and I would say yes, and we would go into the first swamp and I would take their gear and leave them there. They would follow me out soon enough. They had needed the sail for a shelter, I thought dully. After noon I began to think that maybe I could go with them part of the way, just to help them out, prove to them that it was hopeless to go farther.

My fury returned, redoubled. All my life I had managed to live quietly, just doing my job, even though it was a stupid one, but getting paid and trying to live comfortably, keeping busy enough not to think. Keeping busy enough to keep the fear out. Because it was there all the time, pressing, just as the silence here pressed. It was a silent fear, but if it had had a voice, its voice would have been that scream we had heard. That was the voice of my fear. Loud, shrill, inhuman, hopeless. I felt clammy and chilled in the heat, and my stomach rejected the idea of food or drink.

Come back, I pleaded silently, willing the thought out, spreading the thought, trying to make contact with one of them. Come back for me. I'll go with you, do whatever you want to do. Please!

That passed. The storm came, and I shivered alone in the *Loretta* and listened to the wind and the pounding rain. I thought about my apartment, my work, the pamphlets I wrote. The last one I had worked on was titled: "Methods of Deep Ploughing of Alluvial Soils in Strip Farming in Order to Provide a Nutritionally Adequate Diet in a Meatless Society." Who was it for? Who would read past the title? No one, I answered. No one would read it. They were planning for a future that I couldn't even imagine.

The silence was more profound than ever that evening. I sat on deck until I could bear the mosquitoes no longer. Below, it was sweltering, and the silence had followed me in. I would start back at first light, I decided. I would have to take a smaller boat. A flat-bottomed boat. I could row it up the waterway, stay out of the ocean. I could haul it where the water was too shallow or full of debris.

The silence pressed against me, equally on all sides, a force that I could feel now. I would need something for protection from the sun. And boiled water. The beer was nearly gone. They hadn't left me much food, either. I could do without food, but not water and maps. Maybe I could make a small sail from discarded clothing. I planned and tried not to feel the silence. I lectured myself on synesthesia — I had done a pamphlet on the subject once. But the silence won. I began to run up the dock, screaming at Corrie and Delia, cursing them, screaming for them to come back. I stopped, exhausted finally, and the echo finished and the silence was back. I knew I wouldn't sleep; I built a fire and started to boil water.

I poured the water into the empty beer bottles and stacked them back in their original boxes. More water started to boil, and I dozed. In my near sleep, I heard the scream again. I jumped up shaking. It had been inhumanly high, piercing, with such agony and hopelessness that tears stood in my eyes. I had dreamed it, I told myself. And I couldn't be certain if I had or not.

Until dawn came I thought about the scream, and it seemed to me a thing uttered by no living throat. It had been my own scream, I thought, and I laughed out loud.

I loaded an aluminum rowboat the next day and rigged up a sail that might or might not fall apart when the wind blew. I made myself a poncho and a sun hat, and then, ready to go, I sat in the boat and watched some terns diving. They never had asked me what I had wanted to do, I thought bitterly. Not one of them had asked me what I would have liked to do.

J.P. had complained about being forced into teaching, while I would have traded everything I had for the chance to write, to teach — but worthless things, like literature, art appreciation, composition. A pelican began to dive with the terns, and several gulls appeared. They followed the pelican down, and one sat on his head and tried to snatch the fish from his mouth.

I thought again of all the pamphlets I had written, all the thousands of pages I had read in order to condense them. All wasted because in reducing them to so little, too much had been left out. I started to row finally.

When I left the mouth of the bay, I turned the small boat southward. The sea was very blue, the swells long and peaceful. Cuba, I thought. That many people, some of them had to be left. And they would need help. So much had been lost already, and I had it, all those thousands of pages, hundreds of books, all up there in my head.

I saw again the undersecretary's white, dry, dead face, the hurt there, the fear. He hadn't expected me to come back at all, I realized. I wished I could tell Corrie.

The wind freshened. If not Cuba, then Central America, or even South America. I put up my little sail, and the wind caught it and puffed it, and I felt only a great contentment.